SHIMON

~ A NOVEL ~

PERES

SHIMON

~ A NOVEL ~

PERES

#1 *NEW YORK TIMES* BESTSELLING AUTHOR

MIKE EVANS

TIMEWORTHY
BOOKS

P.O. BOX 30000, PHOENIX, AZ 85046

Shimon Peres

Copyright 2018 by Time Worthy Books
P. O. Box 30000
Phoenix, AZ 85046

Cover Photo: Ilan Spira
Design: Peter Gloege | LOOK Design Studio

Hardcover: 978-1-62961-168-6
Paperback: 978-1-62961-167-9
    Canada: 978-1-62961-169-3

This book is dedicated to
Dr. Rami Levi.

He has served the State of Israel for over three decades
on three continents. He is a gifted international relations
leader, skilled in global market development, proficient
in crisis management, and in strategic planning

Rami has served Israel as the tourism ambassador
for both North and South America. In that role, he
managed various international projects, a national task
force, and global partnerships that involved forty-two
governments, world-leading conglomerates, media
networks and international law firms. Success led to his
appointment as the head of the National Government
Tourism Marketing Administration and Task Force.

Rami is my senior advisor and my brother. He is my
partner in defending Israel and in building the Friends
of Zion Heritage Center. He retired from government
service in 2008, entered the private marketplace and
founded several companies utilizing his business acumen
to aid various projects worldwide. It is a distinct honor
to work closely with my dear friend and colleague.

SHIMON PERES

*"Look, we have existed for four thousand years—
two thousand years in diaspora, in exile."*

—VISHNYEVA, BELARUS, 1930—

COFFEE DRIBBLED from his lip as he took a sip from the cup. He wiped it away with his fingertips and returned the cup to the saucer on the table. He cast a glance across the table. "I had a dream last night."

Michael Katznelson was a rabbi. The man seated across from him was Zvi Meltzer, his cantor.

"Oh?" Meltzer said. "Was it an enjoyable dream?"

Katznelson gave a faint shake of his head. "No, it was not."

"I find they rarely are." Meltzer took a sip from his cup. "Even when they aren't particularly troubling, they're almost never. . . enjoyable."

Katznelson looked away. Meltzer waited a moment, then prompted him. "So, are you going to tell me?"

"Tell you what?"

"About the dream."

Katznelson thought a moment longer, took another sip of coffee, then began. "Everyone in the village was surrounded by soldiers. The soldiers were firing weapons at them. Bullets everywhere. People falling over dead. Then we were in the building."

Meltzer frowned. "The building?"

"Yes. The synagogue. The ones who didn't die from the bullets ran in there to be safe."

"Who was there?"

"You. Me. Everyone. As many as could fit. All packed inside. The building was full. And they just kept firing their guns with bullets coming through the walls." Katznelson looked over at Meltzer. "Then I smelled smoke."

"Smoke?"

"Yes. I went to the window and looked out. There were dead bodies everywhere. Lying in the street and on the grass. The entire village—all of them—were killed. And then smoke billowed up before me. Flames rose up in front of the window and I knew. . . " His voice trailed away and a troubled look came over him.

"Knew what?" Meltzer prompted with a hint of urgency. "What did you know?"

"That they were burning the building and we had no way out."

Meltzer had a puzzled expression. "Then what happened?"

Katznelson lifted his cup to take another sip. "I woke up."

They sat in silence, both men sipping coffee, lost in thought. Finally Meltzer spoke. "Well." He had a wan smile. "I'm sure that was a relief."

"It was an important dream," Katznelson replied in an unamused tone.

"You mean like a message?"

"I mean like I was seeing the future."

Meltzer frowned again. "But who would do such a thing? We have all experienced acts of violence, but what you dreamed—who would do something like that? So organized. So intentional."

Katznelson reached to a chair behind him and picked up a newspaper. He pointed to a picture on the page as he handed the paper to Meltzer. "This is the face I saw in my dream."

Meltzer glanced at a picture of Adolf Hitler on the page.

"All night long," Katznelson continued, "standing among the men with the guns." He gestured to the paper Meltzer now held. "That is the face I saw."

Meltzer checked the date at the top of the page and his eyes brightened. "This is yesterday's paper."

Katznelson nodded. "So?"

"So, you read the paper last night before you went to sleep?"

"I always read the paper before I go to sleep."

"I know, and that's what I'm saying. You read the paper, you fell asleep." He tapped the picture with his finger. "His face showed up in your dreams." Meltzer glanced down at the image of Hitler. "Ugly guy. No wonder you had bad dreams."

"It's more than that," Katznelson sighed.

"More than what?"

"More than just seeing the picture, going to sleep, and dreaming about it."

"What more?"

"Well, I've been thinking. Remembering."

"Thinking and remembering what? You aren't making much sense right now, Michael."

"The words of Joel keep coming to my mind."

"Joel. The prophet?"

"'Your old men shall dream dreams, your young men shall see visions.'"

"And you dreamed a dream last night."

"It was more than a dream. It was like a word. A word to my spirit."

Just then, the door opened and a young boy entered. Katznelson looked up and smiled. "Shimon. Finished with school already?"

"It's almost four, Rebbe," Shimon replied. He came to a stop near the table and Meltzer slipped his arm around the boy's waist. Meltzer gave him a squeeze. "How is my grandson?"

"I am well."

"You had a good day?"

"Of course he had a good day," Katznelson said. "All the Perskis are smart. They do well in school."

At seven years old, Shimon wore woolen trousers, a shirt buttoned to the collar, and a woolen jacket. Atop his head was a black hat, and long curls of hair hung in twisted strands from beneath it.

Meltzer tousled young Shimon's hair. "You should be rested after a day with your friends. Now the real education begins. Come." Meltzer stood and glanced over at Katznelson. "We can continue our discussion tomorrow."

"Certainly," Katznelson replied. "I'll look forward to it."

Meltzer lived only a few blocks away and when they reached the house he took a seat at the end of the dining table. Shimon sat to one side. Before them, the table was covered with stacks of books and papers. The books were mostly about the *Tanakh*—the Commandments—and the *Talmud*, the Mosaic law. The papers contained more recent works, primarily the ideas of learned rabbis from the region and recent articles by proponents of an idea known as Zionism—the notion that Jews should return to their native homeland in Palestine.

As they sat at the table, however, Meltzer opened a book on Russian literature, a topic almost as close to his heart as Mosaic law. The book was entitled *The Cossacks*. He handed it to Shimon. "I want you to read from this today."

Shimon glanced at the cover. "Wasn't Tolstoy a Christian?"

"But not at the time he wrote that."

"But he was not a Jew."

"No."

Shimon began slowly, "Why do I have to read the works of a man who was a pagan, who later became a Christian but never was a Jew?"

"Life is complex," Meltzer answered in a professorial tone. "It is not as simple as 'us' and 'them.' The Talmud makes this plain. Have you not been paying attention?"

"Yes, sir. I understand that, but—"

"I know what you are thinking. If we are committed to being a Jew always, why should we care what a non-Jew thinks or says? But even our own traditions point to the complexity of life. The text of *Torah* seems straightforward, but there are always nuances presented by the facts—which is evident from the Scripture itself. And to this very day there are competing ideas among scholars about those nuanced facts."

"But Tolstoy is not Jewish and this is a novel. Not the Talmud."

"Nothing is one-sided," Meltzer explained. "Whatever the issue, if you only see one side of it, then you haven't studied it enough. Tolstoy has much to offer." He gestured impatiently. "Read."

✦ ✦ ✦

Shimon Perski was born on August 2, 1923, in Vishnyeva, a small village with pleasant wooden homes and unpaved streets, nestled beneath a birch forest along the banks of the Olshanksy River. At the time of Shimon's birth, the town was part of the Republic of Poland—known as the Second Polish Republic—a state created in 1918 following the end of World War I. The Republic lasted until September 1939, when Poland was attacked and overrun by the German army, an act that marked the beginning of World War II.

In the first quarter of the twentieth century, European Jews were locked in a debate over the question of assimilation—whether Jews should shrug off their distinctive traditions and practices, rid themselves of their "Jewishness," and simply become European. Or devote all of their strength and will to preserving their ancient beliefs, culture, and lifestyle. In the case of Vishnyeva Jews, the question was whether to become Polish, or Russian, in every way—even to the point of adopting Christian practices and a Christian lifestyle.

For some, assimilation seemed the only way to prevent persecution—Jews had been subjected to centuries of discrimination, hatred, and violence. In Vishnyeva, they'd witnessed a return of the destructive and deadly anti-Semitic pogroms of old.

Others saw assimilation as the intellectually more authentic approach, a natural progression in the development of Jews from an unenlightened sect to one fully embracing Western thought. After all, they and their ancestors had lived in Europe as long as anyone. Why shouldn't they simply see themselves as European?

But not everyone agreed with either of these opinions. Some recoiled from European culture altogether and sought with increasing vigilance to maintain Jewish life in its strictest form. For the *Haredi*—the most authentically Jewish of the Orthodox—the purpose of man was to serve his Maker. That service was achieved by keeping the commandments and observing the old ways—the beliefs, traditions, and practices of ancient Judaism. For them, lifestyle and obedience, culture and faith, tradition and religion were one. Together, they provided the means of fulfilling the obligation of service to God. And it was into that life, that system of thought, that Zvi Meltzer brought his grandson Shimon.

The tradition of the Haredi, though, was nothing new to Shimon's family. In fact, it ran rather deep into their ancestry. His grandparents on both sides grew up in the town of Volozhin, which was twenty kilometers away. Volozhin was home to a famous yeshiva, a Talmudic school, operated by Chaim Nachman Bialik. The school was founded by Chaim Volozhiner, of whom Shimon's paternal grandfather, Zalman Perski was a descendant. As a young man, Zalman studied at the yeshiva, too.

Yet in spite of that, Shimon's father, Yitzhak Perski, and his mother, Sara Meltzer, were not practicing Jews. Yitzhak was a timber merchant and a dealer in commodities of various types, a business he conducted through warehouses he maintained alongside the railroad in a neighboring village. With an acumen for business, he was quite successful and, for the time and place in which he lived, also quite wealthy. The Perskis lived a comfortable life. Shimon and his brother, Gershon—whom they called Gigi—experienced no lack.

As a young boy, Shimon attended a Tarbut school—a secular, Hebrew language school that flourished among Jewish communities in the time between the two World Wars. Classes were taught in

Hebrew, Yiddish, and Polish. The law required the school to teach Polish. Gigi attended the same school.

At home Shimon learned Russian. His mother loved Russian novels, often reading while she went about her daily routine. And there always was a stack of books on the table beside her bed. As soon as he was able to read, she began supplying young Shimon with novels, too.

The stories he read ignited Shimon's imagination and set him to dreaming, at first of worlds that used to be, and then of things that had not yet come to pass. Gradually, those dreams grew beyond mere imagination to the question of "Why not?" Why not a world where Jews could live without fear? Why not a world where machines took us beyond the sky to stars? Why not a life spent exploring the reaches of one's mind and bringing to this world the wonder one found there? It was a perspective that remained with him throughout his life, marking him forever as an optimist but leaving him with the moniker of "Shimon the Dreamer."

SHIMON PERES

*"The Jews' greatest contribution
to history is dissatisfaction!"*

THE NEXT MORNING, Shimon again dressed in wool pants with his shirt buttoned to the collar, then put on his jacket, squared it against his shoulders, and donned his hat. When Gigi was ready, they headed out the door for the walk to school.

Not far from the house, Pawel Stronski approached. About Shimon's age, he was slightly taller and quite a bit heavier. Stocky, in fact, but not muscular. And he talked all the time.

"What does he want?" Shimon mumbled.

"Relax," Gigi said. "He hasn't said anything yet."

"He will, though. I know it. He can't help talking."

"Shimon the Dreamer!" Stronski exclaimed as he came near.

Shimon glanced away, recoiling inside himself.

"What?" Stronski's voice lost any pretense of friendliness as the expression on his face slowly turned cold. "You too good to even say hello?" He gave Shimon a nudge with his forearm. "Think because you're smarter than everybody you don't have to speak?" Then he pushed Shimon with both hands.

Suddenly, Gigi threw down his books and exploded, driving his shoulder against Stronski's side with all the force his muscles could gather. Caught by surprise, Stronski stumbled to one side and flailed his arms in every direction, trying to maintain his balance. But Gigi kept driving with his legs, forcing his shoulder against Stronski's side until a moment later Stronski lay on his back in the dirt. Then Gigi lit into him with his fists.

Before Shimon could react, Ovadia Atzmon, his one and only friend, appeared as if from nowhere and took hold of Gigi's shoulder. "That's enough, Gi," he said. "That's enough." He tugged at Gigi to pull him away, and Stronski squirmed from beneath him.

"I'll get you for this!" Stronski shouted, jabbing with his finger in Gigi's direction. He bent over to catch his breath. "I'll get you."

"You want me now?" Gigi taunted. He started forward as if to finish the fight but Ovadia moved between them. "Let it go," he ordered. And Gigi backed off.

Stronski hurried up the street and disappeared around the corner. When he was gone, Ovadia looked over at Shimon. "You okay?"

"Yeah," Shimon said. "I'm okay."

They continued on to school and for the rest of the morning nothing much happened. At noon the class took a break and Shimon went outside to sit alone in the lee of the building and eat his lunch—a bialy wrapped in tissue that he'd brought from home. The sunshine was warm and as he sat there, eating, his mind drifted to an imaginary meadow filled with lush green grass and dotted with wildflowers. He'd seen a meadow like that once, when he went with his father to inspect a stand of timber, and it had stuck in his mind ever since.

In a few minutes, Ovadia appeared and took a seat at his side. "I heard Stronski and some of his pals talking."

Shimon acknowledged the comment with a nod. "No doubt, planning some new torment for me."

"I think so."

"One day, I will live alone at the edge of the woods and spend my days with flocks of sheep, lounging at the edge of a meadow while they graze quietly in the sun. And then I'll—"

"Are you okay?"

"Yes. Why?"

"You sound a little. . . odd. Like something's wrong."

Shimon gave him a condescending look. "It's a poem, Ovadia."

Ovadia had a skeptical frown. "A poem?"

"Yes."

"I don't remember any poem like that. Who wrote it?"

"I did."

Ovadia looked surprised. "You wrote a poem?"

"Yes." Shimon reached into the pocket of his jacket and took out a small black diary. "I've written many. I keep them in here." The diary fell open near the middle, revealing the words of a poem neatly arranged on the page. Shimon held it for his friend to see.

Ovadia glanced at it, then shook his head. "Don't show the others," he cautioned. "They will only beat you more."

Shimon closed the diary and returned it to his pocket. "Why do they hate me?"

"They are jealous." Ovadia held out his hand. "Give me a piece of that bread."

"You didn't bring lunch?"

"I ate it already. I love that bread."

Shimon smiled as he a tore off a piece and handed it to Ovadia. "You really think they're jealous?"

"Yes," Ovadia replied. "I know they are."

"But what are they jealous about?"

"Your family has money," Ovadia explained. "You want for nothing. And you think thoughts they could never think. They want to think them, they just can't. They don't have the mind for it."

"Well," Shimon sighed, "I can't help who I am."

"Then you'll just have to learn to endure." Ovadia looked over at Shimon with a big smile and held out his hand. "Give me another piece of that bread."

A few days later, Stronski made good on his threat. He and a dozen boys from class grabbed Shimon and Gershon during recess and began pummeling them with their fists. Gershon fought back but Shimon, paralyzed by the violence, covered his head with his arms, doubled over in a fetal position, and endured, all the while shouting, "Why? Why are you doing this to me?"

As before, Ovadia came to their defense but this time his intervention wasn't enough. Stronski and the others overwhelmed him, too. Soon all three boys were on the ground, swarmed upon by their attackers who struck them repeatedly.

After what seemed like a long time, Shimon heard their teacher, Yehoshua Rabinowitz, shout, "Stop this! Stop this right now!" The beating stopped and Shimon glanced up to see Rabinowitz fling Stronski aside. He shoved another away and sent another tumbling backward with a jab of his elbow. "The very idea of you attacking a fellow student. This is completely unacceptable."

When class ended later that day, Shimon remained behind in the classroom until everyone else was gone. Rabinowitz, the teacher, noticed him. "Something you wanted?"

"No," Shimon replied. "Just waiting."

"Oh? To see me?"

"No," Shimon said again. "For the others to go on ahead."

"More trouble?"

"Why do you ask?"

Rabinowitz gestured with his index finger. "You have a bruise on your cheek."

Shimon looked away. "It is nothing." He stood and gathered his books. "It's just. . . why do they hate me?"

Rabinowitz stared at him a moment, then said slowly, "Shimon, it is the life of a man with calling and purpose."

"To be hated?"

"To be misunderstood."

Shimon's eyes brightened. "Is that what it is?"

Rabinowitz nodded. "Yes, that is it."

"They misunderstand me, not hate me?"

"Do you think they understand you?"

"Ovadia says they are jealous."

"Perhaps," Rabinowitz conceded. "But what do *you* think?"

"I think they're mean."

Rabinowitz chuckled. "That might be true, too. But is that all?" When Shimon didn't answer, Rabinowitz continued. "Tell me something. When you think about the future, what do you think of?"

Shimon thought immediately of the meadow that he visited in his mind and of the notebook of poems in the pocket of his jacket. Then he remembered Ovadia's warning that he should keep that part to himself. "I don't know," he shrugged. "I suppose I mostly think of the past."

"Ahh. Right," Rabinowitz nodded thoughtfully. "You have shown quite an interest in history. And in philosophy. The big ideas that have shaped mankind."

"I don't do well in math, though."

"I would agree," Rabinowitz noted. "Nor with science."

"No." Shimon pressed his lips together in a thin, tight smile.

"Perhaps you should—"

"I know," Shimon interrupted. "I should study science and math more."

"Quite to the contrary," Rabinowitz countered. "I was going to suggest you should focus on the things you're interested in. Perhaps that is where your destiny lies."

The comment left Shimon perplexed. "But what does that have to do with Stronski?"

"Stronski and his friends are a distraction."

Shimon touched the bruise on his cheek. "A rather powerful one."

"But a distraction all the same. An obstacle meant to turn you aside from the path to your destiny."

"You mean I must fight back."

"No." Rabinowitz spoke slowly, drawing out the word as if thinking and speaking at the same time, his mind racing ahead to choose the next words carefully. "I mean—"

"Gigi says I should fight back," Shimon interrupted again.

"Gigi *would* fight back. That is who he is. But Gigi is not Shimon. Only you can be Shimon. Only you can fulfill Shimon's purpose."

"But what is that purpose?"

"That's what I'm trying to tell you. Your purpose lies in the direction of the things that interest you. Move in that direction. Study in that direction. Think in that direction."

"Grandfather says there are four levels of understanding for everything. That would mean there are four levels of meaning to why Stronski and his bunch don't like me."

"This is the Sód. The esoteric."

"The mystical."

"Yes. Your grandfather has taught you well."

Shimon tucked his books under his arm and started toward the door. When he passed the front of the room, he nodded to Rabinowitz. "Tomorrow, Rebbe."

"You know, I am head of the local group of Hashomer Hatzair."

Shimon nodded. "The Zionist youth movement."

Rabinowitz noticed the look on Shimon's face. "You do not approve?"

"Grandfather says the group promotes a version of Jewish identity that is cultural but not religious."

"If I didn't already know you I would ask you to define those words, but as I know you know their meaning, I will say, your grandfather is correct. We are political, not religious. But I think you might enjoy our debates."

"Debates?"

"We have quite lively discussions of the issues of the day."

For a moment, Shimon was intrigued. He might not be interested in fighting back with his fists against Stronski, but facing down the challenge of ideas touched an interest deep inside. Still, Hashomer Hatzair was a Zionist group, and Grandfather Meltzer was against Zionism. "Only the Messiah can give us back the promised land," he'd said more than once.

After a moment's hesitation, Shimon straightened the books in the crook of his arm. "Tomorrow, Rebbe," he repeated, then continued toward the door.

✦ ✦ ✦

One evening a few months later, just as the sun was disappearing behind the stand of birch trees to the west and night was coming on, three men appeared on the street near Shimon's house. *Russians,* Shimon thought as he watched from the front-room window. *Or Polish, perhaps. But not Jewish. And not from Vishnyeva.* He knew all the non-Jewish families in town, at least by sight, and these three men were not among them.

After a few minutes the men disappeared, and not long after that a truck arrived filled with a dozen men like the three he'd seen before. White men. Russians for sure this time. Carrying clubs and torches, the flames glowed against the evening darkness.

A little way past Shimon's house the truck came to a stop and the men jumped out. With practiced precision they formed a column two men wide, then marched toward the center of town, stomping their feet and chanting in a heavy, foreboding cadence, "Jews must go. You must go. Jews will not replace us. You will not replace us!"

When the men reached the first synagogue—Vishnyeva had two—they spread out in every direction. A moment later, Shimon heard screams, followed by the sound of breaking glass. Then smoke rose into the sky and flames lit up the night. An awful, angry sound followed. The snarling, brutal growl of violence. Men on men. Fist against flesh. Wood against bone. Shimon stood at the window and watched until a group of women and children ran past and he saw the scared, desperate looks on their faces. Then he ducked below the sill and sat on the floor, his eyes squeezed shut, his arms wrapped tightly around his torso.

In the days that followed, Shimon learned that the men in the truck had come to Vishnyeva from somewhere else. Some said Moscow.

Others said Minsk, though Shimon wondered if either was accurate, given the accent he overheard in the shouts that came from the street. Salo Knaster said the leader of the group was a man from Germany. A Nazi. But no one knew what a Nazi was and gave little attention to what Knaster said.

Regardless of where the men had come from, everyone agreed they'd arrived in Vishnyeva for one reason and one reason alone—to kill Jews. And they'd done just that. By the time the men of Vishnyeva put an end to the violence and forced the intruders to flee, twelve people from town were dead, all of them Jews. Three dozen more were injured. And ten houses were burned to the ground.

A few days later, Rabbi Katznelson came to see Shimon's grandfather. They sat at the table drinking coffee. Shimon, seated in the back bedroom where he studied a Hebrew text, listened to them talk.

"Well," Meltzer said. "You were right."

"About what? What was I right about?"

"You said there would be trouble. That people would die. That houses would burn. And now it has happened."

"What are you talking about?"

"Your dream. The things you saw while you slept. It has now occurred. This is what you saw."

Katznelson shook his head slowly from side to side. "No, this was nothing."

"Nothing? A dozen people are dead. Houses have been burned. Szolem Weiss has a broken leg and he's not the only one. How can you say this was nothing?"

"Zvi," Katznelson said with a somber expression, "the things I saw were much worse."

"Worse?"

"In what I saw. All of us were dead. No one survived. We are still alive." He paused long enough for a sip of coffee. "What happened the other night was nothing."

Just then, Shimon scooted back his chair from the desk where he'd been studying. The sound of it scraping against the floor caught Katznelson's attention. His eyes brightened in a look of realization. "Someone is here?"

"Shimon," Meltzer replied.

"I did not know."

"It's okay."

"He will not be frightened to hear?"

"He saw what happened. Whatever we say cannot add to that."

✦ ✦ ✦

Early in the morning a week later, as Shimon lay in bed asleep, he was awakened by the touch of a hand against his leg. He opened his eyes to see his father standing over him. "Get up. Get dressed," he whispered urgently.

Shimon glanced out the window and saw only the stars in the sky. "It is night."

"Not for long. Hurry. Get dressed. You must come with me."

Shimon sat upright and rubbed the sleep from his eyes. "Is there trouble?"

"We have a trip to make."

"Where are we going?"

"Too many questions," Yitzhak said tersely. "Get dressed and come with me."

Shimon dressed and walked into the kitchen, where his father offered him a bagel and a cup of coffee. As he sat at the table eating, Shimon noticed a suitcase near the door. "We are going away?" he nodded in the direction of the suitcase.

"It is for our trip," Yitzhak replied. "Your mother packed some things for you." He checked his watch, then gestured impatiently. "Eat. We must be going or we will never get there in time."

When he'd finished eating, they walked outside where a truck from his father's business was parked. Yitzhak opened the driver's door and gestured toward the seat. "Get in."

Shimon climbed up to the seat, then slid past the steering wheel to the opposite side. "Where are we going?"

"To see someone special."

"Who is that?"

"Rabbi Kagan," Yitzhak replied.

Shimon knew about Rabbi Yisrael Meir Kagan from discussions at class and with Grandfather Meltzer. He was one of the most influential Orthodox rabbis in the region. He had his own yeshiva in Radun, and was widely known among both religious and secular Jews. Most of his writing and teaching was devoted to encouraging the keeping of the Commandments, but he made no secret of his views on Zionism, which he opposed because of its secular political focus. At the same time, he was a leader in World Agudath Israel, an organization that promoted the teaching of the Torah everywhere and worked to establish religious schools all over the world, including Palestine.

"The Chofetz Chaim," Shimon said softly, noting the Kagan's title, which had been adopted by the public from one of his books, *Sefer Chofetz Chaim.*

"Your grandfather told you about him?"

"Yes," Shimon replied. "And Reb Rabinowitz mentions him often."

"He is very famous, you know."

"Do you mean Rebbe Rabinowitz?"

"No, Rabbi Kagan," Yitzhak explained.

"But why are we going to see him?"

"He is at the yeshiva, speaking. We need to hear what he has to say."

"Yes. But you've never before been interested in hearing from a rabbi."

"Well, I know, but after. . . all that's happened I was. . . more interested."

"Good," Shimon said. He knew better than to press the issue any further.

Radun was more than seven hundred kilometers to the east of Vishnyeva. The drive to get there would take the better part of two days. They reached Bialystok late that afternoon, but Yitzhak pressed on, finally arriving at the home of Jakub Kirshenblatt, a business associate who lived in Lomza.

The next morning, they once again were on their way before sunup and, after another long day on the road, came to the village of Skarszewy, which they reached just before nightfall. Yitzhak had hoped to drive all the way to Radun that day. Kagan was speaking the next morning and he wanted to get there early, but the road from Skarszewy had been more difficult than he expected and nighttime caught them well short of their goal. By then, though, they'd driven past the towns with hotels and rooming houses and had to settle for sleeping in the truck. They parked in a secluded stand of trees off the main road, switched off the engine, and huddled together against the damp night air.

As soon as the sun was up, they continued on their way to Radun and reached Kagan's yeshiva just as the rabbi began his discourse. The room where he spoke was crowded, so they stood in the back. Kagan's lecture was part of his regular instruction to students at the yeshiva, but unlike most days, this presentation was open to the public.

Though tired from the restless night in the cab of the truck, Shimon listened while Kagan taught on the necessity of keeping the Commandments and the manner in which the teachings of the *Soferim*—the Sages, the men of old from Ezra to the Zugot—enlightened the path to obedience.

Late in the afternoon, Kagan finished and the crowd moved toward the doors. Yitzhak, however, took Shimon by the hand and started toward the front of the room where the rabbi collected his papers and greeted the few people brave enough or brash enough to approach him. Yitzhak, who might have been both, showed little inhibition and charged right up and spoke without introduction. "Rabbi Kagan," he said with a smile. "Thank you for that teaching."

"Yes, well. . . " Kagan cleared his throat. "It is always—" He stopped abruptly when he noticed Shimon.

An awkward moment followed, Kagan staring down at Shimon,

Shimon staring up at him, Yitzhak not quite understanding what was happening. He opened his mouth to speak but Kagan cut him off with a gesture for silence, then rested his hand on Shimon's head. "How blessed is a man of peace, in whom there is no guile." He took a deep breath, his eyes closed, head tipped back slightly, as if he'd suddenly fallen into a trance. "A man of peace," he continued. "A man of peace and reconciliation set among a contentious and divisive people."

And with that, Kagan turned aside and walked away. Even Yitzhak did not dare follow after him. Instead, he started toward the door, leaving Shimon to trail behind.

By then the day was almost gone. Rather than starting for home, Yitzhak located a place for them to stay in the home of a rabbi who was friends with Katznelson. They spent the night there and started back the next morning.

From Radun through Skarszewy, Yitzhak said nothing, but as they passed through Bialystok he looked over at Shimon. "What do you suppose he meant by that?"

"By what?"

"A man of peace in whom there is no guile."

"I don't know," Shimon replied.

"It was like a prophecy."

"Grandfather says that is the way things happened to the prophets of old. The word of the One came to them without invitation or expectation. It simply arrived."

"We certainly asked for nothing. I was just interested in hearing him and thought you might be, too."

They talked awhile longer, mostly about the trip. Shimon wanted to ask about the men who'd come to attack the people in town. Wanted to ask about the things he'd heard his grandfather and Rabbi Katznelson discussing. Wanted to ask what it was like to fight back. To defend himself. To defend the town. Instead, he let his father take the lead in the conversation and simply followed along, commenting as best he could. Things worked better that way.

✦ ✦ ✦

A few days later, Shimon resumed classes with Reb Rabinowitz. When school finished for the day, Shimon lingered behind and told Rabinowitz what he'd heard from Rabbi Kagan. Rabinowitz respected Kagan as a scholar, but he wasn't much interested in his work, an opinion he did little to hide.

"He's an interesting figure in Jewish culture," Rabinowitz conceded. "But he is opposed to Zionism. As are most of the leading Orthodox rabbis. Even your grandfather does not favor it."

"He does not see it as his life's work."

"But Zionism is *my* life's work. As you know, I am head of the local Hashomer Hatzair."

"Rabbi Kagan might be opposed to Zionism when he speaks, but he is actively working to establish schools in Palestine."

"Yes. He is. And that is a good thing. But establishing schools for the Haredi is not of interest to me."

"But why would he do that?"

"Do what?"

"Why would he oppose the Zionists but work to establish schools in the land to which Zionists say we should go? Doesn't having the schools in Palestine make it easier for the Haredi to move there?"

"I suppose it does."

"One position is not consistent with the other."

"Ahh," Rabinowitz grinned. "Now you have reached the heart of the Jewish heart."

Shimon looked amused. "The heart of the heart?"

"The center of the center."

"The heart of the Jew is filled with contradictions."

"Yes," Rabinowitz replied. "Rabbi Kagan opposes Zionism, yet works to build schools in Zion, which makes it easier for the Haredi to move there. Your father is devoted to business, leads a secular life, and has little association with rabbis of any kind. Yet he travels all the way to Radun to hear the most celebrated rabbi teach."

"And you, a Jew who never attends *shul*, spend your time educating the most Orthodox of Jews."

Rabinowitz smiled. "You will find there are many inconsistencies among us."

Shimon added, "I should think apparent contradiction would be the hallmark of us all."

"Why is that?"

"Truth always comes wrapped in a riddle."

SHIMON PERES

"Whatever exists we believe can
be changed for the better."

THE ATTACK ON VISHNYEVA that Shimon wit-
nessed from the front window of his house was not the first time
the town had experienced anti-Semitic violence. From the late nineteenth century, pogroms had become a widespread occurrence in that
region—an area of the Russian Empire known as the Pale of Settlement until the Russian Revolution. Often the work of roaming bands
of thugs, sometimes the organized effort of government-sponsored
groups, the marauding attacks sent terror through the Jewish villages
of the region. Vishnyeva had been attacked many times before that
awful evening.

In truth, the attacks had many causes. Economic conditions in
northern Europe were harsh for everyone. Political change—the
collapse of the empire, the struggle for Russia's future—spawned
unrest at every level of society. Fear was a constant source of anxiety
for everyone. The Jews were an easy scapegoat, and blaming them
for whatever social malady the country faced was much easier than
addressing the real causes—namely moral corruption, rampant racism,
and frequent times of poverty.

But anti-Semitism wasn't limited to Russia. Indeed, throughout the whole of Europe, Jews had been subjected to discrimination and violence from the very time of their arrival. And even before that, while they lived in their homeland of the Levant, they were the object of scorn, primarily due to their singular devotion to God—the One—as He'd been revealed to them through history and Scripture. Viewed by pagans as the height of arrogance—that only Jews should be the chosen ones of God—they were repeatedly subjected to ridicule and derision.

Finally conquered by the Romans in 63 BC, the Jews of ancient Israel lived as a client state of the Roman Empire, retaining local leadership but under the ultimate control of Rome. It was an uneasy relationship—pagan Rome exercising authority over a deeply religious Jewish nation—and, as might be expected, Jewish religious leadership pushed back.

Eventually, resistance gave way to sporadic armed uprisings until AD 66, when the Jews of Israel openly revolted. The Roman army, led by Vespasian and Titus, put down the revolt and tightened Roman control of the region. Subsequent uprisings, beginning in AD 115, led to much harsher Roman military action and left the area devastated.

Having dealt with the military aspects of the issue, Roman authorities set out to wipe away even the memory of the nation of Israel. They rebuilt the area as a Roman province, giving it the name of Syria Palestina. Jerusalem was completely destroyed, including the temple and its accompanying buildings, then rebuilt as a Roman city renamed as Aelia Capitolina. Romans ruled Palestine for the next five hundred years until the Levant came under Muslim control.

By then, Jewish families who once occupied Israel had migrated to other areas. Some went west into the Iberian Peninsula and settled in the area now known as Spain. Others moved into interior Europe and settled generally in the area of Poland. Those who lived in Iberia became known as Sephardic Jews, a name derived from *Sepharad*, the Jewish term for Spain. Those who settled in the interior regions of Europe became known as Ashkenazi Jews, a designation derived from the Jewish term for the area. But they were not welcome in either location. From their arrival in Europe, Jews met with opposition. Restrictions on property ownership, occupation, and mobility were common.

Although anti-Semitism was always a problem in Europe, its intensity waxed and waned, yielding periods of relative ease, followed by times of serious peril. By the end of the nineteenth century, many thought European culture was moving beyond the issue, but a series of incidents proved otherwise and the pogroms that followed—of which the violence Shimon witnessed was one—ushered in a new era of rampant and deadly attacks, even in France, which many thought particularly cosmopolitan and beyond prejudice.

In response, many influential Jewish leaders began advocating for a return to Palestine and the establishment of a modern Jewish state. A country of Jews controlled by Jews where Jews could be physically, politically, religiously safe. Theodor Herzl, a journalist and author, began speaking and writing in favor of the cause. His book *The Jewish State* was published to widespread acclaim, and earlier Zionist organizations coalesced around his leadership, eventually forming the Zionist Organization.

Not everyone of Jewish ancestry agreed with the vision of establishing a Jewish state. As Rabinowitz pointed out for Shimon, there were many contradicting opinions among Jews. But it was into that struggle that Shimon would be thrust and through which he would find his calling.

✦ ✦ ✦

Several months after Shimon and his father returned from the trip to Radun, Yehoshua Rabinowitz's cousin, Isidor Talmon, arrived in Vishnyeva. Talmon had spent the past three years living and working in Palestine on a farm—a *kibbutzim*—established some years earlier by Hovevei Zion, one of the larger Zionist groups created to promote Zionism, before the rise of Herzl and the Zionist Organization. The organization and farm initially were supported by a grant from British Jewish financier James Rothschild.

A few days after Talmon's arrival, Rabinowitz invited people from town to his home to hear news of life in Palestine and, more particularly, to learn about the kibbutzim movement. Still inspired by the most recent attack on the village and by what he'd heard from Rabbi Kagan, Shimon's father insisted his family attend the meeting.

Rabinowitz's house wasn't far away, so on the day of the gathering Shimon and his family walked there. They arrived to find the front room of Rabinowitz's house already filled with guests. Someone brought a chair for Shimon's mother and made a place for her near the window, but Shimon, Gigi, and their father stood in back near the doorway to the kitchen.

For the next thirty minutes, Talmon described the journey from Bila Tserkva, the city in Ukraine where he'd been born, to Jaffa, the port at Tel Aviv. First he took a train to Odessa, then a boat across the Black Sea to Istanbul before boarding a ship that sailed along the Mediterranean coast, passing around Turkey, then continuing past Syria and Lebanon to Palestine.

Upon his arrival in Jaffa, Talmon spent a few days with a friend, then caught a ride to Rishon LeZion, the first farming settlement in Palestine established by Hovevei Zion. At night he took turns standing guard against Arabs who sometimes attacked the settlement. During the day he tended orange groves or worked in the cowshed. The collective grew fruit to sell but also produced its own food and operated a small dairy for that purpose. There was always more to be done than could be accomplished in a day. Having been raised in the city, Talmon found farm work hard, conditions sparse, and the fellowship with other laborers rewarding beyond compare.

After three months at Rishon LeZion, Talmon was assigned to a farm at Hadera, where he currently lived. He explained that when he first arrived he was given only menial tasks, working at whatever jobs needed attention. Several months later, he was put to work in the fields, then in the settlement's shop, where he spent long hours repairing broken equipment. That was the work he loved the most and the task to which he was currently assigned, though he thought that assignment might change upon his return.

As his remarks drew to a close, Talmon reached into a leather satchel that Shimon had not noticed before, leaning against a chair in the corner near where his mother sat. With a flourish, Talmon took an object from the bag. It was round and wrapped in tissue and everyone watched as he showed it around.

"And I have here an example of what we produce on our farm."

With all eyes fixed on him, Talmon slowly and deliberately peeled back the paper, one corner at a time, to reveal an orange, which he held aloft for all to see. A collective gasp went up from the room. Mouths fell open in amazement. Tropical fruit of any kind was a rare and exotic luxury in the cool climate of northern Europe. Some who were present that evening had never seen an orange.

Shimon was captivated by the things he heard that night. All the way home and later as he lay in bed unable to sleep, phrases Talmon used kept repeating in his mind. *Eretz Israel*—"Land of Israel." *Aliyah*—"to go up"—a euphemism for immigrating to Palestine, returning to the homeland of their ancestors.

The idea of living on a farm, working in the fields by day, fighting off Arab bandits by night, seemed exotic and mysterious. Like a grand adventure he might read about in a book, with Arabs dressed in robes and turbans, sitting atop large, muscular horses, swinging razor-sharp swords. And the men of the settlement responding with gunfire, then in hand-to-hand combat with clubs and spears made from the handles of farm tools.

Shimon knew his grandfather's position on Zionism. He was opposed to it, though not too much, it seemed. And he knew the admonition of the Haredi, to worship God by keeping the Commandments. But surely, returning to Palestine, devoting oneself to a life of labor, to a life bent on the establishment of a Jewish state, surely that was a good thing. Might it be the ultimate expression of Orthodox worship, the highest form of obedience?

What more could there be in life than to devote oneself to a cause very much like that of Abraham when he first established the ancient land of Israel? What more could one do than commit to a goal bigger than you could attain in a lifetime? Grander than anything anyone could fully imagine, much less achieve?

Shimon was certain his grandfather would never immigrate to Palestine. And he doubted his father would, either. But he decided then that he was going. As soon as he was old enough, he would pack up his belongings, follow the route Talmon had described, and go there to work on a farm. But did he have to wait? What could he do now, without leaving Vishnyeva, to join in the effort?

There was the group Rabinowitz mentioned. Hashomer Hatzair. He could join the local chapter. And he could read on the subject. And he could learn about farming. But was there anything else? Some other way to express his interests?

As he lay in his bed, staring up at the ceiling, imagining life in Palestine, Shimon's eyelids finally grew heavy. Sleep crept close. And in the softness of that moment a phrase from the Psalms came to his mind. *"Pray for the peace of Jerusalem."* His eyes popped open.

That's it! He could pray. That was the something else he'd wanted. He could pray for the work in Palestine and for the state they were trying to create.

"'Pray for the peace of Jerusalem,'" he whispered, then continued with the remainder of the verse. "'May those who love you be secure. May there be peace within your walls and security within your citadels.'" He slid lower in the bed and pulled the covers up to his chin, all the while repeating those words over and over. Until at last he drifted off to asleep.

✦ ✦ ✦

Shimon joined the Hashomer Hatzair group that Rabinowitz led, but he wasn't the only one in Vishnyeva with dreams of Palestine. His father, Yitzhak, was interested, too, though not for political or religious reasons. He saw Palestine for its business potential. A wide-open market, needing almost anything one could sell, with unlimited potential for growth and expansion. It was too good of an opportunity to pass up and he began making plans to take full advantage of it.

As a place to begin, Yitzhak joined the Zionist Organization and attended meetings of all the separate Zionist groups operating in town, which included He-Halutz, Hashomer Hatzair, and Betar. He regularly circulated among each of them, making contacts with as many people as possible, hoping the relationships would pay off once he and they reached Palestine.

Finally, in 1932, Yitzhak could wait no longer. He sold most of his business interests, made provisions for his family's income in his absence, and boarded the train for an overland trip to Istanbul. From there he took a ship to Jaffa and immediately set to work establishing a business in Tel Aviv. It wasn't the best time to make the move. Palestine was long on need, short on supply, and even shorter on the means to pay for it. Things weren't much different anywhere else, either, with the entire world caught in the grip of the Great Depression. But he was determined to make a success of the venture and worked night and day to see it through.

Meanwhile, back in Vishnyeva, with his father gone, Shimon came under greater influence from Rabinowitz, whom he saw every day in class and at Hashomer Hatzair meetings. He also was drawn even closer to his Grandfather Meltzer, with whom he still met every afternoon and evening for study.

Widespread interest in Zionism among the people of Vishnyeva, and among the members of Shimon's own family, produced several consequences. For one, many people who previously lived in town were gone. They'd sold their belongings and headed for Palestine. And all of the talk in the Zionist groups made it easy to strike up a political debate. On the street, around the dining table, in class at school, everyone was ready with a point of view. And not merely a point of view but a side they had chosen to defend, often to the bitter end.

Shimon relished a good debate, but protracted discussions of the issues surrounding Zionism only made the contradictions of Judaism all the more apparent, accentuating the questions he had raised earlier with Rabinowitz.

Why, for instance, did Jews insist on maintaining a distinctly Jewish identity—culturally, traditionally, religiously—but the Zionist groups were decidedly secular in thought, ideology, and in their methods?

And why did the Haredi insist that Palestine was the Jewish homeland, yet resist the effort of Jews to migrate there and establish a Jewish state?

Shimon knew his grandfather's position on the matter, but he also knew that his grandfather had not spoken a word against this father's decision to join the Zionists in Palestine, even though his father talked about it all the time and made no secret of his reasons for wanting to go there. Yet, as intriguing as Shimon found all of that, he had never directly raised his questions with his grandfather. One afternoon, as they sat at the dining room table, he decided to try.

"You are opposed to the return of Jews to Palestine," Shimon began. The tone of his voice made it obvious he was building to a question.

"Yes."

"But you did not argue with Father when he wanted to go."

"What would have been the point?" Meltzer replied. "His mind was made up. Everyone could see that."

"But you had an opinion," Shimon insisted, pressing the point.

"Yes."

"And you did not share it."

Meltzer shook his head. "No, I did not share it."

"So, you chose not to share it."

Meltzer glanced in Shimon's direction. "Does that bother you?"

"It leaves me curious."

"About what?"

"About why you had an opinion, which I've heard you share many times with others, but didn't share it with my father."

"He knew my position as surely as you."

"But the subject seems never to have come up between you. Why?"

Meltzer had an amused smile. "As I have told you before, questions don't always lend themselves to a single answer. You must learn to see all sides of an issue."

"So, for some, Zionism is okay, but for others it is not? Some we should challenge, and others we should not?"

"Zionism is acceptable for everyone. Palestine is our homeland. The desire to live there is laudable. But the notion of a Jewish state, like our ancestors had in the past, cannot be realized until the Messiah comes. That has been our teaching, our tradition, our understanding throughout the ages. Some will listen to that teaching, and understand it, and choose not to go. Some will listen, but never understand. Others will listen, understand, and choose to go anyway."

"And that is why Rabbi Kagan and Agudath Israel are building schools there?"

Meltzer nodded. "Because some of our people will go there regardless." They sat in silence a moment before Meltzer continued, "Do you wish to go to Palestine, too?"

Shimon could sense the question coming before his grandfather asked and knew it would be difficult to answer. "I think I shall go regardless," he said, hoping to deflect the matter. "Father will send for us when he has a place prepared and then we will all be there together."

"You could stay with me if you wanted," Meltzer offered. "I could intercede with your mother."

Shimon knew his grandfather could persuade his mother to let him stay, but he already had decided his future lay in Palestine. He wanted to go. He just didn't want his grandfather to be upset about it. "Father wouldn't like that."

"No," Meltzer sighed. "I suppose he wouldn't. But what do *you* want?"

Shimon knew there was no use trying to dodge the question any longer. To do so risked appearing obstinate. But if he answered now, his earlier attempt to sidestep it would be seen as an act of kindness. So, summoning a bit of courage, he looked over at his grandfather and said softly, "I want to go."

A sad expression came over Meltzer. "Then you prove my point. Some will understand, and go anyway."

"I want to go, but leaving will not be easy. I want to be there. And I want to be here."

"Ah, right," Meltzer conceded. "But you are forced to choose."

"Yes. I am."

"If you want to go, there will never be a good time for it. The present always resists change. You simply pick a time, pay the price, and go. You will have many choices like that in life. If you want something, then decide to get it and pay the price. That is the way life works. Almost everything—even the things that are free—comes at a price." Meltzer reached across the table and took hold of Shimon's hand. "But you must promise me one thing."

"What is that?"

"That you will always be a Jew."

Shimon was puzzled. "How could I be anything else?"

"A Jew. Forever. Promise me that," Meltzer insisted.

"Yes, sir," Shimon replied resolutely. "I promise."

SHIMON PERES

*"Through creativity and innovation, we transformed
barren deserts into flourishing fields. . ."*

NOT LONG AFTER Shimon's father immigrated to Palestine, events in Europe turned toward one of the darkest periods in human history. A period that would transform the need of a Jewish state from the desire of a relative few to the desire of almost every nation on earth, giving the migration of Jews to Palestine the kind of international support needed, support that transcended race, religion, and culture.

Those changes began as a widespread and general German dissatisfaction with social and economic conditions in the decade immediately following World War I. By the 1920s, with the rise of the Nazi Party in Germany, anyone following events in Europe could have easily recognized the change in sentiment. But by 1933—the year after Shimon's father immigrated to Palestine—the movement toward policies specifically targeting Jews in a new and horrendous manner was unavoidably obvious for the world to see.

That year, the Nazi Party became the largest political party in Germany. With a majority in the German parliament—the Reichstag—Nazi delegates elected Adolf Hitler, who already was chairman of the Nazi Party, to the office of chancellor.

As leader of the largest political party in the country, holding a majority in the Reichstag, and now in the chancellor's office, Hitler wielded enormous power. Enormous but not absolute. That changed with passage of two laws. First, the *Decree of the Reich President For the Protection of People and State*, known more widely as the Reichstag Fire Act, which abolished civil liberty. Then shortly after that, the Enabling Act, which gave Hitler the power to make laws on his own, without the involvement or approval of the Reichstag. Together, the two laws had the effect of making him a dictator, his power absolute.

Thereafter, Hitler issued a stream of decrees that steadily and methodically restricted the life of German Jews, first limiting their participation in the professions, then eliminating their right to *any* occupation save that of simple laborer. But the result of those decrees went far beyond mere implementation of government policy.

German citizens, chafing under the terms and conditions of the armistice that ended World War I, and disgruntled by the horrendous economic conditions that followed, viewed the government's policies toward Jews as validation of their own anti-Semitic prejudices. Empowered and emboldened, they turned on the Jews with acts of increasing violence.

Accounts of the atrocities that followed slowly spread throughout Europe, eventually reaching Vishnyeva. Those who were attuned to world events and the rising climate of anti-Jewish violence understood that even worse things awaited. But in 1935, before the tragedy that would befall Germany and the world reached Vishnyeva, Shimon and his family received the fortuitous news from Yitzhak that he was ready for them to join him in Palestine.

On a cool spring morning in 1934, Shimon, Gigi, and Sara, their mother, rode with Grandfather Meltzer to the train station and waited on the platform for the morning train to arrive. They talked in hushed tones about the crispness still in the air, the promise of another growing season, the way the sun shone brightly that morning, but no one mentioned the thoughts that filled their minds. Thoughts that this might be the last time they would see each other. For Shimon, the sense of pending separation was particularly difficult. For twelve years he had enjoyed the companionship of his grandfather. Talking, reading, learning together. Exploring the depths of ideas and concepts to a degree far beyond his age or station in life. All of that now would come to an end.

At last the train arrived and as the baggage was loaded into the car, Meltzer turned to Shimon, placed both hands on his shoulders, and looked the young boy in the eye. "Shimon," he reminded, "always be a Jew."

"Yes, sir," Shimon replied. "I can be nothing else."

"You will encounter many who will try to persuade you otherwise."

"Yes, sir."

"Always be a Jew."

"Yes, sir."

"No matter what the circumstance, or who you encounter."

"Yes, sir," he repeated with absolute certainty, "I will be a Jew forever."

The conductor signaled the engineer, and a belch of steam came from the locomotive. Shimon stepped into the railcar doorway and grasped the edge of the door with one hand, then reached back to extend his hand toward Meltzer. Meltzer rushed forward and clasped Shimon's hand, then slowly it slipped from his grip as the train started forward.

Shimon watched from the doorway until the train rounded a bend in the rails and the station disappeared behind them. He lingered there a moment, wondering if it were all a dream. Wondering if he would awaken to find he was lying in bed at home just up the street from his grandfather's house. Then the train's whistle blew, the rhythm of the wheels clacking against the rails increased, and the train picked up speed.

✦ ✦ ✦

From Vishnyeva, Shimon, his mother, and his brother traveled by train to Istanbul, then by ship to Jaffa, a port on the Palestinian coast, where they were met by Shimon's father. Initially, the family settled in Tel Aviv but soon moved inland to Rehovot, located between Jerusalem and the coast with Tel Aviv in the west, Ashdod to the south, and Jerusalem to the east.

Established in 1890, Rehovot was built by Jews from Poland under the auspices of the Menuha Venahala Society, a group that sought to form a community separate and apart from those funded and established by the Rothschilds. When Shimon arrived, the town had a population of between 3,500 and 4,000 inhabitants and was known for its citrus groves. Agriculture was its primary business.

Already, however, Rehovot was expanding beyond a mere farming community. An agriculture research station established there later became the Department of Agriculture of the Hebrew University of Jerusalem. Rehovot also was home to Chaim Weizmann's Sieff Institute—a research center that began with the study of organic chemistry but later expanded into multiple scientific disciplines. All of which was well underway when Shimon arrived and made Rehovot very much different from the region of Vishnyeva where Shimon had grown up.

As separate and different as Palestine must have seemed, Shimon did not arrive there totally alone. In addition to his immediate family, several of his aunts and uncles already were living there. And, in the same year that the Perskis immigrated, Shimon's teacher, Yehoshua Rabinowitz, also moved to Palestine.

Like everyone else, Shimon came to Palestine thinking the move to be a simple matter. A mere relocation. After all, Palestine had been the Jewish homeland since ancient times. They simply were returning to a homeland that always had been theirs. What he found, however, was a land already occupied, primarily by Arabs, with a history that had grown even more complex than that of the ancient Hebrews. A complexity that confronted Shimon personally in his daily life from the moment he arrived. Palestine of the early twentieth century was a land of conflict, Arabs vs. Jews. Jews vs. Arabs, part of a long history rife with conflict and intrigue.

✦ ✦ ✦

Following the collapse of the Roman Empire, the Islamic prophet Muhammad, supported by a large Arab army, took control of the Middle East on his way to conquering a region that stretched from India in the east to Spain in the west. In the centuries that followed, successive leadership changes brought that area under the rule of an Ottoman Caliphate, which lasted until the end of World War I.

With the collapse of the Ottoman Empire, lesser Arab leaders competed for control of the Middle East. One of those who entered the fray was Hussein ibn Ali al-Hashimi, the Emir of Mecca, a descendant of Muhammad's grandson.

Hussein claimed control of a region known as the Hejaz, a narrow strip of land that extended along the western side of the Arabian Peninsula. Bordering the Red Sea, it included the cities of Mecca and Medina, Islam's two holiest sites, over which he exercised iron-fisted custodial care—a duty that had been the exclusive franchise of the Hashemite family for as long as anyone could remember.

During World War I, the Ottoman Empire sided with the Central Powers against the Triple Entente—the Allies. However, Hussein, realizing that the Ottomans could be defeated, joined the Allies. In exchange for his continued support and assistance, the British promised Hussein a kingdom that included not only the Hijaz, which he already controlled, but also the areas of Iran, Iraq, Syria, Palestine, and Arabia. That kingdom never quite materialized, as the French and British desperately needed oil and would not support Hussein's control of the Middle East, but it did establish Arab independence.

After World War I, Abdul Aziz ibn Muhammad Al Saud led the Saudi family in a revolt against Hussein and took control of the Arabian Peninsula. As the Saudis solidified their domination of the peninsula, Hussein was forced to flee. He retreated northward and settled in Amman where his son Abdullah lived and ruled under British protection.

At the time, the British army occupied the Levant under a mandate issued by the League of Nations, part of the British legacy that arose from the defeat and breakup of the Ottoman Empire. The League's mandate gave the British dominion over an area extending north of Egypt as far as Syria and east to Iran. In 1921, the British established Abdullah—Hussein's son—as Emir of Oman.

In Palestine proper—the area historically comprising the ancient nation of Israel—the Jewish Agency for Palestine, an extension of the Zionist Organization, functioned as the official representative of Jewish residents in Palestine and their official liaison with British mandatory authorities. The Agency coordinated Jewish immigration, supervised the establishment, expansion, and development of farming settlements, and facilitated all other domestic Jewish activities in the region.

At the time Shimon arrived, Chaim Weizmann, longtime leader of the Jewish Agency, had recently fallen out of favor among Zionists because of his reticence to push for an independent Jewish state. The resulting leadership transition brought David Ben-Gurion to office as the newly elected chairman of the Agency. It was a post he would retain until Israeli independence was achieved in 1948. Ben-Gurion would come to have a profound influence on Shimon and shape the future of his life in a direction he could not possibly have imagined at the time he stepped off the boat in Jaffa.

✦ ✦ ✦

In Palestine, Shimon found not only a new land but a new life. It was true, many members of his extended family lived there, but his grandfather, the primary influence on his life to that point, remained in Vishnyeva. With his grandfather's presence no longer a factor, and with neither of his parents practicing the Jewish faith, Shimon encountered the secular influence of the Zionist movement on his own. Swept up in the newness of the moment, his life soon reflected that of the people around him. He no longer attended synagogue, which previously had been a weekly activity, and no longer dressed in a woolen suit and buttoned-up shirt. Instead, he adopted the shorts and short-sleeved shirts of his contemporaries, arguably an attire more suited to the warm climate, and adopted their less-stringent, more carefree and unstructured lifestyle.

In Europe, conditions turned even more ominous than before as Germany rearmed the Rhineland, a region specifically neutralized by the Treaty of Versailles, and the balance of power shifted from France to Germany's favor. But in Palestine, in spite of the tension between Arabs and Jews, life for Shimon took on an idyllic tone. He made friends, spent time studying, and, unlike before, followed a daily routine that included time for play.

For the boys of Rehovot, basketball was the major preoccupation. During Shimon's first summer, they gathered every day for a pickup game. Sometimes on a court in the park or at the school. Other times in a backyard or, if nothing else, on the street with a line on the wall of a nearby building as an improvised basket—take a shot, hit the line, score a point.

Physically, Shimon was big for his age and had an athletic build, but having never played sports of any kind, he knew nothing of basketball technique. After a game or two, his friends began calling him "Two Left Feet," a reference to his penchant for tripping and stumbling over himself as he tried to dribble the ball or take a shot. Not measuring up in ability was difficult for Shimon to accept. Competition ran deep in his personality and he'd always excelled at everything he attempted, but he enjoyed the sense of camaraderie among boys his own age and tried to live with the frustration of not being the best.

Late one afternoon, after a particularly poor performance, Yohai Cohen, a kid who lived a few blocks away, took Shimon aside and gave him some tips. "When you shoot," Yohai told him, "square up to the basket first."

"What does that mean?"

Yohai looked puzzled. "What does it mean?"

"Yeah," Shimon said. "What does it mean? The ball is round. The hoop for the basket is round. What does it mean to 'square up'?"

"Forget the basket," Yohai explained. "Think of the backboard."

Shimon was perplexed. "What's the backboard?"

"That big square board behind the basket," Yohai answered, pointing to the goal.

"Okay."

"Look. The game isn't about the ball, or the basket, or dribbling."

"I thought you said it was about squaring up."

"It is. And that's what I'm telling you. The key to the game is in your feet."

"My feet?"

"Yes." Yohai assumed a stance. "Set your feet slightly apart. Like this." He pointed to his shoes.

"Okay," Shimon said slowly as he adjusted his position.

"Now," Yohai continued, "imagine a line going from the tip of one shoe to the tip of the other."

Shimon looked down at his feet. "Okay."

"Keep that line square with the board."

"What if I'm shooting from the side instead of from right in front of the goal?"

"Easy," Yohai replied. "Just imagine a board behind the hoop, but one set at the angle for where you're standing."

"Oh." Shimon's eyes brightened. "Like this?" He lifted the ball over his head and released it in a perfect arc, but the ball sailed over the hoop and struck the ground on the opposite side. "I'm not sure that helps."

"It does if you remember that the board isn't really there."

Shimon frowned. "Then what's the point of imagining it?"

"Imagine the board that's not there so you can square up to the basket. Then carom the shot off the backboard that *is* there."

Shimon's eyes brightened again in a look of realization. "Like this?" He took a shot. This time, the ball struck the backboard at an angle and bounced through the hoop. A sense of exhilaration swept over him at making the shot and at seeing the greater idea behind it—using something that was not there, to work off something that *is* there, to achieve a third thing he hadn't been able to accomplish before. For a moment he thought of explaining all of that to Yohai, then remembered the reaction he'd received from his classmates in Vishnyeva and decided to keep it to himself.

"Just like that," Yohai laughed.

They played awhile longer, but the sun was sinking quickly and when the light was gone they sat on a bench to relax. As they talked, Shimon learned that Yohai attended Geula Gymnasium, a high school for commerce in Jerusalem. "My parents thought it would be good for me," Yohai explained. "They want me to learn the value of labor."

"And that is what they teach there?"

"They teach everything. It's just, the classes are built around the idea that we will one day work on a farm, engage in business, live the life of the proletariat. Where will you go to school?"

"Balfour."

"Ah. I hear it is a good school."

"That is what they say."

"Your parents must pay a lot for that."

Shimon shrugged. "I wouldn't know. You don't have to pay for the school you attend?"

"I don't think so."

"Where is it?"

"Jerusalem. Yours is in Tel Aviv."

"Yes. I will ride the bus."

"Everyone does."

That evening at dinner, Shimon mentioned what he'd learned from Yohai about schools. "The Cohens are laborites," Shimon's father said. The tone of his voice made his opinion obvious. Shimon knew what it was anyway. He'd heard his father say more than once that neither the labor movement nor those who came to Palestine for religious reasons had the answers.

"I'm not sure that's a word," Yitzhak continued, "but that's what I call them. Devoted to the wonders of the labor movement."

"As is Rebbe Rabinowitz," Shimon added.

"Rabinowitz," his father scoffed. "Would do him good to get out of the classroom and work for a while."

Shimon tried to steer the topic back to his original issue. "Do you think I could attend school in Jerusalem?"

"You're enrolled at Balfour," Yitzhak said flatly.

"Your grandfather thought it was a good idea," his mother noted.

Shimon was surprised. "Grandfather?"

His mother left the table and returned a moment later with a letter. "This is what he said." She handed it to him.

Shimon read the letter eagerly. "I didn't know he wrote."

"It came yesterday."

By Palestinian standards Balfour School was a prestigious educational institution. Founded by Alexander Koler, it offered a classic education much like the instruction Shimon had received from his grandfather, which made the school a natural fit for him. But unlike many schools in Eretz Israel, Balfour was not steeped in the labor movement, which was the heart and soul of Rehovot and the focus of attention for Shimon's neighborhood friends. Attending Balfour put him out of step with the others and impinged on the sense of camaraderie he'd come to enjoy.

After a year at Balfour, Shimon tried again to persuade his parents to let him attend Geula in Jerusalem. This time, he added one more fact. "Tuition is free. Bus fare would be the only expense and we'd have to pay that anyway." He could see the idea of free education struck a chord with his father.

"Hmm," Yitzhak sighed with a note of resignation. "Perhaps it would be for the best."

Shimon's mother looked sad but forced a smile. "You can learn wherever you are," she said.

Shimon understood the response. Earning a living in Palestine had proved to be far more difficult than Yitzhak had imagined. In spite of his effort—rising early, working late, applying himself diligently—business hadn't gone as well as he'd hoped. He tried selling lumber, as he'd done successfully in Vishnyeva, but native lumber was in short supply where they now were, and imports were limited. As an alternative, he opened a café. Business was brisk but required long hours, lots of work, and the profit margin was slim. Saving money on the cost of education was more attractive than it had been the year before.

And so, at the end of his second summer in Palestine, Shimon transferred to Geula Gymnasium. He and Yohai Cohen rode the bus to Jerusalem every morning and back home again in the evening. With plenty of time together in the months that followed, they became fast friends.

In addition to regular classes, Geula hosted a number of labor youth organizations. Hashomer Hatzair, to which Shimon had belonged in Vishnyeva, had a chapter that was active at the school, but Yohai already was a member of HaNoar HaOved. Rather than joining a group on his own, he followed Yohai.

Founded by Histadrut, a central trade-workers union that represented all the major workers organizations in Palestine, HaNoar HaOved was part of the most influential labor group in the country. One that offered students a chance to develop friendships, acquaintances, and connections with the potential to last a lifetime, extending to them the promise of a path to greater and more extensive opportunities in the future.

Like many other youth organizations of the day, HaNoar promoted a form of Zionism that was laced with Marxist socialism. It also included a strong emphasis on life in the kibbutzim. Labor was promoted for its redemptive qualities and as a means for discovering one's true self and ultimate destiny. Weekly meetings included lectures, discussions, and debates regarding various aspects of contemporary labor issues, political events, and ongoing policies. All of which was presented in a dynamic intellectual environment. Very quickly, the priorities of the labor movement became the central focus of Shimon's life and the organizing principle for his thoughts of the present as well as the future.

Through his membership in HaNoar HaOved, Shimon also encountered for the first time the basic tenet that lay at the heart of the Jewish Zionist movement—the labor movement with its emphasis on the politically practical versus Revisionist Zionism with its emphasis on gaining control over Greater Israel. One wanted a secular Jewish political state, even if it meant conceding some of the area that was traditionally part of historic Israel. The other determined to hold out for control of the entire region.

Shimon also learned in greater detail about the paramilitary groups operating in Palestine. Groups like Haganah, well trained and working to protect the kibbutzim, and others like Irgun and Lehi that took a more militant approach, fighting Arab advances everywhere in an attempt to drive them from the region.

Like most of his friends, Shimon was captivated by all of it—the politics, the debate, the kibbutz movement. After class and on the street at Rehovot, they would talk about the kibbutzim, the dominant political parties of the day, and how best to handle Arab opposition. But while his friends focused on which kibbutz to join, Shimon pondered starting one of their own. And while his friends talked about which political party had the better ideas, he talked about the importance of the state and of developing a nation where Jews could be free and safe. Before long, his fellow students again labeled him a dreamer. Friendly banter grew biting and caustic. And then the fights would begin. For Shimon, it was a repeat of the way he'd been treated in Vishnyeva, only this time he fought back, though not nearly as aggressively as Gigi.

One day on the bus ride back to Rehovot, after a particularly troubling day at school, Shimon raised the subject with Yohai Cohen. "Why do they think my ideas are so ridiculous?"

"Who?" Yohai asked.

"You know who. The guys at school. The guys up the street. Everyone we know."

"They never had a serious thought about anything."

"And that's why they dislike me?"

"Look, those guys just repeat what they hear their parents talk about. That's all they know. You actually think for yourself. Things they never considered. Things they lack the ability to grasp."

"But why do they hate me for it?"

"Because they didn't think of it first. And because they know they can't think of it and never will."

Shimon glanced down at the floor of the bus. "I hear them talking. I hear what they say about me."

"I know."

"Calling me a dreamer like it's something bad." Shimon looked over at Yohai. "Is it so bad to dream? To imagine things that don't exist and then work to make them become a reality. Is that so bad?"

"Obviously not."

"Don't they have dreams?"

"I suppose. Surely they must." Yohai grinned. "Pitifully small dreams for most of them, but dreams just the same."

"Well, they never talk about them."

"I think they're too scared to talk about it. Talking about all that other stuff is safer."

"Other stuff?"

"The ideas about collective government versus an open democracy. Or American capitalism and—"

Shimon interrupted. "Do they know what any of that means?"

"I doubt it. I'm not sure I do."

"Me either. But why can't we have both?"

Yohai looked perplexed. "Both?"

"Capitalist economy, collective government. Why can't we have both?"

"Aren't those two ideas opposed to each other? Individual choice, collective control."

"Yes," Shimon replied. "But so is capitalism and democracy. They're opposed to each other, at least in principle."

"You'll have to explain that one to me."

Just then, the bus came to a stop. "Come on." Shimon stood. "This is where we get off. We can talk while we walk."

Yohai slid from the seat and followed Shimon up the aisle. "Think anyone's waiting for us?"

Shimon glanced back over his shoulder. "Waiting for us?"

"To finish the argument. From earlier today."

"I don't know. But I don't care anymore. I've decided. They can argue all they want. I know what I think. They can think whatever they like."

5

SHIMON PERES

"The most important thing
in life is to dare."

WHILE ATTENDING Geula Gymnasium, Shimon learned of Ben-Shemen Agricultural School, a school specifically designed to train students for daily work and life on the kibbutzim. Not merely a place that offered typical elements of education in a labor environment, Ben-Shemen taught the skills necessary for work in the farming settlements—animal husbandry, agronomy, automotive mechanics, and more.

For Shimon, Ben-Shemen seemed exactly the kind of place he'd wanted all along—without even knowing that he wanted it. This was more than a learning exercise, more than the accumulation of knowledge; it was a cause. A cause to which he could devote himself with singular attention. Others might spend their time talking about the kibbutz life, or about politics, or party, or the value of collective wisdom, but for Shimon talk was no longer enough. He wanted to *do*. And doing meant attending Ben-Shemen. All he needed was his parents' permission.

One evening in the spring of his second year at Geula, Shimon talked to his parents about transferring to Ben-Shemen.

"You're already on your second school," his father pointed out. "This would be your third. How many more will you attend? There aren't all that many in Palestine, you know."

"It has taken a while to understand what living in Palestine is really all about."

"And you think this is what it's about."

"Yes," Shimon replied.

"Living on a farm." His father had a condescending tone. "On a communal farm."

"That is the heart of the matter here."

His father looked away. "It's not like the life we knew before."

"We aren't in Poland any longer," Shimon took care to speak respectfully. "And we aren't Poles, either."

"We never were Poles," his mother offered.

"Then what are we?" his father asked.

Shimon stood a little taller. "We are Jews living in our homeland."

"If the Arabs don't kill us first."

"Better to live this way, even with the threat of death, than to live in a cage."

Shimon's father looked over at him. "You think our life before was lived in a cage?"

"I think the Arabs are no more a threat than the Russian thugs."

"Maybe so." His father turned away. "How much will this school cost?"

"Nothing."

His father shot a glance in Shimon's direction. "Nothing?"

"Nothing." Shimon was certain this talk of money and cost would seal the deal. "And it's a boarding school," he added. "I would live there at no expense to us. The only cost would be fare for the occasional visit home."

"More than occasional," his mother interjected. "I hope."

"Frequent," Shimon corrected with a smile in her direction.

"You're fifteen," his father sighed. "I reckon you're old enough to make up your own mind." He started toward the door. "Remember to visit your mother."

✦ ✦ ✦

In 1938, Shimon enrolled at Ben-Shemen Agricultural School and Youth Village. At last, he could prepare for life in Palestine the way the Jews of Palestine had chosen to live. Rebuilding their native homeland, building a modern state. Indeed, the kibbutz movement lay at the heart of the Jewish effort in Palestine not merely as an idealistic cause but as the key to everything else they hoped to accomplish.

When Jewish settlers arrived in Palestine they found no support from local Arabs or the Turkish government. Socially isolated, they were forced to create their own infrastructure—electricity, water, roads, communications—but the key to it all was food production, the source of strength and sustainability that allowed all other things to develop. Without food no settlement, community, or town could survive, much less thrive. The kibbutz movement supplied that need.

Shimon's friend Yohai joined him at Ben-Shemen, where they roomed together. A few days after they arrived they were joined by Nahum Amitsur, who'd recently emigrated from Lithuania. Days were spent in class and working on the farm. At night, they attended lectures, usually from visiting dignitaries, social events in the main hall, or relaxing in their room. Often, they talked late into the night and over the school term that followed, and the bond between the three grew strong.

HaNoar HaOved had a group at Ben-Shemen, and a month or two after arrival, Shimon joined them. Yohai did, too. Much like he'd experienced at Geula, HaNoar meetings were noted for vigorous debate over politics and policy, the desire for an independent Jewish state, and the role of political parties in a free society. Shimon was in his element and became active, speaking up in meetings, offering his ideas, refusing to back down.

Before long, Shimon began talking about his idea of starting their own kibbutz, built around their own ideas, only now it wasn't merely a schoolboy's dream. He talked in specific terms and it became clear he really meant to do it. To finish at Ben-Shemen, locate a site, and establish a collective. Some were intrigued. At Ben-Shemen the notion of starting your own kibbutz wasn't as out of place as it had been at the traditional schools Shimon had attended earlier. But not everyone appreciated his perspective and more than once he was met with a roll of the eye and a snide comment.

Late one afternoon, as Shimon entered the school's main hall, he overheard a group of students talking in a side room. He started toward the door to join them, then heard his name and paused to listen.

"I heard about him," someone said. "Shimon the Dreamer, that's what they called him."

"Who?"

"At Balfour."

"Balfour. You went there?"

"No. But my brother did. He knew Shimon. They all thought he was crazy."

"Or arrogant," someone offered.

"Or both," another added.

"I think he's smart," a girl noted.

Shimon moved a little to the left, placing her in his line of sight. Her auburn hair and dark eyes caught his attention.

The girl continued. "Smarter than you. Smarter than all of us."

"And that's the scariest part."

Just then, Yohai appeared at Shimon's side. "What are you doing?"

Shimon put his finger to his lips in a gesture for quiet, then whispered, "Who is that girl?" Yohai glanced over his shoulder. "Do you know her?"

"Yeah."

Shimon backed away from the door. "Who is she?"

"Sonia Gelman."

"Gelman?"

"Yeah. Her father sometimes teaches the shop class."

"Right. We were in there today."

"Well, that's his daughter." Yohai grinned. "Might be better if he didn't see you gawking at her."

"I wasn't gawking. I was listening."

"I know. I heard part of their conversation."

Shimon looked away. "It's just like before," he sighed.

"They don't matter. Come on." Yohai placed his hand on Shimon's shoulder. "It's almost time for dinner. Let's get in line."

✦ ✦ ✦

During his first year at Ben-Shemen, Shimon joined the student Haganah unit at the village. The school admitted students of every age for class and instruction. Older ones were encouraged to join Haganah and took turns standing guard at night. Shimon was glad to take his place in the ranks.

One evening, not long after overhearing the conversation in the main hall, Shimon was standing guard near a cluster of faculty residences at the edge of the compound. About twilight, a girl appeared on a walkway to his right. He watched as she approached and realized it was Sonia Gelman, the girl he had overheard talking with the others in the main hall. As she drew nearer their eyes met and she smiled at him. He smiled back and she came over to him.

"At least you have a pleasant evening," she noted.

"Yes," he agreed. "At least there's that."

"Have you seen anything interesting out here so far?"

"Well," he said nervously, "there's you."

She grinned. "And they all think you don't know what to say to a girl."

"They all?"

"Ohad. Rafael," she said. "You know."

"Yeah, well, Ohad thinks many things about me, not much of which is true."

"Yes, I suspect so."

He glanced at her, then let his gaze fall to the ground. "I heard you talking the other day."

"Talking? Where?"

"The main hall. That skinny kid. I can't remember his name. The one who said his brother knew me at Balfour."

"Uri."

"Yeah. Uri Goldstein. Talking about what they used to call me at Balfour."

Sonia had a kind smile. "You mustn't think too much of Uri. He's not that smart. . . or perceptive."

For the first time, Shimon looked her in the eye. "You stood up for me."

"They aggravated me that day. They aggravate me a lot, but that day. . . Their arrogance was too much. Their sense that they're better than everyone else. Better than everyone because they think less seriously and do less work and spend more time congratulating themselves for it. It made me angry."

"Well, whether because of anger or. . . something else, I appreciated your kind words."

"You're welcome, Shimon Peres. You're very welcome."

With that, she turned and walked away. Shimon watched as she made her way to one of the cottages and opened the door to step inside. But just before she disappeared, she glanced back over her shoulder. When she saw he was watching her, she smiled at him, gave him a wave, and then was gone.

The next evening, Sonia appeared again and every night after that when he was on duty she came outside at dusk and they talked. At first only for a few minutes, but then for longer and longer periods. Gradually, in the weeks and months that followed, their conversations grew into friendship and he sought her out at times when he wasn't on guard duty. They spent hours talking about the topics they studied in class, his dream of starting a kibbutz—which was a vision they had in common—and the need for a state and ideas about what that state should be like.

"Sometimes I wonder if we'll ever have a state, though," she admitted one day.

"What makes you think that?"

"Well, for one thing, dealing with the Arabs is a challenge. A major obstacle, actually. I think they will always oppose us, state or no state."

"We could solve the Arab problem," he suggested.

"Oh?"

He nodded confidently. "We could solve it."

"How?"

"Make them our friends," he said flatly.

"Ha!" she exclaimed in a burst of laughter. "I think the Arabs might have something to say about that."

"Like what? What could they possibly say except to accept?"

"Well, for one thing, they would have to *want* to be friends. And I don't think they care for our friendship at all."

"Yeah," Shimon chuckled. "I suppose that would be an issue."

"A rather big one," Sonia added.

"But not insurmountable," he offered. "We could find a way to convince them they needed to be friends with us."

"How?"

Shimon shrugged. "Make it worth their while. You know. More beneficial to be our friend than to be our enemy."

"I suppose. But why this thing of friendship? Why is that so important?"

"If we make them our friends—truly our friends—then they won't be our enemies anymore. And friends don't shoot each other."

"Our economic friends."

Now it was his turn to look puzzled. "Economic friends? What are you talking about?"

"You said we should make it worth their while. Worth. Money. Business. Economics."

"Oh." His face brightened in a look of realization. "Economic friendship." He turned toward her with a broad smile. "I like that idea, Sonia. Genuine personal friendship would be best, but economic friendship works, too. On a political level." He looked off into the distance and repeated the phrase, "Economic friendship. Business as a means of diplomacy. I've never thought of that before."

Shimon liked Sonia in a way he'd never liked a girl before. She challenged him at every level—intellectually, emotionally, spiritually—and when they were together, he thought about things he'd never considered before. Felt things he'd never felt before. Came alive in ways he'd never experienced before.

Finally, one night as he walked her home from a study session, they paused beneath an olive tree and he kissed her. After that, they became inseparable, always together, always an item. Sometimes, Shimon's roommates, Yohai and Amitsur, joined them for lunch or dinner and they sat around the table talking, laughing, debating. When not in class or at work, they sat together outside on a bench enjoying the evening sky, or in the library studying. But regardless of where they were, or whether others were present, Sonia and Shimon always were together and he knew they would share their future together. Always. No matter what.

6

SHIMON PERES

*"The key to finding fulfillment is to
find a cause that's larger than yourself
and then to give your life to it."*

WHEN JEWS BEGAN returning to Palestine late in the nineteenth century, many Arabs already lived in Palestine. Particularly in rural and remote areas, however, most did so without owning the land where they resided. Following ancient traditions, they simply took up residence in a favorable location. Many families had been living in the same place for multiple generations.

Jews immigrating to the region purchased land from the Ottoman Turks who actually owned it. Consequently, Arabs in many cases were displaced from houses and farms they'd come to view as rightfully their own. Quite naturally, this led to tension between Arabs and Jews that would at various times erupt in violence.

After the British took control of the region under its mandate from the League of Nations, Jews who wanted to immigrate to Palestine were required to seek British permission before doing so. Permission was sometimes granted liberally and sometimes less so, but for the Arabs any Jewish immigration was seen as a threat to Arab livelihood. In the process, they would very quickly become resentful of what they viewed as British support for Jewish migration. Many blamed the British not only for the presence of Jews but also for the disruption that presence often induced.

In 1936, Arab frustration boiled over in open, armed revolt directed against both Jews and the British. As violence between Arabs and Jews escalated, Arab attacks against the British escalated, too.

In an effort to curb the violence, British mandate authorities banned possession of all weapons throughout Palestine. Both sides of the conflict claimed the ban was unevenly enforced, with Arabs claiming the British confiscated their weapons but not those belonging to the Jews, and Jews arguing the opposite. So, while Arab frustration with the British rose, Jewish frustration with the British rose as well.

To enforce the weapons ban, British authorities first demanded surrender of all firearms in private hands. Announcement of that policy provoked an intense debate among students at Ben-Shemen over whether they should obey and give up their weapons or refuse and keep them. Shimon was one of Ben-Shemen's most vocal opponents of the British policy and one of the staunchest advocates for evading its enforcement.

One night at a HaNoar HaOved meeting, argument over the topic became particularly heated.

"I thought you were in favor of friendship," Yohai chided.

"I am for friendship," Shimon responded. "But friendship with security."

"Maybe that's what the Arabs say, too," Amitsur said.

"And the British," Uri added.

"The British don't care whether we're friends or not," Ohad quipped. "They just want the violence to stop."

"Keep the peace," someone added, "and the British will let us do anything."

"Not quite anything."

Rafael spoke up. "Shimon, you're always talking about one thing and living another. Shimon the Dreamer is now Shimon the Finagler."

"I am not a liar," Shimon retorted with more than a hint of anger.

"No one said—"

"That's exactly what you said." Shimon was angry. "A finagler is one who finagles."

"I didn't mean all that."

"Then why don't you check the meaning of a word before you use it?"

Sonia took his hand. "Shimon, let's stick to the subject."

Rafael rocked his chair on its back legs, his face drawn in a smirk. "If you're going to be all touchy, maybe we should—"

"No," Sonia snapped, cutting him off. "You should learn to debate without resorting to a personal attack on your opponent."

"Well, when things are going your way, you talk one way. All intellectual and everything. All that talk about friendship and 'Oh, we can only find peace if we make them our friend.' You think it makes you sound so smart. Then when they show their true character and you ought to be held accountable for another one of your crazy ideas, you switch sides and want to shoot them dead. So which is it?"

At last, Shimon realized there was nothing for him to do but face the matter at hand, point by point. He took a deep breath and focused on the moment. "When it rains," he began, "you take an umbrella, right?"

"Yes," Rafael sighed. "But what does this—"

"And when it stops raining," Shimon continued, "and the sun comes out, you put away the umbrella. Right?"

"So what? I don't have—"

"When the facts are one way, you have one position and take one form of action. When the facts change, you have another and take a different form of action. You remain the same. The facts are the part that changes."

Rafael lowered the chair, placing all four legs on the floor. His arms were folded across his chest and he looked blankly across the room, as if unable to think of anything else to say.

"So one's position depends on the facts," Yohai added.

"Of course it does," Shimon replied.

"But how does that relate to what we're talking about?" Uri asked with a dismissive tone. "All that umbrella stuff and facts. How does it relate. . . to anything?"

Shimon tried to explain, "Look, our people live in far-flung communities located long distances from British military outposts. When an attack occurs, it takes at least a day for them to respond. By the time they arrive, any attack against us is over and everyone is dead. The only way we can survive is to defend ourselves. To take responsibility for our own security. We have to be able to defend ourselves. With weapons and ammunition, we can respond immediately to any attack. Without that, all is lost."

"Maybe they should disband the British military," someone suggested with a chuckle, "and replace them with burial units."

"Shimon is right," Amitsur said. "I never thought about it before but all of our farms are located in remote areas. None of them is near military installations."

Shimon looked over at Rafael. "I'm not changing my opinion about friendship. I think the long-term solution for us is to be a friend to the Arabs and make them our friends. But friendship doesn't mean naïvely accepting unrestrained Arab aggression. I'm not suggesting we should go on the offensive, as some argue, and attack Arab villages. But if they attack us, we should have the means of defending ourselves. And if the British take our weapons, we'll be left to defend ourselves with rocks and sticks."

"Plenty of that around here," Yohai laughed.

As the British sought to enforce the weapons ban, they engaged in widespread, unannounced searches, even at Ben-Shemen. Students became adept at hiding the school's weapons, practicing ways to do it quickly, while appearing to engage in normal activity. But in 1939, in response to yet another round of intense violence, the British arrived in greater numbers than before and conducted a lengthy and thorough search of the school and the youth village. This time, they located and seized a large cache of weapons. With that secured, they gathered the senior staff, took them into custody, and whisked them away to detention.

✦ ✦ ✦

In the late nineteenth and early twentieth centuries, Zionism brought Jews to Palestine from all across Europe. Their reasons for coming were as divergent as their geographic origins. Each wave of immigration sponsored by different organizations, encouraged and motivated by reasons of their own, brought people with diverse ideas, plans, and expectations. They were, however, very much human and, proved themselves altogether political, coalescing in three major political parties: Mapai, the largest and most dominant, along with Mapam and Ahdut HaAvoda, the most significant of the lesser.

Mapam was led by Meir Yaari and Yaacov Hazan. It was successful with the establishment and expansion of kibbutzim. Yaari, having been educated at the University of Vienna, was a religious ascetic and one of the best intellectuals of the day. Hazan was the more gregarious of the two but not Yaari's intellectual peer. Both were strong, capable men, and Mapam supported policies infused with both their ideas. A Marxist "brotherhood of man" blended with Hassidic religious devotion.

Ahdut HaAvoda was led by Yitzhak Tabenkin. Like Mapam, it embraced Marxist philosophy. Unlike Mapam, however, it shunned the emphasis on the brotherhood of man and, instead, advocated fierce Jewish independence secured by a strong military force, one it proposed to use in a fight for Jewish control of Palestine. All of it. Establishing a state that reflected Greater Israel, or none at all.

Mapai, the dominant party of the day, led by David Ben-Gurion and Berl Katznelson, took a quite different approach. David Ben-Gurion had been trained as a lawyer deeply committed to the rule of law. Katznelson, a self-taught intellectual, was co-founder and editor of *Davar*, the Mapai Party daily newspaper. He also was editor in chief of Am Oved, a publishing house. Both men were anti-Marxist, anti-Leninist, and opposed to every imported value system. They and the party rejected adaptation and synthesis of European political models and, instead, looked to the ancient Torah for guidance. With the support of the major labor unions, Mapai was the emerging Labor Party of Jewish Palestine.

Nuances arising from motivation, structure, and polity were important among party members, but the issue that divided them most was the question of geographic definition. It surfaced as a struggle between pragmatism and idealism. Accommodation and domination. But in the end, it was the question of whether to accept the division of Palestine into separate Jewish and Arab states—with international support—though it meant controlling only a portion of the historic biblical Israel. Or, hold out for Greater Israel—a Jewish political state with complete control of the entire Levant, subjugating the Arab population to Jewish rule—which the international community, including the United Kingdom, would not support.

Mapai, and the majority of Jews in Palestine, favored the immediate, though imperfect, solution of a state now with control of less than the entire region. Mapam and Ahdut HaAvoda adamantly refused to accept anything less than Greater Israel.

Shimon had been exposed to this debate long before he enrolled at Ben-Shemen but once there the issues were placed in stark contrast through discussion in class and a series of lectures held in the school's main hall. One of those lectures was presented by Yoske Rabinowitz, a Marxist who was quite cosmopolitan and appealing to many in his ideas, but mostly in his demeanor.

Shimon was drawn to Rabinowitz's views, too. He had seen how unbridled capitalism had consigned workers, on whom the system relied, to poverty and misery, while those who owned the means of production always prospered, in good times or bad. Yet he was suspicious of Communism.

Monarchies, with the corruption they'd spawned and the profligate lifestyle they'd promoted, had made a ruin of Western civilization. Was Communism any different? As a political system, it concentrated power in the hands of a few, much as the monarchies did. And, like the monarchies, communist government had nothing in its structure to check that power except the ability of the people to revolt, which would produce a political boom-and-bust cycle equally as cataclysmic as the economic cycles of capitalism.

In response to Rabinowitz's presentation, Berl Katznelson lectured for two weeks, three hours each day, addressing the fallacies of Rabinowitz's approach and of the communist ideals in general. Many of the issues he raised were precisely the questions for which Shimon sought answers. He found them in Katznelson's lessons.

Once he'd dispensed with that, Katznelson moved on to argue for the vision of a uniquely Jewish state, based on principles derived from the practices and traditions of old, tinged with socialism but often blended with key democratic ideas. A government big enough to smooth out uncertain cycles of capitalism but not designed to eliminate it. A society in which all were subject to laws derived from an historic Jewish ethic. Laws that respected individual freedom, balanced against social responsibility, evenly applied across socioeconomic distinctions.

Katznelson's lectures captivated Shimon and convinced him that Mapai—the Labor Party—had the correct approach to the Jewish future in Palestine. After immigrating to Palestine, he had wandered off on a freewheeling personal and intellectual tangent, only to be snatched back by the sense of honesty his grandfather instilled in him and which Katznelson reawakened. A nation now, secured against unprovoked attack, yet doing all in its power to live at peace with its neighbors, to transform not only Jewish life but life throughout the entire region. That was the synthesis he had sought and the cause he'd been looking for. A cause to which he could devote himself completely and spend his life working to build.

At the conclusion of Katznelson's final lecture, Shimon approached him to thank him for all he'd done and said. They shook hands and exchanged a pleasant greeting, then Katznelson said, "They tell me you are from Vishnyeva, yes?"

Shimon was surprised a man like Katznelson, a party leader, would know anything about him. "How do you know that? How do you know where I'm from?"

"I know many things," Katznelson replied. "Your grandfather is Zvi Meltzer. Yes?"

"Yes. He is." Mention of Shimon's grandfather made his heart skip a beat. "Do you know him?"

"I met him once or twice. Michael Katznelson is my cousin. You know Michael Katznelson, don't you?"

"Rabbi Katznelson? From Vishnyeva?"

"Yes."

"Sure. I know him. He was our rabbi. My grandfather is his cantor."

"I have been to Vishnyeva. A pleasant place. At least in the past."

They talked a few minutes about life in Poland and the changing politics of Europe. Katznelson was concerned about the direction events were headed in Germany. "Especially the way Soviet leaders are following the Nazi lead. I see only trouble for places like Vishnyeva and all the similar locations throughout Russia."

"We tried to convince my grandfather and grandmother to come with us," Shimon said, "but they refused. My uncle stayed behind to look after them."

Katznelson nodded. "And I did the same with Michael. But he was committed to his congregation." They were quiet a moment, as if remembering their family members and anticipating what might lie ahead for them. Then Katznelson looked up at Shimon and smiled. "I have an apartment in Tel Aviv. You must come there to see me. We can talk more."

"I would be glad to."

"Good." Katznelson raised an eyebrow expectantly. "Sunday, perhaps?"

Shimon was surprised at the immediacy of his invitation. "This Sunday?"

"Is that a problem?"

"No. It's not a problem at all."

"Good." Katznelson seemed pleased. "Sunday, then. Come for lunch. Around noon."

"Yes, sir. Sunday at noon."

"Bring a friend if you like," Katznelson added.

Shimon immediately thought of Sonia. "Yes, I will."

The following Sunday, Shimon and Sonia took the bus to Tel Aviv and made their way to Katznelson's apartment to join him for lunch. Throughout the remainder of their time at Ben-Shemen, those visits became a weekly occurrence as Katznelson took them under his wing.

With Katznelson as his friend and mentor, and with Sonia, Yohai, and Amitsur keeping him focused, Shimon resolved all remaining intellectual debate in favor of the pragmatic Labor approach. To him, it was far better to have a Jewish state than not. To have something, even if that something was imperfect, rather than nothing now—and perhaps nothing later, either. From that time forward, the choice had been made. There would be no looking back.

SHIMON PERES

*"You can kill a thousand; you can bring an
end to life; you cannot kill an idea."*

NOT ALL THE STUDENTS at Ben-Shemen thought Shimon's idea of starting their own kibbutz was a senseless dream. Several, including Yohai and Amitsur, were interested in joining him to see that dream come true. As they grew older their group increased in size and Shimon helped get them organized, becoming their secretary in the process. With an organization in place, they began working to gather the support necessary to start a kibbutz, outlining details of all it might be and how it might function best. More than ever, they focused on acquiring basic skills like proper farming technique, financial planning and management, and the internal controls necessary for efficient and sustainable operation.

At about the same time, Shimon was selected as a delegate to the annual HaNoar HaOved convention held in Tel Aviv. As a youth organization of Histadrut, an umbrella organization for all Jewish labor unions in Palestine, HaNoar HaOved had members from every political party in the country and represented a diverse range of political opinions. That arrangement, however, sometimes produced a skewed leadership mix that masked the ideas and inclinations of individual members.

Although a newly elected delegate, Shimon found an opportunity to address the convention. Notoriety from his remarks caught the delegates' attention and someone placed his name in nomination for a position on the HaNoar HaOved Secretariat, the executive committee that governed the organization throughout the year, in between its annual conventions. As the convention drew to a close, Shimon found himself elected to a Secretariat position. Zorick Dayan, the younger brother of Moshe Dayan, a popular Haganah officer, also was elected and the two became friends.

After completing their education and training at Ben-Shemen, Shimon and the group of students who were interested in starting their own kibbutz were sent to live at Kibbutz Geva, a settlement in the Jezreel Valley, where they received additional instruction specifically about farm operations. By then, the idea of starting a kibbutz had matured into a goal with a name—Kibbutz Alumot. To make Alumot a reality, though, they needed more than farming skills and an understanding of communal operations. They needed funding, equipment, and a site for their community, all of which they hoped to find while at Geva.

Daily life at Geva was structured around hard work supervised by severe and demanding leadership, an experience designed to reflect and prepare Shimon and the others for the harsh and demanding endeavor they were planning to undertake.

Farm work kept them busy during the day, and their evenings where spent organizing youth groups at other kibbutzim on behalf of HaNoar HaOved. On the rare day off, Zorick Dayan, who lived about forty kilometers away in Nahalal, sometimes drove down to Geva for a visit. At other times, Shimon and Sonia rode to Nahalal to visit with him. During one of those weekend visits, they met Zorick's older brother, Moshe. Shimon got along well with him, and the two struck up a friendship.

When Shimon and Sonia weren't otherwise occupied, they would ride to Tel Aviv to visit Shimon's family, or back to Ben-Shemen to visit Sonia's parents. By then, their relationship was sealed. Neither of them wanted to be with anyone else and they talked of a future together.

Before that, however, news was received that Germany and Russia had invaded Poland. A few days later, the calamity that Berl Katznelson had worried might come had finally arrived as nations around the world lined up to oppose the German advance across Europe.

With the coming of World War II, Shimon's father joined the British army. He was assigned to a sapper unit—combat engineers—and went to work building roads, bridges, and other structures for the Allied army. By the second year of fighting he was captured in Greece and spent most of the remainder of his enlistment as a prisoner in a German POW camp.

Shimon's brother, Gigi, joined the Palmach, a semiautonomous commando unit that was part of Haganah. Their mother took a job in a munitions factory making ammunition for the British. Sonia served in the British army as a driver and was sent to Egypt where she worked for the duration of the war.

Shimon, however, remained in Palestine. After concluding their training at Geva, he and the students from Ben-Shemen were sent to Poria, the site of a former kibbutz at the southern end of the Sea of Galilee. A desolate location, it had been abandoned since before the war, and the buildings were in disrepair. Shimon and his group went to work, applied their training, and renovated the buildings. Afterward, they gave the site the name of Poria Alumot as an homage to the name they'd chosen while still in school. Work at Poria was long and difficult, the location was remote, but the social life was great and the students melded into a tight-knit unit.

In 1941, Shimon was elected secretary of HaNoar HaOved. Recruiting new members and establishing new groups at other kibbutzim took even more of his time than before. When he wasn't working on that, his mind was on tasks at Poria that demanded attention, or on Sonia and how they could be together again. Regardless of how his mind was occupied, his thoughts were far from Vishnyeva, Poland, or the things that might be happening there. With the war raging, and mail service irregular at best, there was no way of knowing details about his family or of the conditions they faced. And even so, most of Shimon's extended family was in Palestine. Only his grandparents and an uncle remained in Vishnyeva.

It was just as well that no one had heard news of Vishnyeva, for things had turned very dark there. Very dark indeed.

✦ ✦ ✦

In the summer of 1942, soldiers from the German SS advanced through Poland slaughtering Jews at every turn in an effort to clear the area of inhabitants, making way for the planned resettlement of Germans returning from abroad to take up residence under the Third Reich. On August 30, the soldiers arrived in Vishnyeva.

Outside town, they divided into two units, then entered the village from the north and the south, their advance timed to simultaneously cut off all avenues of escape, preventing the residents from leaving by any means at all. Slowly, methodically, the soldiers moved toward the center of town.

When they reached the first houses, troops in the lead began shooting anyone who appeared. The soldiers who came behind set fire to the houses. The remaining soldiers shot anyone who moved or tried to flee the flames of the burning structures.

Within minutes, dead bodies littered both sides of the road. Houses everywhere were on fire. Screams and shouts filled the air and chaos reigned among the people of Vishnyeva. Still the soldiers, their faces stoic, continued their methodical advance. Firing at will on everyone they encountered.

Those who somehow escaped immediate death retreated toward the center of town, herded in that direction by the oncoming troops, the gunfire, and the horror of the slaughtered and mangled bodies that lay in their path. Before long, the people of the town were gathered on the lawn in front of the synagogue.

With the soldiers closing in and death all but certain, the doors of the synagogue suddenly flew open and Rabbi Katznelson appeared. Next to him was Rabbi Meltzer and behind them their wives.

"In here," Katznelson called, waving his arms for them to hurry. "Get in here. It's our only hope."

Instantly, the crowd surged toward the doorway and pressed inside. "All the way in," Meltzer urged. "Come all the way inside." Men, women, and children rushed to the front of the room, then squeezed themselves into every available space. Within minutes they were standing shoulder to shoulder, back to chest, packed in tightly and unable to move, barely able to breathe.

Outside, the soldiers took up positions around the outside of the building, forming an armed perimeter through which no one could escape. Yet they did not step forward or move on the building in any manner, seeming content to wait as people from the town slipped inside and took the last remaining places.

When the building was filled to capacity, an officer pushed his way through the crowd of townspeople still waiting on the lawn, and stepped to the door. With a cold and sinister smile, he pushed it closed. A soldier came with a heavy chain and together they wrapped it around the door handles, securing it in place with a spike through the links, leaving the door unable to be opened from inside the building.

Then, with the door closed and secured, the officer and soldier made their way back to the troops standing along the perimeter. As the officer reached the ranks, soldiers along the perimeter, who until then had been watching in a relaxed and unconcerned manner, snapped into position, their shoulders squared, their eyes dark and intense.

After a moment, the officer glanced to his right and left, nodded, and then the men raised their weapons—some with rifles, others with automatic machine guns—and opened fire on the people still standing outside the synagogue. Instantly, blood, flesh, and bone fragments filled the air as bullets tore through the bodies. In less than a minute everyone lay dead on the ground, their bodies twisted, mangled, and oozing blood. The odor of death hung over them with a heavy and sickeningly pungent smell.

Before the awfulness settled in, someone arrived with a can of kerosene. The officer nodded again and three soldiers made their way around the building, dowsing its walls with the liquid and setting fire on all four sides. The building was constructed of wood and it didn't take long before flames worked past the windows, licked the eaves, and spread to the roof.

As the heat of the flames became intense, screams rose from inside the building in an eerie, mournful chorus. It only lasted a moment or two, then faded into the roar of the fire as the conflagration engulfed the building. Columns of thick, black smoke that earlier rose in the sky now drifted toward the south and was carried away like puffy clouds on the afternoon breeze.

Several minutes later, the roof collapsed. A shower of sparks flew into the air and the soldiers, still manning the perimeter, began cheering.

Twelve hundred Jews died in Vishnyeva that day. Most, including Rabbi Meltzer and his wife, were members of Shimon's extended family. All were people he'd known and loved his entire life.

✦ ✦ ✦

Meanwhile in Palestine, Levi Eshkol arrived at Poria Alumot late one evening. Eshkol, a key figure in what was rapidly becoming a Jewish government in waiting, had been born and educated in Ukraine. He immigrated to Palestine as a young man, joined Haganah, and rose steadily through the ranks to become an officer. It wasn't long before his bravery and intellectual prowess caught the attention of David Ben-Gurion, who drew him into the Jewish Agency's leadership circles. On the day he arrived at Poria, Eshkol was part of Haganah's high command and worked closely with Ben-Gurion on arms acquisition. He'd come that day at Ben-Gurion's insistence to ask the kibbutz to assign Shimon to HaNoar HaOved for full-time work.

"They would like for him to recruit youth and build youth groups," Eshkol explained.

Yosef Smilansky, president of the kibbutz, seemed perplexed. "Isn't he doing that already?"

"They would like to expand that work. Have him establish additional groups on a broader scope. Throughout the country." Smilansky glanced away. Eshkol caught the look in his eyes. "You seem hesitant. Is something wrong? Is Shimon in some sort of trouble?"

"No." Smilansky shook his head. "He's in no trouble at all. It's just—"

"Out with it," Eshkol said impatiently. "What's the matter?"

"He's always been a bit of a. . . dreamer. I'm not sure he's cut out to be an organizational man."

"A dreamer? What do you mean?"

Smilansky explained awkwardly, "Always looking to the future. Never quite satisfied with the way things are. In the here and now. Always looking over the next hill for the next thing. Something new and better. His head 'in the clouds,' as it were."

"Looking for an improvement?"

"So he thinks."

"Asking questions?"

Smilansky smiled. "All the time."

"Do you disagree with the notion of improving, or just disagree with the improvements he wants to make?"

"Well. . . "

"I see," Eshkol said. "You don't disagree with either of those things. You just don't like it that he's the one who sees the next thing and you don't."

"Look," Smilansky countered, "I don't dislike him. In fact, I like him very much. The youth groups he's been working with in the area all think he's wonderful, and he's doing good things with them. But he's always going on about the need for Jews and Arabs to get along with each other, and it rubs many the wrong way."

Eshkol arched an eyebrow. "You're opposed to that? To Jews getting along with Arabs?"

They both knew Eshkol's question was a subtle reference to the

distinction that separated Mapai from all other parties. A question
that raised the test of whether Smilansky really was devoted to the
party cause.

"Of course not," Smilansky snapped. "But it seems a bit much. At
least right now. Coming from him. With Arabs shooting at us every
day."

"Does he do his work?"

"Shimon? Oh yes. No doubt about that. Outworks just about everyone here. He's just never quite satisfied with the way—"

Eshkol cut him off. "Good. He sounds like exactly the man we're
looking for."

Eshkol stood to leave and Smilansky rose too. "You're sure about
that?"

"Yosef, I assure you, Haganah has thoroughly vetted Shimon
Peres. There isn't anything about him that we don't know. And we're
convinced he's the right guy for what we have in mind."

"Haganah? I thought you said he would be working for HaNoar
HaOved."

Eshkol avoided the question with a smile. "Thanks for your help,
Yosef." They shook hands and Eshkol turned toward the door. "I'm
sure we'll be seeing each other again."

In reality, asking the kibbutz to reassign Shimon was a mere
formality. The work at Alumot was supported heavily by HaNoar
HaOved's parent organization, Histadrut. Members of Poria Alumot
had little choice but to accede to the request and at a collective meeting
the following afternoon they readily gave their consent.

A few days later, Shimon moved to Tel Aviv and took up residence
with his mother at the family apartment. The day after he arrived,
he reported to work at HaNoar HaOved's office a few blocks away.
He was given a Triumph motorcycle and assigned to recruitment,
traveling to settlements at the far reaches of the Negev in the south
and Galilee in the north.

At the same time, Shimon continued to serve as a member of
the HaNoar HaOved Secretariat, but HaNoar HaOved was a large

organization and Mapai, though the dominant political party in the nation, was not the dominant party in the Secretariat. In fact, in a twist of parliamentary nuance that would become a trait of the emerging Jewish state, Shimon was the Secretariat's only Mapai member. The other seats were distributed among a myriad of smaller parties and coalitions, each carefully assembled and controlled by those who favored the Greater Israel approach to Palestine's future. A position Shimon already had rejected.

As the odd member out, Shimon found his proposals to the Secretariat tabled or, more likely, ignored; particularly his suggestions regarding budget allocations. Before long he realized nothing he suggested would ever gain approval unless the composition of the Secretariat changed. That could only be accomplished by the HaNoar HaOved annual convention, and for change to occur there he would have to alter the delegate composition.

Rather than spending his time fighting administrative momentum, Shimon spent it in the field, riding the roads on his motorcycle, setting up new branches in as many kibbutzim as possible. Each of them established under the auspices of HaNoar HaOved but organized around Mapai ideals and policies of statehood now, rather than Greater Israel later. It was a perspective he conveyed through youth group activities like wilderness hikes, camping, and seminars.

The political dispute of the day continued to be statehood now versus Greater Israel and, because of the way membership was divided on the Secretariat, it pitted Shimon against the rest of HaNoar HaOved's leadership. Those in key leadership positions favored Greater Israel. Argument over the two views persisted throughout the year before finally coming to a head at HaNoar HaOved's annual convention.

At that meeting, the first order of business was that of determining HaNoar HaOved's platform for the coming year. As in the past, the Secretary presented the proposed platform, which included support for the notion of Greater Israel. The only other proposal came from Shimon and it was organized around the need for statehood immediately.

HaNoar leadership, entrenched and resting on its past successes, assumed a majority of the delegates supported their view. They fully expected to win. Shimon did, too, but his work in the field proved more effective than anyone realized. Most of the delegates at the convention came from groups that he had established or tutored and, when given the opportunity, they gave him their support. To everyone's surprise, Shimon's platform proposal with support for immediate statehood won and was adopted by the party as its guideline for the coming year.

That victory was a boost to Mapai and the quest for statehood. It also thrust Shimon into the limelight. Suddenly, he was no longer the kid on a motorcycle. Mapai leaders knew his name. He had clout. He had influence. And he had the power to take control of HaNoar HaOved.

Amitsur, who was in town for the convention, was the first to suggest he actually do it. "Do you think the other side would hesitate, if the tables were reversed?"

"I know," Shimon agreed, "but I think it's a trap."

"How could it possibly be a trap? You won. This is the greatest opportunity you've had in your life."

"It is an opportunity, but not for taking over."

Amitsur shook his head. "I don't understand."

"Look," Shimon explained. "HaNoar HaOved is a coalition. A coalition of coalitions. It's a cohesive whole only in appearance, not in reality. In reality, it's a big, unwieldy cluster of competing interests held together by a very delicate balance of ideas, opinions, preferences, and feelings."

Amitsur's face twisted in a look of confusion. "Feelings?"

"Yes."

"This is politics; it's not about feelings."

"It is in HaNoar HaOved. We're young and I'm—"

"It's a youth organization," Amitsur interrupted. "We're supposed to be young. *You're* supposed to be young."

"Yes, but I've been the youngest person everywhere I've gone. And

I'm the youngest member of the Secretariat. If we take over, if I make myself head of the organization, everyone will see it as overreaching and they will be forced to react immediately to stop us."

Amitsur seemed to understand. "So, what are you going to do? Your proposal won. *You* won. Everyone's waiting to see what you do."

Shimon's face brightened in a grin. "I have an idea, one that I think will work even better than seizing power. One that will give us control without taking control."

Instead of using his newfound clout to promote himself, Shimon used it to force an equalization of Secretariat memberships with positions divided among member organizations based on their percentage of the total membership. Parties favoring Greater Israel lost control and were forced to work with all interests, including Mapai. Leadership for the parties favoring Greater Israel—primarily Mapam and Ahdut HaAvoda—were incensed at the move and viewed Shimon with disdain. Everyone in Mapai loved him for it.

✦ ✦ ✦

Not long after the convention, Shimon went on a three-week venture across the Negev. Billed as a HaNoar HaOved member exercise, in reality only half the group was comprised of youth. The other half were members of Palmach, an elite Haganah commando unit. The excursion was accompanied by Dr. Mendelson, an ornithologist whom they brought to provide them cover as an educational expedition. The real purpose, however, was to make maps of the Negev and catalog as much information about the region as possible.

A week into the trip, someone spotted an eagle soaring overhead. "A *peres*," he called out, pointing at the bird and using the Hebrew term.

Mendelson glanced up at it. "It's floating on a thermal updraft—a column of warm air," he explained. "Rises up from the floor of the desert." He looked up at the bird once more. "He'll float up there until he sees a rat or a snake or something, then he'll tuck his wings, dive headfirst toward the ground. Break off at the last moment and snatch his prey with his talons."

Shimon looked up at it. "I sometimes dream of flying."

"I hear you dream of many things," one of the Palmach quipped.

"Is that so bad?" Yohai countered defensively.

"I don't mean dreaming like that," Shimon explained. "In my dreams. At night. When I'm asleep I sometimes dream of flying."

"Even when he dreams he has his head in the clouds," another scoffed.

Mendelson smiled over at Shimon. "It's not as unusual as it seems. Many people dream of flying." He glanced up at the bird again. "Even I have dreamt of it."

"I don't dream," the commander of the Palmach said.

Yohai grinned at Shimon. "At least you have a mascot now."

Shimon looked perplexed. "A mascot?"

"Yes. An eagle. A peres."

"Hey," one of the younger members called out. "That's a good name. Shimon the Peres."

Shimon's eyes brightened. Yohai glanced over at him. "That's a good name."

"Yes, it is," Shimon said quietly. "Shimon Peres."

"You've been looking for a name, haven't you?"

For Jews in Europe, immigration to Palestine meant leaving behind the only life they'd ever known. Not just family and friends, but lifestyle, livelihood, and the knowledge that a troublesome time led to a life of uncertainty.

Stripped of their former lives and, in most cases, their worldly goods, and starting over in a new land, many chose to take a new name. In this way, David Grün became David Ben-Gurion. Levi Shkolnik became Levi Eshkol. Yigal Peikowitz became Yigal Allon. Shimon had been looking for a new name, one that reflected the new life opening up for him, and during that trip into the Negev, he found it. Shimon Perski became Shimon Peres.

SHIMON PERES

"Israel was born under the British mandate.
We learned from the British what democracy
means, and how it behaves in a time of danger. . . "

BERL KATZNELSON DIED in 1944. After his funeral, Shimon gave up his job with HaNoar HaOved and returned to Alumot, where he resumed his work, primarily with livestock. He hadn't been there long when he was elected kibbutz secretary.

As World War II came to an end, Sonia was released from service with the British army and returned to Palestine. She joined Shimon at Alumot and on May 1, 1945, they were married in a ceremony held at Ben-Shemen, the youth school and village where they first met. Sonia's parents still resided there and the service became a sort of homecoming for many of the school's graduates. Sonia was twenty-one. Shimon was twenty-two.

Afterward, Shimon and Sonia took a honeymoon trip to Bitaniya on the Jordan River. They spent warm sunny mornings lounging near the river and in the afternoon raced off through Galilee with the wind in their hair and the open road before them.

A few weeks later, as Shimon and Sonia settled into life at the kibbutz as husband and wife, news reached them that Shimon's father was returning from the war. He arrived by train at Lydda, a community on the east side of Tel Aviv. Shimon and Sonia were there with the family to greet him. He had been gone six years, five of which he spent as a prisoner of war.

Not long after Shimon's father returned, Mordechai Mond arrived in Tel Aviv. Before the war, Mond lived at Traby, a town not far from Vishnyeva. His cousins lived up the street from where Shimon had lived. When the Germans invaded Poland, Mond sensed that things would go badly for everyone, especially for Jews. He escaped to Lithuania and made his way to the coast.

A fishing trawler carried him to Denmark and from there he made his way to England, where he obtained forged documents and used them to enlist in the British army. He was in Germany when the war ended and about that time the British army realized he wasn't a British citizen, so they discharged him on the spot.

With nowhere else to go, Mond returned to Traby and spent three months searching for his relatives, a search that eventually took him to Vishnyeva to check on some cousins.

"And that's when I learned the truth," Mond related to Shimon's family. "The awful truth."

"And what is that?"

"They are all dead."

"All dead? I don't understand."

"Everyone who lived in Vishnyeva. Nahum Sorkin, the grocer. Raya Blumkin, who came from Ukraine and lived on the corner by the synagogue." He looked up at Shimon's mother. "Your mother and father. Rabbi Katznelson and his wife. They are all gone."

"But what happened to them?" she asked.

Choking back his emotions, Mond recounted the day the Germans arrived as best he could, using information he'd pieced together from accounts of two or three residents who returned to town just as the Germans arrived, but escaped and hid in the woods until they were gone.

When Mond was finished telling the story, everyone sat in silence, tears streaming down their cheeks. Not an eye in the room was dry.

Shimon stared blankly ahead, thinking of his grandfather. The smell of his coat when he hugged him. The look in the old man's eyes when he was pleased with an answer. And his last words that morning as they stood on the platform at the train station. "Always be a Jew."

Finally, Shimon's father broke the silence. "These were German soldiers?"

"SS. Schutzstaffel."

"The paramilitary organization formed by the Nazi Party," Shimon's father nodded. "They were accountable solely to Hitler."

Shimon had a look of disbelief. "You mean, Hitler ordered them to kill our family?"

"Yes," Mond nodded. "At least, that was the effect."

"More likely," Shimon's father added, "he ordered the cleansing of the region. What happened in Vishnyeva was part of that."

"Still, the death of our family was the result of his order," Shimon said. "And those men were under his command."

"But why?" Shimon's mother asked. "Why kill them? They had never done anything wrong. And certainly nothing that should concern the Germans."

"Hitler's grand scheme was to clear the area of all who lived there," Mond explained. "Jews, Russians, Poles, and everyone else. So he could relocate the Jews from Germany there."

"And kill them, too?"

Mond agreed. "Eventually, I think they wanted to repopulate the region with Germans."

"Eventually?"

"Hitler was a madman," Mond sighed. "There's really no other explanation."

"The personification of evil," Shimon added.

"Yes," his father acknowledged. "The personification of evil."

✦ ✦ ✦

In May 1946, the country of Jordan, known then as Transjordan, was granted independence by British mandate authorities. Abdullah Ibn al-Hussein was installed as King Abdullah I. The country became known as the Hashemite Kingdom of Transjordan.

In October, Sonia gave birth to a daughter. She was born at the Scottish Hospital in Tiberias. They named her Tsvia, a feminine version of Zvi in honor of Shimon's grandfather.

Not long after Tsvia was born, Shimon received news that David Ben-Gurion had decided to include him as part of the Mapai delegation to the Zionist Congress, to be held in Basel, Switzerland. Traditionally, delegates to the Congress were older and well established in the party, but that year two places were reserved for younger delegates. Shimon was one of those delegates. Moshe Dayan was the other.

Moshe was thirty-one years old. Shimon was twenty-three. The two knew each other but not well, and before embarking on the trip they met in Tel Aviv to discuss their views on the issues they expected the Congress would address. They hadn't talked long before they realized they were in complete agreement on the topics that mattered—to support Ben-Gurion no matter what; to promote the free and unhindered immigration of Jews to Palestine, whether by means deemed legal by the British or otherwise; and to establish an independent Jewish state, even if it meant taking up arms against the British. For Moshe and Shimon, their visit was the beginning of a lifelong friendship.

The first Zionist Congress had been convened by Theodore Herzl in 1897. Delegates to that meeting agreed to make the meeting an annual occurrence and established the Zionist Organization for continuing the work of Zionism between congresses. Almost from inception, it became the central organization for the Zionist movement and for the continuing organization of the Jewish people. The 1946 Congress was the first to meet after the end of the war in Europe, and the first since the Holocaust.

The delegation departed for Switzerland in the first week of December, sailing from Jaffa aboard a steamer. It was Shimon's first trip by ship since arriving in Palestine as a young boy. Rooms were assigned by lottery. Shimon drew a berth in the room with Levi Eshkol and Pinhas Lavon, two Mapai stalwarts. This was Shimon's first time to see Mapai leadership up close.

Once underway, Shimon and Dayan spent their time strolling the main deck or sitting in lounge chairs on the fantail, comparing observations about the delegation, discussing the Congress they were about to attend and the future they saw unfolding before them.

Shimon was an editor for *Ashmoret*, a newspaper for younger Party members, and planned to write articles about the Congress for the paper. He also was commissioned to write for *Yediot Hadashot*, the evening Mapai newspaper. When he wasn't talking to Dayan or visiting with his roommates, he worked on his first series of articles, scratching out sentences on a notepad as he sat in a chair on the leeward side of the ship.

The delegation arrived in Basel to a Congress that was deeply divided on almost everything. The issue of leadership for the Zionist Organization, statehood for Palestinian Jews, and whether partition of the region—dividing it into separate Jewish and Arab states—under *any* design was an acceptable solution. Even those who supported immediate statehood and a division of Palestine disagreed about how to implement it. The Mapai delegation, which included those handpicked by Ben-Gurion, was also divided, mostly along those same lines.

The Congress opened on December 7, and by end of the first day Ben-Gurion was thoroughly frustrated with the whole affair. The next morning he was noticeably absent as Shimon and the delegates from Palestine gathered outside the hall before the first session. By the time the doors opened, he still wasn't present. Shimon followed Arye Bahir to a row of chairs near the front and took a seat, wondering aloud if Ben-Gurion intended to join them.

As other delegates filed into the hall, Paula, Ben-Gurion's wife, appeared in the row behind where Shimon and Bahir were seated.

She leaned over Bahir's shoulder and whispered, "Arye, he has gone crazy this time."

Bahir had a puzzled frown. "What do you mean?"

"He's upstairs in the room," Paula explained. "Packing."

"Packing?" Bahir turned to look at her, a stricken expression on his face. "Packing for what?"

"To go home. He insists he won't stay another minute with. . . " Paula paused as if wondering whether to repeat what Ben-Gurion actually said. "He won't stay another minute with such a crowd as this. I've argued with him all night. He won't give in. You have to talk to him."

"Certainly," Bahir replied. He stood and tapped Shimon on the shoulder. "Come with me."

Shimon rose at once and followed Bahir as they made their way toward the aisle. A few seats from the end they passed Moshe Dayan. Bahir took him by the shoulder and looked down at him. "Take the floor." It was an order, not a request. "And start talking. Keep talking until I get back."

Dayan looked perplexed. "How long will that be?"

"A while," Bahir continued toward the aisle. "Just keep talking."

Shimon followed Bahir from the hall as he hurried upstairs to Ben-Gurion's room. When they opened the door, sure enough, there he was, angrily stuffing clothes into a suitcase. "Arye, it's no use," Ben-Gurion snapped as they entered. "Nothing you will say can change my mind."

"It's true," Bahir began, "they are—"

"Petty," Ben-Gurion snarled, finishing the sentence. "Simple-minded." He threw up his hands in a gesture of frustration. "Millions died at the hands of the Nazis and all they talk about is position papers on the quality of life for Jews in Europe! Millions more are trapped in Europe right now, most of them living in the same death camps where they watched their families being slaughtered before their eyes, and all these delegates can talk about is what to eat for dinner. I'm through with them. The whole lot of them. I am through!"

"We have to—"

"And our own delegation!" Ben-Gurion fumed. "Our own members! Can you imagine? I thought they were serious-minded people. I thought they understood what is at stake. But they're talking all night about whether to divide Palestine, how to accommodate the other side, wringing their hands and piously saying, 'Oh, we must have unity.'" His voice was even louder by then. "Let them and unity be cast into—"

"David," Paula said sharply, cutting him off. "That isn't going to help."

Ben-Gurion looked over at her, his eyes ablaze with anger. "It surely would help us if they were gone. Gone from here. And gone from Palestine." He made a slicing gesture with his hand.

"But using offensive language," she said calmly, "doesn't move us forward at all. Stick to the point."

"Listen," Bahir said, trying again. "I know it's frustrating. And I know they're being small-minded. But you are right. Millions languish right now in European detention centers. And you are right about statehood. We can't wait. We have to do it now, while we have the opportunity. This moment may never come again. But if we bolt now, we'll lose the chance. If we walk out now, we will be giving up this moment and handing it over to the other side."

"Nonsense. We can do it on our own."

"No, we can't," Bahir argued. "Not without the party. And not without international support. To get that support, we need the backing of an international organization." He pointed with his index finger. "This is the organization we begin with."

Ben-Gurion paused and looked over at Bahir. "What do you mean?"

"If you walk out now, you'll not just walk out on the Congress. You'll walk out on Mapai. A party you created. You'll walk out on the millions in Europe who need our help. And you'll walk out on the dream of a Jewish state in Palestine."

"They can—"

"No, they can't," Bahir argued. "It will never happen. Not without the Congress. Not without Mapai. And not without you."

"So what are you saying?"

"Let me convene a party meeting."

"Right now?"

"Yes, right now."

"What about the Congress? The session has already started."

"No, it hasn't. Moshe Dayan asked for the floor and when we left to come up here he was just getting warmed up with a story about some daring military exploit." A smile came to Ben-Gurion. Bahir pressed the point. "Let me gather the delegation. You can tell them about your frustration, about why they must back you, and you can win them over to our point of view."

"And if not?"

"If not, we'll go home and try something else."

"Okay."

"But there's one more thing."

"What's that?"

"You have to stay with this meeting until we convince them we're right."

Ben-Gurion looked disgusted. "Stay with them—"

"David," Bahir interrupted, "as long as it takes. You'll stuff your anger in your pocket along with your ego and your pride. You won't do it for me. You won't do it for the Congress. But you'll do it for the sake of the Jewish people. And you'll keep this delegation meeting going for as long as it takes to convince them. You won't walk out."

Ben-Gurion took a deep breath. "Okay. As long as it takes."

With Ben-Gurion back on board, at least for the moment, Bahir and Shimon left the room and started downstairs to gather the delegation. "Don't forget what you saw in there," Bahir said as they hurried toward the stairs.

"I don't think I'll ever forget a word of it," Shimon replied.

"I may not always be available. You may have to talk him down sometime."

Shimon didn't know whether to be flattered by the comment, or terrified. "I'm not sure I could."

Bahir glanced over his shoulder in Shimon's direction. "When the time comes, you'll find the words. Just remember. However much praise you give him, give him twice as much guilt."

While Shimon rounded up the Mapai delegation for a meeting, Bahir interrupted Dayan, who still was talking, and asked the chairman for a recess of the session. Weizmann, who chaired the session, readily agreed. An hour later, the Mapai delegation was assembled in a room down the hall from the one where the sessions were held.

Ben-Gurion addressed them: "Since arriving here yesterday, it has become apparent that we are a deeply divided group. I called this meeting because I want to settle those differences." He spoke in a serious tone but without anger or vindication. When he finished, he invited a response. One by one, delegates rose to speak. Most did so without the restraint Ben-Gurion had shown in his opening remarks. Some supported his views, others vehemently opposed them.

The delegates argued all night but, true to the commitment he'd made to Bahir, Ben-Gurion stayed with them. He refused to let them leave, though only one or two raised the issue of a recess.

Just before sunrise, the issues were enumerated in the form of a platform, most of it focused on support for immediate statehood rather than waiting for control of the entire region, and the matter was put to a vote. When the votes were counted, Ben-Gurion's platform was approved. Moreover, Ben-Gurion sealed his position as head of the party.

As delegates filed from the room looking tired and weary, Shimon sat quietly and watched. Outwardly, he appeared as exhausted as everyone else, but inside he was at peace, certain that more had happened in that meeting than anyone realized. With Ben-Gurion in charge of the party and the party behind him at last, Shimon sensed the Jewish state they'd longed for was being born. Independence was no longer a question of if, but now only a question of when.

The Zionist Congress adopted the plan to establish a Jewish homeland in Palestine and rejected a proposal, favored by the British, for an Arab–Jewish conference. Weizmann, whom many thought too accommodating—both to the British and to the Greater Israel groups, was not reelected as president of the Zionist Organization. He'd served as president since before the war and kept the organization together even when biennial congresses were suspended but he'd relied too much on British benevolence, a reliance that proved misplaced.

The end of Weizmann's tenure marked a changing of the guard and it struck Shimon as a sad moment. In aligning the Zionist Organization more closely with British preferences, he'd chosen a path that kept Zionism moving forward in the short term, but Weizmann emerged from the war out of step with the long reach of the issues and the momentum of history those issues generated. Things were different. People were different. And they had no choice but to press forward into a future that already was opening to a vastly different world than had existed before.

✦ ✦ ✦

When the Zionist Congress ended, Shimon traveled to Palestine with Meir Argov, who was fifteen or twenty years older. They stopped in Paris and one night while they were there Argov took him to dinner with Louis Danjou.

Tall, slender, and dignified, Danjou made quite an impression when he appeared in the hotel dining room and even more so when he spoke. They talked that evening about many things—the Soviet drive for dominance, the future of Europe, whether NATO could provide the long-term stability the region needed, and the kind of support the West owed to Jews in Palestine. Shimon found it an interesting mix of topics and came away from their meeting sensing that Danjou was a friend and someone who was willing to extend himself as far as possible to be of help in their efforts to create a free and independent Jewish state.

Later, in the hotel room, Argov explained, "Louis Danjou is a member of what used to be Labor and Socialist International."

"Used to be?"

"The war threw us into disarray."

"Us?"

"Yes. I was a member, too."

"But you talk about it as if it's still around." Shimon found Argov's language a little confusing.

"We've been trying to reorganize. Change the structure. Adjust our goals. Find a new name."

"What kind of name?"

"Right now we're calling it Socialist International."

"Never heard of it."

"As I said, the war caused quite a bit of confusion. And, as you can imagine, rather a lot of soul-searching."

"I think we've all been doing some of that," Shimon noted.

"Ben-Gurion has been working with us. He asked me to bring you here and introduce you around."

Shimon was flattered that Ben-Gurion had thought to include him and he questioned Argov about Danjou well into the night in an effort to learn all he could. Conversation on that topic led naturally to the broader discussion that was on everyone's mind—the future of Palestine, their relationship with Arabs, and the reaction they might expect from neighboring countries. And somewhere after midnight, Argov asked about what had been going on with Shimon and the kibbutz he'd been working with.

"We've been searching for a permanent location," Shimon explained.

"I heard about that. You're at Poria now?"

"Yes, but it is not a very good location."

"Location is what you make of it, but I have seen that site. It's not really conducive to farming."

"Then you know the salts in the ground make growing anything very difficult."

"I am certain it's the reason the place was abandoned. And probably the reason you were sent there."

"As a test?"

"Many groups of your age think they want to start a settlement, until they actually try it."

"We've been there awhile," Shimon countered. "Anyone who reviews our work would see that we're serious."

Argov was on the board of Petah Tikvah Workers Council and the Jewish National Council, the executive committee aspect of the Jewish Agency. That Shimon brought up the subject of the kibbutz with him was no accident. Of all the people on the trip, Argov was one who could open the door for their own settlement.

The following year, Shimon attended a Mapai meeting in Tel Aviv. While there, Meir Argov handed him a letter notifying him that the settlement group from Ben-Shemen had been given their own kibbutz location—at a site located not too far from Poria. When Shimon returned home, he shared the news with the others in the group and they made plans to move to the new site immediately.

SHIMON PERES

"If a problem has no solution, it may not be a problem, but a fact—not to be solved, but to be coped with over time."

BY 1947, BRITISH CONTROL of Mandatory Palestine was collapsing and violence between Arabs and Jews was once again on the rise. As a solution, British officials began discussions at the United Nations about dividing Palestine into two separate states: one for Jews and another for Arabs. For Jews, division—commonly known as partition—posed both advantages and disadvantages.

Backed by British support, and with growing international acceptance, the idea of a Jewish state was closer than ever to becoming a reality. Moreover, it offered the very real possibility of creating a Jewish state immediately. However, in giving effect to that idea of partition some suggested dividing the region according to population percentages, rather than actual land currently controlled. Dividing Palestine by a ratio based on population could easily give the Jews a state, but one that lacked enough geographical size to be sustainable. An outcome that some thought was precisely what the British intended.

At the same time, granting Jews a state with geographic borders that included too many Arabs meant the creation of a state ostensibly Jewish but with an Arab majority. In that instance, the state could easily be voted out of existence, with laws enacted to restrict Jewish rights—or banish them entirely. That would only be a repeat of the treatment they'd received in Europe, and Ben-Gurion was determined none of that would happen.

Early in 1947, preparations began for what all assumed would be the coming day of Jewish independence. With that moment fast approaching, one of Ben-Gurion's primary concerns was the establishment of a national army, one that looked and functioned like every other national army. An army that would demonstrate an aura of legitimacy among nations of the world and one capable of defending the new state. Ben-Gurion knew that many in the international community would view it for form as much as function. He also knew, perhaps as no one else did, that the Jews of Palestine would have to fight for independence against an armed Arab opposition. If they couldn't win against the Arabs, no one would support them regardless of how authentic the army might appear.

As a central core for his emerging army, Ben-Gurion drew heavily on officers from the Jewish Brigade, which had been formed and trained by the British during the war. Their training was among the best any in Haganah had received and, having fought under British direction, they understood the way armies were supposed to work.

At the same time, he ordered the dissolution of Palmach and folded it into Haganah with the notion that Haganah would provide the bulk of a national army once independence had been declared. More than anything else, Ben-Gurion's decision to end Palmach brought the age-old dispute—statehood immediately versus holding out for a Greater Israel—to a decisive confrontation.

For several of the smaller but more belligerent paramilitary organizations, like Lehi and Irgun, the idea of Greater Israel was central to their existence. They viewed the dissolution of Palmach as a prelude to their own disbanding once statehood by partition had been achieved. In response, they refused to acknowledge the Jewish Agency's authority and asserted a right to fight on their own for complete control of the region. They also insisted on conducting their own weapons-procurement program, in effect creating an alternative Jewish government in Palestine. Ben-Gurion and the Jewish Agency could not allow that to happen any more than they could allow partition of the region to go awry. Very quickly, a showdown loomed.

Shimon watched these developments with interest, but he did so from a distance at the Alumot kibbutz. That distance, however, did not keep him from talking among his friends about what lay ahead and it became a favorite topic for extended conversations. One evening after supper, he, Sonia, Yohai, and Amitsur sat at a table in the settlement's main hall after everyone else had finished eating and moved on.

"I am certain there will be trouble once the British leave," Shimon began. "That much I know. I just don't know how bad it will get."

"You think the Arabs will wait for the British to leave?" Yohai asked.

"That's a good question and I'm not sure what the answer is. They haven't shown any restraint or sense of diplomacy in the past."

"They don't have any one person in control, either," Sonia observed.

"One thing I think is clear," Shimon offered. "And that is that Ben-Gurion will wait until the British withdraw before declaring our independence. If he did it before they left, they might not depart and I think he and everyone else knows that. So, they'll at least do the British the courtesy of waiting until they are gone. But once they leave, he will declare independence."

"And then the fighting will start," Yohai added.

"War is coming," Amitsur agreed. "And this time it won't be just raids here and there. This time Egypt and Syria and all the others will join in against us. It will be a fight for our survival."

"Literally," Sonia added.

"Yes, but isn't that what we've wanted?" Yohai grinned. "The chance to fight for a future?"

Amitsur nodded. "But we have to also win. Not just fight. But actually prevail."

"We will win," Shimon assured. "I have no doubt about that. But first we must win the war among ourselves."

Yohai had a knowing smile. "Ben-Gurion against Lehi."

"And Irgun, too," Shimon added.

"He can't let any of them go their own way," Amitsur offered. "If he does, we'll never have a country, even if we defeat the Arabs."

Yohai looked over at Shimon. "Do you think they'll come around?"

Instantly, scenes from the all-night meeting at the Zionist Conference flashed through Shimon's mind and he smiled at the memory of it. "I think Ben-Gurion will get them to see that his way is the right thing."

"Or," Sonia added, "at least get them to accept that statehood is inevitable."

Yohai glanced across the table at her. "You don't sound too happy about that."

"I'm glad for independence, but I've lived through one war and I would rather not go through it again."

"We don't have much choice," Shimon noted. "But I agree. It won't be easy."

"Well, it might be easier for you than some of the rest of us," Yohai suggested.

Shimon had a questioning frown. "What do you mean by that?"

"They will come for you. They will come for us, too, and we'll all take up a rifle and dive into the trenches. But they'll come for you first, just like they did before."

"Before?"

"When Eshkol came to get you."

"I doubt he'll do that again," Shimon replied in a dismissive tone. "What would they want with me? Someone like Moshe Dayan, yes. He's a fighter and a soldier at heart. But not me. I have no military expertise and they know it."

"But you are smart," Yohai said.

"And you do favor a strong defense," Amitsur offered, "in spite of all you say about peace."

"And they know you," Yohai added.

Later that evening, when Shimon and Sonia were alone with Tsvia, Sonia turned to him. "Yohai and Amitsur are right, you know."

"About what?"

"They will come for you."

"Look," a frown wrinkled his forehead and he had an irritated tone in his voice, "you know I—"

"Not for your soldiering skills," she said, cutting him off with a finger gently to his lips. "They won't come for that. But they will come for your mind. The Jews of Eretz Israel have not many like you." Sonia put her arms around his waist and leaned against him. "Your mind will be your contribution to the struggle for independence."

"Maybe so," Shimon conceded as he wrapped his arms around her shoulders. "But if they come for me, will you go with me?"

"I am your wife," Sonia snuggled closer. "And whether I am in Alumot or Tel Aviv or anywhere else, I will always be with you." She leaned her head back and smiled up at him. "You are my husband. I am your wife."

Shimon bent over and gave her a kiss. "Then I am sure I will win," he smiled. "No matter what happens."

✦ ✦ ✦

In May 1947, the British government submitted a formal request to the United Nations asking for recommendations regarding the future of Palestine. In response, the UN General Assembly created the United Nations Special Committee on Palestine, known by the acronym UNSCOP, to conduct an investigation and report to the General Assembly with recommendations.

Shimon was at Alumot, high up on the mountain tending sheep when the UN committee was announced. Not long after that announcement was made, Yohai came and found him. "Levi Eshkol is here."

"I know you're joking," Shimon laughed.

"No," Yohai insisted. "I'm not kidding. Eshkol is waiting to see you."

Shimon stood. "Well, he'll have to wait a bit longer while I gather the flock. I can't leave them out here alone and unattended."

"I will tend them," Yohai offered. "You must hurry."

That's when Shimon realized the news Yohai reported wasn't a joke and, more than that, knew his life would never again be the same. Reluctantly he handed over his shepherd's staff and made his way down the slope toward the compound.

Shimon arrived at the main hall to find Eshkol, indeed, waiting impatiently. This time he came with a letter from Ben-Gurion asking the kibbutz to assign Shimon to Haganah command. That evening, after dinner, the members of Kibbutz Alumot met to consider the request. As before, it was only a formality and everyone knew it. Though no one wanted to see Shimon and Sonia leave, they readily gave their assent.

Later that night, as Shimon and Sonia packed to leave, Amitsur came by for one last visit. He glanced around at the clutter. "So, you will be on your way."

"Just for now," Shimon replied. "It's only temporary. We'll be back."

"I think we both know better than that."

"This is my home. I will do what they ask. The war will come and go. And then we will return."

"Trouble is coming," Amitsur warned. "We all know that. And soon all of us will be called to the fight. Most of us will return one day, but for you. . . I think this is a bend in the road that will take you to places you've never imagined."

Sonia shot a look at Shimon. "Remember his words."

"You think he's right?"

"I think there are words, and then there are *words*."

Amitsur realized he'd struck a nerve between them. Rather than pressing the point, he took Shimon by the hand. "Take care of yourself."

Shimon placed a hand on Amitsur's shoulder. "And you also."

The following day, Shimon met Yohai for breakfast and one last good-bye. Then he, Sonia, and Tsvia traveled to Tel Aviv, where a small apartment awaited them.

Once his family was settled, Shimon reported for duty at Haganah headquarters—known as the Red House—where he was directed to the office of Yosef Yizreeli, deputy director of Haganah's general staff. Yizreeli assigned him to the manpower department, where Moshe Zadok was in charge.

"Great," Zadok announced flatly. "You're finally here."

"I came as soon as I could. I just got word two days ago."

"You can work from there," Zadok pointed to an empty desk across the room. He thrust a stack of files at Shimon. "I'll handle issues regarding the men we already have. You're in charge of recruitment."

"Haganah recruitment?"

Zadok took a sarcastic tone. "Has someone changed our name and forgotten to tell me?"

Shimon chuckled. "It's just. . . Haganah. . . "

Zadok paused and finally turned to face him. "I know. It's Haganah and we've all dreamed of what it might be like to be a member." Then he turned abruptly back to his desk. "You'll get used to it." Zadok gestured over his shoulder in Shimon's direction. "Those files contain lists of people who've been identified as potential members. Some notified us. Others were recommended by someone else. Regardless, find out everything you can about them, weed out the bad ones, and convince the rest to join us."

"Just like that?"

"Just like that." Again Zadok paused and turned to face Shimon. "Look, it's no different from what you've been doing with HaNoar HaOved. Only, we can't accept people we haven't properly vetted. So, vet them, recruit them, get them on board. And get busy." He turned back to his desk once more. "We don't have a lot of time."

The job was intimidating at first, but soon Shimon got the hang of it and by the second week he was totally absorbed in the work, quickly falling into a routine of eighteen-hour days. Some nights he slept on a cot in the office and didn't go home.

✦ ✦ ✦

In addition to his general responsibilities, Eshkol had four areas of detailed oversight. He served as Ben-Gurion's deputy in Haganah, head of Settlements for the Jewish Agency, secretary of the Tel Aviv Labor Council, and he was in charge of Military Intelligence. All of which kept him occupied and gave Zadok and Shimon a free hand with their assignments.

Meanwhile, Teddy Kollek was in America working on behalf of Haganah, recruiting volunteers and rounding up arms, ammunition, and supplies. Like everyone else, his workload was overwhelming and on more than one occasion he had threatened to resign unless he received help. He especially needed someone who spoke English and understood American culture. Shimon met none of those qualifications. Nevertheless, a few months after Shimon arrived in Tel Aviv, Eshkol turned to him for help and appointed him head of Haganah's American department anyway. Needless to say, a fight with Kollek followed but when the dust settled, Shimon still was head of Haganah's American department.

The arrangement was confused with overlapping duties—Shimon was in charge of American operations and general recruiting, which meant working for Zadok and Eshkol at the same time. Before long, however, things sorted themselves out, not just on the operational side with Shimon but also on the strategic side with Ben-Gurion and the general officers in Haganah.

In addition to the dispute about dissolving Palmach, a fight erupted over placing the military under civilian control. Control of the military by an elected head of government would have been tough enough for seasoned Haganah officers to accept, but placing the military under the purview of a civilian minister of defense was more than they wanted to bear. Yet that was the model Ben-Gurion and the Jewish Agency leadership envisioned for the government after independence. As their position became known, dissension that had been mostly internal erupted into open opposition.

The fight, and its resolution, was further complicated by the fact that Haganah's chief of staff, Yaacov Dori, was absent. Dori—an experienced, capable, and respected officer—was ill and Ben-Gurion had not replaced him. In Dori's absence, Yigal Yadin was the highest-ranking general officer, but lacked the authority to implement the sweeping changes necessary to resolve differences among the rank and file.

Compounding the issue was a noticeable disparity in training among senior Haganah officers. As if that weren't enough, operating for decades as an underground organization had created traditions and practices that ran counter to those of a disciplined national army with set rules, regulations, and procedures.

Much of the dissension came from Yisrael Galili. As former head of Palmach, he was as affected by the changes Ben-Gurion enacted as anyone. He objected to the structure being imposed on Haganah and bristled at the thought of being made accountable to anyone.

Galili put up a fight, but eventually Ben-Gurion prevailed and Galili resigned. A number of generals left with him, too. Their departure left Haganah's highest levels of leadership in disarray. To restore order, and to turn the culture of Haganah toward that of an army and away from its freewheeling paramilitary past, Ben-Gurion appointed Eshkol to take charge of the group as its first civilian leader. Yigal Yadin, Dori's deputy, took over field command of the troops.

When Eshkol assumed his new duties, Shaul Avigur, who'd been working as Eshkol's deputy, joined him. Before that, one of Avigur's primary duties had been that of procuring arms. In that regard, he and Shimon had worked together in acquiring arms from sources in the United States. With Avigur gone, Ben-Gurion moved Shimon over to weapons procurement.

SHIMON PERES

"From my earliest youth, I have known that while one is obliged to plan with care the stages of one's journey, one is entitled to dream, and keep dreaming, of its destination."

MEANWHILE UNSCOP, comprised of representatives from eleven nations, conducted a series of visits to Palestine. During those visits the committee held separate hearings in areas controlled by Arabs and in areas that were predominantly Jewish. That work took up most of June and July. Arabs, for the most part, refused to participate.

In August 1947, the committee withdrew from Palestine and reconvened in Geneva, Switzerland, where it conducted further hearings and thrashed out the details of its report. By then, Arab leaders realized that the British were serious about withdrawing from Palestine and that the international community was committed to dividing Palestine into two states. They also finally awakened to the fact that their earlier refusal to interact with the committee had only served to leave the entire matter under Jewish influence. Hurriedly, they assembled a delegation and sent it to Geneva to lobby, first in opposition to the plan as a whole and then for a scheme of division that favored Arab interests.

By September, the UN committee's work was finished. Its final report recommended partition of Palestine and included a map of the proposed division. Acting as representatives of the Jews who lived in Palestine, Ben-Gurion and the Jewish Agency lobbied for several changes to the map but otherwise accepted the division as proposed. Those changes were adopted and on November 29, 1947, the UN General Assembly approved the plan of partition. The grand mufti of Jerusalem, acting as Arab spokesman as expected rejected it as soon as it was announced.

With a UN plan for Palestine in place, British authorities announced their withdrawal from the region by August 1948. Even before the British fully withdrew, conflicts broke out between Arabs and Jews. Buses were bombed. People from both sides were attacked in the streets.

Under orders from Ben-Gurion, Haganah retaliated and conducted preemptive raids against Arab strongholds. Irgun, with Menachem Begin as its leader, still refused Ben-Gurion's order to disband and conducted raids of its own, most of which were not coordinated with Haganah's actions. Ben-Gurion was frustrated with Begin but felt that a confrontation would be premature. He wanted to wait until the British were gone and Jewish independence had been declared. "Then I will force him to join us," Ben-Gurion announced. "He can join us or become an outlaw and face the consequences."

At the time, the British held some ninety Jews and several hundred Arabs at a prison located in Acre, a town on the coast of northern Palestine. Most of the Jewish prisoners were members of Irgun and Lehi. They had been captured when British troops responded to Arab–Jewish violence or in the course of raids conducted to interdict the supply of arms. Four Irgun members had been summarily tried at the prison and scheduled to be hanged.

Two days before the scheduled hanging, a team from Irgun attacked in an effort to free the condemned men and two dozen others.

The escape was successful but seven Irgun members were killed and four were taken prisoner.

Officials at the prison announced the four Irgun men they'd captured were to be hanged. When their sentences became known, Menachem Begin, head of Irgun, ordered the capture of several British soldiers, which he intended to use in bargaining for release of Irgun members.

A message from Irgun delivered to British mandatory authorities announced that Irgun was holding two British soldiers that they intended to execute unless the four Irgun members who faced death sentences were released. British authorities refused to negotiate, and the four prisoners were hanged. The morning after the hanging, the bodies of two British soldiers were found hanging from trees by the side of a road near Jerusalem.

News reached Haganah headquarters shortly after sunrise. Ben-Gurion was furious and demanded an investigation. "I want to know who did this!" he shouted.

Eshkol was in the room when the news arrived. He'd arrived for a meeting on arms procurement and brought Shimon with him. "I think we both know who ordered it," Eshkol offered.

"Menachem Begin is out to ruin us," Ben-Gurion fumed. "That short-sighted—" He caught himself and took a deep breath. "I want an investigation, Levi. Find out who did this. Get us the proof."

"That may not be possible," Eshkol replied slowly.

Ben-Gurion's eyes were ablaze. "Why not?"

"David," Eshkol began carefully, "no one in Haganah will want to investigate this. They all know what they'll find and they don't want to be the ones who find it."

"I don't care whether they want to do it or not," Ben-Gurion retorted. "Order them to do it and get it done."

"You'll never find the truth that way."

Shimon was standing near the door and spoke up. "I think Moshe Dayan would do it."

"Good," Ben-Gurion said. "Send for him right away."

Eshkol started from the room. He took Shimon by the arm and hustled him out to the hall. "Don't ever do that again," he ordered.

Shimon was startled. "Do what?"

"I wasn't suggesting no one really wanted to do it," Eshkol said. "Or that they wouldn't do it if he asked."

"Then what was all that—"

"I was trying to talk him down from it."

"Talk him down?" Shimon was puzzled. "You don't want to find out who hanged those men?"

"I know who hanged them," Eshkol replied through clenched teeth. "Ben-Gurion knows who hanged them. All of Haganah knows who did it," he gestured with a sweeping motion. "But right now we don't have proof of *anything*. We can deny knowing about how it happened, or who was behind it, because we don't know."

"And that's—"

Eshkol interrupted. "If there's an investigation, we'll learn the facts and then we will know for certain that our suspicions are correct."

"And we'll be unable to deny it without lying."

"Exactly." Eshkol gestured over his shoulder in the direction of Ben-Gurion's office. "I don't want him in a position where he has to lie."

Shimon had a knowing look. "If he knows—actually knows—he's in a tough position."

"Right again. In spite of Begin's difficult nature, and in spite of this tragic event, Irgun is popular with the people. We're trying to avoid a confrontation with them before we declare independence."

Just then, the front door opened and General Cunningham, the British High Commissioner for Palestine, entered. Eshkol nudged Shimon in the opposite direction and whispered, "Find Moshe and get him down here immediately."

"I thought you didn't want—"

"Never mind about that. We need him now. Go!" Eshkol gave him a gentle push. "He turned to Cunningham. "General," Shimon heard him say. "How may I help you?"

As instructed, Dayan reported to the Red House that afternoon.

Two days later, he returned and met with Ben-Gurion. "The short answer," Dayan reported, "is that members of Irgun did it. No one knows for certain who actually hanged the two men but it was an Irgun operation."

"No." Ben-Gurion shook his head slowly from side to side. "You mean, no one will *say* who did it."

"Correct," Dayan acknowledged. "Everyone says it was Irgun. No one will say who actually put the rope around their necks."

"Irgun's own people admit it was them?"

"Yes."

"Who told you this?"

"If I tell you," Dayan answered, "they will never talk to me again."

Ben-Gurion wasn't happy. "You value their friendship?"

"I value the contacts," Dayan explained. "We exchange information on a regular basis. They are the reason we've had any coordination at all."

"Well," Ben-Gurion scoffed. "You need better contacts. We haven't had much cooperation from them at all."

"I need more contacts," Dayan urged.

"You need better contacts," Ben-Gurion retorted.

"The ones I have are good enough. I just don't have enough of them."

When Dayan was gone, Ben-Gurion called Eshkol to his office. Eshkol brought Shimon and Zadok with him. Golda Meir was there, too. Meir had come to Palestine with her husband, Morris, in 1921. She joined Moetzet HaPoalot—the Working Women's Union—and rose through the ranks to play a strategic role in the Jewish Agency's pre-state activity.

"So," Ben-Gurion began. "We know it was an Irgun operation. But what do I do now? The British want justice."

"The British will be gone soon," Meir explained. "All we need to do is stall until they're gone."

"The British aren't the only problem," Shimon offered.

"What do you mean?" Ben-Gurion questioned.

"The international community is watching."

"They're always watching," Meir replied.

"They're watching to see what kind of leader you are," Shimon continued. "What kind of government we are."

"We aren't a government at all," Meir retorted. "I think you should leave this to us."

"For all practical purposes, we are a government in waiting," Shimon corrected. "Everyone knows what will happen. Everyone knows who will be in charge once the British leave. They know the grand mufti will be the voice of the Arabs, as much as they have a voice, and that the Jewish Agency will become the transitional government of the new Jewish state. The world knows that will happen and they know we will be the ones who do it. They're watching now for a preview of what is to come."

"So, what does that mean?" Meir asked.

"If we believe in law and order, then we should show it. Now. If we shirk our responsibility now, others might be reluctant to take a chance with us when we need them."

"So you think we should arrest two or three Irgun members and turn them over to the British?" Ben-Gurion questioned.

"They will hang them for certain. David, don't listen—" Meir began.

"Arrest the men who did this," Shimon said quickly. "Announce to the world that you have in custody the men who were responsible. Tell the world they will be given a fair trial and if found guilty, they will be punished. But not by the British. By us."

"We have no system to handle this sort of thing."

Shimon explained, "If we want to be a state, we have to act like a state."

Ben-Gurion liked the idea, but before he could act, General Cunningham responded with force. A dozen key Irgun leaders were arrested along with those from Mapam and two smaller right-wing parties. Riots broke out in Jerusalem, and British troops quickly leveled several hundred Jewish homes.

Later that week, the British Foreign Ministry in London announced that the British army and all civil staff would withdraw from Palestine earlier than previously planned. The new withdrawal date would be May 14, 1948. A new sense of urgency enveloped Ben-Gurion and the staff at the Red House.

SHIMON PERES

*"Israel must appear as a country
which has a deterrence."*

WITH LESS THAN five months remaining until the British withdrawal was complete, Ben-Gurion redoubled his efforts to prepare for independence. A committee was formed to draft a constitution for the new state. That work necessitated numerous meetings to discuss the kind of government that would work best and to decide on a model around which to construct the legal framework. That proved to be a contentious debate and meetings became increasingly long.

Because of the proximity of his office, Shimon was often drawn into those discussions but did his best to avoid them whenever possible. He spent more and more time on the road, recruiting new members for Haganah and procuring arms for the troops already enlisted. Still, he often found the discussions unavoidable, even when he'd managed to dodge the formal committee meetings.

One day, early in 1948, Shimon returned to the office from a recruiting trip. Ben-Gurion's office door was open. He waved Shimon inside. "Just the man I need to see."

Shimon approached Ben-Gurion's desk and handed him a document. "Take a seat and have a look at this."

Shimon dropped onto a chair across from Ben-Gurion, scanned down the first page of the document, and realized it was a draft of a proposed constitution. "A president," he commented as he turned to the second page. "But a limited one."

"I think we should divide the two functions. Head of state. Head of government. That system has worked well for European countries."

"Our friends in America might disagree."

"America has states that are ten times our size."

"Easily."

"And they can afford to disagree with anyone they like. We have other issues to address."

"Such as?"

"Other than being Jewish, there is no national identity for us. We have no collective consciousness of what it means to be a citizen of our own state. America has a national concept that encompasses all the different ideas of what it means to be American. We have no such story. No such collective identity."

"One day we shall."

"But we don't live in 'one day' right now. We live in the here and now. Someone later can change the government if they like."

"And we have a process for—"

Just then, Golda Meir appeared in the hallway outside Ben-Gurion's office. He noticed her and when he looked up, Shimon turned to see who was behind him.

"What are you two doing?" Meir asked as she entered the room.

"Looking at the most recent version of the committee's constitution."

"Oh?" Meir cast a disapproving look in Shimon's direction, then over to Ben-Gurion. "I wasn't even aware they were finished with the revisions."

"They just released it this morning."

Shimon sensed the tension in Meir's voice. He handed the document back to Ben-Gurion, then stood and offered his chair to Meir. "Please," he motioned. "I was just leaving."

Meir took a seat and Shimon left the room. A few steps down the hall from the office door he paused and heard Golda ask, "Why is he barging in on the committee's area of responsibility? He has no right to see our work before the committee has had time to review it."

"You mean before *you* have seen it."

"I am a member of the committee. That ought to stand for something."

"Golda, he wasn't barging in," Ben-Gurion retorted. "I called him in here. I showed him the document."

"The committee should have seen it first. He's not a member of the—"

"Golda," Ben-Gurion snapped. "Am I the chairman of the committee?"

"Yes, but—"

"Why are you always questioning me?"

"Because you—"

"And why are you always so suspicious? Every day you think someone's out to get you. Every day it's someone new. Yesterday you thought Eshkol was trying to move you out. Today you think Shimon is trying to butt in."

"As the only woman on a committee of men, don't you think I ought to be a little bit suspicious?"

"I am not aware that anyone has ever given you reason to think they're after you. And certainly not because you're a woman. That fear exists only in your mind."

"Well, I don't think—"

"Golda, I am chairman of the committee and chairman of the Agency. I'll invite the comments of anyone I please on any topic I please." He took a seat at his desk. "Don't you have something better to do than to sit here arguing with me about controversies that don't exist? We have enough to worry about with the problems that actually exist. Don't go inventing new ones that don't matter."

A few months later, the executive committee finally agreed on a plan of transition and introduced its proposal to the National Council, including a declaration of independence, a transitional roadmap, and a permanent constitution. The Council members discussed and debated the measures but in the end gave their approval. They also approved the date, May 14, for declaring independence and began work on a signing ceremony.

✦ ✦ ✦

With independence approaching and an Arab–Jewish war growing more certain by the day, Ben-Gurion called yet another meeting of the Jewish Agency executive committee to discuss their options and refine their strategy. Eshkol and Golda Meir attended along with other members of the leadership circle. Shimon and Zadok were present, too.

Meir glanced around warily as they gathered. "I thought this was a meeting of the executive committee," she commented dryly.

"It is," Ben-Gurion replied. "I think we're all here. All who can be."

Meir gestured toward Shimon and Zadok. "But why are they here?"

"Because I invited them," Ben-Gurion huffed. He looked over at Meir with a dour expression. "Are we going through this again, Golda?"

"I'm just asking," she said with an argumentative tone. "We have—"

"And I'm just saying," he responded without waiting for her to finish. "Time is running out. We need all the help we can get. I invited Shimon and Moshe. Let's get on with the things we have to do."

"Besides," Eshkol added. "Shimon and Moshe are in charge of personnel and arms procurement. We need their participation so we know the resources we have on hand and so they understand the resources we will need to execute the strategies we plan."

"Okay, okay," Meir held up her hand defensively. "I was just asking."

"Where's Dayan?" Ben-Gurion asked.

"In the field," Eshkol replied.

For the next hour they received reports on Haganah readiness and reviewed the latest information on arms procurement, immigration, and funding. That discussion took them to an analysis of the threats Haganah anticipated once the British withdrawal was complete. "For certain," Meir ventured, "all of the Arab nations will line up against us."

"War is a certainty," Ben-Gurion nodded.

"All of them will move against us the moment the British leave," another added.

"Perhaps not all of them," Eshkol interjected.

"Levi," Meir said, turning to face him, "the Arab League has already announced its intentions. They mean to crush us before we get established. They've said so repeatedly."

"I know what they've said," Eshkol nodded, "but thus far, only Egypt has initiated military preparations." He produced a map and photographs from a briefcase that sat beside his chair, then used them to brief the committee on the information they'd collected to support his claims. "Syria might yet be a problem," he stated in conclusion. "But Iraq won't send large contingencies of troops, if they send any at all. Arab League members from North Africa don't have the strength to participate either." He tapped the map with his index finger for emphasis. "Egypt will be the major combatant."

"And Jordan," Meir added.

"Perhaps."

"For certain," she rejoined.

Shimon finally spoke up. "I'm not sure about Jordan."

Meir had a condescending expression. "I think you're a little beyond your depth on this one, Shimon."

Ben-Gurion glanced in Shimon's direction. "You have an idea about Jordan?"

"I think we should attempt to make a deal with King Abdullah."

Meir gave an exasperated sigh.

Ben-Gurion ignored her. "What kind of deal?"

"I think we should see if he will agree to stay out of the fight."

Meir glared at Shimon coldly. "And why would he do such a thing? Every member of the Arab League would condemn him for it. He would be an outcast immediately. They're suspicious of him already."

"They think he wants to control all of Palestine," someone noted.

"And he does," Meir added.

Shimon shook his head. "They don't have to know about the deal."

"Ha!" Meir exclaimed in mock laughter. "You think something like that could be kept secret."

"It's possible," Shimon replied. "Abdullah would have no reason to tell them. We certainly wouldn't. But more importantly, Abdullah has no reason to fight us. We pose no threat to him and he knows it. And we know it from our discussions with him." Shimon gestured to Meir. "Discussions you've conducted."

"That's true," Eshkol noted. "We pose no threat to Abdullah. In fact, we are a buffer for him and he knows that, too. With us here, his western flank isn't something he has to spend much time defending."

"And," Zadok added, "they can hardly sustain themselves as it is. They can't afford a war and Abdullah might welcome the opportunity to sit this one out."

"Unless the British continue to support them," someone offered.

"Which brings up an interesting point," Meir observed. "Will the British support Abdullah if he attacks us?"

"Well," Ben-Gurion answered, "I don't think they will abandon him no matter what happens."

"Do you think the British will encourage him to fight us?"

"I think many in London would like to do that very thing," Meir noted. "But ultimately, I don't think they would actually encourage it. Not officially."

Ben-Gurion looked over at Shimon. "You really think Abdullah would agree to stay out of the war?"

Shimon nodded. "I think he might."

Ben-Gurion turned to Meir. "Golda, you've dealt with him. What do you think?"

"Of all the Arab nations, he is by far the friendliest. But I think in the end he will prove to be like the others—weak and unwilling to take a stand that contradicts the accepted Arab line."

"But would he be hostile to an overture from us?"

She shook her head. "He would agree to receive an envoy. And he would discuss the matter civilly. But—"

"Then I think you should go," Ben-Gurion announced.

Meir's eyes opened wide. "Me?"

"Yes, you."

"It was Shimon's idea," she chuckled.

"You have the relationship," Ben-Gurion reminded. "You've spent more time with Abdullah than any of us. I want you to talk to him. See if you can convince him not to attack us. At least, not now." Ben-Gurion turned to Eshkol. "Tell Yigal Yadin and Moshe Dayan to form a plan based on the latest intelligence. We have to move forward with a strategy and work with what we have." He looked across the room to Shimon. "Find us weapons and ammunition. Rifles, ships, tanks, armor. Cannon of any kind. Our lives depend on it."

"Yes, sir," Shimon replied.

✦ ✦ ✦

As Ben-Gurion instructed, Golda Meir met with King Abdullah. He was happy to receive her, and the two got along well. Abdullah refused to commit himself to a nonaggression pact but instead suggested the Jews of Palestine should wait to declare independence. "Allow me to seize the entire region. Then you can set up your country as a canton under our protection. You would have representation in the Jordanian parliament."

Golda Meir reported this to Ben-Gurion and he presented the results to the Jewish Agency executive committee. Some were in favor of accepting the offer, and someone added, "We don't have to declare our independence now. We could do it later."

Ben-Gurion looked over at Shimon. "What do you think?"

"We can't wait. Our people need a state now. We need a place of our own. The millions of our fellow Jews still trapped in Europe need a place to live. We all need a place that is safe. Not just physically safe, but politically safe. Making ourselves subject to an Arab king would put us at the whim of Arab influence. And waiting will only make Abdullah's position stronger. We may never have the opportunity for freedom and security again."

"I agree," Ben-Gurion replied.

"Should we inform the Council?"

Ben-Gurion instructed, "We should inform them of our decision to reject Abdullah's offer. If they want to convene and debate the matter, that will be up to them."

SHIMON PERES

"Israel is moving from the realm of poetry to the realm of prose."

ON THE MORNING of May 14, 1948, messengers were dispatched throughout Tel Aviv and the surrounding area with invitations for guests to attend what was called a concert that afternoon. The event was set for the Tel Aviv Museum and included a ceremony for the establishment of the new State of Israel. Invitees were carefully selected and told to keep the event secret out of concern the British might attempt to intervene if the event's actual business were to become public.

Guests arrived to an orchestra and a festive but elegantly subdued atmosphere. Promptly at four o'clock, Ben-Gurion made his way to the podium positioned at one end of the room. With little fanfare, he read the declaration of independence and announced that as of midnight that night, the time at which the British mandate in Palestine was to end, the State of Israel would exist as a separate, independent nation. That state, he asserted, would exert sovereign authority over all areas designated for a Jewish state as referenced in the United Nations' recently approved plan of partition. The announcement was carried live and broadcast to the world as the first official transmission of the Voice of Israel radio station.

When he concluded his remarks, Ben-Gurion made his way to a table where he was joined by members of the Jewish Agency for Palestine. Seated together, they signed the declaration document and posed for pictures. Afterward, while the orchestra continued to play in the main hall, Agency members adjourned to a separate room where they adopted the plan of a transitional government and approved appointments to key leadership positions. David Ben-Gurion, head of the provisional government, was named prime minister and also minister of defense. Moshe Sharett was named foreign minister.

Sharett had been born in Ukraine and came to Palestine with his parents in 1910. They lived for a time in Jaffa, then became one of the founding families of Tel Aviv. Sharett graduated from Herzliya High School and studied law at Istanbul before serving in the Ottoman army during World War I. Afterward, he studied at the London School of Economics and upon return to Palestine became active in regional economic development. He was a longtime friend and staunch supporter of Ben-Gurion.

Within minutes of Ben-Gurion's announcement, the United States issued a statement from President Truman formally recognizing the State of Israel and acknowledging the transitional government. That statement had been arranged by Chaim Weizmann as yet one more imprimatur of legitimacy.

In spite of its euphoric beginning, Israel faced enormous challenges. Of immediate concern, all seven members of the Arab League, including Egypt and Jordan, announced again their refusal to recognize the new state and reaffirmed their intention to wipe it away. As Eshkol suggested earlier, Egypt, which possessed by far the largest and best-equipped army, presented the most immediate and serious challenge. Indeed, within hours of Israel's announcement, the Egyptian army began amassing troops and equipment on its border.

Yet as great as those external challenges might have been, internal obstacles to national unity were, in some ways, even greater. In one of his first acts as head of government, Ben-Gurion designated Haganah as the Israel Defense Forces (IDF). General officers who already were disgruntled remained so after independence. Continuing efforts to mold the disparate paramilitary organizations into a single, national army only made matters worse. Still, even with war in the offing, Ben-Gurion insisted on pressing forward with the plan that Israel would have a single army under one hierarchy and one command structure.

Domestically, Israel faced a political fight, also. Like Haganah, the Jewish Agency, Histadrut, Lehi, and Irgun—powerful organizations that were instrumental in establishing a Jewish presence in Palestine—existed long before the creation of the state. Each had its own political structure, goals, and leadership. Persuading them to put aside their differences and work together proved to be a major challenge only made worse by independence and the establishment of a single entity to rule them all.

As if that were not enough, on the international front most UN members approved the creation of the new state. Almost all thought its time had come and viewed the establishment of a Jewish state as necessary to prevent a recurrence of the atrocities perpetrated by the Nazis. Yet, as soon as Israel declared its independence, every UN member save one imposed an arms embargo against the new state, denying it the weapons and equipment needed to defend against armies bent on destroying it. Arms procurement, already a critical issue for Israel, became a test of survival.

The lone nation refusing to impose an embargo against the State of Israel was the Soviet Union. With its approval, officials from Czechoslovakia agreed to sell the new state armaments and munitions. Much of it was surplus left over from World War II but, for a new nation facing the threat of annihilation, it was like manna. Along with equipment and materiel, the Czech government permitted the use of its airfields and facilities as transit points for items procured elsewhere, provided mechanics to retrofit used equipment, and trained IDF personnel to operate and service it.

Establishing and coordinating relationships with the Czech government required someone on site in Czechoslovakia. To handle that, Ben-Gurion turned to Ehud Avriel, who had been born and educated in Vienna and immigrated to Palestine in 1940. He joined Haganah and spent most of World War II assisting Jews in their attempts to flee from Europe. That experience, along with his family background, gave Avriel invaluable contacts throughout Europe and a thorough understanding of European culture.

While Avriel worked the Czech side of the arms deals, Shimon was put in charge of coordinating the Israeli side. His office in Tel Aviv became the central point of coordination, addressing payment and logistical issues for each of the shipments. And not merely for Avriel's work in Europe, but for the efforts of others around the globe who stepped up to help circumvent the arms embargo and obtain the items necessary to properly equip IDF for the coming battle.

Because of the difficulty in traveling between Palestine and Europe, and in order to avoid the scrutiny of Arab agents, Avriel rarely came to Israel. He and Shimon communicated through coded telegrams and in face-to-face meetings in Paris, London, and other European cities. It was intense work and kept Shimon away from home, occasionally for weeks at a time, but he found it exhilarating and it awakened in him an interest in international affairs.

At first, Avriel was suspicious of Shimon and worked with him only out of necessity. He doubted Shimon had the discretion or experience necessary for sensitive international work. Then, on a rare trip to Tel Aviv, Avriel met with Moshe Sharett, Israel's new foreign minister. At Ben-Gurion's direction, he briefed Sharett on his activities in Europe, for the first time disclosing the contacts he'd developed.

They sat in Sharett's office for over an hour and as their conversation came to a close, Sharett offered, "I would be glad to assist with communications between you and Ben-Gurion, if that would help."

"Oh, I don't think that will be necessary," Avriel replied. "Shimon seems to be doing a good job so far."

For the briefest of moments Sharett appeared taken aback. "Shimon? Oh. Yes. Right," he recovered. "I just meant if you need additional help. So much is going on around here these days. I wanted you to know that you can call on me if you need me. Don't feel like you can't use me if the moment requires it."

And that's when Avriel realized that Sharett didn't know about Shimon's involvement in coordinating the arms purchases. A smile came to him as the thought crossed his mind, *Perhaps Shimon wasn't so naïve after all.*

Indeed, Shimon's work in arms procurement was far more discreet, and more extensive, then either Avriel *or* Sharett understood. Although Czechoslovakia was their largest supplier, Israel's needs were even larger and Shimon knew it. Working night and day, he established an arms acquisition program that reached literally around the world.

One source, second only to the Czechs, was the United States. An early and vocal proponent of the arms embargo, it nevertheless became one of Israel's largest suppliers. Not officially and not because of government policy but in spite of it through the help of volunteers.

One of the most important US volunteers was Al Schwimmer. American by birth, Schwimmer served in the US Air Force during World War II, then went to work for Trans World Airlines. With Ben-Gurion's prompting, he left a promising career in aviation to assist in acquiring aircraft for the fledgling IDF Air Corps. Using contacts developed over years of service, along with a healthy dose of courage, he acquired surplus US aircraft and recruited pilots to fly them to Israel.

One of Schwimmer's first groups to arrive were three B-17 Flying Fortress bombers. Traveling a circuitous route, they went first to the Canary Islands off the Moroccan coast, then across Europe to a base in Czechoslovakia, where they were rearmed with machine guns and equipped with navigation devices that had been removed before sale.

While the airplanes were being refitted, Shimon and Avriel met at a café in Vienna. As they sipped coffee, Avriel slid a note across the table. "Take a look at this man. He's in Italy."

"Okay," Shimon said cautiously.

Avriel glanced warily around the room as he spoke. "He supposedly has access to things we can use."

"You know this person?"

"No." Avriel shook his head. "Not personally. But we have a mutual friend. Get someone to look into him. Shiloah maybe."

Shimon frowned. "Reuven Shiloah?"

"You know him?"

"We've passed each other in the hall a few times."

Avriel nodded. "He's a good man. Someone you should get to know."

"From what I hear, not many people get that close to him."

"Yeah," Avriel smiled. "He likes to keep things close. But he's trustworthy. Ask him to look into it."

Later, when he was alone in his hotel room, Shimon took the note from his pocket and glanced at it. It contained a single name. Eduardo Casparello. Shimon knew nothing of the man, but when he returned to Tel Aviv he walked down the hall from his office and found Shiloah seated at his desk.

Unlike most people with whom Shimon worked, Shiloah was actually a native Palestinian. Born in Jerusalem, he grew up under the Ottomans and was fluent in multiple Middle Eastern languages. He was educated, articulate, and known by everyone, but exactly what he did remained a mystery, even to those at the highest levels of leadership. Shimon recognized who he was, but that was all he understood and from talking to others that was as much as anyone knew of him. Shimon was certain, however, that Shiloah was aware of far more about him.

"Got a minute?" Shimon asked from the doorway.

"Only a minute," Shiloah replied.

Shimon stepped inside the office, pushed the door closed, and took a seat. "I received a name from Ehud Avriel. He suggested you might be willing to look into this fellow."

Shiloah glanced up for the first time. He had a questioning look. "You want me to investigate Ehud?"

Shimon took a slip of paper from his pocket and handed it to Shiloah. "No, this guy."

Shiloah glanced at the paper, and his eyes opened wider. "Casparello," he said softly.

"You know him?"

"I'll look into it." Shiloah tucked the paper into the pocket of his shirt and turned his attention back to the files on his desk. "Leave the door open when you go."

A few days later, Shimon found a note on his desk that read simply, "He's good." It was signed "R. S." He assumed the note came from Shiloah but his first instinct was to ask around and make sure. He didn't want to plunge into a transaction with Casparello only to learn later it was a mistake. Then he thought better of it. He'd asked no one else about anything that would have generated such a cryptic response and asking about it would only reveal the issue to more people—most of whom needed to know nothing about it. Asking would also make him appear as out of touch as some already thought he was. So he slipped the note into a desk drawer and walked up the hall to Ben-Gurion's office. If Shimon was to pursue Avriel's lead, he would need someone to help coordinate it. The work in Europe with Avriel already kept him busy sometimes twenty hours a day.

In a meeting almost as brief and cryptic as the one he'd had with Shiloah, Ben-Gurion offered Pinchas Sapir as Shimon's assistant. Born in Russia, Sapir immigrated to Palestine as a thirty-year-old. He had been involved in business before emigrating and had a good grasp of how industry worked. Making contact with Casparello took time, but once the relationship was established it proved as helpful as Avriel had suggested. Through him IDF obtained large quantities of Carcano and Fucile rifles, along with ammunition, grenades, and a number of cannon.

Paying for the necessary arms was difficult at first, but Golda Meir traveled to the United States to solicit aid from American Jewish organizations. She had grown up in the United States, understood the culture, and spoke English without a Russian or Polish accent.

As the size of weapons purchases increased, funding increased as well, the money often arriving just ahead of major payouts. In spite of her earlier suspicions about Shimon, Golda never once questioned how the money was being spent, a fact that did not go unnoticed by Shimon.

SHIMON PERES

"They are not as courageous or brave as you think. They are cowards, and if they will see strength, they will retreat. . . . The minute you appear determined and strong, you will win."

AS EXPECTED, less than a week after Ben-Gurion announced Israel's independence the Egyptian army crossed the border and advanced northward, moving up the coast at a rapid pace. Heavy resistance from IDF troops stalled that advance north of Gaza long enough for Schwimmer's B-17s to arrive from Czechoslovakia. The bombers were followed by Czech fighter aircraft and a week later the Egyptian advance that had looked so threatening earlier turned into an IDF rout.

To the north, Syrian forces advanced into Galilee but reached only as far as the southern tip of the Sea of Galilee. There, Moshe Dayan and his armored troops fought the advancing army to a standstill.

Meanwhile, forced by threats from neighboring Arab states, King Abdullah ordered his army to advance westward across the Jordan River. It seized control of East Jerusalem and the territory lying between the city and the river. At the same time, Abdullah opened Jordan to Palestinian refugees. Thousands fled there for safety.

By mid-June, Israel's army had regained much of the territory lost to the initial enemy attack and began encroaching on areas allotted to an Arab state in the UN plan of partition. Members of the UN Security Council, alarmed by the outbreak of war, brokered a ten-day truce. It came just as Israel was running low on ammunition.

Along with the truce, the UN announced the appointment of Folke Bernadotte to mediate a solution to the conflict. Bernadotte was a Swedish diplomat who developed a reputation for handling difficult situations during World War II when he arranged the release of some 31,000 prisoners being held by the Germans.

Ralph Bunche, a rising young diplomat from the United States, was appointed to assist Folke. Bunche was an African American and a native of Detroit. He'd graduated from UCLA and held a PhD in political science from Harvard.

The negotiating team arrived in Tel Aviv as the truce went into effect and immediately requested meetings with Arab and Israeli representatives. Ben-Gurion directed Moshe Sharett to represent Israel. The grand mufti of Jerusalem represented Arab interests.

Bernadotte attempted to find a political solution that would salvage the two-state partition plan previously approved by the UN. Sharett was willing to listen and offered suggestions on how that might be accomplished. Arab leaders, however, held fast to their original position, denying that Israel had any right to exist and refusing to recognize its borders no matter how they were drawn.

While those discussions went on, Eshkol learned that Irgun had gone forward with its plan to acquire arms independently of the provisional government. Weapons, including much- needed ammunition, had been loaded aboard a cargo ship known as the *Altalena*, which now lay off the Mediterranean coast near Jaffa. Upon hearing the news, Ben-Gurion was livid and ordered Menachem Begin brought to his office at once. Eshkol was certain seizing Begin would only lead to an armed confrontation with Irgun soldiers. Instead of arresting Begin he sent a message asking him to come to the Red House.

A few hours later, Begin arrived and was immediately ushered into Ben-Gurion's office. A loud and angry argument ensued, heard by everyone in the building, and when it was over Begin left in a huff. "Why does he have to be so stubborn?" Ben-Gurion shouted.

Eshkol grabbed Shimon. "Come with me."

"Where? I have a lot to do here," Shimon argued.

"This is more important."

With Shimon in tow, Eshkol led the way to Ben-Gurion's office. Ben-Gurion was standing behind his desk when they entered.

"He insists that weapons aboard that ship belong to Irgun," Ben-Gurion railed. "And he won't agree to have them distributed by IDF."

Eshkol nodded. "I'm sure he thinks we'll deny him the best."

"Yes," Ben-Gurion agreed. "He's worried you won't give Irgun any at all."

"So, what do we do?"

Ben-Gurion folded his arms across his chest. "Sink it," he ordered in a resolute tone.

Eshkol look surprised. "Excuse me?"

"Sink the ship," Ben-Gurion repeated.

"Sink it?"

"We are the government. I am the prime minister of Israel. And I'm the defense minister of Israel. Menachem Begin is head of a private organization."

"This isn't about you and Begin."

"Yes, Levi. It is," Ben-Gurion insisted. "This is about me as prime minister. And this is about every other prime minister that comes after me. We are the government and when we speak we speak for the government. If he won't comply with our lawful orders, then we have no choice. Sink the ship!"

"Very well," Eshkol answered, then he turned toward the door and Shimon followed him out to the hallway.

"Why did you need me?" Shimon asked when they were away from the office.

"When you go in to talk him down, never go alone."

"I don't think I'll ever have the opportunity, one way or the other."

"Yes, you will," Eshkol insisted. "Arye Bahir told me what you did in the hotel room at the Zionist Congress."

"But I didn't do *anything*," Shimon protested.

"Exactly. And that's another thing. When you choose someone to go in there with you, pick someone who Ben-Gurion likes and who knows enough to keep quiet. Without being told."

"If you're not around, maybe I'll get Bahir."

Eshkol stopped and turned to face Shimon. "Listen. This is serious. We're all committed to the work we're doing and the cause we're fighting. But we are all human. Sometimes personalities get in the way and every now and then even a brilliant leader runs up against the limitations of his personality. That's where we come in." He tapped Shimon on the chest. "That's where *you'll* come in. We have to talk them around their limitations and help them get to the things that really matter."

"Okay," Shimon nodded. "But how do we talk him past this?"

"I don't think we can."

"Why not?"

"Because he's right," Eshkol turned away and started down the hall.

For the next two days Eshkol did his best to reach an agreement with Begin and Irgun but as the original cease-fire neared an end, and with fighting expected to resume the moment it expired, Eshkol gave the order to Yigal Yadin.

The next day, artillery cannon manned by IDF troops opened fire on the *Altalena* as it ran aground off the coast of Tel Aviv. The ship caught fire with the second round of shelling, and thick black smoke billowed into the air. Not long after that, secondary explosions ripped through the hull. A crowd formed onshore to watch and everyone agreed it was an awful sight. They also agreed that Ben-Gurion had no other choice. Reluctantly, Menachem Begin and Irgun agreed also and brought his units under IDF control.

As the end of the ten-day truce approached, Bernadotte raised the question of extending it to permit further discussion. Arab representatives, however, would not agree. Faced with no option but to resume fighting, Ben-Gurion and Sharett convened a meeting to review Israeli strategy. Golda Meir, Pinchas Sapir, Shimon, and others were in attendance. The room was filled to capacity and the air inside quickly became stuffy.

Eshkol and Yigal Yadin briefed the group on IDF's current positions. "So, that's where we are," Eshkol summarized. "We have stopped the Egyptian advance up the coast and are holding them just north of Gaza. And in the north we're sitting just south of the Sea of Galilee. The Jordanians hold Jerusalem and the western bank of the river."

A voice from the corner said dryly, "Our people in Jerusalem are dying."

"I think our first priority should be to cut a way through to them," Shimon suggested, no longer intimidated by those in the room. "Drive a wedge across the country. That would relieve the city and split the region in half. Separate the north from the south."

Yadin seemed to like that idea. "That would put us in a good position in many respects."

"We need all of Galilee, too," someone added.

"But that would take us beyond the area designated on the map."

"The map?"

"The UN map. The plan of partition."

"I think we moved beyond that when the Egyptians invaded."

"What about Gaza?"

Yadin shook his head. "I'm not sure we can drive the Egyptians out of Gaza. I mean, given enough time we could cut them off and lay siege to the city, but that would occupy troops and equipment that might be better employed elsewhere. We have them contained. They won't move any farther up the coast and we can push their northern perimeter closer to the city itself. But I think we should turn our attention to other areas that are more important to us."

"And besides," Meir spoke up, "we might not want Gaza at all."

"Why not?"

"It would leave us with too many Arabs."

"But we need Eilat," Sharett noted, referring to a settlement at the northern end of the Gulf of Aqaba.

"Yes," someone agreed. "We need it as a port. As an outlet to the east."

"Otherwise," Sapir offered, "our ships have to sail through the Suez Canal, where they would be subject to the Egyptians."

"I don't think they'd let us through."

"Exactly. With Eilat, we don't need the Egyptians."

Someone seated near the door spoke up. "And we need all of Galilee, too."

"But, again, that takes us beyond the areas assigned by the UN plan. Is that going to be a problem?"

"And what about the Jordanians?"

"I think we should avoid the Jordanians," Ben-Gurion insisted. "Unless they move on us, we should leave them alone. A fight with them gives the British a reason to intervene and we don't want that."

"You mean give them East Jerusalem?"

"For now."

"That includes the Temple Mount."

"We can negotiate access," Ben-Gurion countered.

"You think Abdullah will agree to that?"

"I think we should take that risk."

"So, what are we doing? What's our strategy?"

"Let's go on the offensive," Eshkol suggested. "Sweep up the remainder of the Negev. Push toward Eilat. Drive north into Galilee as far as we can."

"And take Arab territory," Sharett added.

Ben-Gurion nodded. "I agree. They chose this war. We would have accepted the UN plan and let them have their state, but they wanted all of it and chose to fight."

"They aren't fighting for what the UN was willing to give *them*," Sharett added. "They're fighting for what the UN was willing to give *us*. They want it all. The whole of Palestine. We'll take as much as we can get, too."

"That would certainly give us a better negotiating position," someone added.

"We're not negotiating," Ben-Gurion snapped. His voice was tense and his tone terse. "We're building a country."

When the original truce expired, Arab leaders refused to grant an extension and fighting resumed. In the south, IDF units swept through the Negev capturing Arab villages with little or no resistance. Several attempts by the Egyptians to mount an offensive were repulsed.

Near the center of the country, an expansion of Israeli control to the east of Tel Aviv opened a corridor to West Jerusalem, bringing relief to Jewish residents who'd been trapped there since the war began. As planned, IDF troops avoided a direct assault on Jordanian positions, taking defensive positions in the western half of the city.

In Galilee, a push northward led to the capture of Nazareth and all of the southern half of the region. However, an attempt to drive out Syrian troops from the eastern side bogged down with little success.

Two weeks later, a second UN-sponsored truce was arranged, and through the month of August and into September Bernadotte once again attempted to find a diplomatic solution. With Israeli control of areas well beyond those designated for a Jewish state, and with Egyptian troops unable to deter them, Arabs were in a precarious position. They still demanded that the Jews leave but their bargaining position had rapidly deteriorated and they had little means of pressing their point, either in talks or on the battlefield.

At the same time, elements of the Israeli transitional government were inclined to negotiate an end to the fighting. Money spent on the war could be used in any number of other areas and some wondered if there wasn't a way to bring the conflict to a successful end without fighting all the way to a conclusion.

When word of that possibility leaked out, operatives who'd been part of the more radical paramilitary groups became concerned that Bernadotte might actually succeed in convincing the Arabs to accept a Jewish state. They also worried that Ben-Gurion might agree to cede occupied territory to make that happen.

Rather than waiting to find out, on September 17 former members of Lehi attacked Bernadotte's car in Jerusalem. In a hail of gunfire, Bernadotte and several who were traveling with him were killed. Ralph Bunche, Bernadotte's assistant, escaped injury and later that week was appointed to continue the work of mediating a settlement, but fighting resumed and IDF units continued their advance into Arab territory.

By the end of the year, Israel controlled Galilee, the western side of Palestine from the coast to Jerusalem, and all of the Negev except Gaza. Arabs held Gaza and an area south of the city to the Egyptian border. Jordan held East Jerusalem and the region known as the West Bank, which lay between the city and the Jordan River. Then, in March 1949, IDF troops reached Eilat at the head of the Gulf of Aqaba. At about four in the afternoon of March 10, the flag of Israel was raised over the settlement and the war was declared over.

SHIMON PERES

*"Nobody in the Middle East speaks their
original language but Israel."*

NOT LONG AFTER the war ended, when Israel's independence was established and her security firmly in hand, general elections were held. Ballots included a referendum on the form of government and the election of an initial slate of candidates to public office. As everyone expected, Ben-Gurion was chosen prime minister. Chaim Weizmann was elected president, a nod to his significant, though recently troubled, role in the cause of Zionism and creation of a Jewish state in Palestine. Members of the national legislature, known as the Knesset, were chosen as well.

After the elections, Moshe Sharett was appointed to continue as foreign minister. With the government now officially adopted by voters and the Foreign Ministry's mission expanding, Sharett decided to hire an assistant. Shimon suggested his friend from the kibbutz, Yohai Cohen. Sharett met with Yohai and a few days later offered him the job.

During the transition from the farm, Yohai stayed with Shimon and Sonia for a few days while he found a place of his own. They talked and caught each other up on what had been happening in their lives, but after that they didn't see much of each other, occasionally meeting for lunch but not much else.

After a month or two went by and Yohai no longer came around, Sonia was suspicious. "It's not right," she commented one night after dinner.

"What's not right?" Shimon asked.

"The situation with Yohai."

Shimon shrugged. "It's nothing. He's just busy."

"No." Sonia was unconvinced. "There's more to it than that. You two used to be close. We all used to be close."

"Times change. People move on."

"Do you think you've moved on?"

"I never thought about it much." He looked over at her. "But now that I do, you know, we haven't been back to the kibbutz since we left."

Sonia gave him a knowing look. "That might have something to do with it."

Shimon disagreed. "I don't think so. I don't think anything is wrong."

"Was he glad to have the job?"

"Yes," Shimon nodded. "You heard him when he was staying with us."

"And then once he actually went to work, things changed."

"Yeah." Shimon thought for a moment. "I guess it did."

"Did you have anything to do with him? Officially. Have you been working with him on something?"

"No."

"Then maybe it has to do with Sharett."

Shimon dismissed the comment with a wave of his hand. "Moshe Sharett and I are on good terms."

"I'm not so sure," Sonia said in a doubtful tone. "I think something's not right."

Shimon slipped behind her and wrapped his arms around her shoulders. "What's not right is you and me standing here talking." He leaned over and nuzzled her neck. Sonia giggled in response, then turned to kiss him.

✦ ✦ ✦

After the election, Ben-Gurion retained his position as minister of defense, in addition to being prime minister. Golda Meir was appointed ambassador to the Soviet Union. At the Defense Ministry, Shimon remained in charge of IDF recruitment and weapons procurement, but to those duties was added the role of acting secretary of the navy. At the time of his appointment, he was twenty-six years old.

Until the spring of 1948, Haganah had no navy. That year, Ben-Gurion appointed Gershon Zak to the task of forming one, both for its tactical advantages and as a further expression of legitimacy for the then government-in-waiting.

For personnel, Zak cobbled together elements from Palmach's small naval service, a smattering of volunteers who'd come over from the United States with shipments of supplies and a small cadre of people who had been trained at a naval school in Italy under arrangements negotiated by Ze'ev Jabotinsky, a Revisionist Zionist activist. For ships, he commandeered three vessels that had been previously used to ferry displaced persons from Europe.

With those rudimentary pieces in place, Zak's sea service patrolled the coast, monitoring port activity and, during the war, interdicting Egyptian seaward resupply of Arab and Egyptian units fighting in Gaza. Israeli ships also bombarded shore positions in and around Gaza and south to Port Said, Egypt. In its most significant action, and to the surprise of almost everyone except Zak, the Israeli navy sank the Egyptian flagship, *Emir Farouk*.

During the war, Zak had been assisted by Paul Shulman, an American whose mother was an early supporter of Zionism. A US Naval Academy graduate, Shulman served in the navy during World War II. Ben-Gurion met him while on a fund-raising trip to New York and placed him in charge of procuring ships for transporting smuggled material from the United States. Later, he was involved in bringing immigrants from Europe.

Shulman was a trained naval officer but lacked depth of practical naval experience. He was also noticeably younger than many of the older Haganah officers who were serving in the fledgling navy.

That made for a difficult relationship from the beginning. Nevertheless, his work immediately prior to and during the war for independence helped not only the war effort but also the plans to add a navy to Israel's military.

The navy's inauspicious beginning, and its less than critical role in the War of Independence, meant that during the conflict it received the least logistical support of the IDF's branches. When Shimon took over as acting secretary of the navy, that service was deficient in almost every respect. To address the situation, Shimon went to work purchasing ships, arming and equipping them, and training sailors to operate in accordance with modern naval standards. He also spent time defining the new branch's mission.

From the time of the first *Aliyah*—the return of Zionists to Palestine beginning in the late 1800s—Jewish life in the region centered primarily on the kibbutzim. The labor movement, which played such a big part in establishing the settlements, was focused in that direction, too. Israelis came to statehood with a well-defined relationship to the land; the relationship of modern Israel to the sea was the least. Defining the mission of a new navy took quite a bit of thought, planning, and exploration.

During the war, a lack of resources forced the navy to use lighter craft. That worked well for patrolling relatively shallow water along the coast. Israel's navy lacked heavy firepower. At that time, purchasing that kind of presence on the sea was cost prohibitive. A light, nimble fleet, however, offered the ability to strike quickly and without much notice. Shimon liked that idea and used it as the central focus of a long-term strategy.

Aside from overall equipment, training, and mission issues, one of the biggest issues facing Shimon was that of resolving conflict between Zak and Shulman. Zak came to the navy after years of service in Haganah. He brought with him much of that agency's freewheeling, plan-as-you-go paramilitary culture. Shulman came from the US Navy, which demanded a disciplined, organized, methodical approach to naval operations. From the beginning of their association, the two did not agree on much of anything and sorting out a working relationship between them took much of Shimon's time and attention.

To resolve the matter, Shimon placed Shulman in command of the navy from a military perspective and positioned Zak as the civilian naval executive under the Ministry of Defense. That satisfied the issue in one respect but still made for an awkward arrangement. At any rate, things sorted themselves out soon enough.

Zak served in his naval position through the year, then resigned to embark on a career in education. Not long after he departed, Shulman left, too. He continued to serve as an adviser to Ben-Gurion but was no longer part of the Ministry of Defense. Munya Mardor, a Haganah veteran, replaced him as military commander of the navy. With Mardor, the navy turned toward an iteration that would carry it through the next decade.

✦ ✦ ✦

In 1950, Shimon was appointed leader of the Defense Ministry's delegation to the United States. He, Sonia, and their children moved to New York City, where they lived in a seven-room apartment on Manhattan's Upper West Side. With room to spare it was a far cry from where they'd lived in Tel Aviv, and the apartment soon became a rendezvous spot for single members of the delegation. It also served as a stopover for visitors from Israel needing a temporary place to stay.

Living in New York City provided Shimon and Sonia an opportunity to relax and spend more time together. Their personal relationship, always close, grew deeper and, in a sense, recovered from the stress they'd experienced as a result of Shimon's long hours at the office during the war. They attended plays together, visited art museums, dined at nice restaurants, and encountered a social life neither of them had ever known.

For Shimon, exposure to new ideas and a new lifestyle had another effect, too: It raised concerns for him about the depth of his education. As a child, he had attended the yeshiva in Vishnyeva and had been tutored by his grandfather, which provided an excellent intellectual and religious foundation. He'd built on that foundation at high schools in Tel Aviv and Jerusalem, then added intense instruction and lectures at Ben-Shemen. And he'd further expanded his understanding with the help of Berl Katznelson. But that was the extent of his education and not much of it had been anything like the formal education students received in the United States.

In New York he encountered people from every level of society whose formal educational experience seemed to have gone much further, much deeper, and much wider than his. Interacting with them left Shimon with the sense that he'd missed something; that intellectually he was lacking.

One night, as he and Sonia prepared for bed, he mentioned his misgivings to her. "If I'm going to deal with the world, with people who have ideas that matter and who are in a position to do something of significance—if I'm going to do my job—I need to be closer to their intellectual level."

"You are," Sonia replied. "In fact, you are superior to them."

"But not in what I know."

"You can learn."

"Yes," Shimon agreed. "And I think I would like to do that."

"Good. You can read more. We can buy books. Get a library card."

"No. I mean I want to take some classes."

"Classes?" Sonia paused with a puzzled look. "Here? In the United States?"

"Yes, while we're here in New York."

"But where? How?" she asked. "Your English is adequate for daily life but is it good enough to learn in a class?"

"I can learn that, too."

Not long after they talked, Shimon applied to study English at New York University. As his language skills improved, he enrolled in economics and philosophy courses at the New School for Social Research, a university located in Lower Manhattan that catered to intellectual progressives. The school fostered a sense of unbridled academic exploration and, at various times, was home to people like James Baldwin, W. E. B. Du Bois, Bertrand Russell, Reinhold Niebuhr, and John Maynard Keynes. It was the perfect place for Shimon and, as much as his time in New York exposed him to new cultural life, his time at the New School opened his mind to new ideas.

✦ ✦ ✦

Although he lived and worked in New York, Shimon remained in charge of IDF recruitment and arms procurement. In that capacity, he received regular updates and briefings of important events and policy decisions in Israel. Most of that information came through cables and encoded telegrams but occasionally it came by way of a visitor to the apartment. One of those visitors was Pinchas Sapir.

Since the end of the war, Sapir had moved from his position at the Israeli Defense Ministry and had taken a post with the Ministry of Finance, an area more suited to his skills and interests than clandestine arms acquisition. He passed through New York on his way to a meeting in Washington, D.C., and late one night as they relaxed in the living room he briefed Shimon on recent events in Israel.

Sapir reminded, "Ben-Gurion has been intrigued by the possibility of an arrangement with King Abdullah."

"We tried that before the war."

"Yes. And Abdullah wanted us to agree to become a kind of autonomous zone under his authority."

"Something like that."

"Ben-Gurion wanted me to bring you up to date on the latest with that."

"Oh?" Shimon had expected a discussion of financial issues, a subject in line with Sapir's current position. That the topic was something else left him suspicious, a fact that his voice belied by its tone.

"I know," Sapir continued defensively, apparently sensing Shimon's sentiment. "I'm not with the Foreign Ministry, but I think the Old Man wanted you to know what was happening and he wanted it delivered in person. Too much detail to put in a cable and all."

Shimon nodded. "He asked you to see me about this?"

"Yes. He briefed me about it himself, then had Golda meet with me as well."

Shimon raised an eyebrow. "I bet that was an interesting meeting."

"She's not as bad as you think," Sapir replied. "Though she is deeply suspicious of you."

"I knew she used to be."

"She still is."

"I never understood why."

"She seems to think you're always exceeding your authority."

A frown wrinkled Shimon's forehead. "My authority?"

"Yes."

"Interesting. I'm not sure what that means exactly, but it's an interesting choice of words."

"When we were buying arms from Italy and you were involved with the Czechs, you saw it as doing deals to get our troops what they needed."

"That's exactly how I saw it, because that's exactly what we were doing."

"She viewed it as you conducting foreign policy on your own."

"Well," Shimon scoffed, "it was foreign in that we were dealing with a foreign country. And relations in that we had a relationship with the people in that country."

"And," Sapir added, "the whole thing was overlapping—everyone stepped on everyone else's area of responsibility, at least to some extent."

Shimon sighed. "Almost everyone had overlapping duties."

"I know."

"I always sensed something wasn't right between us," Shimon continued. "Something fundamental. Like something that was a part of me that not even she could specify, it just made her react. We got off on the wrong foot. But I have no idea where it comes from."

"Well, for one thing," Sapir continued, "she sees foreign affairs as her domain."

"But she's not the foreign minister."

"I know, but—"

"She's an ambassador."

"I know. But that's how she sees it. Actually, she sees all of Israel as her domain."

"I'm sure she sees herself as Ben-Gurion's logical successor, too."

"Unless you get in ahead of her," Sapir quipped.

Shimon's eyes opened wide. "Me?"

"She sees you as the Old Man's chosen boy."

"Thinks I'm getting ahead of people who've been around longer?"

Sapir nodded. "I think so."

"She shouldn't worry about me. I mean, Ben-Gurion and I get along well and we like each other, but I'm pretty sure the next prime minister will be Moshe Sharett. I think that's what Ben-Gurion wants."

Sapir glanced away. "I don't know." A cloud came over him and for a moment Shimon wondered if Sapir thought the role of prime minister should come to him.

Shimon wanted to steer the conversation back to the topic at hand. "But you came to tell me about Abdullah."

"Yes." Sapir sat up straight and his countenance changed. "So, Ben-Gurion is still interested in the Jordanians and he sent Golda to talk with King Abdullah."

"Right there. She's the ambassador to the Soviet Union, yet here she is going off to visit with the king of Jordan. And why? Because it's part of her job? No. Because she has a long-standing relationship with Abdullah. They've been talking with each other for two decades. So, even though she has responsibility in one area, she's the logical person for work in another, too. And it's the same with all of us."

Sapir kept going. "So she talked to Abdullah. He's not opposed to peace with Israel and reminded her that he had hoped to avoid war altogether in '48. But now he's not just dealing with his own people. He's caught between the other Arab states, too. There's a rising Arab sense of ethnic identity all over the region. Not just among Arabs in Palestine but everywhere. And he thinks nationalism runs counter to the monarchies."

"The monarchies haven't helped themselves in that regard, either," Shimon noted. "Most, if not all of them, are corrupt. The Egyptian monarchy is the worst of all. They're the ones most at risk."

"Perhaps so, but Abdullah is worried about his own position. He annexed the West Bank and extended Jordanian citizenship to Palestinian Arabs. More recently, he's been trying to develop the East Bank, the Jordanian side of the river, in an effort to entice Palestinians to settle there and become true, traditional Jordanians."

"A tacit acknowledgment that his claim to the West Bank is tenuous at best."

"Probably," Sapir agreed. "Opening Jordan to Palestinian Arabs and giving them citizenship seemed like a good idea during the war, but it had the effect of immediately giving Jordan a Palestinian population that outnumbers existing Jordanians."

"Which is why we didn't want Gaza and don't really care to have control of the West Bank. I assume the shift in Jordanian majorities didn't go unnoticed."

"Not at all. Political instability is on the rise. And with that instability, Abdullah thinks other Arab nations have come to see Jordan as weak."

"And vulnerable."

"Right," Sapir acknowledged. "Abdullah would prefer peace with us, but in light of all of that, he is walking a fine line between the various Arab groups and interests. Trying to hold on to power."

"And if he makes a deal with us it will tip the balance against him and he'll be out of power."

"Something like that."

"So, where does it stand now with Jordan?"

"Golda reported all of that to Ben-Gurion, but I don't think he's made up his mind what to do. Or even if there is anything he *can* do right now."

The conversation with Sapir proved more interesting than Shimon had expected. More revealing, too, and later, as he lay in bed, he recounted the conversation once more in his mind.

What he'd learned that evening about the situation with Jordan was intriguing, but even more interesting was the information he'd picked up about Golda Meir. She'd been involved in Jewish organizations since the age of fourteen and came to Palestine in 1921, two years before Shimon was born. That she had a sense of being ahead of him in the line of succession to authority was understandable. Zionist leadership was decidedly male, too, and her wariness of being discounted simply because she was a woman was likewise understandable. But she knew him and she'd seen his work. Didn't she know by now that he was no threat to her? Didn't she know he was committed to Israel, just as she was?

And then it hit him. "That was the difference."

Golda Meir was a member of Histadrut, a faction in the Labor Party movement, but one that engendered deep loyalty to itself. An "us against them" approach where "us" was Histadrut, not the State of Israel. "She is committed to the labor union," Shimon whispered. "I am committed to Israel."

SHIMON PERES

"I don't think anybody who carries a rifle carries the future. Because I don't believe you can really change the world by killing and shooting."

BEN-GURION REMAINED interested in reaching a rapprochement with Jordan and in the summer of 1951 decided to try once again to reach an agreement with King Abdullah. This time, instead of using Golda Meir, he turned to Reuven Shiloah.

By then, Shiloah's secretive and highly compartmentalized job had been transformed into the government's Institute for Intelligence and Special Operations, commonly known as the Mossad. Israel's intelligence service, of which Shiloah was the director.

Using his own contacts, developed outside of those Golda Meir had maintained, Shiloah arranged a series of high-level discussions with key Jordanian officials. Those talks were designed to raise the level of those conversations from mere talk to actual negotiation. To move from abstract concepts to practical measures in an effort to reach a definitive peace agreement between the two countries or, at least, to find ways of cooperating more closely on issues affecting the West Bank and Jerusalem.

As talks proceeded, the diplomatic parties developed an amicable relationship and participants found many areas of agreement. So much so that Shiloah and King Abdullah began meeting face-to-face. Most of those meetings took place in Amman but one was scheduled in conjunction with Abdullah's regular Friday visit to Al-Aqsa Mosque in Jerusalem. He'd been coming there for prayer each week since Jordanian troops seized East Jerusalem during Israel's War of Independence. The meeting with Shiloah was set for a Friday in July.

During that visit, Abdullah and Shiloah met for talks and afterward the king went to the mosque for Friday services. As he approached the mosque entrance, a gunman rushed forward, pushed his way past security guards, and fired shots from a pistol at point-blank range into the king. The king fell dead on the spot. The gunman, later identified as Mustafa Ashu, a Palestinian reacting to rumors that Abdullah was negotiating a peace agreement with Israel, was killed immediately.

By right of inheritance, King Abdullah's son, Talal, immediately succeed him to the throne. Martial law was declared in Jerusalem and a curfew was imposed throughout Jordan. Talal took the throne but suffered from severe mental illness and later the next year abdicated in favor of his own son, Hussein—Abdullah's grandson—who became King Hussein of Jordan.

✦ ✦ ✦

In 1952, Shimon returned with his family to Israel. They rented an apartment in Tel Aviv and began reconnecting with old friends. After two years of exposure to a different culture and lifestyle, Sonia began to distance herself from the daily rhythms of Israeli politics and worked to reclaim the sense of purpose and mission that had motivated her to join Shimon in the labor movement. Instead of adopting the normal routine of a politician's wife, she began volunteering at a hospital that worked with special-needs children. And not the glamorous kind of volunteering some did, like serving on boards and attending luncheons. Sonia volunteered for the kind of service no one wanted and for which no one received acclaim. She spent her time out of the public eye, scrubbing hospital floors and cleaning patients' rooms.

Shimon, on the other hand, immersed himself in government service. He was appointed deputy director general of the Ministry of Defense, a civilian position that oversaw administrative details for the Defense Ministry, including the budget. Work on spending priorities put him at the heart of defense policy debate and he spent long hours sorting through stacks of requests, turning spending and payments into workable policy.

On the military side, Yigal Yadin was chief of staff for IDF. Moshe Dayan was IDF's chief of operations. Those two positions were filled by IDF officers—both Yadin and Dayan held the rank of general—and were responsible for actual military command with direct authority and control over military units. As had proved too often to be the case, conflict arose between the old guard military leadership and civilian accountability.

For one thing, Yadin was six years older than Shimon. He'd been a university student and field commander, while Shimon worked from an office in the Red House. That was part of the problem, but the primary trouble lay in the fact that Yadin resented being accountable to a civilian. "If I am to be accountable to anyone," he said more than once, "it should be to the minister of defense. To him and him alone. Certainly not to someone at a sub-ministerial level who has never served a day in the military." The difficulty between them simmered from day one, but it finally came to a head when Shimon proposed changes to the defense budget.

Yadin favored spending increases for uniforms, housing, and food for the soldiers. Shimon understood his reasoning—military success still came down to placing troops on the ground—but armies in the region were ahead of the IDF in weapons sophistication that provided advantages on the battlefield that human bodies could never match.

Weapons upgrades were necessary not merely to keep pace with Israel's Arab neighbors but also to maintain even minimal defense capabilities.

In an attempt to get the most benefit for their money, and to move as much as possible into the acquisition of critical components, Shimon wanted to rid IDF of its major support facilities—military hospitals, bakeries, and laundry facilities—and contract with private companies for those services. He encountered resistance to this idea from several levels of the military. One afternoon, following yet one more round of discussions with Defense Ministry planners and analysts, he brought up the subject in a conversation with Moshe Dayan.

"Do you think I'm wrong?" Shimon asked.

"I think there are very few right-and-wrong answers in life," Dayan replied. "Some are better than others, but not that many are clearly right. Or clearly wrong."

"Someone told me today that I am a dreamer. Do you know how many times I've been told that? It's like a cliché. 'Shimon, always with his head in the clouds. Shimon, always thinking he's so smart.'"

"You are so smart. You intimidate men twenty years older than you and with a lifetime of military experience."

"You mean Yigal Yadin."

Dayan smiled. "Well . . . yes. Now that you mention him."

"I'm not trying to act smart. I just want to get the most out of our money. We don't get enough of it, so we have to spend it in a way that gives us the most possible. The best weapons systems. The best airplanes. The best tanks."

"Machines."

"The day has passed when we could win a war solely with foot soldiers."

"We couldn't have won the first one that way, either."

"Right," Shimon agreed. "We had to have the airplanes from the Czechs and the ones Schwimmer brought from America. Yigal and his group want an army designed like the ones that fought three wars ago. When men lined up across from each other and had at it with swords and axes."

"That was more than three wars ago."

"You know what I mean. We don't need an army designed to fight the last war. We need one designed to fight the next one."

"And that's what you're trying to do by getting rid of the bakery?"

"And the laundry. And the hospital. We can't afford an army that is fully integrated from top to bottom."

Dayan had a puzzled frown. "Fully integrated? You mean they want to enlist Arabs and other ethnic groups?"

"No," Shimon replied. "Not racially integrated. Fully integrated. It's a term. A business term. For a business that does everything—mines the natural resources, smelts it into usable material, builds something, markets and sells it."

Dayan had a mischievous grin. "Been to New York and now you're getting all fancy on us?"

"That's how some of them see it."

"So how would that work in the army? A fully integrated army. What does that mean?"

"An army that recruits and trains soldiers for combat but also cooks, cleans, and clothes them. And gives them healthcare. All with military personnel in military facilities."

"And how does contracting for that save money?"

"Well, for one thing, those operations involve expensive fixed assets. Because of that, they have to be built with excess capacity. They never operate at peak capacity."

"Which is a good thing, I suppose."

"If you have one, yes. But you have to maintain it completely, whether you use it all or not."

"Ah." Dayan's eyes brightened. "And that's where you find the savings. You only contract for what you need at any given moment. Not for excess capacity of some unknown future demand."

Shimon ginned. "You always sandbag me on this topic."

"Sandbag?" Dayan shrugged. "What do you mean?"

Shimon wadded up a piece of paper and threw it at him. "You know exactly what I'm talking about. Every bit of it. Probably even thought about it before I was born."

"I'm not that much older than you. But yes. I've been lobbying for this kind of change since I joined Haganah. Our leaders are from a time that has passed. They think of an army as an army of soldiers. The world now has armies of machines."

"We can't fight solely with soldiers anymore. And even if we wanted to, we don't have enough people for it."

"Or a war of attrition, either," Dayan added. "We have to fight smarter than our enemies."

"And smart is with the use of the latest technological advances."

The Defense Ministry debate continued for another two weeks with additional meetings, arguments, and discussions. Finally, Ben-Gurion called Shimon to his office. Ben-Gurion was seated at his desk when Shimon arrived.

"Yigal came to see me," Ben-Gurion began.

"About the budget?" Shimon was unsure how this meeting was going to turn out, but whatever Ben-Gurion decided, that's what they would do. He crossed the room toward the desk as Ben-Gurion continued to talk.

"Yes. Isn't there a way to work this out?"

Shimon took a seat in a chair near the desk. "You mean the differences between him and me? Or the issues of budget policy and IDF mission?"

"A way to accomplish both goals. More for the troops while continuing to acquire the weapons we need."

"Get us more money and we can do anything."

"How much do we need?"

"We need a lot," Shimon replied.

"And you think your ideas will get it for us?"

"Yes."

"And cutting expenses for the troops is the way to go?"

"In any organization," Shimon explained, "personnel costs are the single biggest expense. Even under the changes I've proposed, personnel expenditures will still exceed weapons purchases. But to do any of it, to make any changes at all, we have to find ways to save. To get more and do more with the money we have. That's all I'm trying to do." He scooted closer to the desk, picked up a blank piece of paper, and began to write. "These are the figures on what we're currently spending."

For the next ten minutes, Shimon outlined the Ministry's current budget, then showed Ben-Gurion the difference between the costs in the areas he wanted to change versus the price of contracting for those services from the private sector. "And then, when you look at the cost of maintenance on the facilities—"

Ben-Gurion held up his hand to interrupt. "I've seen the reports. Yigal thinks you want a budget for machines, and he wants a budget for soldiers."

"I know." Shimon nodded. "That's how he sees it. That's not how it is, but that's how he sees it." He leaned forward. "Look, 'machines,' for want of a better term, are becoming more and more a part of our lives on every level. Not just in the military but in every sector. They are becoming an increasing factor in every economy of the world and in every army of the world."

"And we have to adapt to keep pace."

"Yes," Shimon agreed. "Foot soldiers on the ground are no match against an armored vehicle with a fifty-caliber machine gun. A propeller-driven airplane will be no match for the newer jet aircraft. Wars in the future will be fought by men using machines, not by men staring at each other across no-man's-land between trenches. We have to be ready for that day because that day is already here."

"Okay," Ben-Gurion said finally. "I've decided to go with your ideas. We'll use your budget proposal."

Shimon was relieved but he didn't want to gloat. "You understand," he cautioned, "General Yadin will resign."

Ben-Gurion leaned back in his chair. "He already has."

Shimon was puzzled. "He resigned already?"

"I talked to him a little while ago and gave him the news."

Shimon felt a smile crease his cheeks. "And you put me through this for an exercise?"

"I wanted to be sure I made the right decision."

"Well," Shimon sighed. "I'm sorry it came down to Yigal leaving. He's a good soldier, especially in the field."

"Just not one for the future?"

"Not for the future that is coming our way." Shimon stood to leave.

Ben-Gurion looked up at him. "Shimon, I'm counting on you to be right."

Shimon looked down at him. Civility, the general angst of human existence, told him to reply with the expected sense of self-doubt, to say that he hoped he was right, too. But Shimon had come to understand the politics of the office, of the government, of the internal staff better than to respond that way. The battle over the budget wasn't merely a battle over money but of policy and he wasn't giving an inch on that. "Yes, sir," he replied with confidence. "I'm sure I'm right."

✦ ✦ ✦

With Yadin gone, Mordechai Makleff was named IDF chief of staff. Shimon thought things might be different, that the tug-of-war between the way things used to be and the way things needed to be might finally lay behind them, but he soon found Makleff to be as petty and territorial as Yadin. Makleff preferred the same loose operational approach that permeated Haganah leadership of the past rather than the discipline necessary for a traditional, well-trained standing army. And he didn't want to be accountable to a civilian administration, either.

Makleff was a blustery guy but Shimon wouldn't back down. When Shimon stood his ground, Makleff complained that his authority was being undermined. "No civilian can tell me what to do," he muttered. But Shimon remained unmoved.

Eventually Makleff presented Ben-Gurion with a list of thirty senior officials he wanted fired. Shimon was among those on the list. Ben-Gurion refused and, instead, dismissed Makleff, appointing Moshe Dayan to take his place as IDF chief of staff. When Shimon heard the news he was overjoyed. "At last, we have someone I can work with."

The two enjoyed a warm relationship and met regularly to discuss policy, administrative issues, and the needs of the troops. During one of those meetings Dayan warned Shimon, "Golda and Pinchas Sapir have been comparing notes about you."

"About me?"

"They've been watching you."

"Why?"

"Golda's not happy with Ben-Gurion's decision to side with you against Yadin. She blames you for Yadin leaving."

"She ought to leave me alone. She's always trying to stir up trouble for me."

"Hey," Dayan laughed. "I'm just giving you a heads-up."

"I'm not angry with you, but this has been going on for a long time. Golda has questioned my loyalty since the day we met."

"She defines loyalty as loyalty to Golda. And, perhaps, loyalty to the union, too."

"Histadrut?"

"Yes. And you aren't loyal to either."

"So, what do they plan to do?" Shimon asked.

"Nothing, really—at least, as far as I know. I think they're just waiting for you to self-destruct."

Shimon was puzzled. "Self-destruct?"

"They think Ben-Gurion will keep moving you up until you over-reach and expose yourself for the pretender they think you are."

"They're jealous."

"Probably," Dayan shrugged.

"No. It's jealousy," Shimon insisted. "You're right about Golda valuing loyalty to Histadrut over the state and loyalty to herself most of all. But deep down, the problem is jealousy. She thinks I'm getting ahead of her. And she's convinced Sapir I'm getting ahead of him, too."

Dayan had a questioning look. "Why would Sapir think that? He wasn't in leadership before. And he's never been a minister until now."

"I don't know why he thinks it," Shimon shrugged. "But Sapir came to New York and we had a discussion while he was there. I think he and Golda have been talking a lot about who should follow Ben-Gurion as prime minister."

Dayan sat up straight. "You mean they've been talking about which one of *them* should follow him?"

"I doubt the discussion included much about Sapir's chances but I'm sure they talked about Golda's and I'm also certain Sapir came away from that thinking he had as much chance, or as much right, as she did in getting the post."

"And what did you say?"

"I tried to persuade him that what she was saying was wrong, but he said she thought I wanted the job and that I would probably get it because Ben-Gurion liked me. I told him that we got along well but that Moshe Sharett was Ben-Gurion's choice. Which he is."

"Everyone knows that." Dayan leaned back in his chair. "Even Golda knows that's who he wants."

"She talks that way to us. But I don't think she talks that way to everyone."

"No?"

"I think she's telling some of them that she ought to be next."

"And Sapir is one of the people she's talked to about it."

"Right," Dayan nodded.

"Maybe that's how he got the job with Trade and Industry."

Shimon raised an eyebrow. "You think Golda got him appointed to that ministry position to fill out his résumé?"

"Wouldn't be the first time someone got a hand up the ladder."

"No," Shimon agreed, his voice trailing away in thought. "It wouldn't."

SHIMON PERES

*"The most complicated thing
in life is to be afraid."*

ISRAEL WASN'T the only country in the region where leadership succession was being discussed. Throughout the Middle East similar questions were being raised, not only about succession but about governmental legitimacy as well. Some of those questions were being asked in the form of discussion and conversation among the intelligentsia, analyzing the viability of a monarchy—most, if not all, of the Arab countries were ruled by monarchies—and about the likelihood of avoiding more interference from Western or Western-allied interests.

Others were raising questions about the monarchies in the form of violent protests and radical plots. Many supporting those more sinister expressions were members of groups fully capable of effecting the change they sought, either by coercion or by force.

The Kingdom of Jordan confronted succession issues when King Abdullah was assassinated. That event forced them to address the problem of how to deal with less-capable members of the royal family while quelling open rebellion in the streets.

In Egypt there had been no assassination, but the trouble Abdullah had foreseen from the rise of Arab nationalism burst into the open not long after the crisis in Jordan. For the first time, demonstrators clogged the streets of Cairo, openly defying the government's ban on public assembly and calling for an end to the monarchy. Those protests were organized by a group known as the Muslim Brotherhood, and the sense of frustration they raised among the Egyptian public did not bode well for the monarch.

The Muslim Brotherhood had been founded by Hassan al-Banna in 1928, in the city of Ismailia, Egypt. Beginning with six workers from the Suez Canal Company, whom al-Banna sought to protect from abuse, the Brotherhood grew steadily, reaching a membership of more than 800,000 by 1938 and two million by 1948.

In line with al-Banna's conservative Sunni beliefs, the Muslim Brotherhood followed Sharia law, seeing it as the norm for daily life of all Arabs and the organizing principle of local and national governments. According to al-Banna and the Brotherhood, this had been the way Arabs lived until traditional Muslim practices were corrupted by Western influence. That, they suggested, came from Western military intervention and Western businesses that exploited the region's people and natural resources.

In practice, the Brotherhood followed a powerful blend of political activism and Islamic charity. They addressed the long-neglected physical needs of Egyptians by founding hospitals and schools. With success in those ventures, they found opportunities to disseminate their brand of nationalism, fueled by an appeal to religious belief and authority as a way of returning Arabs to the supposed prominence of a prior era. It proved a powerful and effective combination, and by 1950 the growing dissatisfaction with monarchical rule that it incited had become a serious threat to the monarchy. A threat the monarchy unfortunately ignored and did nothing to address.

Since the nineteenth century Egypt had been ruled by the Muhammad Ali dynasty, formed by Muhammad Ali, an Albanian commander in the Ottoman army who had been sent to the region to drive out Napoleon's army. When the French left, Ali remained, seizing Egypt for himself in 1805. His descendants followed him, serving as governors of Egypt under British control, until Egyptian independence was recognized in 1922. Thereafter, they were known as kings, though they ruled through a constitutional monarchy.

Egypt enjoyed a stable government until 1936, when the reigning king, Fuad I, died and was succeeded by his son, King Farouk. Sixteen years old when he took the throne, Farouk indulged in a lavish lifestyle that far exceeded anything the country's economy could support. By 1952, with the help of the Muslim Brotherhood, a majority of Egyptian citizens came to understand the extent of their young king's excesses and his insensitivity to their situation.

Aside from being out of touch with ordinary Egyptian citizens, King Farouk presided over a corrupt government. Bribes, favors, and intrigue were the rule of the day. Law of any kind was routinely ignored. His ministers, appointed to serve the people, were more interested in accruing power and wealth for themselves, regardless of the pain and suffering it caused the masses.

All of that, however, paled in comparison to the disgust for Farouk caused by his inability to prevent the formation of a Jewish state in Palestine. "Even a Muslim child can call upon Allah," they said in the streets. "And would he not answer?" Egyptian army officers were upset, too, and in the end, that proved to be Farouk's undoing.

After World War II, the British, who had ruled Egypt throughout most of the Muhammad Ali dynasty, withdrew their control. They retained control over the Suez Canal, which was viewed by authorities in London as a vital shipping link, but their continued presence only heightened tensions in the region.

With the Egyptian government no longer functional under Farouk, and society fracturing into irreparable disruption, officers in the Egyptian army took steps to provide an orderly response. Two army officers, General Muhammad Naguib and Lieutenant Colonel Gamal Abdel Nasser, an instructor at the Royal Military Academy, formed a group known as the Association of Free Officers. A small group at first, it sought to work for change at the higher levels of military and government leadership. When that proved unworkable, they turned to lower-ranking officers and began recruiting members on a broader scale.

As a first step, the Association sought to make the Egyptian military independent of the monarchy and recruited members for that purpose. In reality, however, Naguib and Nasser had decided it was time to end the monarchy's rule. They planned to accomplish that by taking over the government, at least in the short term, and sought control of the military to bring that plan to pass.

Though initially formed as part of the Muslim Brotherhood, Naguib and Nasser soon became suspicious of the Brotherhood's religious motives. The Brotherhood, they feared, would follow through on its stated religious goals and impose Sharia law, eventually establishing themselves in power through a theocracy. Both men and most of the Association members preferred an elected secular government.

Gradually, Naguib and, to an even greater extent, Nasser moved members of the Brotherhood out of leadership positions in the Association. Having accomplished that, they went on to purge Brotherhood members from all levels of the organization.

✦ ✦ ✦

Amidst the turmoil in Egypt, Dayan and Shimon met in Shimon's office to discuss the defense budget and to review progress on plans for establishing a new air base in the Negev. As their conversation continued, talk turned to the situation in Egypt.

"Change is coming," Dayan declared. "We might need to rethink that base."

"We've come a long way into the project," Shimon anwered. "We can't just drop it now."

"I wasn't thinking of dropping it," Dayan replied. "I was thinking it might not be large enough."

Shimon had a questioning frown. "You think change in Egypt might be a problem for us?"

"It could. Have you seen the latest intelligence reports?"

"Yes. Rather unsettling with the officers demanding to separate the army from the king. Isn't that tantamount to demanding control of the government?"

"I suppose," Dayan replied.

"The king will never agree to it. His ministers won't let him."

"You're probably right, but Naguib and Nasser aren't mere officers."

"Nasser is a colonel," Shimon pointed out dismissively.

"Yes, but Naguib is a general and these aren't ordinary guys. They aren't just soldiers."

"Oh?"

"These are men of intellect, men of passion and commitment."

"You know them?"

"I've met them once or twice. They won't sit quietly for long and they won't simply meet and talk like we do," Dayan said with a laugh. "They will do something."

"What do you think they will do?"

"I think," Dayan replied matter-of-factly, "that they mean to overthrow King Farouk."

Shimon nodded slowly. "From what I hear that wouldn't be too difficult. I don't think there's much left to overthrow. They could probably pay off the palace guard and remove him without firing a shot."

"Well, however they do it, I think they'll move him out just the same."

Shimon had a twinkle in his eye. "That could create an opportunity,"

Dayan grinned. "That's exactly what it will create. An opportunity. We could take all of the Sinai in the confusion. Set up camp on the Suez before they even know we're out of the barracks."

Shimon shook his head. "I wasn't thinking about that."

"What were you thinking of?"

"Peace."

Dayan threw his hands up in mock frustration. "Ahh! It's

always the same with Shimon. Peace. Peace. Peace." When Shimon's eyes opened wide in disbelief, Dayan roared with laughter. "I had you."

Shimon grinned, realizing Dayan was joking. "Yes, you had me."

"You're too easy," Dayan was still laughing. "But you're right. It just might be the opening Ben-Gurion has been looking for. He's been trying to find *one* of our neighbors who will make peace with us. He tried Jordan and they turned him down. So, if not Jordan, then why not Egypt."

"That would shift things."

"Yes, it would," Dayan agreed. "Egypt is our strongest enemy and peace with them would mean we could stop always looking over our shoulder, wondering when they are coming back again."

"That would make the base in the Negev less of a necessity."

"I didn't say that," Dayan replied quickly. "We must always be ready. We're not like the United States with our enemies on the other side of the ocean. Ours are just a short distance away—and in every direction. Whatever peace you find, you find it from a position of strength. Never let your guard down. The stakes are too high for an unguarded moment."

A month or two later, one of Shimon's aides rushed into the office carrying a small portable radio in his hands. "It's happening," the aide blurted out as he came through the doorway.

"What's happening?" Shimon asked, more than a little perturbed by the sudden interruption.

"The coup."

A frown winkled Shimon's forehead. "Where? Here?"

"No. In Egypt." The aide turned up the volume on the radio and they listened to a broadcast as a reporter in Egypt described how the Association of Free Officers took charge of the military and sur-rounded government administrative buildings. With the buildings secured, armed officers entered them and removed King Farouk's ministers, bringing most of them out in handcuffs. "And the crowd is still cheering," the reporter added.

Shimon listened to the news, amazed that events were happening just as he and Dayan had discussed and equally amazed that he was hearing a description of it almost as it was happening.

In the days that followed, the Free Officers created a Revolutionary Command Council which, with the army's support, took control of the country. Naguib was named president of Egypt. Nasser served as his assistant. The Command Council acted as the national legislature.

When Naguib and the Free Officers were in control and order had been restored, King Farouk was allowed to leave the country. He fled in disgrace to Monaco to live in exile.

+ + +

Whether trouble in Egypt offered Israel an opportunity for peace or not, events there heightened Shimon's determination to modernize and improve IDF weaponry and operational methods. Regardless of what Ben-Gurion might attempt to achieve diplomatically, Dayan was correct. They had to be prepared to defend themselves against all comers and at a moment's notice.

Although Israel needed arms and munitions of almost any sort or kind, Shimon was unwilling to settle for anything less than the best equipment. He searched far and wide for sources that could supply what they needed at a price they could afford. Lately, however, he'd been interested in moving those purchases away from covert arrangements toward actual government-to-government transactions. Ideally with partners they could deal with on a long-term basis.

After sorting through the options for such an arrangement, Shimon decided the French government, with whom they had a longstanding though clandestine relationship, was their most likely legitimate supplier. He reviewed the matter with Ben-Gurion, who had the final decision.

"As you are aware," Shimon began, "we have been purchasing arms through a broker in Paris for quite some time."

"Yes. And he's been very helpful."

"Yes. But I think we need to change that relationship."

"Oh?" Ben-Gurion's eyes opened wider in a look of concern. "Has something happened that I don't know about?"

"No. Not at all," Shimon assured. "I just think we can get a better deal if we work directly with the French government. We're a government now and we need to be dealing on a legitimate basis. Not sneaking through the back door with a third party."

Ben-Gurion nodded thoughtfully but gave no hint of his opinion. "You think the French are ready for that?"

"Yes, I do. Current French leadership is very different from the French leadership of World War II. The people in power now are much closer to us than those in the past."

"I should think so. Many who were in charge under the Nazis are now in prison for war crimes. Most of the ones in control now spent the war serving in the French Resistance."

"And they saw what happened to the Jews."

Ben-Gurion agreed. "They saw it up close and in gory detail. I've heard some of their accounts. It was awful."

"I think," Shimon continued, "given the chance, they will gravitate instinctively toward us."

"Okay," Ben-Gurion nodded. "Then you should make contact with the French and see what you can do."

"Yes, sir."

"Start with Marrast. I think he's the better of the brokers. Or perhaps that man you were dealing with last time."

"Lescot."

"Yes, start with him."

Since shortly after the War of Independence, Shimon had been dealing with several French arms dealers who were based in Paris. He'd met them through Louis Danjou, to whom he'd been introduced by Meir Argov on their way back from Shimon's first World Zionist Congress.

Of the several brokers, Jules Marrast had proven to be the most reliable but he had been selling only lighter weapons—mostly rifles and grenades. He'd provided a few armored vehicles, most of which were only one generation beyond World War II surplus, but most of his sales had involved only items for infantry soldiers.

Recently, however, Shimon was able to purchase a number of handheld missiles. The missiles had been developed for the French army but after testing, the government decided not to go forward with production. At the time Shimon heard about them, ten crate loads of the missiles had been sitting in a warehouse since the program ended. He was able to get them at a deep discount.

That transaction had been handled through Marrast but unlike other transactions, the missile sale required at least tacit government approval. Getting it done had involved direct contact with Henri Lescot, a low-level official with the French Defense Ministry. He and Shimon met on three separate occasions to work out the necessary details for shipment. They had kept in touch since then and as Shimon planned a trip to Paris in his attempt to elevate future dealings to an official government arrangement, he decided a visit to Lescot should be his first stop.

The connection with Lescot turned out to be very beneficial, and a relationship that began as a friendship of necessity soon became a back-channel means of communicating directly with members of the French government. It was back channel in that it operated outside the normal government apparatus of the respective foreign ministries, which meant it excluded Israel's ambassador to France and its foreign minister, Golda Meir.

Through Lescot, Shimon was introduced up the ranks to Prime Minister Pierre Mendès and, eventually, to President Charles de Gaulle. In the process, Israel reached her first actual, legitimate, government-to-government defense relationship—the way nations of the world conducted their business. That first straightforward deal was an agreement with the French to sell Israel long-range cannon for use by the IDF Artillery Corps. It was negotiated between Shimon and Paul Reynaud, the French deputy prime minister. Moshe Dayan assisted with contract details.

17

SHIMON PERES

"Books are my constant companions. If you eat three times a day you'll be fed. But if you read three times a day you'll be wise."

BY THE MID-1950s, Ben-Gurion had been active in Israeli politics in one form or another for forty years. After arriving in Palestine, he had worked on a kibbutz at Petah Tikva and joined Hashomer, one of the early paramilitary groups that defended Jewish farming settlements, and served on the executive committee of Poalei Zion, one of several Jewish labor unions. During World War I he helped form a Jewish militia that offered its services to the Ottoman Empire. However, being non-Arabic, he was deported and found his way to the United States, where he lived for three years.

After the war, Ben-Gurion returned to Palestine and, with Berl Katznelson, formed Ahdut HaAvoda, a labor political party. Not long after returning, he became chairman of the Jewish Agency executive committee, a position from which he oversaw the move toward statehood, and prepared the Jews of Palestine for independence. When independence was declared, Ben-Gurion became head of the transitional government. He directed the defense of Israel during its

War of Independence and served two terms as prime minister while at the same time serving as minister of defense.

By 1954, Ben-Gurion was sixty-eight years old. No longer a young man. The years of work and worry had left him mentally and emotionally drained and he showed signs of physical fatigue. His fiery disposition and pragmatic decisiveness had made him an ideal revolutionary leader and brilliant military strategist. Yet after independence was won he'd been forced to govern in a time of peace and stability. Doing so took him to the limits of his ability and strength.

At the same time, the mood of the people of Israel had changed. No longer a band of disparate idealists, they had become a unified nation with a growing national identity. The country then needed to move forward, becoming a nation defined by the people who resided there rather than by European immigrant priorities.

Israel faced a transition in leadership, but it had not come as a surprise. Moshe Sharett, the foreign minister, had been groomed by Ben-Gurion as his successor and everyone knew it. Like Ben-Gurion, Sharett had held leadership positions in a number of pre-state organizations. He'd been a member of the Jewish Agency executive committee, a signatory to the Declaration of Independence, foreign minister in the transitional government, and continued in that post as part of the permanent government. Ben-Gurion liked Sharett and made no secret that he thought he was the best person for the prime minister's position.

Shimon thought Sharett was a good choice, too, but when he raised the subject with Dayan in one of their regular office visits, he found Dayan less than enthusiastic.

"I don't know about him," Dayan announced in a skeptical tone.

"What do you mean?"

"I don't know. There's just something about him."

Shimon was puzzled. "Like what?"

Dayan shrugged. "I'm just not sure he can handle being in charge."

"He's done a good job at the Foreign Ministry."

Dayan nodded. "He's done well."

"And he's defended Ben-Gurion on more than one occasion."

"Yes, and they seem to be friends. But I—"

"So, why the reservation?"

"There's just something about him," Dayan continued. "Something about the look in his eyes. Or the set of his jaw. I don't know. I just don't think he'll be the same once he gets in office."

"Well, how could anyone know that?"

"You can't know it for certain, I guess. It's just one of those things. If you know it you just. . . know it."

"You're not making much sense."

Dayan sat up straight and leaned closer. "Look, I've seen guys who were great as squad leaders. Some of them moved up and made excellent platoon leaders. But when they advanced one more position and became company commander, they changed."

"And you think Sharett is one of those."

"Yeah." Dayan leaned back in his chair. "I think he might be."

Having a new prime minister meant creating a new government. Every ministerial position would be up for review. Shimon thought that would be a good thing. He also thought it was time to separate the position of minister of defense from prime minister. The country needed new ideas, fresh perspective, and leadership tailored for each specific area of government. They needed a defense minister who understood defense led by someone who could concentrate solely on that area. Shimon thought Pinhas Lavon could fill that role.

Like many of his contemporaries, Lavon had been born in Ukraine. As a young man, he studied law at Lviv and worked as an organizer for Histadrut. At the age of twenty-five, he came to Palestine and continued that work. After independence, he won a seat in the Knesset and later Ben-Gurion appointed him minister of agriculture. Shimon broached the idea of moving Lavon to defense in a meeting with Ben-Gurion and found him quite acceptable. Having received that approval, Shimon began talking Lavon up to others, trying to smooth the way for Lavon's appointment. No one had any reservations about him, not even Dayan, and the issue appeared to be settled.

In the months that followed, Shimon felt satisfied with himself. He'd identified a candidate for defense minister—in effect, selecting his own new boss—and he'd engineered the appointment of that person well in advance of the election. Then he'd promoted that person and paved the way for his appointment, an appointment to which no one objected. Everything seemed in place for a smooth transition assuring continued progress toward making IDF the kind of military the country needed and the era demanded.

✦ ✦ ✦

As time for his departure drew near, Ben-Gurion seemed to have second thoughts. Leaving something he'd worked all his life to promote was more difficult that he'd imagined, but he was certain the time had come and he was determined to go. The country needed to move on and *he* needed to move on.

In preparation for leaving, Ben-Gurion conducted a review of the Defense Ministry. That review developed into an eighteen-point plan. When it was complete, Ben-Gurion submitted the plan to the Knesset and then resigned. He and his wife, Paula, moved to Sde Boker, a kibbutz in the Negev, where he studied biology, worked on the farm, and tried to relax.

The following year, elections were held to fill the vacancy of prime minister. Moshe Sharett was duly elected to the office. As Shimon had hoped, Pinhas Lavon was confirmed as minister of defense. Sapir was named minister of trade and industry. Shimon was named director general of defense.

Shimon's new position was a promotion, and he thought it meant he had the confidence of Lavon and Sharett. But very quickly, Sharett became suspicious and dismissive. Not long into the term, Sharett began refusing to meet with him, preferring instead to handle all defense matters through Lavon at a ministerial level. Shimon had never been frozen out of the prime minister's office and wasn't sure he could do his job effectively without direct access to Sharett.

The whole thing didn't make much sense to him and in an attempt to find out what was going on, he sought out his old friend Yohai Cohen.

After working for Sharett at the Foreign Ministry, Yohai had been brought in as cabinet secretary for the new administration. It was a busy position, responsible for coordinating communications and policy initiatives between ministers as well as controlling the agenda for cabinet meetings. He and Shimon had met more frequently than when Yohai first came to Tel Aviv as Sharett's assistant, but neither of them had much time for socializing after hours. Still, Shimon needed to get to the bottom of whatever was going on in the prime minister's office and he persisted with Yohai until they arranged time for coffee together. They met one afternoon at a shop near the administrative offices in Tel Aviv.

"You sounded like this was more than just an old friend wanting to catch up," Yohai began. "What's going on?"

"That's what I need you to tell me," Shimon responded.

"Nothing's going on," Yohai demurred. "I'm just busy and haven't had time to—"

"Not about us. I want to know what's going on in the prime minister's office."

"You know I can't tell you that." Yohai took a sip of coffee. "It's confidential."

"Look," Shimon continued, "when Sharett was foreign minister he and I got along well together. We worked on a dozen projects together. His door was always open to me. I came to his office. He came to mine. Now he's prime minister and he doesn't want to deal with me. When I try to talk to him, he tells me to take my issues to Lavon and that he and Lavon will address whatever needs their attention at a ministerial level."

"You know, he's not Ben-Gurion."

Shimon scowled, "What does that mean?"

"From what I understand, things were rather loose back then. Sharett doesn't want to operate like that."

Shimon leaned back in his chair. "There's more to it than that."

Yohai took another sip of coffee and glanced away. Shimon caught the look in his eye. "What is it, Yohai?" When Yohai didn't immediately answer, Shimon pressed the point. "We may not have seen each other much lately, but I know that look and I know you're not telling me everything about this. What's going on?"

"Well. . . it's just. . . people talk."

"Yeah? Who's talking?"

Yohai looked over at Shimon. "Pinchas Sapir for one."

"And who else?"

"Golda."

Shimon felt angry. "And I bet I can guess what they're saying."

"Look, Shimon." Yohai had a conciliatory tone. "It's just the same old stuff you've heard before."

"I don't understand why they have it in for me."

"I don't know about all of that. Not with them. Back when we were in school it was just jealousy. Here, I don't know what it is. But those two have been talking about you since I first arrived."

"Is that what happened between you and me? At first? When you first took the job here. Is that why you stopped coming around?"

"That and I just got busy." Yohai had an apologetic look. "I'm sorry."

"That's okay. We're friends. Things happen."

"Yeah, but I should have known better."

Shimon let the comment pass without response. There was nothing to be gained by rehashing all that had happened between them. "Is that all there is to this, though? Is it just Sapir and Golda filling Sharett's ear?"

Yohai had a puzzled expression. "What do you mean?"

"Does Sharett have something against me, personally? Have I done something that offended him?"

"I don't think you *did* anything," Yohai explained. "But Sharett sees you as a Ben-Gurion man. One of Ben-Gurion's young men."

Shimon gave an exasperated gesture. "Specially selected to get ahead of those who're older and entitled to leadership roles. I know. I've heard that before, too."

"That's Golda's view," Yohai conceded. "With Sharett, it's just that you're too much of a Ben-Gurion man for him. He knows where your loyalties lie and he thinks they aren't with him."

"He thinks I'm still more committed to Ben-Gurion than I am to him?"

"Yes."

"But Ben-Gurion isn't in office."

Yohai nodded. "But he's a little paranoid about it. And a little unsure of himself in the prime minister role."

"Will it work out over time?"

Yohai shrugged. "I don't know. I'd like to think so, but I don't know."

Shimon sighed. "Neither do I."

Several days later, Shimon rode down to Sde Boker, the kibbutz in the Negev where Ben-Gurion and Paula lived. He found Ben-Gurion cleaning a stall in the barn.

Ben-Gurion was using a shovel and continued to work as Shimon approached. "If you came all this way, there must be trouble."

"I'm not sure."

Ben-Gurion threw one more shovelful toward the end of the stall, then took a break. "Well, you came all this way." He stuck the shovel blade into the ground and leaned against the end of the handle. "Go ahead. Tell me about it."

For the next ten minutes, Shimon described his experience with Sharett. When he finished, Ben-Gurion took the shovel in hand and turned back to the stall. "The problem is that Israel has many visionary people." He scooped up a shovelful and tossed it toward the growing pile at the far end. "But she has not many visionaries with a practical approach to putting the vision into action."

"And you think that's Sharett's problem?"

"Sharett is a good man. But that's not your problem."

"What's my problem?"

"He's not me."

"No, he's not."

"And you shouldn't expect him to be."

"I'm just trying to do my job. Procure weapons and equipment. Give the soldiers in IDF what they need to defend us."

"And that's the problem, I think."

"That I'm doing my job?"

"You're a person who takes the initiative," Ben-Gurion replied between scoops with the shovel. "You get things done without constantly coming back to discuss the details."

"Isn't that what I'm supposed to do?"

"It was with me, but I think what you see as doing your job, Sharett sees as you going behind his back. Like when Golda says you're always stepping beyond your authority. Influencing foreign affairs to further your personal ambitions."

"You knew she said those things?"

Ben-Gurion glanced over at him with a grin. "I wasn't always asleep at my desk."

"Well, I'm not interested in furthering my own ambitions."

"I know that. And I imagine Sharett knows that. Or he would if he stopped and thought about it. But for him, it's probably more about control. He knows that if he tells you to do something, you'll go do it. But you won't come back to him until it's done. And that means *he* won't be in control of things. *You* will."

"He wants to manage everything himself?"

"Not really. He just wants to know that the person in your position will do things his way, not my way. And he doesn't have that kind of confidence in you. At least, not yet."

"So, he would prefer his own people in every position?"

"He would prefer people he thinks are loyal only to him."

"He's already moved his staff from the Foreign Ministry to similar positions in the prime minister's office."

"That's to be expected."

"Is this same thing going to happen with Lavon? Is he going to be suspicious of me and want me out?"

"I don't know. Perhaps." Ben-Gurion paused with the shovel and turned to face Shimon. "Look, I didn't support Sharett because I thought he was a good version of me. Or Lavon, either. I supported them because I thought they were as close as we could get to people who are both visionary and practical. They're not perfect."

"I know, but—"

"You and I got along well together, Shimon. I like you and I've always thought you were good for the country. Berl thought the same thing. We helped you along and I think you have a wonderful career ahead of you. And Israel will be the better for it. But I've taken you about as far as I can take you right now. I think you'll have to use what you've learned to this point and find your own way. Build your own career."

Shimon grinned. "You're kicking me out of the nest."

Ben-Gurion laughed. "I hadn't thought of it that way, but yes. The Peres—the eagle—is finally learning to fly."

The conversation with Ben-Gurion hadn't gone quite like Shimon had hoped. But as he drove back to Tel Aviv he realized that perhaps it had gone better than he'd expected. He'd gone there looking for answers. Looking for Ben-Gurion to tell him what it all meant and what he should do. Instead, he found perspective and an admonition to work things out for himself, on his own terms. And that, after all, was what he really wanted to do. To make his own way and to make it for himself. "And if Ben-Gurion thinks I can do it," he said aloud, "then I think so, too."

18

SHIMON PERES

*"I am perceived by many to be a
man of great contradictions."*

LAVON ARRIVED at the Defense Ministry with the reputation of being a dove—someone predisposed against the use of military force as a means of solving Israel's issues with her neighbors. Very quickly, though, he began displaying hawkish tendencies.

Near the end of Ben-Gurion's term as prime minister, cross-border raids against Jewish villages by Arabs from the West Bank had increased. After Sharett took office and Lavon became minister of defense, the raids escalated. Not long after taking office, Lavon ordered development of a strategy for reprisals against villages on the Jordanian side of the border. Shimon and Moshe Dayan argued against the action but Lavon was set on going forward. Dayan wasn't so much against the raids as against the targets. IDF attacks on unarmed Arab civilians, he argued, would be just as bad as Arab attacks on unarmed Jewish civilians. There were other ways of stopping the raids.

Lavon, however, was convinced that reprisals were the correct response and he convinced Sharett that he was right. The first attack was planned against the town of Qibya, which lay just inside the West Bank territory. Command of the attack was given to Ariel Sharon, pending a final approval order from Sharett.

Sharon had been born at Kfar Malal, located north of Tel Aviv near the coast, about halfway to Netanya. As a young person, he joined HaNoar HaOved and later became a member of Haganah. When Haganah was transformed into the Israel Defense Forces, Sharon became one of the army's best commanders, leading troops into battle at Latrun and in several other decisive confrontations during the War of Independence. Afterward, he was given command of Unit 101, a special group created to perform clandestine operations.

In spite of internal opposition within the Defense Ministry, and with command and control murky at best, the attack on Qibya went forward. Sharon led the assault. As a result, sixty-nine Arab civilians were killed and there was widespread destruction of private property.

When news of the attack reached the international press, the response was quick and decisive. The United States condemned the attack and announced the suspension of economic aid to Israel. Other nations reacted as well, and the United Nations Security Council convened to deliberate the matter. Days later, the UN issued a resolution censuring Israel for the Qibya attack.

Condemnation was so widespread and so vehement that the Israeli government was forced to respond. Statements from the Foreign Ministry suggested the attack was a civilian uprising, but most doubted the plausibility of that explanation. Lavon described it as a successful military operation that became a political disaster.

In the days that followed, Lavon became obsessively suspicious of those in the Ministry who had served with Ben-Gurion. Even more suspicious than Sharett. At the time Lavon took over, Dayan ran the military side of the Ministry and Shimon the administrative—handling the budget, reaching deals with arms suppliers, and the like. Lavon, however, decided to do all of that himself. As the new operational procedure became clear, Shimon turned again to his friend Yohai for help. He found Yohai at home one weekend and they sat on the balcony of Yohai's apartment to talk.

"Lavon giving you trouble?" Yohai asked.

"It's just like with Sharett."

"Except this business with the attack at Qibya has magnified things."

"I tried to tell them not to do it."

"Well, that's not what Lavon is saying."

"He's saying I was in favor of it?" Shimon asked.

"He's saying you gave the order."

"*I* gave the order?"

"That's what he's saying."

Shimon shook his head. "Ridiculous."

"Golda seems to think it might be true."

"Golda? She doesn't know the first thing about this."

"Well, you know. That never stopped many of us."

"Look," Shimon pointed out, "Dayan was opposed to the operation. And he's a military man, oriented toward following orders. I'm not in the chain of command. I can't order him to do anything."

"I don't think he sees it that way."

"Is that why Lavon won't work with me?"

Yohai had a knowing smile. "When trouble comes, everybody looks for cover."

"Well, tell Sharett to ask around—talk to the people who were in the meetings about this operation and decide for himself. He'll find out what actually happened. Not what Lavon wants people to believe happened."

"I can suggest it. I can't tell him what to do."

Shimon nodded in agreement. "Ask him. He'll find out the truth."

✦ ✦ ✦

Meanwhile, in Egypt the politics of the revolutionary regime deteriorated into a power struggle. Naguib wanted to move the army back to its barracks and return the nation to civilian control. Nasser and other members of the Revolutionary Command Council opposed that move, arguing the people weren't ready for it yet. "If we remove the military now," Nasser argued, "we will only give the

Muslim Brotherhood an opportunity to gain undue influence over the country."

In October 1954, members of the Muslim Brotherhood lent credence to Nasser's warning when they attempted to assassinate him. Nasser was unharmed, but seized the incident as an opportunity to wrest control of the country for himself. Using Naguib's apparent friendliness with the Brotherhood against him, Nasser forced Naguib to resign. With Naguib gone, the Revolutionary Command Council named Nasser to the presidency.

As president of Egypt, Nasser quickly cracked down on the Brotherhood. Key leaders of the organization were arrested and executed. He also took steps to purge politicians who had been sympathetic to Naguib, replacing them with people of unquestionable loyalty. Within a matter of months, he had solidified control over the country.

With the rise of Arab nationalism, the Soviet Union became more active in the region, supporting Arab groups and initiatives throughout the Middle East. To counter the growing Soviet influence, the United States sought ways to intervene. When Nasser came to power, US officials viewed him as an Arab leader with whom they might be able to work. As a result, US policy toward Egypt moderated and officials adopted a supportive stance.

In London, Arab nationalism and a strong US–Egypt alliance were viewed by government officials as contrary to the United Kingdom's long-term interests. Of particular concern was continued British control of the Suez Canal. England was also worried about access to Middle Eastern oil reserves.

Authorities in Israel were concerned, too. US encouragement of Egyptian nationalism was seen as empowering Nasser toward a more militant approach in dealing with Israeli issues. Perhaps even encouraging Nasser to attempt military action.

To counter the perceived threat to Israel's national security, Lavon began searching for ways to disrupt the US–Egyptian relationship. He hoped, by some means, to drive a wedge between the United States and the United Kingdom, while simultaneously alienating both the U.S. and U.K. from Egypt.

For that to happen, Lavon needed a way to cast Egyptian nationalists in an unfavorable light. Doing that with Nasser would be difficult. People who resided outside the region tended to view him as a moderate. The Muslim Brotherhood, however, was seen by many Western nations as a militant and dangerous group. Exploiting that militancy required the expertise of someone who understood the ins and outs of covert operations. He found that person in Binyamin Gibli.

Gibli had been born at Petah Tikvah, one of the kibbutzim where David Ben-Gurion had lived. As a young man he joined Haganah and became a member of Shai, Haganah's intelligence corps. He rose through the ranks and, shortly before the War of Independence, became head of the intelligence organization. Later, after independence, Shai was dissolved and its assets were rolled into IDF's Directorate of Military Intelligence, commonly referred to as Aman. Gibli was Aman's first director. He was experienced, capable, and enthusiastic. Just the kind of person Lavon sought to plan and execute his reprisal strategy.

As the United States made clear its intention to support Nasser, Lavon convened a series of meetings at the Defense Ministry to discuss Israeli options. At those meetings, Lavon reviewed the situation in Egypt and laid out his view of the threats that situation posed, then asked for options to address those threats.

Gibli was quick to respond. His plan favored a covert operation. As he explained it, "Operatives, posing as Egyptian nationalists, would set off bombs in theaters, train stations, markets, and anywhere else that might disrupt normal daily Egyptian life. The key is to do it in a way that blame for the explosions falls on the Muslim Brotherhood. That would force the United States and other nations to back off. Except that the British won't leave because to do so would mean abandoning control of the Suez Canal, which they will never do. So, with the U.S. stepping back, the British military would remain in place as a stabilizing force, as far as Egypt was concerned. For us, their presence will prevent an Egyptian move against us."

Shimon thought Gibli's plan was a bad idea and he said so more than once. "This is the kind of thing the United States, even with its CIA, can rarely do effectively," he pointed out. "We don't have the resources of the United States or the capability of the CIA. We will never pull it off and I don't think it would work even if we did what you suggest and got away with it."

Gibli bristled at the suggestion his intelligence unit lacked the capability. "Why not?" he asked in an imperious tone. "Why wouldn't it work, even if we got away with it?"

"Because," Shimon replied forcefully, "to be effective and accomplish what you want to accomplish, one or two incidents won't be enough. If you only do a couple of these, everyone will pass it off as sporadic violence of an isolated group. To be effective, you'd have to do this with multiple detonations in multiple locations over a persistent stretch of time."

"I'm not talking about one or two incidents," Gibli retorted in a dismissive voice.

"But that's just it," Shimon continued. "We don't have the resources to sustain this kind of thing over a period of months. And we don't have the resources to make it look like anything other than what it would be."

"Which is?"

"An incursion by Israeli agents into Egyptian territory and Egyptian domestic affairs."

"I think you underestimate our ability."

"And I think you underestimate the size and scope of what it would take to actually do what you're trying to do." Shimon glanced around the room. "Listen," he advised the others, "if the Muslim Brotherhood wanted to actually do this sort of thing, they would have to plan it for months in advance. Then recruit a sizeable group of people to carry it out. And they'd have to orchestrate the collection of bomb-making material and the construction of dozens of bombs.

Maybe a hundred or more of them. That would be a year-long project and involve an extensive organization. We don't have that kind of presence in Egypt. We can't pull this off in the short time frame you envision."

Others joined Shimon in opposing the plan, but still Gibli went forward with his detailed design that became a scheme to detonate bombs in Cairo and Alexandria. Attribution to the Muslim Brotherhood would be accomplished by stories leaked to the press, by the kind of bombs used for the incidents, and by creating one or two staged bomb-making sites where Arab extremist literature would be left for investigators to find.

Over Shimon's continuing objections and the doubts of Moshe Dayan, the plan nevertheless advanced beyond the planning stage. Gibli enlisted the help of six operatives who traveled to Egypt under various cover stories and began recruiting Egyptian Jews to carry out the attacks.

Under the supervision of Gibli's agents, bombs were prepared in Cairo and in Alexandria, and potential sites for the attacks were located. But as the day of the first attacks approached, Egyptian police and military personnel raided one of the bomb construction sites. Four conspirators were captured and documents implicating Israeli intelligence units were discovered. Only one bomb, planted in a theatre in Alexandria, was detonated.

In the weeks that followed, two of the captured conspirators inexplicably died in prison. The other two were tried, convicted, and executed.

News of the explosion in Alexandria and the arrest of the attackers spread quickly through the international media. Censorship of Israeli media outlets, however, kept the details of Israeli involvement secret from the country's public. Gradually, however, news of what actually happened was impossible to contain and the truth became known. When asked about it, Sharett, who hadn't been informed of the details of the plan and thus hadn't been involved in authorizing the actual attack, denied Israeli involvement.

Over the next several weeks and months, as more details of events in Egypt became known, culpability seemed to rise no further in the government than Lavon, the minister of defense. Journalists began referring to the incident as the Lavon Affair, and the plot that Gibli proposed became a full-blown political controversy.

With the public increasingly demanding the full story, a committee of inquiry was convened to investigate what happened and determine responsibility. Gibli said Lavon authorized the operation. Lavon denied it and tried to pin responsibility on Gibli and Shimon. Newspapers ran daily stories on the controversy. Many of the articles included extensive accounts of the planning and background information on the covert agents, details few could have known who weren't directly associated with the operation. Sharett, always suspicious of Shimon and anyone else who hadn't worked for him at the Foreign Ministry, assumed most of the information being made public came from Shimon.

When Yohai Cohen heard Sharett's accusations, he suggested Sharett might need to talk with those who were present during the planning of the operation. "To avoid saying anything you might have to publicly retract later."

"You think I should actually get into this?" Sharett asked.

"I think you're into it already. The only way out of it is to go on through to the other side."

"I suppose you're right," Sharett conceded.

At home, Sonia read the newspaper articles without comment until the committee of inquiry was convened. The evening the news of it broke, she raised the matter with Shimon after dinner.

"We need to talk about this Lavon Affair I've been reading about in the papers."

"I can't—"

"Shimon, tell me!"

Shimon knew from the tone of her voice and the look in her eyes that she wasn't going to back down. "Pinhas Lavon," he began reluctantly, "is the most suspicious, untrusting person I've ever known."

"Were you involved?"

"You know you can't ask me that. And even if I wanted to, you know I can't tell you what you want to know."

Sonia gestured with a sweep of her hand, and cautioned, "Look around this house. We have children to care for. A home to give them. And I need to know if the police are going to show up here in the dead of night, turn us out into the street, and upset our lives."

"Come on, Sonia." Shimon had a pained expression. "It isn't going to—"

"Shimon," she sternly cut him off again, "is there going to be trouble for us?"

He nodded. "There may be trouble, but I had nothing to do with this except to oppose it. Anyone who was at the meetings will know it."

"The meetings? There were meetings?"

"Nothing like this happens without planning."

"So, you knew about it."

"Yes."

"And you opposed it."

"Yes," Shimon sighed. "And that's—"

"And someone went ahead with the plan even though you, the director general, opposed it."

"Yes. Now, that's all I can say about this." He looked her in the eye. "Things are not like they used to be. There may be trouble. But as long as they tell the truth, we'll get through this."

Sonia looked away. "You have more faith in them than I do."

In the course of the investigation, Shimon received a request from the committee for information regarding the plot. Moshe Dayan received a request, too. Both responded with the asked for information. When Lavon learned they provided information to the committee, he accused Shimon of disloyalty. "Shimon the liar," he growled. "Merely covering his own involvement at my expense."

Labor Party leadership responded unfavorably, too. Several in leadership positions asked Shimon to take a leave of absence. Others blamed the fiasco entirely on him, saying that only he could concoct such a convoluted and devious plot.

As the pressure mounted, Shimon grew increasingly distraught. He kept it to himself at the office, but at night when he was at home he vented his frustration to Sonia. "They always blame me for everything," he growled. "Always."

"Just like when you were young."

"Yes. Exactly like that." He ran his fingers through his hair in a gesture of frustration. "There must be something wrong with me. A sign on my back I can't see that says, 'I did it. Blame me.'"

"You're the kid in the class who speaks up, that's all." Sonia ran her hand over his shoulder. "You're the one who always speaks up. Who answers the questions." She grinned at him. "You're the teacher's pet."

"Not this teacher."

"No, but you were for Ben-Gurion, and that's how the rest of them still see you. So, this is their chance to get back at the teacher."

A frown wrinkled his forehead. "What do you mean?"

"They can't get to Ben-Gurion directly," Sonia explained. "That would be too costly, politically speaking, but they can get to you."

Shimon shook his head. "This has nothing to do with Ben-Gurion."

"I think everything has something to do with him. One way or the other. Especially for Lavon and Sharrett. Maybe the others, too."

Sonia was right, of course, and Shimon knew it. The hardest part, though, was not being able to do anything about it. All he could do was sit and wait for things to play out. To run their course. And hope that maybe, somehow, Sharett would realize what was really happening. Maybe, after all, Yohai could help him take a look at what actually happened in the meetings.

✦ ✦ ✦

To his credit, Sharett reviewed the information supplied by the committee of inquiry, then talked to those who were present at the planning meetings for the Egyptian operation. None of them would say who authorized the attacks, but they all said Shimon was against the operation.

"And he said so?" Sharett asked more than once. "Shimon actually spoke out against the plan?"

They all agreed. "He spoke up against it from the beginning. And not just to voice an objection. He argued against it. Made some really good arguments against it, actually."

"But the plan went forward anyway?"

"Lavon wanted it."

"He said that?"

"Not in so many words, I don't think," someone answered. "But we all came away from those meetings with the clear sense that Lavon supported it. I mean, dreaming up a plot against the Egyptians was his idea in the first place. That's what got Gibli going. After that, there wasn't much Shimon or anyone else could do to actually stop him. I mean, if Gibli chose to do it, and Lavon gave his approval, tacit or otherwise, Shimon couldn't have stopped him. But he spoke up against it in the meetings right down to the day the news broke that it had happened."

"Lavon knows this?" Sharett asked.

Someone else spoke up, "Lavon was there. He was told. He was at the meetings. He knows Shimon was opposed to it."

In light of that information, and with the controversy threatening his government, Sharett sided with Shimon and told Lavon to resign.

Lavon resisted, "I'm not resigning. If I resign, it will be an admission of guilt."

"And if you refuse to resign," Sharett warned, "I'll be forced to fire you."

Reluctantly, Lavon resigned from his position as minister of defense, and Sharett invited David Ben-Gurion to return as his replacement. He accepted the position, but Sharett's government was in trouble.

Israelis remembered how decisively Egyptian soldiers had crossed from Sinai into the Negev and how handily they swept up the coast beyond Gaza. The existential threat was very real to the people of Israel, and anyone reckless enough to tempt a repeat of that was inviting trouble at the polls. When the issues raised by the Lavon Affair continued to linger, Golda Meir and Levi Eshkol put pressure on Sharett to step aside. Like Lavon, he resisted at first, but in a matter of weeks he bowed out and the cabinet ran the government until elections were arranged.

SHIMON PERES

"You know when civilization began?
With the invention of the mirror."

IN SPITE OF THE Lavon Affair—the botched operation
that it entailed, the execution of Israeli agents, and the public outcry
when it became public—Ben-Gurion still viewed the shift in Egyptian
leadership and the ouster of the monarchy as a potentially positive
opportunity for Israel. Young Egyptian idealists appeared more amenable to change than the former deeply entrenched monarchy. He
was certain the moment was right to attempt a peace agreement with
Nasser.

"Who should we ask for approval?" Shimon wondered.

Ben-Gurion had a wry smile. "We're not asking."

"No?"

"No. The cabinet is coordinating things, but none of them have
more rank than I do. We're all equal ministers right now."

"Okay."

"Are you all right with that?"

"Yes," Shimon replied. "How do we get a message to Nasser?"

"I was thinking about Shaike Dan."

Shimon grinned. "Good choice."

He was. . . an interesting guy. To begin with, Shaike Dan wasn't his real name, or his only name. According to some accounts, he was born Dan Yeshayahu. Others said his name was Isaiah Sheyke Dan Tranchtenberg. . . or maybe it was. . . well. . . any of the dozen other names associated with him. It just depended on who asked the question and who gave the answer. At the Defense Ministry—among those who actually knew of his existence—Shaike Dan was known less by the truth of his actual name and more by his reputation as a man who could get things done, which was all the name he needed.

During World War II, Dan worked with a British artillery unit stationed in Lebanon. But when a call went out for volunteers to parachute into Yugoslavia to locate captured British pilots, Dan didn't hesitate to enlist for that duty. He was eager to go, but not merely for the sake of the pilots. Dan had another motive. He wanted to locate Jews and help them escape to Palestine. And for the duration of the war, he did just that. In that effort, he developed relationships with a wide array of resistance members who, after the war, rose to influential levels in the governments of Yugoslavia, Romania, Czechoslovakia, and a number of other countries.

At Ben-Gurion's direction, Shimon prepared a note to Nasser, hinting at the possibility of direct talks. On a trip to Paris, he met with Shaike Dan, who was serving as Israel's ambassador to Yugoslavia. They met for lunch and Shimon gave him the note.

"We would like for you to give this to Josip Tito."

"We?"

"Ben-Gurion and I."

"Do I need to know the contents?"

"No. Just give Tito the note and ask him to give it to Nasser. I understand they are friends."

Dan nodded. "They are."

"And you can pass the note to him?"

"Certainly."

Two weeks later, Ben-Gurion came to Shimon's office and handed him an envelope. "This arrived today." The back flap had been opened but Shimon could see it had been sealed with wax and imprinted with a signet ring. A note was inside and he took it out.

"He says it's an intriguing offer," Ben-Gurion said while Shimon read the note. "But he's turned us down."

"'If I made peace as you suggest,'" Shimon read aloud, "'I would forfeit not only my position, but also my life.'" He returned the letter to the envelope and handed it back to Ben-Gurion. "I suppose he has a point."

"Perhaps, but we need to make peace with one of them."

"You mean Jordan or Egypt?"

"Or Syria. We need to reduce the number of fronts we must defend."

"Syria will never reach an agreement with us. They won't fight. At least, not much. And they might even engage in talks. But that's all they will do. They'll never agree to anything."

✦ ✦ ✦

Elections to fill the office of prime minister were held in November. Ben-Gurion won with a resounding majority. His return to power brought a sense of stability to the government, but it was an awkward time. Shimon and Dayan discussed it one night a few days after the result was announced.

"Ben-Gurion is capable," Shimon assured, "but he represents the past. Israel has turned toward the future."

"Whatever that might be."

"In the beginning, when the Jewish Agency was formed and we began working toward independence, the goal of doing what was the dream of those who returned here. The idea of a state was their idea."

"Our idea."

Shimon agreed, "Yes. But since then, many more have come here and been born here."

"And not all of those who came here came from Europe."

"Exactly. What began as our dream has now become their dream. But it's a very different dream from what it was."

"And who said you weren't Shimon the Dreamer," Dayan joked. He took a breath to compose himself, then said, "So, what is your point?"

"We have many people who want to serve in government. They want to hold office. And everyone has an idea of what the nation should be. But there is no one in all of Israel with Ben-Gurion's blend of ideal and practical—vision and pragmatism."

"Now, *that* I agree with," Dayan nodded. "There is no one like him. And even though he's tired and not as quick as he once was, he's still far beyond anyone who's available to serve in office today."

After the election, Ben-Gurion returned to his former practice of serving as his own defense minister. Shimon continued in his position as director general of the Defense Ministry. Moshe Dayan remained IDF chief of staff. Sapir continued at Ministry of Trade and Industry and Golda Meir was appointed foreign minister.

As the new Ministry positions were announced, Ben-Gurion called Shimon to his office. "I've decided to replace the cabinet secretary," he announced. "I know Yohai Cohen is your friend and I wanted you to hear the news from me."

"Have you told him yet?"

"No. I wanted to pay you the courtesy of telling you first."

"Has there been a problem with him?"

"No. Not at all. But he was one of Sharett's advisors. They go back a ways. I just think the office needs a clean sweep of it."

"I suspect it does. Any objection to me bringing Yohai to the Defense Ministry?"

Ben-Gurion seemed curious. "As what?"

"I was thinking I could make him my assistant."

"Sure," Ben-Gurion replied after a moment. "You could probably use the help."

"Yes, I could."

"Don't misunderstand me. He's a good man. I just think that we need things to be—"

"It's your office," Shimon interjected. "You're entitled to the working arrangement you prefer."

Ben-Gurion smiled. "Exactly! Exactly."

✦ ✦ ✦

In the fall of 1955, Nasser announced that Egypt had reached an arms agreement with Czechoslovakia. Shimon was concerned about what that might mean. He didn't have to wait long to find out.

Two weeks later, Nasser ordered the Strait of Tiran closed to Israeli shipping. The strait provided Israeli ships the only way out of the Gulf of Aqaba and the country's only sea link to the East—from Eilat, down the Gulf, to the Red Sea, and eventually out to the Indian Ocean. When news of the order arrived, Dayan and Shimon went to see Ben-Gurion.

"You've heard?" Ben-Gurion asked as they arrived.

"Yes," Shimon replied. "I assume you'll want to respond."

Ben-Gurion glanced away. "I... don't know."

"I would remind you," Dayan noted, "on previous occasions you have stated that closing the strait would be a cause for war."

"Yes," Ben-Gurion acknowledged. "But I'm not certain we can take military action. Or that we should. Not right now."

Dayan frowned. "Why not?"

"We need a peace agreement," Ben-Gurion answered.

"With Egypt?"

"I thought it might be possible."

"Thought?"

"Right," Ben-Gurion replied. "I thought it might work, but now it seems it may not."

"So, if it isn't going to work out with them, why the hesitancy?"

"All might not be lost." Ben-Gurion glanced over at Shimon. "Perhaps."

"If Nasser is at all interested," Dayan continued, "he has a strange way of showing it."

Shimon spoke up. "You don't think peace with Egypt isn't a lost cause?"

"It might be for now," Ben-Gurion answered.

Dayan scowled in frustration. "I think closing the strait is a rather clear indication he's not interested."

"But what changed him?" Ben-Gurion wondered aloud.

"I don't think he changed at all."

Shimon spoke up again. "Perhaps this is more about Egyptian politics than it is about us."

Ben-Gurion seemed interested. "What do you mean?"

"One of the reasons the coup received widespread support," Shimon explained, "was because King Farouk's government was seen as unable to prevent our independence."

Ben-Gurion nodded. "I think that's right."

"And if that is the case, couldn't closing the strait merely be a gesture to the public? A way of saying that he is aware of their sentiment?"

"Perhaps," Ben-Gurion responded. "But even if that's all this is, it's still about us. I mean, if he closed the strait because he's just mean and aggressive or if he closed the strait to show he's opposed to us, it has very little difference. It's still about us. And the result is the same—our ships can't sail from Eilat."

Dayan spoke up. "So, what should we do?"

Ben-Gurion paused a moment and took a deep breath. "Make plans for an action to open it," he said finally.

Dayan appeared relieved. "Yes, sir."

"Plans, Moshe," Ben-Gurion cautioned. "That's all. Just plans."

"Yes, sir."

"I don't want a repeat of the Lavon debacle."

Over the next several days, Shimon assigned Yohai Cohen to work with Dayan and the IDF general staff. They reviewed options for opening the strait, then put together a plan to execute the most viable of those options. In December, Ben-Gurion and Moshe Dayan presented the plan to the cabinet. After a lengthy briefing and even lengthier debate, the cabinet remained divided on what to do. Dayan recommended a preemptive strike, but others were not convinced it was necessary and even Ben-Gurion seemed less than enthusiastic about it.

✦ ✦ ✦

While the government debated its response to Egypt, Shimon continued to work toward modernizing IDF weaponry. That effort required almost constant travel not just to France—Israel's primary weapons source—but to other countries, too, as Shimon attempted to find additional sources.

Beyond that, though, Shimon was interested in pursuing other aspects of Israel's defenses. IDF had made great strides in training soldiers, equipping them with shoulder weapons, and in modernizing the mechanized divisions. The air corps was moving toward the elimination of piston-driven fighters, and missile systems were becoming an integral part of their armaments. That was good but it was all merely an extension of conventional weaponry. Israel needed an edge. Something that would give them a decisive advantage. A defensive weaponry that not only involved the latest technology but also an entirely new and different philosophy. Something no other country in the Middle East had. They needed a nuclear option.

One of Shimon's primary contacts in France had been Pierre Mendès, the one-time French minister and a short-term premier. No longer in the French cabinet, he remained a member of the National Assembly and one with connections to almost every level of France's government. Shimon had kept in touch with him even after Mendès left office. They met one evening for dinner while Shimon was in Paris.

"I understand the Egyptians have closed the Strait of Tiran," Mendès commented. "That must be difficult for you."

Shimon didn't really want to discuss that topic but he didn't want to appear rude, either. "Yes, it has closed our access to the East."

"Any plans to do something about that?"

"The ministers are discussing their options."

"Ah. Yes." Mendès had a knowing smile. "Ministers do like to discuss things."

"Look, we need a way to change the conversation."

"Oh." Mendès sounded taken aback. "I'm sorry. I didn't mean to touch a sensitive issue."

"Not that," Shimon grinned. "I wasn't talking about our conversation. I meant the regional conversation. Metaphorically."

"Ahh." Mendès nodded. "The metaphoric Middle Eastern conversation. Israel shouldn't exist. 'We're here and we aren't going away.'"

"Yes. And the related one. We will attack you. We will defend ourselves. We will attack you again later."

"I'm not sure you can stop that conversation," Mendès noted. "That's the way people in your part of the world have been doing things for a long time."

"We need to change that, too."

"Anything come to mind?"

"Peace with one of our neighbors would be a start."

"That would help," Mendès commented. "But I'm not sure it's possible."

"Who do you know with influence in Syria?"

"I know many people who deal with the Syrians. But I don't know any who could have much success influencing the Syrian opinion of your country."

"Of all our neighbors, they are the least friendly. Not that any of our neighbors are particularly friendly. But Syria is the least friendly among them."

"I'm afraid your options are limited in that regard."

"What do you think about nuclear energy?"

Mendès raised an eyebrow. "As a defensive option?"

Shimon deflected the point of the question, "Well, in terms of power generation."

"You mean generation as a beginning."

Shimon shrugged. "As a way to create a new capability."

"And raise a new issue with your neighbors."

Shimon gave a tight smile. "That wouldn't be so bad, either."

"I can tell you this: they all are asking for it."

Now it was Shimon's turn to raise an eyebrow. "They've been to see you?"

"The Syrians have. And the Iranians. Not so much the Egyptians."

"Not so much?"

"Before the coup," Mendès explained, "one or two ministers had broached the subject with us. Since then, those men are gone and the ones who have replaced them have been busy with other things. But they are thinking in this direction. Nasser has been thinking of electrical power generation. Building a dam. Buying turbines. That topic is very much on his mind."

"So, what do you think of it?"

"I think most of the West would be opposed. The U.S. for certain."

"They haven't been very friendly to us of late."

"No. And they see the region is very unstable. If you get nuclear power, others will demand it. And their interest will go beyond merely a means of generating electricity."

"But beyond that?" Shimon inquired.

"It is expensive. But political opposition would be your biggest obstacle."

"US engineering firms are pushing it in other areas that I would think are not so stable. They're trying to sell it to India."

Mendes nodded, "They're looking for ways to capitalize on the new technology. And the government goes along with them because they want to show it can be used for peaceful means. The United States needs to build its own nuclear power facilities. Oil and coal will only increase in expense."

"If we can solve the financing and work around the political issues, what do you think of it?"

"It might be helpful," Mendès conceded. "And you don't have to develop the weapons. Just the hint of it."

"You mean bluff?"

Mendès sighed. "You could call it that."

"Isn't bluffing about them more dangerous than actually having them?"

"With other weapons, yes. With nuclear, not really."

"Why?" Shimon wondered.

"The threat of nuclear weapons isn't that anyone expects them to be used. It's that the other side thinks they *might* be used."

"The potential is the thing."

"Yes. The uncertainty of the potential. That's the real power." Mendès seemed to enjoy explaining his ideas. "When the United States and the Soviet Union face each other, everyone wants them to talk. To negotiate. And they fall all over themselves doing everything to get the two sides together for conferences and summits. And why? Because they think these two countries are ruled by madmen and will destroy the world? No. It is because everyone thinks they might. Not that they *will*. Just that they might."

Shimon decided to ask a further question. "Do you think your country would help us do that? Help us create such a program?"

Mendès seemed unfazed by the question. "We might. We just might. But is Ben-Gurion ready for it?"

"I don't know."

"I am correct in assuming you have not talked to him about this?"

Shimon nodded, "Yes. You are correct."

Mendès reached over and patted the back of Shimon's hand. "You will make a good foreign minister one day."

"I am just trying to do my job."

"And that is one of the things that makes you so good at it." Mendès wiped the corners of his mouth on his napkin. "You should pay a visit to Gaston Millerand."

"I don't know him."

"He's an under-minister of defense. In charge of our program. I can arrange an introduction."

When Shimon returned to Israel, he met with Ben-Gurion and briefed him on the meeting with Mendès. This wasn't the first time the issue of nuclear energy had come up in conversation between them but it was the closest they'd come to actually moving forward with a nuclear project.

When Shimon finished, Ben-Gurion leaned back in his chair. "I'm not sure this is the time for such a thing."

Shimon found the response a curious one. "What do you mean?"

"With this situation with Egypt unresolved. I'm just not sure we need to do this now."

"You mean it might complicate things if we did it now and it became known?"

Ben-Gurion looked over at him. "That's exactly what I mean. I'm already up against the statements I made earlier about this being a cause for war. The Egyptians are moving troops around. No one knows what they're up to. If we did this, and news of it got out, it could push things over the edge before we're ready."

"We at least need a research reactor to develop our own scientists and physicists."

"That part might be good," Ben-Gurion concurred. "But I'm not sure we need to acquire nuclear weapons. And I'm worried about touching any of it right now."

"There is some advantage in the mystery of it."

A frown wrinkled Ben-Gurion's forehead. "The mystery of it?"

"If someone *thinks* we have nuclear weapons, whether we have them or not, won't they react the same?"

"You've really been talking to Mendès," Ben-Gurion smiled.

Shimon felt flush. "Why?"

"He and I had the same conversation once."

Shimon laughed. "I was being played."

"Not really." Ben-Gurion leaned forward. "Look, you're thinking in the right direction. We need a new option. I was hoping for peace. First with Jordan, then with this latest effort with Egypt. Syria is a lost cause, but either of those two might just reach an agreement with us. Under the right conditions. That was my idea of a new option." He leaned back again. "This nuclear idea might be something that would help." He looked away as if considering the matter, then said, "See what you can find out. But no commitments yet."

"Yes, sir."

Shimon stood to leave. Ben-Gurion called after him, "Just explore the idea, and keep me informed."

Over the next several months, Shimon continued to deal with officials in France for the purchase of arms for IDF, only now he added discussions about nuclear research, construction of an experimental reactor, and acquisition of the material necessary to power it. Gaston Millerand had proved helpful in that regard, providing tours of France's nuclear facilities and introducing him to scientists who could answer his questions.

Talks led to a comprehensive security agreement with the government of Guy Mollet, who had become French prime minister in 1956. The agreement included arms sales and even greater cooperation on defense issues than they'd had before. It also included an agreement for exploratory talks between Israeli and French scientists about the inner workings of nuclear power.

That summer, Shimon arranged a conference with French military leaders. That meeting led to Israel's purchase of seventy-two Mystère aircraft, two hundred AMX tanks, and large quantities of ammunition. And all of it negotiated and concluded through the Defense Ministry under Shimon's watchful eye.

At the request of Shimon's French counterparts, Golda Meir and the Israeli ambassador to France were not included in the discussions, though Shimon went out of his way to keep her informed of the details. She was suspicious, as always, that Shimon was actually conducting foreign affairs on his own and promoting his own version of foreign policy, rather than simply negotiating financial transactions, but Ben-Gurion supported him in that effort and there was little she could do about the situation except to note it and move on.

SHIMON PERES

"In the Middle East, the conflict today is a
matter of generations and not of cultures."

AFTER WORLD WAR II, British forces withdrew from Egypt and most of the Middle East, leaving the Egyptian monarchy in control of the Suez Canal. Cargo transiting the canal was subject to Egyptian supervision. Following Israeli independence, Egyptian officials became particularly harsh in dealing with shipments bound for the new nation, detaining shipments for lengthy periods, subjecting them to extensive inspections, and imposing special taxes and duties. That treatment only intensified after the monarchy was ousted and Nasser took over as president.

At the same time, Nasser condoned, promoted, and supported cross-border raids by Arab gangs into Israeli territory. Most in Israel, including Ben-Gurion and Shimon, viewed Nasser's participation in the raids as an attempt to establish credibility among his fellow Arab leaders. Proving to the Arab League that he was the foremost anti-Semitic leader and that Egypt was the foremost anti-Semitic country. Closing the Strait of Tiran had been part of that effort.

While attempting to establish himself in the region, Nasser also pursued an ambitious domestic policy at home. That policy included construction of a dam across the lower reaches of the Nile River. Known as the Aswan High Dam, it was designed to provide flood control and create the potential for generating electricity, both of which Egypt needed.

In the summer of 1956, Nasser approached President Eisenhower about obtaining financial help from the United States in funding the Aswan Dam project. Eisenhower was amendable to the idea, but in the course of exploring it further US officials learned that Nasser also had been negotiating with the Soviet Union about participating in the same project. When Eisenhower heard that news, he declined to participate. Nasser responded to the rebuff by nationalizing the Suez Canal, supposedly to divert revenues from the canal to fund the dam's construction. Countries in the West, who saw the canal as a vital shipping lane, were furious. None of them more so than France.

Not long after the Egyptians nationalized the canal, Shimon was in Paris on yet another weapons-procurement mission. While there, he received a note asking him to pay a visit to Maurice Bourgès-Maunoury, the French minister of defense. After concluding his meetings for the day, the two met in Maunoury's office.

"As you are no doubt aware," Maunoury began, "this business with Nasser and his recent decision to nationalize the Suez Canal concerns us very much."

"I'm sure it does," Shimon acknowledged. "It concerns us all."

"Historically, we have deep ties with that tiny strip of Egypt. France undertook to finance the canal's construction in the nineteenth century and we've remained quite attached to it ever since."

Maunoury's account of the canal was a bit overstated—French banks and businessmen backed the construction, not the French government—but Shimon let that pass. "I understand your concern," Shimon remarked, "but I'm not sure there is much any of us can do about Nasser's decision. At least, not right now."

"Well, that's what I wanted to see you about," Maunoury responded. "We've come up with a plan we'd like to discuss. One that might address our concerns while also dealing with those cross-border raids you've been experiencing. And," he added with a smile, "perhaps even to resolve the issue you've had with the Strait of Tiran."

For the next twenty minutes, Maunoury outlined a plan that called for Israel to invade the Sinai. Egypt, Maunoury suggested, would no doubt respond in force. With the two armies facing each other, France and England would then intervene to separate them and in the process take control of the canal.

Shimon listened with interest but he was in no position to agree. "I'll have to take this up with Ben-Gurion," he opined when Maunoury finished.

"Of course. I am sure he will see the merit of it."

"I'm sure he will be quite intrigued."

"You think it is a good plan?"

Sharon nodded. "It has some merit. Have you discussed this with the British?"

Maunoury's eyes darted away. "We have. . . engaged them in discussions and. . . they are ready to take back the canal."

Shimon smiled in response. It was just as he'd thought. This was a French idea. The British weren't onboard yet.

By the time Shimon reached Israel, he was convinced Maunoury's plan to liberate the canal was an unworkable trap. One that exposed Israel to all the risk, while leaving France and Britain all the reward. Israel would be fully committed, risking the safety of its citizens and gambling with the future of its independence. France and England, if England indeed chose to participate, could walk away from the venture without consequence.

Nevertheless, Shimon briefed Ben-Gurion on Maunoury's plan, noting for him the risks that Israel would entail. To his surprise, Ben-Gurion did not dismiss it out of hand. "Run it by Moshe," he ordered. "See what he thinks."

Dayan was even less reticent than Ben-Gurion. Enthusiastic, actually. He'd been arguing for months that Israel needed to make a preemptive strike against Egypt, and the thought that the French might agree with him seemed to energize him all the more. "The plans we've developed for opening the strait will easily accommodate taking the canal," he noted. "All we have to do is increase the scale."

"Still," Shimon argued, "it's a lot of risk, for us. They get the gain. We get the risk."

"There's gain in it for us, too," Dayan countered. "We have as much right to sail the Strait of Tiran as anyone. Egypt has no right to close it. I see no risk in standing up for ourselves. In fact, it might even improve our stature among the nations of the world."

"If we win."

"If?" Dayan roared, only half in jest. "You doubt we can defeat them?"

"We would be fighting the Egyptian army."

"We've done it before. And we've learned a few things since the last time. We've also modernized our weaponry, thanks to you."

"It still seems like a very big risk. And it seems like the French are taking advantage of us."

"I understand why you might think there is some risk. War, by its very nature, involves risk. But it's not really that great for us."

"Oh?" Shimon was skeptical.

"For one thing," Dayan explained, "the Sinai is, strictly speaking, Egyptian territory. But they have no real presence there. Their supply lines will be longer than ours. And they will be fighting farther from their bases. They might think of it as defending the homeland, but no Egyptians actually live there. It's just desolate desert."

"Perhaps you are right."

"Of course I'm right," Dayan boasted in humor. "And think of it this way: Working with the French on *their* plan will give you leverage to get more weapons from them."

Shimon grinned. "It might just do that."

"And," Dayan continued, "it might give you a chance at that other thing you've been working on."

Shimon frowned. "Other thing?"

"That exponential option you don't like to mention by name."

"Yes." Shimon had a look of realization. "The reactor."

"Ho!" Dayan howled. "He actually said it."

"You make it sound like some taboo."

"Well, you *have* held it rather closely."

"You'll admit," Shimon countered, "it would be a bit too much of a topic to discuss at a cabinet meeting."

"Right now, yes. But I think it will have to be discussed there. Eventually."

Shimon glanced away. "Maybe."

A week later, Ben-Gurion presented the French plan to the cabinet in nonspecific terms. Dayan accompanied him and provided the barest of information to support the presentation. The cabinet deliberated the matter for most of an afternoon, then gave its preliminary approval. After the meeting, Ben-Gurion directed Dayan to proceed with detailed plans and initial preparations.

That August, Ben-Gurion discussed the French proposal for the Suez with Golda Meir. As foreign minister she had heard the presentation to the cabinet. She'd voted in favor of moving forward with it, primarily because she knew Dayan and the IDF needed time to prepare, but she remained noncommittal regarding final consent. "I don't like it," she reflected. "I think we should do something, but I'm not enthusiastic about this plan. It's a little overboard."

Ben-Gurion added, "The French are always concocting some complex gambit when the straightforward approach would do just fine."

In spite of her misgivings, Meir agreed to pursue the matter with the French and traveled to Paris as head of a delegation to work out the details. She was accompanied by Dayan, Shimon, and Moshe Carmel, a decorated IDF soldier who now served as minister of transportation.

Upon arriving in Paris the delegation learned that Guy Mollet, the French prime minister, would not be participating in the Suez discussions, as had been previously planned. According to his office, the French military had seized an airplane with Algerian rebel leaders aboard and Mollet was involved in sorting that out with the National

Assembly. Meir suspected it was a ruse contrived merely to get Mollet out of the meetings.

The French foreign minister, Christian Pineau, took Mollet's place, but Pineau wasn't any more enthusiastic about the plan than Meir and did little to hide his contempt for the idea. Meir interpreted all of that—Mollet's absence and Pineau's lack of interest—to mean that Shimon had overstated the French position on the matter, had failed to properly prepare for the delegation's trip, and otherwise had not the slightest idea what he was doing.

"All this time, he's been attempting to manipulate the situation," she railed in the privacy of her hotel room. "Merely dreaming of something when in fact no such thing exists. The French don't care about this idea. It was *his* idea, not theirs. Just one more example of Peres the Dreamer overreaching."

But the idea to liberate the Suez *was* a French idea and, moreover, Shimon was prepared for the meetings. Not only that, he'd developed close relationships with all of the key French officials. So much so that he arranged a private meeting for Meir with Mollet at which the two had a full and frank discussion. That meeting seemed to placate Meir's concerns somewhat, and the conference continued.

For his own meetings, Shimon did as Dayan suggested and arrived with detailed requests for additional military equipment needed for the operation. The French readily agreed to the requests and, with Dayan's help, approved delivery schedules for shipment.

When they returned to Israel, Golda Meir gave Ben-Gurion a dour report. "Once again," she complained, "Shimon has underestimated, overstated, and misrepresented French support for this so-called plan." Shimon, Dayan, and Carmel, however, gave a very different view and the operation moved along with the estimated timetable worked out at the conference.

As the plan continued to unfold, Ben-Gurion was concerned the Egyptians might bomb Israeli cities and towns. "The IDF air force may not be adequate to support a Sinai Operation *and* protect the remainder of the country at the same time." Shimon relayed those concerns to his French counterparts. Mollet responded by ordering two squadrons of the French air force to be stationed in Israel.

Ben-Gurion also wanted the British actively involved in the operation. He was concerned because of the British response to an earlier Israeli reprisal raid against Jordan. During that incident, British diplomats raised the issue of their mutual defense treaty with Jordan—in effect, threatening Israel with military action. "I don't want a repeat of that," Ben-Gurion groused. Shimon relayed those issues as well and the British stepped up their involvement.

That October, a final meeting was held in France. Ben-Gurion, Shimon, and Dayan attended, along with a number of aides and assistants, Yohai Cohen among them. Parties to the meeting engaged in lengthy discussions, and there was considerable back-and-forth with the British over the extent of their participation. Various ruses were suggested to provide cover for the parties, but Ben-Gurion refused them all. "I'm not going to lie," he stated flatly. "We either find a way to do this in a straightforward manner, or we don't do it at all."

Dayan presented a proposal for a Sinai Operation designed, on Israel's part, as an action to open the Strait of Tiran. "At the same time," he explained, "our forces will sweep through Gaza to eliminate terrorist activity and cover our western flank as the main force drives into Sinai. We can reach the Suez Canal before the Egyptians have time to respond."

Some thought Dayan's projections were unreasonable and questioned whether he could retake the Suez as quickly as outlined. In the end, however, the participants reached a Seven Point Agreement, which became known as the Sèvres Protocol, so designated after the location near Paris where the meetings were held.

While discussion of the Suez attack proceeded, Shimon seized the opportunity to pursue talks with Gaston Millerand on a planned-for nuclear reactor deal. He'd hoped merely to move the conversation forward and keep the idea alive. However, Millerand and officials from the Defense Ministry had worked on the project with him long enough that they were ready to commit. Before the Suez conference dismissed, Shimon reached an agreement for French assistance in constructing a reactor. The exact location, tentatively set for a site in the Negev near Dimona, was still undetermined, but the French were committed to constructing a reactor and supplying uranium to power it. He discussed the agreement with Ben-Gurion while they were still in Paris and received tentative approval from him.

Five days after the final Suez meeting, the Suez War broke out. As Dayan had suggested, IDF troops swept through Sinai in a week, leaving the Egyptian army devastated. At the same time, additional IDF units moved through Gaza, eliminating terrorist strongholds.

In accordance with the plan, British and French officials decried the threatening situation unfolding on the Sinai Peninsula, and jointly deployed forces to take positions to separate the Israeli and Egyptian armies. Those units arrived at Port Said on the coast and quickly moved inland. However, they bogged down before reaching the Suez Canal.

With the British and French hopelessly entangled, making the situation more perilous than before, the United States and the Soviet Union denounced the operation and demanded that all foreign troops be withdrawn. England and France complied, but Israeli forces pushed past Eilat all the way to the Strait of Tiran. In quick succession, IDF units destroyed Egyptian batteries overlooking the strait, once again opening the passage to Israeli ship traffic.

SHIMON PERES

"Let all of us turn from bullets to
ballots, from guns to shovels."

IN ISRAEL, the Suez Crisis was followed by a decade of domestic stability, consolidation, and growth. The country, not even ten years old, needed the time to consolidate its economy, strengthen its infrastructure, and simply live.

Yet for all that was going right, the Lavon Affair lingered in the background, kept alive by Lavon's persistent demand for exoneration, and by smoldering resentment of some in the Labor Party over what they perceived as Ben-Gurion favoritism. For the disgruntled, the Lavon Affair became a *cause célèbre*, a controversy around which they could whip the uninformed into a force of internal party opposition—backstabbing of the worst kind—which Shimon found deplorable.

Ben-Gurion wanted to resolve the Lavon matter once and for all. Having been trained as a lawyer, he had a deep and abiding devotion to the rule of law and wanted it to be the bedrock of the government. Consequently, he insisted on handling the matter through a judicial inquiry, an extension of the court system, where it could be investigated by trained, independent professionals and adjudicated by equally independent prosecutors and judges.

"We in the executive wing of the government cannot be investigator, judge, and jury at the same time," he argued. "The law must be applied to these situations by an independent judiciary."

Members of the cabinet, Golda Meir among them, were just as strongly insistent that it be handled through a Commission of Inquiry appointed by the cabinet, and over which it could exercise supervision. Shimon was certain that was their goal all along—to control the investigation.

He felt that, "If they simply investigate, in an objective manner, and look only at the evidence, everyone else would be exonerated. Lavon and Gibli would be the only ones implicated. The problem for them is if they did that, they would also find that there isn't enough evidence to exonerate Lavon or Gibli. The evidence exonerates everyone else, totally and completely. But it neither absolutely convicts nor absolutely exonerates Lavon, which is what they're trying to do and the only way they can do that is through a commission that they appoint and they control."

After a lengthy investigation, the commission did, in fact, clear Lavon. With an exoneration in hand, members of the Labor Party's old guard convened a Court of Honor—a party device to investigate internal matters. Formally, the Court of Honor was to investigate the manner in which the affair had been handled by party officials, primarily Ben-Gurion, Shimon, and a select list of operatives. Lavon was intent on rehabilitating his torn and tattered political career. His erstwhile supporters were intent on having retribution for any number of supposed offenses and slights they might have endured over the years, including the sense that they'd been "passed over" for Ben-Gurion's younger favorites.

Golda Meir, Moshe Sharett, and Pinchas Sapir were among those who used the party inquiry as an opportunity to vent their anger and frustration. Meir, in particular, saw herself as the rightful successor to Israel's leadership positions, whichever she chose to hold, and seemed to think she'd only been deterred from free reign of that by Ben-Gurion's supposed decision to elevate others ahead of her. Party members who had no claim of historic priority, if any such claim were possible, saw the moment as an opportunity to advance their own careers and rallied around her in what could only be described as a pure, partisan bloodletting—no matter the effect it might have on the party or the nation.

When the outcome became apparent, Ben-Gurion, Shimon, Dayan, and others resigned from the Mapai faction of the Labor Party and formed a new entity known as Rafi. At first only a short-term parliamentary move, they soon seceded from the Labor Party altogether. Rafi became an entirely separate organization and, with Ben-Gurion as the standard-bearer, not an inconsequential one at that.

Shimon was chosen as Rafi's initial secretary-general and he went to work immediately doing what he'd done before—establishing local Rafi groups, recruiting new members, and raising money. Over the previous ten years, his work with the Defense Ministry had taken him away from Sonia and their children for weeks at a time. Now his work with Rafi threatened to keep him away even longer. He loved them and wanted to be with them, but the tug of Israel and allure of the national cause was more than he could resist. Sonia, who had never been interested in politics, withdrew even deeper into family, her work with the poor and disadvantaged, and the quiet life she'd envisioned for herself. "The man I married worked in the cowshed," she once said. "I did not marry for a life of politics."

✦ ✦ ✦

In spite of the Lavon investigations and the changes those inquiries brought, Shimon retained his position as director general of the Defense Ministry and continued to work on weapons acquisition. He pursued the nuclear option as well. With Ben-Gurion's support, and the help of the French, that project slowly unfolded. One of the first steps was the establishment of the Israel Atomic Energy Commission and from there the program advanced toward reality, albeit in small, incremental steps. Not all ministers in the cabinet favored the program, and convincing them to support creation of the commission took an enormous amount of work.

Israel's established scientists were not in favor of the program either, and Shimon decided early on that attempting to convince them of the program's merits would be fruitless. However, two of Israel's brightest minds—Ernst David Bergmann and Israel Dostrovsky—expressed an interest in what he was doing.

Bergmann was a physicist who had studied at the University of Berlin. Afterward, he worked for Chaim Weizmann and became head of the Weizmann Institute. Somewhat younger, Dostrovsky studied at University College London and lectured at University College North Wales before joining Bergmann at the institute. Both men had distinguished themselves in the academic study of radioactive materials and were Israel's leading minds on the subject. They understood the significance of what Shimon was attempting to establish and, along with the staff at the Weizmann Institute, provided the core of Israel's nuclear program. They also were instrumental in recruiting recent university graduates whom they could train as a cadre of nuclear physicists to support the program into the future.

As director general of the Defense Ministry, many of the decisions regarding details of the program's development were left to Shimon's discretion. After establishing a team of scientists, one of the crucial issues was that of finding a suitable location for the reactor. Dimona had been previously selected as a site based on its remote location and the availability of water from the established system created for irrigation. As the project moved forward and construction drew nearer, the site came under closer scrutiny. Long hours were devoted to collecting physical samples from the area, the extraction of subsurface borings, and a review of Dimona's geological history. Almost the entire Negev had been surveyed by oil companies earlier in the century in their quest for Middle Eastern oil. No oil reserves were found but a vast library of geological surveys and findings was created. Shimon's staff, with Yohai coordinating their work, collected copies of those documents, then combed through them for even the minutest details.

After lengthy deliberations with geologists, engineers, the growing team of physicists, and Shimon's staff, Dimona was, indeed, determined to be the best site for Israel's nuclear energy research. Officially entitled the Negev Nuclear Research Center, the facility's existence was a matter of utmost secrecy.

While construction of the reactor site moved forward, Shimon also initiated construction of a residential neighborhood to house the program's construction crews and operating technicians. Built on the outskirts of Beersheba, which was not far away, it included paved streets, lush parks, and modern recreational facilities.

✦ ✦ ✦

In 1963, Ben-Gurion left office, this time for good. He remained a member of the Knesset but no longer served in a ministerial position. Levi Eshkol, the Labor Party candidate, was elected to succeed him. Eshkol appointed Golda Meir as his minister of foreign affairs but three years later she left office, too, citing exhaustion and health issues. Sapir, by then minister of finance, seemed interested in filling the Foreign Ministry vacancy. Shimon thought Dayan should have it. Dayan thought the job should go to Shimon.

"I'm too young for the party leadership to accept," Shimon submitted as he and Dayan talked one night in Dayan's office. "Besides, all the old guard hate me."

"Not all of them," Dayan corrected.

"Whoever those supporters might be, they certainly keep their opinions to themselves."

"The problem is—"

"I know, they're just jealous," Shimon interrupted. "I've heard it all my life."

"If it's jealousy, it's not really about Ben-Gurion favoring you or anything like what Golda argues."

"It's certainly what she says."

"Maybe. But I think for most of them, the problem is that things come naturally to you. They have to work at it."

Shimon scowled. "So they hate me because I'm a natural fit for my work?"

"You were born to be a diplomat," Dayan explained. "Most of the ministers we've known were born to be politicians. But instead of sticking to politics, they try to make themselves into diplomats because foreign affairs has a lot of public appeal. It's a sexy occupation, so to speak."

"Politics is dirty business."

"Exactly! So, you are a natural at diplomacy, but that's an area that easily bleeds over into politics. An area in which you, my friend, are not so naturally suited."

"I'm a born diplomat, not a born politician?"

"Yes."

"Most people couldn't tell the difference."

"Most people think a politician is someone who can talk to opposing groups and make them all think he's totally on their side. But that's not a politician; that's a diplomat."

"Then what's a politician?"

"A politician is a guy who can look at a complex issue and instantly reduce it to a simple equation. Menachem Begin is going to be prime minister one day."

Shimon's face contorted in a doubtful expression. "Begin?"

"Not because he's the best at planning our future, and not because he's a naturally likeable guy, but because he sees things in black and white. Yes and no."

"That part I agree with," Shimon acquiesced. "You're either for him or against him."

"And when he runs for office he will cast that as for *us* against *us*. And it'll be like this—Arabs are complex people with a complex culture and complex religious beliefs. Menachem will take all of that and package it as a yes-or-no vote. They're against us, they want to kill us, they mean to destroy us. Vote for me. I won't let it happen. People will vote for a person like that because they know what they're being asked to do. It simplifies their choices, their solutions, their lives."

Shimon thought for a moment, then raised the obvious question. "And me? What am I like?"

"You see every side of every issue," Dayan observed. "And not just see it. You understand all of those perspectives. When you think of Arabs, you see subtlety, nuance, and a long history. You not only see them, you empathize with them. You know instantly why they think what they think, believe what they believe, do what they do. But you can't put that into a yes-or-no equation. An Arab is too complex for you to do that. Too much of a real person for you to cast them as good or bad. For us or against us."

"Most of them aren't against us," Shimon noted. "They're just more for themselves than they are for us."

"Exactly my point," Dayan concurred. "Exactly my point. You belong in foreign affairs."

"I like foreign affairs because it's the direction of the future. Our future. Israel's future. Here, at defense, we are always fighting or preparing to fight. And the country needs a military that is ready. But the future will be in learning to get along with our neighbors. Making peace. Constant war is not sustainable for us. We can't flourish as a nation this way. We spend too much money on defense."

"And that's why defense works for you," Dayan grinned.

"What do you mean?"

"It lets you straddle the fence. You can work both sides. Preparing for war, while building relationships for peace."

Shimon smiled. "I suppose so. It also gets me in trouble. What I see as doing my job others see as invading their portfolio."

Dayan chuckled. "You know, one day you will have to choose. You'll have to make your choice and pay the price."

"The price?"

Dayan adopted a parental tone. "Shimon, everything comes at a price. Peace is no different."

A few days later, Eshkol surprised Shimon and Dayan by appointing Abba Eban as minister of foreign affairs. Born in South Africa, Eban was educated at Cambridge. During World War II he worked for the Zionist Organization in London, then came to Jerusalem as an intelligence officer with the British army. After the war he worked for the Jewish Agency in the areas of foreign affairs and diplomacy, becoming Israel's first ambassador to the United States and then first ambassador to the United Nations.

The year after Eban's appointment, Syria cut the flow of water into the Jordan River, a vital source of irrigation for Israeli agriculture. Loss of water from the river threatened not only the country's crops but also its livelihood, even its very existence. An extensive system of canals and pipes moved water from the Jordan south to the Negev where it was used to bring the desert to life. That same system also brought water to Dimona where the newly formed Israel Atomic Energy Commission was constructing a reactor. Syria's action threatened all of that.

As a response, Eshkol and Eban decided to dispatch combat aircraft on a flyover above Damascus. One hundred planes were sent in a gesture meant as a show of force, a protest about the water situation in the Jordan River. Syria, however, saw it as an invasion of sovereign territory and an act of war.

Egypt, ever quick to take sides against Israel, came to Syria's aid and once again closed the Gulf of Aqaba to Israeli shipping, blocking it at the Strait of Tiran. At the same time, Nasser ordered Egyptian troops to mobilize, and sent units to positions along the border with Israel.

With events again moving toward war, Shimon, in his capacity as secretary-general of Rafi, issued a call for Labor Party unity. Secretly, he hoped to return Rafi permanently to the party fold. To accomplish that, he needed to work out a deal that Eshkol and the Labor Party would accept, but also one that Rafi members would agree to. Emotions were still frayed from events that compelled Rafi's formation.

Late one night, he discussed the situation with Yohai. "Well,"

Yohai opined, after hearing Shimon's dilemma, "we could ask them to offer *you* a position."

Shimon disagreed. "That wouldn't mean much to Rafi members. Now, if we could give them Ben-Gurion or Dayan, they might go for that."

"I think we've moved on from Ben-Gurion. And he's moved on from us." Yohai noticed the look on Shimon's face and quickly added, "I mean, he's done a great job but I think retirement is what he needs right now and that seems to be what he's chosen. I don't think he wants to come back again."

"I know what you mean. And you're right. He's moved on. We've moved on. I just don't like not having him around."

"What you said, though. About Dayan," Yohai continued. "What about that? Would they make him foreign minister?"

Shimon shook his head. "Eshkol likes Abba Eban too much to replace him. But they might make him defense minister."

"That would be great," Yohai responded enthusiastically. "But how do we get Eshkol and Labor to accept it?"

"Offer to dissolve Rafi."

"Do they need Rafi gone?"

"They need national unity. And they need Moshe. The country needs Moshe. This is the only way they could get him to become part of the government."

"The only way?"

"He's as angry as anyone about what they did with that Lavon situation."

"Will Moshe go for it?"

Shimon smiled. "He will if I ask."

"And what about Eshkol? Will he agree to it?"

Shimon's smile widened to a grin. "That's your responsibility."

Yohai had a startled look. "I don't know him that well."

"But you know the people in his office. Sound them out. See if he'll go for it."

The next day, Yohai met with members of Eshkol's staff and key people he'd come to know in Labor Party leadership, then reported back to Shimon. "Eshkol will accept Dayan as defense minister, but the offer has to come from you, personally. Also, you can't have a Ministry position until after the next round of elections."

Shimon rolled his eyes. "Golda."

"Yes," Yohai acknowledged. "Everyone has someone to please. They have Golda, we have Ben-Gurion. Speaking of which, will Ben-Gurion agree to this?"

"We're going to see him and find out." Shimon stood and came from behind his desk. "Get your jacket."

Yohai frowned. "I'm going with you?"

"Absolutely." Shimon was at the door already and paused to wait for Yohai. "When you need to convince him of something, never go alone."

Late that evening, Shimon and Yohai met with Ben-Gurion. Yohai sat to one side and listened as Shimon explained the agreement he'd reached with Eshkol and the Labor Party. Ben-Gurion seemed to accept the arrangement and asked only a few questions. "The part about you," Ben-Gurion said, "you know that comes from Golda."

"I realize that." Shimon also knew that everyone who'd been involved in the negotiations had pointed this out to him. Telling him, in effect, that Golda still held something against him. It was frustrating, knowing that she felt that way yet not knowing why. But at the same time oddly reassuring to know that everyone else knew it, too.

After a short conversation and a cup of tea, Ben-Gurion gave his consent. "You'll have to submit this for party approval," he remarked as they were leaving.

"Yes, sir," Shimon replied. "I'll call a meeting. Perhaps we can get this done by the end of the week. You'll chair it?"

Ben-Gurion patted Shimon on the back. "No. After tonight, I'm done with politics. The party is yours. You'll have to run it."

Later that week, Shimon submitted the question of dissolving Rafi to its members for a final decision. He'd taken a nose count beforehand and knew they would agree to join Eshkol's government. Whether they would agree to dissolve Rafi was less certain. After a lengthy argument, they agreed to join the government majority but balked at dissolving the party.

The following day, Shimon went to see Eshkol at the prime minister's office. In a meeting that was remarkably brief, cordial, and to the point, Shimon offered his proposal. In exchange for an appointment of Dayan as defense minister, Rafi would join Labor in support of Eshkol's government.

"You understand," Eshkol warned, "if we do this, I can't appoint you to a ministerial position until after the next round of elections."

"I understand." Shimon wanted to say more, to unleash years of frustration over Golda and the way she'd treated him—frustration he was sure Eshkol would understand and might even, in some measure, share—but instead he kept quiet. This was a good deal for Rafi. It got them back inside Labor where they belonged. He would work on dissolving the organization later but for now, this was enough.

The two men shook hands and that was it. Rafi was part of the Eshkol government and Dayan was in charge of the Defense Ministry.

Once again, Shimon had selected an appointee to serve as his own boss, arranged the offer of that appointment, and won its acceptance. He went home that evening feeling confident about his future and the future of the country. Moshe would know what to do, no matter what action the Egyptians chose.

✦ ✦ ✦

In June 1967, with the Egyptian army poised on Israel's border, Dayan and his IDF generals devised a strategy to make a preemptive strike. Shimon, as director general of defense, was involved in the planning. He and Dayan shared similar views of IDF's capability. Neither thought the fight would last very long.

Dayan briefed Eshkol, then Eshkol brought Abba Eban into the discussion. Eban gave the plan full support but was concerned the cabinet might delay a decision. "We need to move quickly," he urged.

"The longer we wait the greater the risk this might slip out. And then we'd lose the element of surprise."

In an effort to smooth the way for cabinet approval, Eban met with Pinchas Sapir, thinking Sapir would be supportive and help the others decide promptly. Sapir listened, then went to see Golda Meir and talked to her.

"Shimon is involved?" she asked.

"I'm sure he's involved in the planning," Sapir replied. "He's director general."

"And we're stuck with Moshe Dayan."

Sapir thought it an odd comment. "Didn't you want him?"

She shook her head. "No, not at all."

"Then why did you agree?"

"Eshkol wanted him," Meir explained. "I wanted Rafi back in the government. Officially part of it."

"Why did you want Rafi's support?"

"Circumstances appear to be taking us toward war," Meir advised. "That being the case, I want them in the government so they get the blame, too, along with us. Otherwise, they would be outside the government, free to blame us at will, and free to criticize Eshkol's policies."

"Blame? You think we'll fail?"

"I think no one can know what will happen. Not for certain. And if things go wrong, we don't want Shimon and Ben-Gurion out there telling everyone it was Labor's fault."

"And what about Dayan?"

"Shimon wanted Rafi back in the party. He didn't like being on the outside. Eshkol wanted Dayan."

"How do you know all of this?"

Meir glanced away. "I have sources."

"I still don't understand," Sapir persisted. "You did this for Shimon, or Eshkol, or who?"

"Listen," Golda shouted. "I didn't do it because of them. Shimon wanted Rafi back on the inside. In the Labor Party. Part of the coalition.

He couldn't leave Rafi because he's too loyal to Ben-Gurion. And now that he's there—"

"But if he's in the party—Labor Party—won't he be a force to contend with?"

"Maybe. But he would have been much stronger with Rafi on the outside; he just didn't see it. And that's not what he wanted. He wanted to be inside. So I gave him what he wanted. Rafi's a part of the Labor Party and soon it will disappear completely."

"They'll be absorbed."

"No. Shimon will take them apart. That's part of his plan."

"You know this for a fact."

"Like I said, I have sources."

"So, Eshkol gets Dayan, which is what *he* wanted. Shimon gets back in the Labor Party, which is what *he* wanted. And Rafi will disappear, which is what *you* wanted."

"Plus Rafi is eliminated as an outside threat to Labor," Meir added. "If this thing with Egypt goes badly, which it very well might, Shimon with an independent Rafi behind him would end up as prime minister." She closed her eyes and shook her head. "That must never happen."

✦ ✦ ✦

Later that week, Eshkol presented to the cabinet the strategy for a preemptive attack. Dayan provided details of the operation in a briefing that included schedules, maps, and diagrams of planned troop movements. The cabinet debated the matter, asking questions and exploring options in a meeting that ran late into the night, but before they adjourned they voted to approve the plan.

It was after midnight when Dayan returned to the Defense Ministry, but Shimon was still in his office, seated at his desk, working through a stack of files. Dayan paused outside Shimon's doorway and leaned inside. "It's a go," he announced.

"The generals are waiting for you down the hall," Shimon replied.

"This will take a while. You should go home and get some sleep," Dayan suggested. "We'll need you sharp tomorrow."

Shimon followed Dayan's advice and went home. Sonia was in bed when he arrived but she got up to sit with him while he ate. She knew war was coming—the newspapers had been talking about it for weeks—but she avoided the topic and told him about her day, the children, and the latest news from relatives in the United States. It was a quiet moment, just the two of them. Almost surreal as he thought about what was to happen the next day.

The next morning, IDF aircraft launched widespread strikes against Egyptian airfields. Almost the entire Egyptian air force was destroyed while it sat on the ground. The air assault was followed by a two-pronged ground offensive: one into Gaza, the other into the Sinai. Israeli forces quickly swept through both areas, inflicting heavy losses on the Egyptian army.

In spite of the Israeli rout, and taking advantage of the regional confusion that followed, Nasser called on Jordan and Syria to enter the fight. Claiming that Egypt had repelled Israel's attacks and destroyed the Israeli army, he chided them for sitting idly by while his armies crushed the Jews beneath their heels.

Nasser's demand put King Hussein in a tough spot. Since Israel's War of Independence, Jordan had welcomed a large Palestinian population inside its borders and under its protection in the annexed West Bank. A Palestinian majority now occupied Jordanian territory on both sides of the Jordan River. Moreover, Nasser was immensely popular and anti-monarchy sentiment ran strong throughout the region. With only a word from him, rebellion might engulf all of Jordan.

Fearing a threat to his own reign if he refused, Hussein acceded to Nasser's demand and ordered the Jordanian army to attack Israel from the east. Syria joined the fight from the north and began lobbing artillery rounds into Galilee.

Israel responded with a counter strike. In two days of fighting, IDF troops drove Hussein's army back to the east, beyond the Jordan River, and seized control of both East Jerusalem and the West Bank territory. Rather than solidifying Hussein's claim to the area, the Jordanian army lay in ruin and its population was sent fleeing for the hills.

With Egypt eliminated as a threat, and the Jordanian army no longer an issue, Dayan and the IDF turned their attention to Syria. In two days of heavy fighting, the IDF destroyed Syrian artillery positions on the Golan Heights and seized control of the ridge.

The entire operation, from beginning to end, on all three fronts, took only six days to complete: Two days to defeat Egypt, two days to remove Jordan from Jerusalem and the West Bank, two days to take the Golan Heights from Syria. When fighting ended, the Israel Defense Forces was victorious, Moshe Dayan was a national hero, and the conflict would be forever known as the Six-Day War.

SHIMON PERES

"I have one weakness. I don't like
vacations. I like to work."

LEVI ESHKOL SERVED as prime minister until February 1969, when he died in office from a heart attack. Yigal Allon became acting prime minister, holding the office for two months while a general election was arranged.

With Eshkol gone, Golda Meir returned to political involvement in the Labor Party and was selected as the party leader, which made her the candidate for prime minister in the upcoming election. She won handily and reappointed Moshe Dayan as minister of defense. David "Dado" Elazar became IDF chief of staff. Pinchas Sapir returned as finance minister, and Shimon was named minister of immigrant absorption.

The ministerial appointment was Shimon's first cabinet position. As with all his dealings with Meir, he was both glad and frustrated at the same time. Honored to be included but frustrated at being moved out of the Defense Ministry. He also found the change of pace from the high intensity of the Defense Ministry to the less-stressful rhythm of immigration unsettling.

"This is the first time I've worked outside the Defense Ministry since... before independence," he told Dayan.

"But, hey," Dayan countered, "you're a minister now. That counts for something, doesn't it?"

"Yes. It does. But I can't help thinking she put me there to table my interest in foreign affairs. Although the name—Immigration—implies otherwise, this is one area that has no contact with other countries. The Ministry deals only with the domestic needs of immigrants. That is, *after* they've arrived here."

"She had to appoint you," Dayan offered. "She couldn't risk offending former Rafi members or they might leave the party."

"I realize that," Shimon noted. "And I think the reason she gave me a ministerial appointment at all was because she wanted to be cordial about it. But I also know she doesn't want me involved in the areas she's really concerned about, so she put me in immigration, out of the way. Solves several problems at once."

"You mean keeping you out of foreign affairs?"

"And out of defense."

"Well," Dayan grinned, "if I know you—and I know you better than most—you won't let a minor thing like your title slow you down."

The Ministry of Immigrant Absorption was in charge of settling new immigrants, coordinating government benefits specifically designed for new arrivals, and working with local government to accommodate emigres. One of the central themes of statehood had been the universal right of all Jews everywhere to return to Israel to live. The Ministry of Immigrant Absorption handled the government's programs that were created to implement the domestic side of that policy. Dealing with foreign governments and issues that involved the immigrant's country of origin fell under the Foreign Ministry's purview.

Not long after taking office, Shimon attended a meeting regarding issues related to immigrants and communities in East Jerusalem. Yehoshua Rabinowitz served as mayor of Jerusalem and was at the meeting. Rabinowitz had been Shimon's teacher in Vishnyeva and had known Shimon most of his life. They visited after everyone else left, and Rabinowitz asked Shimon about the work. "You've done well for yourself," he noted. "And now you are a minister in the cabinet."

"It's been an interesting life so far. Thanks to your help."

Rabinowitz smiled pleasantly. "Has coming to Israel turned out as you first wanted?"

"Yes, but it has been different."

"Most certainly," Rabinowitz acknowledged. "As it must always be. The imagining of anything is quite different from the actual doing of it. The encounter is always more real than we imagine it beforehand."

"Do you remember when your cousin Isidor Talmon came to Vishnyeva?"

"How could I forget? That was the meeting that changed everything. The people who attended that meeting survived the Germans. Those who did not attend died."

Shimon was astounded. "I hadn't thought of that."

"I think of it many times. Talmon and I talk almost every day and we speak of that evening often. It was the most momentous in all of our lives." They sat in silence for what seemed like a long time, as if remembering the evening and people they knew who were no longer with them. "But," Rabinowitz continued, "you were saying. . . "

"Just that the way Talmon described life here made it sound like one long vacation."

"He did," Rabinowitz laughed. "He has a way of telling a story."

"I already knew it would be hard work. That's what the whole labor movement was about. You taught us that."

Rabinowitz chuckled, "Glad you paid attention."

"But it was very different from what I expected."

"In what way?"

"The biggest thing I've noticed is how divided we are."

Rabinowitz nodded in agreement. "We are deeply divided. And even within the various Zionist groups, where one would expect to find a high degree of commonality, we are divided into factions."

"Every organization," Shimon added. "They're all actually coalitions made of factions that have very different views of what we should and shouldn't be, what we should and shouldn't do, how life in Israel should and shouldn't develop. And it's even that way in the supposed majority that runs the government."

"Yes. Very much so." Rabinowitz nodded once more. "A year or two ago I finally met Golda Meir. She is not much like I imagined her to be."

"I can imagine."

"Sometimes I think she might be divided within herself," Rabinowitz added with uncharacteristic candor. "Rather like your experience with Palestine."

"She's plainspoken and forthright in whatever she's doing, whether public or private, and everyone knows it. But there is a side of her that one only sees by working with her on a daily basis."

"I've only met her. I don't have much to do with her or her office. What is it like to work with her?"

"You should drop in to see her," Shimon suggested. "You might fit in well with her. She is more oriented toward the party than the government, as I think you are. Or, at least, you were."

"I support the government," Rabinowitz huffed in a defensive tone. "As mayor, I am part of the government."

"And Golda supports the government, but she can't get away from her original orientation toward the party. The movement. It is a view she developed before statehood and it's deeply ingrained in her mind and in her personality."

"It's not a bad thing to find a cause to which one can devote one's energy and effort."

"You have said that often in class."

"It is the way to find fulfillment," Rabinowitz explained. "Find a cause. Devote yourself to it."

Shimon replied thoughtfully, "My grandfather used to say that, too."

The next morning, Shimon awakened early and sat in the living room thinking about his conversation with Rabinowitz, remembering his grandfather Meltzer, and remembering the life he'd had as a child in Vishnyeva.

It was true that he'd never identified a cause for which he could devote his life. Not a single cause. But that was because the cause changed, sometimes frequently, sometimes daily. He'd always been devoted to a cause, just not the same one all the time. The kibbutz they'd dreamed of at Ben-Shemen, the creation of a Jewish state, building up the IDF; those had been his causes. But to say one of them was the defining one—the single thing that tied them all together—that was something he'd never known and maybe he—

Just then, Sonia entered the room still looking sleepy. She was dressed in pajamas with a housecoat over the top and her hair was in disarray, but seeing her brought a smile to his face as it had since the moment he saw her for the first time. "I'm sorry I awakened you."

"You didn't awaken me." She dropped onto the sofa beside him, curled her feet beneath her, and leaned against him. "Your side of the bed got cold. That's all."

Shimon took her hand in his and they sat quietly for a moment.

Her eyes were closed but he could sense her smiling. "I could get used to this part of the new job."

"Used to what?"

"It's almost dawn and you're still here. And not only here, but sitting quietly on the sofa."

Shimon chuckled. "Not quite the pace of the past."

"You were doing too many things at once," she continued. "At defense. It was too much."

"I know," he sighed. "But our lives depended on it."

"Well, you're not there now. You have a different job and you're here with me on the sofa in the living room, so I think you should tell me what's wrong."

"I just needed time to think."

She leaned away from him. "Shimon, it's early in the morning, the kitchen is dark, and you haven't been anywhere near the coffeepot. So, tell me, what's on your mind?"

"I saw Rabinowitz yesterday."

"Your old teacher?"

"Yes."

"What did he have to say?"

"He asked me if I'd found my cause." Shimon felt Sonia's cheek move against his shoulder as she smiled once more. "That amuses you?"

"You've always had a cause."

"I know," he sighed, "but I don't think I've ever had a single cause that tied everything else together."

"A mind like yours is too big for one idea."

"Not just an idea," Shimon said. "A cause."

"Israel is your cause."

"Maybe."

"You've given your life to it." Sonia moved her feet to the floor, let go of his hand, and stood. "Come on," she gestured.

He looked up at her. "Where are we going?"

"To the kitchen. I'll make your breakfast."

Shimon stood and put his arm around her shoulder. "You're better than I deserve," he whispered.

The next afternoon Shimon rode up to Netanya, a city north of Tel Aviv, for a meeting with area planning officials. On the way back, he stopped at the cemetery where Berl Katznelson was buried. Standing at the grave, he remembered the many times he'd visited Katznelson's apartment, the hours they had spent talking, the way learning had consumed them both.

"Knowledge is a good thing," he whispered. "But it's not enough, is it?"

Shimon remembered his grandfather had taught him that everything had four levels of meaning. From the obvious to the mystical. Since coming to work first with Haganah then with IDF and the Defense Ministry, he'd not had time to think much about that. Most days, there was hardly time to grasp the value of what passed across his desk and no time to reflect on any deeper significance, much less discern three levels below the surface. Now, in a different Ministry, where work moved at a much slower pace, he realized how much he'd only scratched the surface of the issues that had challenged him along the way.

"Perspective," he whispered. "I've missed the way the pieces fit together."

The Middle East was like a giant puzzle. A puzzle of puzzles, actually. Each piece—Israel, Jordan, Syria, Lebanon, Egypt—stood in relationship to one another, but each of those separate countries was comprised of various competing groups, all of them competing for the primacy of their own agenda. But what did that mean for him, personally, and how did it relate to his own life?

Katznelson had been motivated by the desire to teach and to give the next generation a love of learning. Shimon's grandfather had been motivated by that same desire. *He wanted to teach me,* Shimon thought. *Knowledge for knowledge's sake. Knowledge that made me who I was supposed to become.*

Teaching kept the table in his grandfather's dining room loaded with books. But he'd also been motivated by a devotion to God and a sense of mission in caring for those who attended the synagogue near his home. Being a rabbi, fulfilling his religious calling, ultimately cost him his life. And as tragic as that end had been—even knowing beforehand that it might come to that—his grandfather would have lived no other way.

"That's what I want," Shimon whispered as he turned away from the grave and started back toward his car. "That's what I need. A calling. An overarching purpose to which all the pieces of my life fit. Like a puzzle. A puzzle of meaning, joined together at all four levels by something bigger than any of the single pieces. But what?"

Work kept Shimon occupied the next several days, but on Thursday he went out for lunch and on the way back to the office stopped by the Great Synagogue on Allenby Street. Though he wasn't a member he'd visited there on occasion to pray or think or be alone just for a moment. That day, he found the cantor rabbi, Yaakov Rosen, near the lectern in the main sanctuary of the building.

A young boy was standing at the lectern, pointer in hand, slowly reciting a verse from the scroll. "'Pray for the peace of Jerusalem,'" he read. "'May those who love you be secure. May there be peace within your walls and security within your citadels.'"

Hearing those words brought back a rush of memories—the night Talmon spoke to the families of Vishnyeva at Rabinowitz's house, hearing him talk about life in Palestine, the desire that welled up inside to do something about the challenges the Zionists faced, and the commitment he'd made to pray. And he *had* prayed, almost every night as a young boy. And he *still* prayed. . . sometimes. . . but somewhere along the way he'd stopped reciting those verses from the Psalms. Maybe now he would do that again. Maybe that was—

"Very good," Rosen said to the boy and the sound of his voice brought Shimon back to the moment. "I think you're ready," Rosen added. "Do you?"

"Yes, Rabbi," the boy grinned. "I am ready."

"Good. Now run along and play. Do you have a way home?"

The boy pointed to the back of the room. "My mother is waiting to walk with me." A woman stepped into the aisle and as the boy caught up to her she took his hand, then they disappeared into the hall beyond the doorway and were gone.

Rosen turned to Shimon and smiled. "You are back again. It has been a while since I saw you. Is something on your mind?"

"Just needed to catch my breath."

"And now you have it?"

Shimon nodded. "Now I have it."

Over the next year, Shimon followed through on his commitment to pray, and focused on the verses from Psalms. Peace, which always had been an interest for him, became more than an interest and more than a mere cause, or even a calling, but a philosophy. A way of viewing the world—Israel, Palestinians, Arabs—and even his own life.

"Constant war," he commented to Yohai, "is not sustainable for Israel."

"I think you've said that before," Yohai needled, harkening back to a time when they were young and used to debate issues like this late into the night.

Shimon grinned. "Only now it means even more than it did back when we were in school. Now I can see for certain, a future of continued conflict would remake the people of Israel into combative, unforgiving, hardened warriors—but warriors only. God has created us for more than that. For a much larger purpose. To be creative, innovative writers, researchers, scientists, doctors. Technology is the coming wave of culture. Israel needs to be at the forefront of the electronic age."

"Business transformed America," Yohai noted. "I suppose it could transform Israel."

"And not just Israel but the entire Middle East. But there's more to it than just technology. We could transform farming and agriculture. Aaron Aaronsohn was a world-class agronomist. We could develop others like him. But to do that, we have to find a way to make peace with our neighbors."

"You know," Yohai suggested, "this sounds really interesting when we talk about it, just the two of us, but very few people see peace as the chief characteristic of our future."

Shimon sighed, "I know."

"And not many see innovation as important. They certainly don't see us as transforming the region. That would mean changing the lifestyle of the Arabs, and most of the people you and I deal with would like to take the Arab lifestyle in the opposite direction."

"They see only war."

"Only conflict."

"Well, I'm sure peace is the right path," Shimon responded, the confidence returning to his voice. "It's the only way we'll ever have a future in which all Israelis can flourish. Not merely survive, but flourish."

"Make the Arabs our friends?" Yohai quipped, reminding them again of what Shimon had said years before.

He nodded. "Yes, make them our friends."

✦ ✦ ✦

In September 1970, Golda Meir moved Shimon from head of the Immigrant Absorption Ministry to the office of minister of transport. The Transport Ministry handled issues regarding development and maintenance of Israel's internal and external transportation system—highways, railways, airports, seaports, and the like.

Shimon understood the importance of infrastructure to Israel's economy. He'd seen the difference between their road system and that of other countries, and he'd seen the way a national highway system had transformed the United States' post-war economy and culture. But he didn't understand why he'd been selected to run that Ministry. He'd never dealt with transportation issues, other than to schedule delivery of weapons. Transportation was about rails, bulldozers, road graders, concrete, and asphalt—or so he thought. News that he was to head that Ministry left him. . . confounded, and after cleaning out his office at Immigrant Absorption, he went to see his old friend Moshe Dayan.

"She did it to make room for Natan Peled," Dayan explained.

"Peled?" Shimon frowned. "Why?"

Dayan shrugged. "He's a party member."

"Do you know him?"

"Sort of. Secretary of a kibbutz, became active in Labor politics, elected to Knesset."

"But he lost his seat in the election."

"She wanted to keep him in the government. Thought he could do the job in Absorption but wasn't sure how he would be a good fit at the other posts."

"And even though I know nothing about roads and bridges, she thought I could handle Transport."

"You have great administrative skills. Nobody disputes that. Not even Golda."

"Just another attempt to keep me out of the way," Shimon groused.

"Keep me out of the way without making you or Ben-Gurion angry. That's all she was trying to do."

Dayan grinned. "You'll take the job, though, right?"

"Yes." Shimon looked over at him. "I'll do it. The roads might never be the same, but I'll take the job."

Dayan rose and walked from behind his desk. "That's the spirit. Come on. Let's get a drink."

Talking to Dayan helped; it always did. He leaned on his friend for support more than he cared to admit, but by the time Shimon returned home that evening he was once again in a dour mood. Sonia cornered him in the bedroom as they prepared for bed. "Out with it," she said.

"Out with what?" he frowned.

"Whatever it is that has you in this mood."

"It's nothing."

"It can't be nothing. What's the matter?"

"It's the same old thing."

"Shimon the Dreamer?"

"No. Not so much that. It's just—"

"You wanted something different from Transportation?"

"I wanted to go back to the Defense Ministry."

"Well, you wanted something different from Immigration and now you have this. So, what happened to peace?"

Shimon was puzzled. "Peace?"

"That all-encompassing cause you were looking for."

He chuckled. "It rather evaporated, I guess."

"It's a choice, Shimon."

"What's a choice?"

"Peace. It's a choice."

"Yes, but—"

"No buts. It's a choice. If it's peace you want, then make the choice—choose peace, then find a way to make it happen. Use that big mind of yours and figure it out." She tossed a pillow toward his side of the bed. "And you could begin by making peace with yourself."

"What does that mean?"

"You are who you are, Shimon. You can't be anyone else. You just have to be you and let everyone else worry about the consequences."

"But is it enough? Me being me. Is it enough?"

She put her arms around him and drew him close. "It's enough for me. More than enough." Then she pulled him over and they tumbled onto the bed.

✦ ✦ ✦

From his first day as minister of transport, Shimon applied himself to the task of learning all there was to know about transportation and infrastructure. He toured highway construction sites, visited seaports, and inspected railroads, bridges, and trestles. And at every turn he viewed it all through the lens of peace, imagining ways to organize the movement of people and goods around the philosophy of cooperation, friendship, and mutual benefit for all who lived within Israel's sphere of influence. At first only a mental exercise, it soon became a challenge he was determined to conquer and it didn't take long to see how the two—as incongruous as they might seem—were actually very much related.

Although generally thought to work with the physical aspects of infrastructure, like most other ministries Transport tended to drift into areas beyond the scope of its initial focus. Movement of farm products naturally involved agriculture. Transportation of finished products involved the manufacturing sector. And activity at seaports or border crossings naturally touched on areas of foreign policy and international affairs. Before the end of his first year in office, Shimon was enmeshed in all those areas and more.

One of the first projects to see the imprint of Shimon's approach was in the development and improvement of border crossings. Checkpoints into and out of Gaza and the West Bank were notorious bottlenecks that delayed traffic at every level. Whether commercial or domestic, vehicle or pedestrian, it all came to a crawl as police and military personnel meticulously inspected every person, truck, or car crossing the border. Shimon convened a series of conferences with representatives from all of those organizations, including counterparts from Gaza and the West Bank, to explore better ways of moving traffic in and out of those areas.

Highway-development projects were under way in both places, but it was easier in West Bank because the region was more politically stable and not the home of as many militant Arab groups. Funding, however, was limited for construction in Arab areas, mostly from a security standpoint. As Shimon would comment often, "If we build better roads, it will only assist Arab terrorists in attacking our towns and villages. They'll be able to hit us and flee more quickly."

After meeting with Arab community leaders during that first year at the Ministry, Shimon realized that trust was the key issue. He remembered his grandfather talking to him about Tolstoy and Tolstoy's ideas for how people should live together. "He spent much of his life trying to reconcile the diverse people of the Russian Empire to each other," his grandfather had instructed. Shimon had spent many hours reading Tolstoy's books and essays, and as he continued to wrestle with how Jews and Arabs might coexist peacefully, he reread those books. When he'd finished with that, he picked up a copy of Mahatma Gandhi's early writings, then moved on to read Thoreau.

All the while, Shimon searched for ways to build bridges of understanding between Jews and Arabs, even as he oversaw the construction and maintenance of roads, bridges, and other forms of transportation. Finally, he turned to Yohai, who came with him first to Immigrant Absorption and then over to Transport, and assigned him the task of finding practical ways to develop relationships between Jews and Arabs.

Shimon outlined the issue he wanted to address. "They don't trust us, and we don't trust them. I'm not sure where we could begin but there must be some trust somewhere in our society. At some level. It might be way down, in the simplest form. But somewhere there must be some activity, some common endeavor, something that we all do, where they trust us and we trust them. Find out where that is and come up with ways to build on it."

A month or two later, Yohai came back with an answer. "Sports," he announced. "That's what you're looking for. Baseball, to be specific. Baseball for children. That's the most common place where people trust each other."

"They have teams that play each other?"

Yohai shook his head. "Not teams. But they play the game in the neighborhoods and they don't care who is Arab and who is Jewish. They only think about who can hit, who can pitch, who can run."

"So, we need to play baseball? Would we organize it? Gaza versus Tel Aviv? Or... what?"

"To work, we'd need to do it like they're already doing it. Arab kids and Jewish kids all mixed up together. Not an Arab team against a Jewish team. That would simply be a rehearsal of what we already have—one group against the other. This would be something different. A game where the players aren't divided by their ethnic origin. And we wouldn't want to over-organize it, either. More like helping them, not forcing them."

Shimon liked the idea. "Okay, how do we do it?"

"I was thinking we could make baseball fields part of the road and highway grid."

"We already include parks, right?"

"Yes. If those parks included baseball fields, we could build them all over the country."

"Okay," Shimon replied, thinking through the details.

"But," Yohai cautioned, "there's one problem."

"What's that?"

"We need to convince kids to play there."

Shimon had a twinkle in his eye. "I can take care of that."

23

SHIMON PERES

"I never was after money. It never attracted me."

WHILE SHIMON WORKED with Immigrant Absorption and Transportation, events in the Middle East continued to move the region toward change. Energized by sentiments with deep historic roots, compounded by momentum long in the making, those events unfolded in a cascading effect that propelled everyone toward an increasingly uncertain future.

Beginning in 1948, when Palestinian refugees fled to Jordan during the Israeli War of Independence, Palestinian Arabs steadily gained political influence in Jordan. The Muslim Brotherhood did its best to exploit that growing political advantage but the Brotherhood was active throughout the region, not solely in Palestine. In addition, the Brotherhood was a readily identifiable entity, its actions easily observed, all of which afforded King Hussein ample opportunity to blunt its effectiveness.

In 1964, however, the Arab League founded the Palestinian Liberation Organization—known by the acronym PLO—which was specifically created to represent Palestinian Arabs. The PLO's primary goal was the establishment of a homeland for Palestinians and it was dedicated to an armed struggle against Israel to accomplish that objective. That bolder, more militant approach seemed to catch the spirit of the times and the PLO grew rapidly, quickly eclipsing the Muslim Brotherhood as the dominant influence among Palestinians. Capitalizing on the large Palestinian population living in Jordan, and casting King Hussein as out of step with the prevailing Arab sentiment, the PLO became active in Jordanian politics, entering its own slate of candidates for elected offices. Backed by its Palestinian majority, the PLO quickly won control of almost half the seats in the Jordanian parliament. Some of those officials were appointed to ministerial positions in the Jordanian cabinet.

With its widespread popularity among the public, and with the support of Nasser and leaders of other Arab countries, the PLO became increasingly militant. Members were organized into armed units that patrolled the streets of western Jordanian cities and towns. It established an alternative passport system, set up checkpoints to enforce its own regulations, and authorized raids on nearby Israeli towns and villages.

During the 1967 War, Israeli troops entered Jordan and destroyed several PLO camps and training facilities. The PLO responded by moving its operations deep into the Jordanian mountains, where it became firmly entrenched. It also acquired more sophisticated weapons and turned increasingly toward acts of terrorism as a means of exerting its influence.

Throughout the remainder of the 1960s the situation in Jordan grew increasingly worse and in September 1970, the PLO attempted to assassinate King Hussein. Hussein responded by declaring martial law and conducting military operations against the PLO. For a time, Jordan teetered on the edge of civil war, but after a prolonged struggle the Jordanian army defeated the PLO and forced its members to flee the country. In the aftermath, the PLO moved its headquarters and base of operation to Lebanon.

Meanwhile, in the fall of 1970, Nasser died and Anwar Sadat became president of Egypt. Abba Eban, Israel's foreign affairs minister, believed Sadat was more open to peace talks than even Nasser had been. He also thought the situation in Egypt had changed enough to permit those talks to go forward. On his own initiative, Eban broached the subject through several mutual acquaintances at the United Nations. Sadat's representatives indicated some interest and the two sides began secret preliminary discussions.

As those secret meetings progressed, Eban briefed Golda Meir and asked about raising the nature of their conversation to a more actionable level, perhaps involving Sadat himself. Meir was willing to address issues regarding the Sinai, which Israel had occupied since the war of 1967, but only at a ministerial level. At the same time, she made it clear she wasn't interested in exploring any other topics.

Talks continued to move forward and eventually, at the request of both sides, the United States introduced a proposal to the United Nations, calling for negotiations between Egypt and Israel with the help of a mediator. The General Assembly adopted that request as a formal resolution and appointed Gunnar Jarring to mediate. His efforts to move the parties toward peace became known as the Jarring Mission.

Negotiating sessions with Jarring were held alternately in Israel and Egypt. As talks proceeded, the Israeli delegation indicated its willingness to address Sinai issues and put forward proposals to that effect. Sadat, however, insisted they also discuss removal of IDF troops from Gaza and the West Bank. That was precisely the kind of broadening of the discussion that Meir wanted to avoid. Eban attempted to work around it in order to keep the talks on track. Doing so, however, proved difficult.

Then, at a meeting in Cairo, Sadat went further, stating that IDF withdrawal from Sinai and from the West Bank was a precondition to discussions of peace between the two nations. Meir was categorically opposed to withdrawal as a condition for talks, rejected the proposal out of hand, and withdrew from further negotiations.

Two years later, in the summer of 1972, the Summer Olympic Games were held in Munich, West Germany. During those games, the Olympic Village, the site where athletes and coaches lived, was attacked by eight members of Black September, a Palestinian terrorist group. Eleven members of the Israeli Olympic team were taken hostage. West German police attempted a rescue, which failed, and in the course of that attempt the eleven Israeli hostages were massacred.

German police, though poorly equipped to address the situation, killed five of the eight terrorists. The other three were captured and taken into custody. However, a few months later the three terrorists were released by West German authorities in an exchange toward resolving the hijacking of a Lufthansa airline flight. Golda Meir responded by ordering Mossad to track down and kill Black September members, which they did.

Meanwhile, Sadat indicated a willingness to restart talks over the Sinai. As an initial proposal, he offered to recognize Israel's rights as an independent state, in accord with UN resolutions, in exchange for an Israeli withdrawal from the Sinai. Various ideas were proposed but ultimately Meir refused them all and in the weeks that followed, tensions in the region began to rise.

At the time, Israeli defense policy was built around the notion of a preemptive first-strike capability as key to the nation's survival. That first-strike perspective required advance warning, and Israeli intelligence was thought to be capable of giving the government a forty-eight-hour notice of any potential attack. That was more than enough to mobilize IDF units. This strategic policy was a well-known fact, though the details of defense planning and strategy were closely guarded secrets.

With tensions between Israel and Egypt rising, President Richard Nixon and Henry Kissinger, his national security adviser, were worried that Israel's defense policy might start a war that would engulf the entire MiddleEast. In separate messages, both men warned Meir not to initiate hostilities. Heeding that warning meant refraining from a first strike, which left the nation vulnerable to attack by its neighbors. Even so, Meir's advisers assured her that Israeli intelligence still could give adequate warning of any pending attack.

By the fall of 1973, with no progress on negotiating an end to

Israeli occupation of the Sinai, Sadat decided to force a solution. In October of that year, Egypt led a coalition of troops from Syria, Iraq, Jordan, Saudi Arabia, Algeria, and Morocco in a surprise attack against Israel, crossing cease-fire lines in both the Sinai and Golan Heights. The sneak attack, which came during the Jewish celebration of Yom Kippur, caught Israel totally off guard. In the initial hours, Arab forces made great inroads into Israeli-held territory. IDF units responded, however, and mounted a counter-strike.

While fighting raged, citizens and government officials alike voiced their anger at the early success of Arab forces. Many questioned why Meir hadn't launched a preemptive attack, as had occurred in 1967. Accusations against her came even from members of the Knesset, and when representatives began raising their arguments on the floor, Shimon got angry. "I've had enough of this!" he shouted as he rose to take the floor.

"Some of you," Shimon began, "who are attacking the prime minister the loudest and the most vehemently should stop to consider this: If we had attacked first we would have been seen by everyone in the world as the aggressor. Leaders from around the world who have already made that position known in public addresses—remarks that members of this body would have known if they'd bothered to read the newspapers—have made their position on that matter quite clear and unmistakable. Had we attacked first, we would have been castigated by them as unruly aggressors, and isolated by the rest of the world."

"We've been isolated all along," someone shouted.

"We have not been isolated," Shimon countered. "Our weapons come from France, from Czechoslovakia, and from the United States—countries that would have withdrawn their support had we attacked first. All the countries that supply us with the weapons we need to defend ourselves would have refused to sell to us. Can we fight without weapons? We cannot survive as a nation without the support of our allies. And sometimes we must act in accordance with the wishes of our friends. We cannot always insist on our own way and expect everyone to accommodate us."

"Shimon would put our families at risk," someone shouted. "Solely for the sake of the praise of the United States."

"We are not putting our families at risk," Shimon argued. "We are acting like a responsible nation of self-governing people who have a mind and aren't afraid to use it."

"Now he is attacking—"

"Listen to me," Shimon interrupted. "Our intelligence service spotted the threat. Our military responded to the threat. We have suffered no greater harm than had we attacked first. And now the world sees the Arabs as the aggressor we've always known them to be. Yes, we are in a position we've not been in since the war for independence. It is an uncomfortable position with Egyptian troops crossing the border. But our position as a nation is in a far better strategic position than we've ever been. And when our troops have repelled the Arabs, driving them back on every front, the world will know that we are fully capable of defending ourselves. And they will know that the Arabs are the unjust parties to the issues that remain between us."

As he spoke, Shimon's remarks appeared on a television screen in the prime minister's office and an assistant brought them to Meir's attention. She watched in silence but when Shimon finished she responded with a smile. "Perhaps I have misunderstood him after all."

Public animosity—and even the ire of some Israeli officials—also turned on Moshe Dayan, who as defense minister was seen as equally responsible for Israel's military situation, a position viewed as both a risk and an embarrassment. Criticism against him came from within the Labor Party, too, and Dayan was deeply offended. Frustrated and angry, he appeared at Shimon's office one evening and dropped onto a chair in front of the desk.

"You look beat," Shimon chided. "Fighting a war wears you out?"

"Fighting the Arabs I can handle," Dayan responded. "It's the Jews who are killing me."

Shimon shook his head in disbelief. "Have you ever heard of anything like this?"

"I heard Golda was pleased with what you said the other day."

Shimon grimaced. "Sometimes the Knesset can be a great place. And other times it's a collection of whiners."

"Well, I doubt she'll ever say anything to you directly, but I heard she was pleased and said maybe she'd misunderstood you after all."

"She's right," Shimon frowned. "She has misunderstood me."

"People always see things from their own perspective." Dayan sighed. "And they have such short memories."

"They aren't on the inside," Shimon said, turning to the trouble Dayan first raised. "The public doesn't know what you know. And what they *do* know they don't understand. You couldn't have done anything about the situation even if you'd wanted to. Not without Golda's authorization."

Dayan wasn't satisfied. "The public might not know, but they ought to remember. Six years ago, they sang my praises. Said I should be prime minister. Now they turn on me."

"Politicians are just as fickle."

Dayan raised his voice suddenly, "The party! What a waste." He slumped back in the chair and lowered his voice. "You should never become a politician, Shimon." He wagged his finger in a cautioning gesture. "Never become a politician. Give yourself to diplomacy. Leave the politics to someone else. Someone without a heart or a mind."

"It wouldn't matter."

"What do you mean?"

"When things go wrong everyone gets blamed, regardless of their true connection to events."

"Don't I know it!"

"And they'll find a way to pin all this on me before it's over. Especially now that I've spoken up."

"Do you regret it?" Dayan asked

"Speaking up?"

"Yeah. Do you regret taking up for her?"

"Not one word."

"Then what they say doesn't matter. Let them complain. They can always vote for someone else next time."

"And I would say the same to you." Shimon stood. "Come on."

"Where are we going?"

"Somewhere besides here."

"I have a war to oversee."

Shimon slipped on his jacket and started toward the door. "After we get a drink."

Dayan grinned. "That's a good idea." He followed Shimon out into the hall.

By the end of October, Israeli forces had regained control of the war and advanced across the Sinai Peninsula to a point beyond the Suez Canal. In the north, the IDF expelled the Syrian army from the Golan Heights and once again maintained the position it held at the end of the war in 1967. With Israel proving once again that her Arab neighbors were both the aggressor and outmatched by the IDF, the Soviet Union and the United States launched a joint effort to broker a cease-fire through the United Nations. After a flurry of diplomatic meetings, an agreement was finally reached that halted the fighting and opened the way for preliminary talks on a permanent agreement.

While those talks were under way, an Israeli national commission of inquiry—known as the Agranat Commission—was established to investigate the manner in which Israeli officials conducted the war and to determine why Israel had been caught so completely by surprise. And, to further compound domestic political life, a general election was held in Israel. When the result was tabulated, Meir was returned to office as prime minister, but dissatisfaction with the government's handling of the war still ran high.

In mid-November, David Ben-Gurion suffered a stroke and was taken to a hospital in Tel HaShomer. At first, he was well enough to receive visitors but then his condition began to deteriorate and he declined rapidly. He died on December 1 and was buried at Sde Boker in a grave next to his wife, Paula, who had passed away a few years earlier. His funeral was attended by the entire cabinet. He was mourned by the entire nation of Israel.

Ben-Gurion's death marked the beginning of the end for an era that had been dominated by larger-than-life figures. Heroic men and women who came to Palestine, sight unseen, and carved out a nation with, almost literally, their bare hands from land many deemed uninhabitable and against opposition many thought insurmountable. Ben-Gurion had been a dreamer, of sorts—he would have described himself as a visionary—but with a practical perspective. An appreciation of the ever-present distance between what one might wish to obtain and what can realistically be achieved. He took the dream of a Jewish homeland and, often by the force of his own personality, made that dream a reality. The nation he helped found was not perfect, nor was it everything all of the disparate factions wanted it to be, but it was a nation, it was decidedly Jewish, and it was free.

Later that month, after Ben-Gurion was laid to rest and while the Agranat Commission continued to delve into Israeli domestic affairs, a formal peace summit was convened in Geneva as an international attempt to resolve matters regarding Israel and her neighbors. The summit was sponsored jointly by the United States and the Soviet Union. A further extension of the previous cease-fire talks, all parties—Israel and members of the Arab League—were invited to attend. Egypt and Israel sent delegations, as did Jordan, but Syria refused to participate. Nevertheless, the meetings proceeded as scheduled and continued into January, but the summit ultimately adjourned without making notable headway.

Undaunted by the lack of progress in Geneva, Henry Kissinger sensed that an agreement between Israel and Egypt remained a viable possibility. Acting on behalf of the United States, he continued to work for a permanent agreement between those two parties, shuttling from one capital to another, negotiating terms and conditions, inching the parties along on an incremental basis.

Through that work, leadership in both Egypt and Israel came to realize that their most recent war, known by then as the Yom Kippur War, had changed the context between them. It provided enough of an Egyptian victory to permit Sadat to reach an agreement with dignity.

He'd flexed his military might and had vindicated, after a fashion, his country's embarrassment over Israeli occupation of the Sinai, an area Egypt rightly claimed as its own. From an Israeli perspective, the war also had been enough of an Egyptian defeat to show Egyptian officials, and the Egyptian public, that they would never be able to impose their will on Israel by force.

Early in 1974, Kissinger's efforts at shuttle diplomacy paid off when Egypt and Israel reached an agreement, known as the Sinai Separation of Forces Agreement. Under that arrangement, Israel withdrew from beyond the Suez Canal, creating a security zone between the two armies. Israel still controlled most of the peninsula, but the armies were separated far enough to prevent incidental contact and the cease-fire became permanent.

The following April, the Agranat Commission released its interim report, which called for the dismissal of four high-ranking Israeli military intelligence officers and Dado Elazar, IDF chief of staff at the time of the war. The report was controversial and protestors took to the streets to vent their displeasure. Public demonstrations created an uproar so intense and widespread and of such a duration that Golda Meir, though not directly implicated by the report—and ultimately exonerated in the final version—resigned from office as prime minister.

At the time of her resignation, Golda had lived in Palestine for more than fifty years. She'd been involved in building a Jewish homeland as long as anyone then alive, most of that involvement spent at the heart of the effort to form an independent Jewish state. Her exit from office, coming on the heels of Ben-Gurion's death, was yet one more reminder that the country was leaving its founding era.

When Meir assigned Shimon to Immigrant Absorption and later to the Ministry of Transport, he had not been happy. He'd seen it as a demotion and an attempt to move him out of the way. But as she left office he realized that, without intending to do so, Meir had done him a huge favor, at least politically if not personally. He would have rather been at the Defense Ministry embroiled in the thick of the fight, but by being at the Ministry of Transport, most of the controversy over the

Yom Kippur War had passed him by. While others came away from that conflict with their careers in tatters, Shimon looked forward to the future with hope, peace, and the sense that perhaps now he could get back to working in areas of the government where he had the most experience—in defense and foreign affairs. The two areas he was certain would be at the center of whatever the next decade might bring.

SHIMON PERES

*"The problem of the Middle East is
poverty more than politics."*

IN JUNE 1974, the Labor Party held an election to determine
Golda Meir's replacement. Yitzhak Rabin and Shimon ran as candidates for the post. Though the two men were roughly the same age,
they had come to that moment by quite different paths.

Shimon was born in Poland and immigrated in the 1930s. Rabin
was born in Jerusalem and grew up in Palestine. Shimon had been
raised in a household that valued education and learning, while Rabin
had been raised in a Labor Zionist home that valued agriculture,
farming, and the redemptive nature of work. Although Shimon had
been involved in every aspect of Israel's history from the War of Independence to the present, his involvement had been from a desk at
headquarters in Tel Aviv. Rabin, on the other hand, had spent almost
thirty years in the military. He fought in the War of Independence,
rose through the ranks, and became IDF chief of staff.

Rabin was supported by the party machine. Establishment people;
contemporaries of Ben-Gurion and the founding generation who felt
it was their right to pull the levers of power. Of the two, they saw

Rabin as much more like themselves, or rather how they wanted to see themselves; a war hero, rising through the ranks, leading the troops in battle.

Though he'd been at the heart of Israeli politics all his life, Shimon was seen by many as an outsider. In a version of the way he'd been treated since childhood, the charitable ones referred to him as a dreamer, obsessed with lofty ideals, always looking off into the future. Less polite members, those who were put off by his natural ability to see and empathize with all sides of an issue, thought of him as duplicitous. Someone who would say one thing to one group and something else to another. It was true, Shimon really could see all sides of an argument and not merely understand alternate views on an issue but empathize with those who held them. And that, more than anything else, was the thing that made the difference in the race. Rabin knew how to cast complex issues in concise, yes-or-no terms. You're with us; you're against us. No equivocation.

During the party's short but intense campaign season, Shimon relied heavily on Yohai Cohen. Yohai worked tirelessly and was unflaggingly loyal, but he knew very little about politics and was equally as solicitous of others as Shimon. By then, Shimon had decided that if he wanted to move Israel forward on the thornier issues—finding peace with her neighbors, resolving the Palestinian issues, and developing an innovative, transformative economy—he needed to become prime minister. Policy, he'd seen, worked best when it emanated from the top down rather than from the bottom up. If he weren't in charge, he'd always be misunderstood, opposed, castigated, and cast aside. But to have a successful political career, he needed the help of a fresh perspective. Someone whose skills added the things he lacked.

One night after a rigorous round of speeches, Shimon ran into Menashe Beinart in the restaurant at the King David Hotel. Beinart, a journalist, was covering the election for *Davar*, one of the daily newspapers.

"We have something in common," Beinart opined.

"Oh? What's that?"

"I write for *Davar*, a newspaper co-founded by your friend Berl Katznelson."

Shimon's face brightened at the mention of his old friend and mentor. "That's right, but you're too young to have known him." Beinart was easily twenty years younger than Shimon.

Beinart shook his head. "No, Katznelson died before I came along. But they still tell stories about him sometimes at the office."

"And well they should. He was a remarkable man."

Beinart took a sip of coffee and changed subjects. "You know, this would be a different campaign if Golda had served out her term."

"Not if she chose to run again," Shimon responded.

Beinart again shook his head. "I don't think she would have done that."

"Why not?" Shimon was of the same opinion but wanted to hear what Beinart might say on the topic.

"I think Ben-Gurion's death, the public protest over the war, all of it sort of highlighted for her that the times have changed. It's not like it was before."

"I can't imagine her being concerned about that."

Beinart shrugged. "Maybe, but she's not the young lady she was when you were coming up. And I think all this helped her realize that."

"You might be right."

"And," Beinart continued, "she's had some health problems."

"I know."

"That's the kind of thing that gives a person a different perspective."

Shimon changed the subject. "What do you think of the campaign we actually have?"

"It's an odd mix in a way. The old guys still can't accept you."

"I know."

"They think you're one of Ben-Gurion's young men. That he reached over them to appoint you to places that should have been theirs."

Shimon nodded and repeated the comment he had heard said previously, "I should have waited my turn."

"Yes, but they support Rabin. Who happens to be a man of almost the exact same age as you."

"But he wasn't that close to the old man."

"Right. Still, it's odd. The old guys don't like you because you're seen as one of the young guys who was lifted past them. But they support a young guy who has also surpassed them."

Shimon lifted his gaze to look past Beinart and the tone of his voice became more distant. "They like Rabin because they think of him as a man's man. Me, they think of as someone who rose to the top by manipulating the system. By swaying Ben-Gurion."

"They could say the same thing about Moshe Dayan," Beinart noted.

"Yes," Shimon agreed, returning to the moment. "And they do. Except that he won battles for them, which seems to temper their opinion."

"Well. . . perhaps. . . until now."

"Yeah." Shimon sighed and leaned back in his chair. "We won the war with Egypt. And Moshe is a big reason we did. But the way people complain, you'd think we lost." He leaned forward suddenly. "Yet we won. Our troops pushed the Egyptians back below the Suez Canal."

"I guess the public thinks they live in a free and open society. One that really does allow them to voice their opinion."

Shimon felt a flash of anger, then just as quickly realized Beinart had made a point. He leaned back in his chair once more and assumed a relaxed position. "Yes, I suppose they do."

"Ben-Gurion liked you both. You and Dayan."

"You knew Ben-Gurion?"

"I met him a few times. Interviewed him once or twice. Nothing extensive. Just to get a quote for a story."

Shimon smiled. "He liked us. But there again, Moshe earned his notoriety on the battlefield. I won mine from the safety of an office," he chuckled. "Though a few times it didn't feel so safe."

"Do you feel it when people say that? When they say those things, does it sting?"

"I think each of us serves with the gifts we have. We each live our lives as opportunities open up to us. Moshe Dayan is well suited for the life he lives." He looked over at Beinart. "As are you."

Beinart grinned. "But then, I'm a guy who served at IDF headquarters during a war, too."

Shimon's eyes brightened with interest. "You were at headquarters?"

"Yes, I was a journalist before the war, so when fighting started they put me in a job that suited my situation."

They continued to talk for almost an hour and Shimon came away impressed. Beinart seemed to understand politics and people and wasn't afraid to say what he thought about either. Shimon made a note to remember him as someone who might be helpful in the future. It didn't take long for him to find that use.

Yitzhak Rabin won the Labor Party election, but only by two percent of the vote. The narrowness of that victory was something Rabin couldn't ignore and forced him to give Shimon a significant position in the government. Initially he appointed Shimon as information minister, a post primarily responsible for communicating with Jews who lived outside Israel. Two weeks after taking office, Shimon invited Beinart to lunch where he offered the reporter a job working for the Ministry. "I've been a minister. I know how to run an office," Shimon said. "But I don't know much about media or how to use it effectively. I need some help."

"I think you need to work your job in at least two directions."

The comment seemed odd to Shimon. "What do you mean?"

"There's the obvious need to communicate Israel's position, policy, and priorities to the Diaspora abroad. But you also need to communicate yourself to the nation and to your fellow ministers."

"Why?"

"Think of this. Yehoshua Rabinowitz was your teacher back in Poland, wasn't he?"

"Yes."

"He's now been appointed minister of finance. He's your peer in the cabinet," Beinart noted, "but he has known you since you were a child. He was your teacher. He's at least twenty-five years older than you."

"Okay. What about it?"

"You are serving as a contemporary with many others who are much older than you—some, like Rabinowitz, who was your teacher and mentor, and some who see you as operating above the station normally given someone of your age or experience. The whole complaint we've discussed before that you wouldn't be so high in government if Ben-Gurion hadn't promoted you."

"But I'm the same age as the prime minister they seem to adore."

"I know. But not in their minds," Beinart emphasized. "And that's my point. You need to communicate this to your fellow ministers, without doing it in an obvious manner."

"That gets me in trouble, too."

"Shimon the Manipulator?"

"That's what they'll say. The kinder ones. Others will say something worse."

"It's important to change this internal conversation. Their perception of you encourages gossip about how you were handpicked by Ben-Gurion, don't know your place—that kind of thing. And it leaves you open to unfounded accusations when things go wrong. That's how you got swept up in the Lavon Affair and how you were sideswiped by the controversy over the war with Egypt, even though you weren't even part of the Defense Ministry at the time. They say things about you and it sticks because those accusations fit with the ongoing conversation some of them have about you every day, good times and bad. You need to change that conversation."

"They'll believe I had something to do with it because I'm the dreamer, liar, and a cheat."

"Right."

Shimon smiled. "See, I told you I needed you, and you just proved my point. Come work for me."

Beinart took the job with Shimon and began organizing the Information Ministry around his ideas for how best to communicate their message. In June, however, Rabin moved Shimon to minister of defense, an area in which he had worked most of his professional career. He was excited to be returning to familiar territory and convinced Beinart to join him in that work. Mordechai Gur served at the time as IDF chief of staff.

The campaign and election to succeed Golda Meir left Rabin and Shimon rivals in the Labor Party—sometimes bitter rivals. That, in turn, made them deeply suspicious of each other. So much so that they found it difficult to work together.

After witnessing several confrontations between the two men, Beinart realized something had to be done to change the situation. While Shimon was away on a trip to France, Beinart went in search of Sonia. He found her at the hospital where she worked as a volunteer on the children's ward. They met in a dayroom at the end of the hall.

"He likes you, you know," Sonia commented. "Talks about you all the time. . . when I get to see him."

"He's away a lot."

"Yes, he is. But this is the life we have chosen. I detest politics. He loves it." She shrugged. "What can I do? I love him."

"I was wondering if you could help me," Beinart said, steering the conversation to the topic he wanted to discuss."

"How could I possibly help you?"

"Shimon and Rabin. . . they don't. . . "

"They don't like each other. I know."

"Well, that's just it. Do they really not like each other?"

"Actually, Shimon likes Rabin and he doesn't like Rabin, at the same time."

"That's what I'm trying to understand."

"Shimon knows Rabin is a good man. And that he wants the best for the country. But they can't both be prime minister. And Rabin is liked by all the people who hate Shimon. So it is tough for Shimon to let himself like Rabin."

"How can I work things out between them?"

Sonia shook her head. "You can't. It is impossible to untangle that knot."

"I was wondering. Do they have anything in common? Maybe someone they both know and trust?"

Sonia thought for a moment. "Giora Eini," she said finally.

"The lawyer?"

"Yes. Giora is a friend of Rabin and a friend of Shimon. And Giora is an honorable man. A lawyer," she added wryly, "but a good man just the same."

Beinart met with Giora, and together they worked out a plan to slowly interject Giora as a mediator between Shimon and Rabin. He understood both men well and, working patiently, began to smooth out some of the difficulties between them, bringing them to a working relationship that allowed both men to do their job successfully. They still were rivals, but rivals with a deeper understanding of each other.

As minister of defense, Shimon once again focused on rebuilding and strengthening IDF. Arms acquisition, replenishment, upgrading. Insuring their reserve stores were adequate. But Shimon was now a man committed to peace and he looked for ways to use his role as defense minister to further the goal of regional peace. One of Shimon's first attempts toward peace was with Jordan.

Ben-Gurion had wanted an agreement with at least one of Israel's neighbors as a way of eliminating an enemy. He thought King Abdullah was the most likely prospect, but when Abdullah was assassinated and replaced by his grandson, King Hussein, the younger king seemed even more likely to reach an agreement than his predecessor.

Reaching that agreement had been complicated by regional Arab politics. It was also a painfully tedious process and each of their previous efforts had failed. But years had passed since then and things had changed. Shimon thought he might have another try at it. This time, however, he would try a different approach. One that drew on his grandfather's teaching about the four levels of meaning and the patient approach he'd learned from Berl Katznelson—using this, to influence that, to make something else open up.

To put his plan into effect with Jordan, Shimon decided to open a dialogue with Zaid Rifai, Jordan's prime minister. First, though, he needed research, and for that he turned to Beinart.

"We need information on Zaid Rifai," Shimon ordered.

"The Jordanian prime minster?"

"Yes."

"What kind of information do you want?"

"Whatever you can find."

"Can you tell me what you want to do with it?"

"I want to meet with him. I just need to find the point at which I should engage him. Something that has nothing to do with Israel or Jordan or anything else."

"Oh," Beinart replied with a look of realization. "Okay. That I can do."

A week later Beinart returned with an answer. "Rifai's mother has been ill. She's in a New York hospital right now. Probably getting out soon. But that's the thing you're looking for."

Shimon nodded, "That's what I need."

Rifai and Shimon were scheduled to attend a UN conference set for New York. With the help of two intelligence officers and a London travel agent, Shimon determined the hotel where Rifai was staying. One afternoon between conference sessions, he waited in the hotel lobby until Rifai appeared. The two knew each other from Shimon's work as minister of absorption. It wasn't difficult for Shimon get past the security detail and approach him.

After a brief conversation, Shimon and Rifai agreed to meet in a conference room at the United Nations building following the end of the upcoming session. Their conversation that evening was cordial and mostly about things that mattered little to anyone else. Children. Families. And, finally, Rifai's mother. Rifai seemed surprised Shimon knew of her condition and talked about her at length. Apparently, he'd been close to her all his life and her illness had hit him hard. The two men connected at a new and more significant level than ever before.

Just before they parted, Shimon raised the topic he'd come to address. "I think we should meet again," he suggested. "After we get back home."

"Yes," Rifai replied. "I would enjoy that very much."

"I will have someone contact your office."

"Very well. We shall be awaiting your call."

When Shimon returned home he instructed Beinart to contact Rifai's office and arrange a meeting. "Should we alert the Foreign Ministry?" Beinart asked.

"No, this isn't about foreign affairs."

Beinart looked puzzled. "Then what is it about?"

Shimon had a twinkle in his eye. "Defense. It's about defense."

A few days later, Shimon and Rifai met for lunch at a residence in East Jerusalem. Afterward, they sat in the front room of the house and discussed mutual issues—Palestinian dissatisfaction with conditions in Gaza, organizations operating in the area, their increasingly militant nature, and the threat all of that posed to both Israel and Jordan.

As they were about to depart, Shimon suggested, "We should do this again."

Refai replied, "Yes, perhaps on a regular basis."

"I would like that. Do you think King Hussein would ever agree to join us?"

"He might. . . " Rifai said tentatively. "But what would we talk about with him?"

"Our countries made a lot of progress in understanding each other. He talked with Golda Meir and with Ben-Gurion. Perhaps he would like to continue those talks through me."

"Perhaps he might. I will pass along the message."

In the spring, Shimon received a message from Rifai indicating King Hussein would meet with him, but only at a location inside Jordan. Shimon, using Beinart as an intermediary, arranged the meeting for later that summer at a resort in Aqaba. Shimon was accompanied by Beinart, Hussein was accompanied by Rifai. They discussed their mutual interests and the obstacles they faced in reaching an agreement. Nothing of any real substance came from the meeting, but both sides left feeling confident that progress could be made in relations between the two countries.

✦ ✦ ✦

Beginning in the second half of the year, two events occurred outside Israel that would have an effect on events in the region. The first, which happened near the end of the summer that year, was the resignation of US president Richard Nixon. He'd spent much of his second term under the pall of corruption allegations, and that August the US Congress voted to approve articles of impeachment. Nixon resigned from office rather than face legal proceedings to force his removal. Vice President Gerald Ford replaced him. The transition disrupted US participation in Middle East peace efforts, leaving the parties there to continue on their own.

The second event occurred in April 1975, when conflict broke out in Lebanon between the PLO, which had fled there after being expelled from Jordan, and Kataeb Regulatory Forces. Fighting spread to Beirut and soon escalated into a full-scale civil war, which became known as the Lebanese Civil War. Lebanon was not a strategic challenge to Israel but the dispute affected Israel nonetheless, especially northern Galilee.

Later that year, the peace process continued to move toward a broader resolution of the Israeli–Egyptian conflict. The work of hammering out an agreement was conducted by the parties themselves. Rabin, Yigal Allon, who was the Israeli foreign minister, and Shimon were the primary participants for Israel. The key disagreement was over where to locate the line of disengagement.

After a lengthy process, talks between the Egyptian and Israeli delegations resulted in the Sinai Interim Agreement, which was agreed to in Geneva on September 4, 1975. Representatives from the United

States were present for the signing as a matter of courtesy and with an eye toward participation in the process going forward. As an interim agreement, the accord addressed two areas. It obligated the parties to resolve future differences by peaceful means, not by military conflict, and it required further withdrawal of Israeli forces from the Sinai. It wasn't a complete resolution by any means but it was a step forward. As Shimon had learned long ago, "A move here, to get us to there, so we can ultimately reach a third spot."

By 1976, fighting in Lebanon pushed the country toward total collapse. Sensing it might be threatened by that demise, Syrian troops advanced across the border and entered Lebanon under the guise of helping to stabilize the situation. Fighting continued, however, and in March, Lebanese president Suleiman Frangieh asked Syria to formally intervene on a broader scale.

In May of that year, and in spite of the ongoing war, Lebanon held its previously scheduled presidential election. Elias Sarkis won the election but Frangieh refused to step down. Fighting grew more intense. As a result, Syria stepped up its military operation in Lebanon and began purging the country of leftist organizations.

Although Israel and Syria were actually on the same side in the conflict—they both supported groups loyal to the Lebanese government and opposed the PLO—the advance of Syrian troops southward through Lebanon alarmed many in Israel as those troops moved toward the border. Because of that, Israel imposed a red line across southern Lebanon beyond which Syrian troops would not be allowed to advance. Once again, the region moved toward war, this time on Israel's northern border.

SHIMON PERES

*"I felt that if I could make the world
better for the young, that would be
the greatest we could do."*

ON JUNE 27, 1976, Mordechai Gur rushed into Shimon's office. "There's been a hijacking."

"Where?"

"An Air France flight from Athens to Paris."

"Why is that a problem for us?"

"The flight originated here. In Tel Aviv. It left here with almost two hundred fifty people on board."

Shimon sank back in his chair. "They're targeting Jews."

"It looks that way."

"Where is the plane now?"

"They've diverted it to Benghazi."

"Any idea who the hijackers are?"

"Our information indicates the plane was taken by four terrorists. Two from the Popular Front for the Liberation of Palestine and—"

"Why am I not surprised?" Shimon interrupted.

"And two more from Revolutionary Cells. It's a German group.

"Think Benghazi is their ultimate destination?"

"I doubt it. Libya hasn't shown any interest in this sort of thing. I think they'll only be there a short time. And that's assuming the Libyans will even allow them to land."

"We should call someone and get them to allow it."

"We want them to land there?"

"We need to string this out. Give them room. Let them tell the world what they want."

"I think we know what they want."

"Yeah. They want us gone. Have we confirmed the hijackers' identities?"

"We're doing that now. We should think about how to coordinate this."

"Let's use the command center for now. Use it as a clearinghouse for information. That way we can relay it to the other ministries without sending the raw information to everyone. At least for now."

"I'll get moving on it."

The airplane landed in Libya and was there for seven hours. One passenger was released for medical reasons, then the plane took off to Entebbe, Uganda. While the plane was en route, Gur returned with confirmation of the hijackers' identities and of the passengers. "Eight-five of them are ours. Israeli citizens."

"The PLO won't care about nuances of citizenship. If they're Israeli, they're Jews today." Shimon thought for a moment. "Do we have people in Entebbe?"

"Yes. We've alerted them. They're preparing now to be at the airport before the plane arrives. They'll be able to feed us on-site intelligence in an hour or so."

"Good. We'll need to brief the prime minister on what we know."

"Is anyone else working this?"

"The Foreign Ministry is trying to establish diplomatic contact but that's rather difficult right now. Uganda isn't very friendly with us, and the PLO. . . well. . . you know what we're up against there."

"Right. We'll make sure our people are covering as much as possible."

A few hours later, the hijacked airliner landed at the Entebbe airport. Passengers were removed from the aircraft and herded into an abandoned terminal building. Not long after that, the attackers announced their demand of $5 million for the return of the airplane. For the hostages they wanted the release of fifty-three Palestinian militants. Forty of the people they wanted released were being held in Israeli prisons. The hijackers set a date of July 1 for compliance. After that, they announced that they intended to start killing the hostages.

When news of the attack and demands reached the Rabin government, a debate ensued over whether to negotiate or attempt a rescue. Rabin favored negotiating. Shimon favored a military rescue. At their initial cabinet meeting, Mordechai Gur presented a rescue proposal that called for an assault on the airport from Lake Victoria. The plan included use of a naval commando unit thought to include troops who were specifically trained and equipped for such an operation. That plan, however, relied on the Ugandan government for return of the men after the rescue had been launched. After hearing Gur's presentation, the cabinet dismissed it as too complex and tenuous.

"I will consider a military rescue," Rabin ventured. "But only if it is workable and has a reasonable chance of success."

After the cabinet meeting, Rabin and Yigal Allon, along with Allon's staff at the Foreign Ministry, went to work establishing contact with the hijackers. Late that evening they were successful in opening negotiations through the French embassy in Uganda, which already had established contact with the hijackers on behalf of Air France.

Shimon returned to the command center at the Defense Ministry and went to work with Mordechai Gur on a new, less-complicated rescue plan. IDF commanders and analysts joined them in that effort.

Late that night, agents on the ground at the airport in Entebbe radioed their first report. "Israeli passengers and the airline's flight crew have been separated from the other passengers."

"How many hijackers?"

"Eight now. The original four plus four more who joined them after they arrived here."

Agents also reported that Ugandan leader Idi Amin arrived shortly after the plane landed and he appeared to welcome the terrorists, offering them the full support of his government. Non-Israeli passengers had been released. And the total number of detainees—Israelis plus airline crew—stood at ninety-four.

The following day, Shimon began making the rounds, lobbying other ministers for support of a military option. Haim Zadok, the minister of justice, agreed that they needed to rescue the hostages. As did Yigal Allon, the foreign minister, but several others weren't so sure a rescue would work.

"I think it has about as much chance of success as a diplomatic attempt," one minister suggested. "Which I don't think has much hope at all."

Another chided Shimon for turning to the military. "I thought you favored peace?"

"I do. But this isn't that kind of situation. This is about dealing with thugs and thieves. I'm not a pacifist. These hijackers are a threat to our existence and the safety of our people. If we give in to them now, no Israeli citizen will ever be safe."

Meanwhile, Rabin made little progress with diplomatic negotiations, and IDF planners were hampered in devising a workable plan due to the time constraints imposed by the hijackers' deadline. "We just need more time," he complained.

"Maybe Rabin and Allon should focus on that if they want to use the diplomatic approach," Beinart suggested. "Use it as a first step, but at the same time give us something we actually need. Time to prepare a rescue."

Shimon nodded. "That's a good idea." He left at once to meet with Rabin.

Rabin saw the advantage of negotiating additional time. "But how can we get them to extend the deadline?"

"Ask the Americans to lean on Amin," Shimon suggested. "And ask Sadat to help, too."

"Sadat?"

"He's been talking to us on other topics. I think he really wants to change the relationship with us. So, give him a chance." When Rabin hesitated, Shimon added, "We've got nothing to lose by asking."

Rabin brought Yigal Allon into the conversation and they began making telephone calls to every contact they could find. Sadat contacted Amin for assistance, then placed a call to Yasser Arafat, who was head of the PLO. Arafat agreed to send an emissary to Entebbe to negotiate with the hijackers. At the same time, Allon contacted the US State Department for assistance. They pressured Amin as well. The following day, the hijackers agreed to extend the deadline to Sunday, July 4.

While all of that was happening, the Defense Ministry was moving forward with military options. The first issue of any plan was that of reaching Uganda without being detected by Ugandan authorities. To do that, Israeli aircraft needed to refuel at a secure site. Kenya agreed to allow use of one of its airfields. Detailed plans and photographs of the Entebbe airport were located and crews worked feverishly to establish a mockup of the facility that would permit troops to rehearse a rescue operation.

At the Defense Ministry command center, analysts worked out an exact schedule for each hour of the operation, then broke it down by the half hour, then to the quarter hour. Precise tables of equipment, supplies, and weapons were created along with troop rosters and leadership selection. And, finally, Gur and Shimon moved the proposed operation date up to Saturday, July 3.

When the plan was complete, Gur and Shimon took it to Rabin. This time a representative from Mossad was present along with a number of aides. Gur briefed Rabin on the details and when they were finished Rabin scheduled a cabinet meeting for that Saturday morning. With the deadline looming and defense officials anxious, Shimon, acting on his authority as defense minister, ordered the strike team, equipment, and airplanes moved to the IDF base at Sharm el-Sheikh, the last secure point on the flight path that also was in Israeli territory. That move gave the team an extra couple of hours on the schedule.

On Saturday, the cabinet meeting convened with its members sitting as the ministerial defense committee, a measure that added a layer of security to their deliberations. Rabin presented the rescue plan in brief. Shimon followed with an argument in favor of adopting it, then Gur revealed the operational details. The cabinet deliberated over the matter, then gave its approval. Shimon and Gur departed for the Defense Ministry immediately. Rabin left shortly afterward to brief the opposition party's leadership.

Orders to proceed in hand, Shimon and Gur notified IDF commanders, who then radioed instructions to the hostage rescue team. Within minutes of the cabinet meeting adjournment, the team took off from Sharm el-Sheikh aboard four C-130 cargo planes. Two Boeing 707s followed—one outfitted as a medical unit, the other equipped as an airborne command center to monitor activity on the ground once the troops deployed at Entebbe.

The aircraft flew along an international route, traveling most of the way at extremely low altitude to avoid being detected by radar. As planned, they refueled in Kenya, made a final check of the situation at Entebbe, then took off for Uganda.

While the airborne command center circled overhead, the four cargo planes descended to the runway at the Entebbe airport. They landed with the cargo doors already open and the troops deplaned as soon as the aircraft came to a stop. Using a black limousine and two Land Rovers painted to look like Amin's entourage, the lead group approached the airport, breached the security perimeter, and started toward the terminal.

As the team passed through the checkpoint, one of the IDF soldiers in the rear fired a round from an unsuppressed rifle at a Ugandan guard. Worried that the sound of gunfire might have compromised the operation and deprived it of the element of surprise, the team hurried toward the terminal and burst inside.

The hostages were being held in one of the terminal's waiting rooms and were guarded by seven armed hijackers. As the IDF rescue team entered the room, a gun battle ensued. In the crossfire, three hostages were killed. One by Israeli gunfire and two by gunfire from the hijackers. The exchange lasted only minutes and when it ended all seven hijackers lay dead on the floor.

To that point, save for the indiscreet gunfire at the airport perimeter, the entire operation had been conducted with flawless precision. Once on the ground, the rescue operation lasted all of fifty-three minutes. Twenty minutes to secure the airport and thirty-three minutes to suppress the hijackers, retrieve the hostages, and load them into the waiting aircraft. Several IDF soldiers were injured but none had been killed.

As the rescue team prepared to board the cargo planes, however, Ugandan soldiers opened fire on them from an airport control tower. The rescue team returned fire while the aircraft crew made the plane ready for takeoff. When all was set, IDF soldiers protecting the planes jumped on board and the planes rolled quickly toward the runway.

In Israel, the operation was greeted as a rousing success, which it was, but it was a success tinged with sorrow. Of the one hundred IDF combat troops involved with the rescue team, only one—Jonathan Netanyahu—was killed, the victim of a gunfire exchange outside the airport terminal.

International reaction to the rescue was mixed. African countries deplored it as a violation of Ugandan sovereignty. Members of the United Nations raised similar arguments in debate over resolutions that addressed the incident. Western countries, however, praised it as an act of self-defense brought on by state sponsorship of organized terrorist activities. In perhaps the most poignant response, the United States developed its own hostage rescue teams using a model created from Israel's organization and execution of the Entebbe raid.

✦ ✦ ✦

Through the remainder of 1976, formal negotiations between Egypt and Israel stalled. Since the end of the Yom Kippur War, the United States had been the primary sponsor of those talks, but US leadership was preoccupied with the political controversy surrounding Nixon's impeachment, his resignation, the installation of the Ford administration that succeeded him, and by the US elections of 1976. As a result, formal, traditional methods of international dispute resolution went unimplemented. Behind the scenes, however, representatives of Israel and Egypt continued talks, conducting their own negotiations aimed at reaching an agreement to finally settle the controversies between them.

At the same time, Shimon met again with King Hussein of Jordan. He hoped by some means to resolve differences between their two nations that had gone unaddressed since the end of the Six-Day War in 1967. Chief among those outstanding matters was Israeli occupation of East Jerusalem and control of the area known as the West Bank.

As he met with Hussein, Shimon realized that the issue of Jerusalem was too big and too important for either of them to resolve at the moment. Both sides, Jews and Muslims, valued the city from traditional and religious perspectives that ran to the core of their respective identities. Attempting to resolve that first would prove the undoing of any effort at all. Instead, Shimon sought an incremental approach, working on issues that might actually be resolved as a way of building trust, establishing a relationship, opening doors to further possibilities. Moving this, to get to that, to open up yet a third thing.

During his conversation with Hussein, Shimon suggested they might find a mutual solution with issues regarding the West Bank. "That is an area that has enormous potential and isn't tangled in the issues that paralyze Gaza."

Hussein agreed. "The people of the West Bank are more accustomed to dealing with both sides. Somewhat less suspicious of Jewish priorities."

"And," Shimon added with a smile, "more accommodating to a monarchy."

Hussein laughed. "That is true, too."

"What if we administered the region jointly," Shimon suggested. "Some sort of joint commission with representatives from both sides."

"From Israel and the PLO?"

Shimon shook his head. "No. From Israel and Jordan."

"As a permanent solution?"

"We could begin with a short-term arrangement. An interim agreement. Work together while we continue to discuss a permanent solution."

"It is an intriguing idea," Hussein replied. "But it would require further study on our part before we could say."

Hussein's noncommittal response did not surprise Shimon. He already knew from information collected by Menashe Beinart and Yohai Cohen that Jerusalem had been the focus of Hussein's interest, and he was certain that lay behind the king's response on the West Bank.

As a Muslim, Hussein would find it difficult to reach an agreement on the West Bank that omitted the Jerusalem issue, or that might even forestall its resolution in the future. This much was plainly obvious to Shimon and his team. From Hussein's perspective, if joint administration wasn't an honest interim proposal but a permanent one after all—if this was all Israel would *ever* agree too—then the problem of Jerusalem would have to be addressed. And, no matter how appealing joint administration might be to Hussein personally, he could not afford to appear to surrender the city to the Jews—even though Israel now controlled it absolutely.

Still, the idea of joint administration had intrigued Hussein, and Shimon thought it might be an area in which they could make progress in the future. For that option to remain viable, however, Israel had to address a key ongoing issue—the continued establishment of Jewish settlements in the West Bank.

After the Six-Day War in 1967, Israel controlled all of Jerusalem and the West Bank. Jewish messianic groups were empowered by that victory. Unification of control over Jerusalem was a featured emphasis of apocalyptic literature and became the focus of the groups as well. Devoted to ushering in the day of the Messiah, those groups were committed to establishing Greater Israel—Jewish control over historic Israel at the height of its Davidic glory—by political action. Settling the occupied territories with Jewish settlers was part of their strategy and ideology. As a result, Jewish messianic groups pushed for the establishment of new Jewish settlements in the controlled areas.

Israeli government policy, however, opposed creation of new West Bank settlements. The Defense Ministry and the IDF were assigned the mission of enforcing that policy and had long-standing strategies and procedures for blocking settlement construction without using brute force.

In the Rabin government, Yisrael Galili served as minister without portfolio—a cabinet member with the right to vote on cabinet decisions but with no specific area of responsibility. The areas in which he worked were assigned to him by Rabin on an issue-by-issue basis, or developed by Galili on his own with Rabin's approval. Galili had previously served as Haganah chief of staff but had been removed from that position by David Ben-Gurion during the generals' revolt when Ben-Gurion sought to transform Haganah into a national army. Galili was a somewhat controversial figure but was not without administrative gifts and abilities.

As a minister and cabinet member, Galili had access to IDF information and strategy through briefings provided to the prime minister's office in the course of normal operating procedure. As a former Haganah official, he knew how to interpret that information and how best to use it. While IDF and the Defense Ministry worked to block the creation of new settlements by Jewish messianic groups, Galili helped members of those groups circumvent those efforts. He coordinated with them through Haim Gvati, the minister of agriculture.

Frustrated by the messianic groups' success in avoiding IDF and Defense Ministry attempts to block their settlement construction, Shimon dispatched Yohai Cohen to find out what was going on. That's when he learned about Galili and his connection to the messianic groups. As an Orthodox believer, Shimon understood the religious motivation, the part it played in personal lives of the believers, and the role it played in the life of Israel. He also understood the politics of the situation—Rabin's interest in accommodating a highly motivated group with significant influence—but he was frustrated by Rabin's apparent willingness to ignore the long-term implications of his policy decisions for Israel's future, a future he saw as desperately needing the hope of peace, which Rabin's actions in the West Bank seriously undermined. "This is the kind of situation Ben-Gurion warned about," Shimon complained. "We are saddled with politicians who have no vision beyond the next election cycle. And not the first idea how to take a grand vision of Israel's future and translate it into incremental, practical steps."

✦ ✦ ✦

During the fall of 1976, Rabin nominated Asher Yadlin to become the next governor of the Bank of Israel. At the time of the nomination, Yadlin was head of Kupat Holim, a large health insurance company. His appointment was submitted for cabinet approval in September with the position taking effect in November.

At the same time, reports began appearing in the Israeli news media suggesting Yadlin and other Labor leaders had been complicit in illegitimate financial transactions. Yadlin had been involved extensively in Labor Party fund-raising but the transactions supposedly went much further than that and actually involved Kupat Holim, the health insurance firm that he led.

After Yadlin's nomination was submitted to the cabinet, but before he actually took the position, ministers learned that elements within the Israeli police had opened an investigation into the allegations against Yadlin. Yadlin denied any wrongdoing.

In the course of investigating Yadlin, police raised questions about whether Avraham Ofer, Rabin's housing minister, had been involved in the conduct that gave rise to questions about Yadlin. By then what began as a mere political problem seemed on the verge of becoming a genuine imbroglio. Already some noted that both men, already tied to the heart of the Labor Party, appeared to have links to Pinchas Sapir, who served as finance minister under Eshkol and Golda Meir. The implications of a controversy pinned together in a string of relationships that ran deep into Labor's history did not go unnoticed. The issue with Yadlin threatened not only the reputation and effectiveness of the Rabin administration but appeared to call into question the integrity of the Labor Party's history and purpose as well.

Controversy over Yadlin continued to build. Finally, near the end of 1976, Rabin faced a confidence vote in the Knesset. As might be expected, he lost that vote and his government dissolved. Elections were set for the following May 1977.

Rabin continued in office pending the outcome of those elections but without control of a legislative majority. However, in March 1977, news reports alleged that Rabin and his wife held dollar-denominated accounts at a bank in Washington, D.C. Accounts of that nature were illegal under Israeli currency laws. An investigation revealed that the accounts had been opened at a time earlier in Rabin's career when he had been Israel's ambassador to the United States, but they had never been closed. Charges were brought against Rabin and his wife and they were subsequently fined for the infraction. By then, however, the damage had been done. Faced with a deteriorating political situation—allegations of corruption that tarnished the Labor Party and now the currency violations—Rabin resigned.

At the time of his resignation, Rabin recommended that the Labor Party name Shimon as his replacement, both as party leader and as the party's candidate for prime minister in the upcoming election. Shortly thereafter, the Labor Party central committee did just that, endorsing Shimon for both positions. The move made him Israel's de facto prime minister until elections in May.

SHIMON PERES

*"It's better to be controversial
for the right reasons, than to be
popular for the wrong reasons."*

IN THE MAY 1977 general election, Shimon faced Menachem Begin, leader of the Likud Party. Formed in 1973 by Begin and Ariel Sharon, Likud was an amalgamation of conservative Israeli political parties all of which were dedicated to establishing a Greater Israel.

Begin had been born in Russia, but in 1939 he lived in Poland. When the Germans invaded he escaped and eventually enlisted in the Free Polish Army. He was sent to Palestine with the army but resigned to join Irgun, the Zionist paramilitary group active before Israeli statehood. Begin rose through the ranks and had become Irgun's leader at the time of independence.

By contrast, Sharon had been born on a moshav, a cooperative community, in mandatory Palestine. He joined Haganah at a young age and had a long career, first with Haganah, then as a commander with the IDF. Forming Likud marked his entry into Israeli politics.

Since the time of independence, the Labor Party had been the dominant political force. Labor's candidates had faced conservative challengers in every election, but none of those candidates had posed any viable challenge or had a serious possibility of winning. Every prime minister had come from Labor, but public outcry over the Yom Kippur War surprise and repercussions from corruption allegations against the Rabin administration threatened to change all that.

With the first wave of immigration in the nineteenth century, Zionism—the return of Jews to Palestine and the creation of a modern Jewish state—had been the primary focus of Palestinian Jews. Once the state was created, that focus shifted to defense and security. During the first twenty years, Labor-led governments addressed those issues well, but the Yom Kippur War—the surprise attack, the advance of Egyptian troops well into Israeli territory, and a simultaneous attack by Syria in the north—cast all of that in doubt.

Allegations of corruption hadn't helped either, but that wasn't all. Labor had grown complacent. Resting on success in the past, party leaders had assumed the future would be no different. Yet all the while, life in Israel was changing. Israel itself was changing.

By 1977, divergent bands of Zionists, dedicated to land and labor, had slowly evolved into a complex cosmopolitan society. One influenced by freedom at least as much as earlier generations had been influenced by European oppression and persecution.

Israeli demographics had changed, too. Unlike the early years, when most Jews came to Palestine from Europe, after independence immigrants arrived from all parts of the world. Many came from Northern Africa, bringing with them traditions and priorities that were very different from their predecessors.

As with human migration in other countries, assimilation into existing Israeli culture was problematic. North African Jews were particularly dissatisfied by what they perceived as discriminatory treatment in finding housing and jobs, supposedly discrimination occasioned by the differences in their physical appearance. Their presence and dissatisfaction upset the balance of social order and revealed smoldering tension between Ashkenazi and Sephardi Jews, between early comers and late, between Jews from North Africa and those from Yemen.

Menachem Begin understood the nation's concern about security and felt the tension of its seemingly alienated ethnic groups. He also knew how to use those emotions to distinguish himself from Shimon. He knew, as Dayan had suggested earlier, how to reduce all of that to us-and-them language. The art of turning a complex issue into a yes-or-no question; I'm for you. He's against you. Casting himself and Likud on the side of the populous as *us*—with Shimon and Labor as *them*—Likud handed Labor a resounding defeat and swept Begin into office as prime minister backed by a solid majority.

After the election, Begin appointed Ezer Weizman as defense minister. Most of the remaining cabinet positions were filled with obvious choices from among Likud members and the coalition Begin assembled to create a Knesset majority. In a surprising move, however, he invited Moshe Dayan to join the government as foreign minister.

Dayan had been elected to Knesset from the Labor Party, but he still was angry at party leadership for turning on him after the Yom Kippur War. When Begin asked him to join the cabinet, he readily accepted the position. The Labor Party responded by expelling him. The evening after Dayan's appointment and expulsion were announced, Shimon had dinner with him at a restaurant in Jerusalem.

"Why didn't you talk to me about this?" Shimon asked. "Before you made your decision."

Dayan gave him a playful smile. "Because you would have told me not to do it."

Shimon nodded. "That's exactly what I would have told you."

"I was going to accept the position anyway. I just didn't want to do it after having that talk with you."

Shimon was touched by the gesture and took it as one more indication of their deep and abiding friendship. "I appreciate that."

"So, you don't mind that I'm with Begin now."

Shimon looked up from his plate. "No, you can be a member of any party or no party at all."

"You don't care?"

"No. I don't care. I mean, I would rather you and I were in the same party. And I would rather that was the Labor Party. It needs all the help it can get. But Israel needs you, too."

"Israel could do just fine without me."

"Israel needs you more than you know," Shimon argued. "And there isn't anyone else I want in charge of the Foreign Ministry than you."

"But this is your area of expertise. Not mine."

Shimon smiled. "You're better at diplomacy than you'd ever admit. You just get tired of all the details."

Dayan laughed. "I hate details. They're so tedious."

"Just remember, it's all in the details."

✦ ✦ ✦

The result of the election meant Shimon was no longer a minister, but he continued to serve in the Knesset and as Labor Party leader. When not attending to Knesset business he was hard at work rebuilding the party. Haim Bar-Lev, a former IDF chief of staff, was named Labor Party secretary-general. Menashe Beinart agreed to serve as Labor Party spokesman, and Shimon appointed him to the task of redrafting the party's message.

"We need a new version," Shimon insisted.

"No," Beinart replied. "You need a complete rewrite."

"Yes, but we can only do so much and hold the membership together."

"The real problem is the old guard."

"Most of the old guard are dead."

Beinart shook his head, "Not the founders. They aren't the problem. The trouble comes from the next generation. The group slightly younger than Ben-Gurion and slightly older than you."

"I'm not sure I understand."

"You were one of the youngest. Ben-Gurion one of the oldest. But between you and him there was—"

Shimon nodded, "Golda. And a lot more besides her."

"And they all have their allies."

"Like I said, we can only do so much. There's a limit to the scope of change they will endure."

✦ ✦ ✦

Although Shimon was relegated to the Knesset's political opposition, he nevertheless remained active in a broad range of organizations that addressed a wide variety of issues. One of those issues was foreign affairs, and he found an outlet for that interest through his continuing membership in the Socialist International, the labor-oriented group to which he'd belonged since coming to work for Ben-Gurion in Tel Aviv years earlier. Through that organization he met many influential leaders, politicians, and statesmen. One of those was Bruno Kreisky.

Born in Vienna, Kreisky was Jewish but grew up in a non-practicing family. When the Nazis invaded Austria, Kreisky escaped to Sweden. He returned after the war and became active in the Austrian government, eventually rising to the level of foreign minister. In 1977, he became Austria's chancellor.

Throughout his long and active career, Kreisky had cultivated relationships with leaders and politicians throughout the world. One of those friendships was with Hassan Tohamy, an Egyptian official who had served as Egypt's ambassador to Austria. Tohamy, in turn, was close friends with Sadat. With formal peace talks stalled, Kreisky was concerned about the lack of progress in settling the differences between Egypt and Israel. In an effort to nudge things along he met with Tohamy to discuss the topic. "I think the time is right to do something big," he urged. "To do something momentous in moving Egypt and Israel toward peace."

Eventually, Kreisky convinced Tohamy to raise the issue with Sadat, and through careful but persistent pressure Sadat agreed to send a representative to meet with someone from Israel. "We will talk," Sadat said. "But that is all."

With Sadat on board, Kreisky contacted King Hassan II of Morocco and asked him to host the proposed talks. Hassan readily agreed. After those two pieces of the puzzle fell into place, Kreisky contacted Shimon and asked him to pass news of these developments on to Moshe Dayan, along with an invitation for him to attend.

Shimon delivered the message and encouraged Dayan to accept the invitation. "This is too good of an opportunity to pass up," he insisted.

Surprisingly, Dayan was skeptical and suspicious. "You orchestrated this?"

"No," Shimon replied, caught off guard by Dayan's mood. "I had nothing to do with it. I am merely the messenger."

"Then why did Kreisky contact you and not me directly?"

"We're old friends," Shimon explained. "I've known him since. . . since about the time you and I went to our first Zionist Congress together. Why are you acting like this?"

"How?" Dayan questioned. "How do you know him?"

"Through the Socialist International." Shimon glared at him. "Don't get suspicious of me now."

"I'm not suspicious of you. It's just—"

"Yes, you *are* suspicious of me," Shimon argued, doing little to hide the frustration in his voice. "You hear them talking about me every day. Begin and all the others. And now you wonder if what they say about me isn't true."

Dayan glanced away. "Well. . . "

"You can't listen to them." Shimon's voice was tense. "Not about me. You've known me longer than Begin or anyone else in his cabinet. Trust me, Moshe. Trust our friendship."

"But if I meet with the Egyptians, what would I say?" Dayan asked, abruptly turning the conversation in a different direction. "I have no idea what to do."

"Mostly," Shimon sighed, suddenly deflated, "just be Moshe. That's all. Just be you."

"That's it?"

"Look, you'll know who their representative will be before you get to the meeting. I'll help you prepare." Shimon looked him in the eye. "You can't pass up this opportunity, Moshe. No matter how uncomfortable it makes you. No matter what you believe about how it came together. You have to take the meeting. If for nothing else, just to keep the process alive."

That summer, Dayan and Tohamy met in Morocco. Talks were cordial, and though the meeting produced little in terms of signed agreements it went a long way toward developing a sense of cooperation between representatives of the two countries. When he returned, Dayan briefed Begin, then discussed the situation with Shimon.

"Tohamy was a little distant at first."

"That's to be expected," Shimon assured. "Trust has always been the biggest issue between us and them. Between us and all our neighbors. They don't trust us. We don't trust them."

Dayan nodded. "I've found it easy to get along with Arabs on a daily basis, but at the governmental level things are different. I want to trust them, but I'm not sure I can. Everyone's motives are suddenly... clouded and uncertain." He caught Shimon's gaze. "We need to change that."

"Yes, and I think the way we can do that is by creating experiences that give us an opportunity to get to know each other. More talks like you and Tohamy had, for instance. You and I didn't suddenly one day fully trust each other. It happened gradually. Our understanding of each other developed over time. We need to do that with the Palestinians. Only, to make that happen on a government-to-government level we have to be intentional about it."

Dayan thought for a moment. "I don't think that's enough. I mean, what you're saying is right, in one sense. But maybe we also need to do that on a personal level, too. Citizen to citizen. Create opportunities for individual Israelis to meet and experience individual Egyptians. Individual Palestinians. From Gaza. From the West Bank. From Jordan."

"I think they've met each other," Shimon replied. "It was just while looking down the barrel of a rifle."

"And that is a big part of the problem. All of our experiences with them have been in the midst of battle. While shooting at each other."

Once again, Shimon was intrigued by the idea of finding ways to build trust between Israelis and Palestinians. "When I was at the Transport Ministry," he remembered, "we tried this with children. We built parks with baseball fields. Worked them into the highway and road development projects and helped create leagues where Arab children and Jewish children could play ball together."

"Maybe we could also do that on a business level. Haven't I heard you talking about creating points of contact for businesses to cooperate?"

"A cooperative zone," Shimon nodded. "Like the one they've been developing in Europe since the war."

"I don't think the Middle East is ready for something that extensive. Not yet, anyway, but maybe we could find a way to start moving toward it." Dayan grinned. "One of your four-level maneuvers." Shimon looked puzzled. Dayan laughed. "You know, moving this, to move that, to make something else work out."

Shimon had a look of realization. "Right. Cooperative zones. Maybe we could start with two businessmen. One Arab, one Israeli. Meeting for coffee."

Shimon liked the idea of creating ways to build trust and he filed the conversation away, thinking one day he might have the opportunity to do something about it. He also began thinking of two businessmen he might coax into having coffee, too.

✦ ✦ ✦

Meanwhile, in the United States, controversy regarding the presidency sorted itself out with the election of 1976. Jimmy Carter won that contest and was sworn in to office in January 1977. He and his administration spent much of that spring getting organized, but very soon thereafter Carter began casting about the Middle East for leaders who were willing to work with him toward a regional peace agreement. Younger than Nixon or Gerald Ford and far more energetic, Carter was idealistic, confident, and certain he could solve the Middle East's problems if he could just find the right people with whom to talk.

As a point of beginning, Carter wanted to restart the process begun by Henry Kissinger and hoped to bring all the parties together in Geneva for multilateral peace talks. King Hussein of Jordan, fearing further isolation from the Arab world and reprisals from his neighbors for working with Israel, refused to participate. Syrian leaders were not interested, either, and formal peace talks stalled before they really got started.

Private meetings between Dayan and Tohamy, however, had opened up the relationship between the two countries, more so than either of them realized at first. In 1977, Dayan received word that Sadat would agree to direct contact with Menachem Begin in Jerusalem. Dayan asked Shimon about it.

Shimon was genuinely excited. "This is unprecedented," he exclaimed, his eyes wide with excitement. "The president of Egypt visiting the prime minister of Israel. In Jerusalem. You have no choice but to follow through on this."

"But how do we do that?" Dayan wondered.

"What did Begin say about the offer?"

"I haven't told him yet."

Shimon's mouth dropped open in surprise. "Then deliver the message to him," he exclaimed. "Tell Begin he should telephone Sadat and invite him to come to Jerusalem."

"We can pick up the phone and call him?"

"Yes. When a head of state wants to meet like this with another head of state, someone broaches the idea at a lower level of the government, so that if the event never occurs the public never finds out the suggestion was even made."

"So if the idea fails it does so out of the public eye."

"Exactly. If the idea of a meeting survives the initial suggestion, then each side confirms the deal. The invitee wants to know if an invitation will be extended. The inviting side wants to know if it will be accepted."

"And both want to know that before either of them makes a move? Sounds easy enough," Dayan observed.

"Sadat has already indicated he'll accept if asked. Just convince Begin to make the call and extend the invitation."

To Dayan's surprise, Begin was very much interested in pursuing the matter. The day after Dayan spoke with him, Begin telephoned Sadat and invited him to Jerusalem. That visit took place in November and included an address by Sadat to the Knesset, making him the first and so far only Egyptian leader to address the Israeli parliament.

By then, Dayan had learned that part of Sadat's motivation for the meeting was to win US support for Egypt. Dayan was upset by that but Shimon talked him down. "Don't focus on that. Begin has motives for talking to him, too. Just talk. You can always refuse to agree. But if you don't talk, you get nothing."

After speaking to the Knesset, Sadat and Begin met in the prime minister's office. Dayan attended part of the meeting, along with his Egyptian counterpart. "We have many psychological barriers to peace," Sadat noted.

"Yes," Begin replied. "There are many suspicions on both sides."

"I think we might get past some of that," Sadat continued, "if we tried working toward a peace agreement that could be implemented in stages."

"I agree. But that will be very difficult with Jordan and Syria. I'm not sure they will even participate."

"Perhaps we could reach an agreement between ourselves. Without the participation of other Arab countries."

Begin's eyes opened wide. "Yes, perhaps we could."

"But I must insist," Sadat continued. "Whether they participate with us or not, any agreement we reach must include resolution of the West Bank and Gaza issues."

By the end of their visit Begin, wary of what he already knew were Sadat's broader motives, was noncommittal. Sadat had hoped for more but seemed to accept their conversation as a positive step nonetheless. A way forward seemed to be opening and, according to aides, Sadat did not want to be the one to squelch that possibility.

After Sadat had gone, Begin invited Shimon to his office. Dayan was present for their meeting and listened while Begin briefed Shimon on the substance of his talks with Sadat.

"Interesting," Shimon commented when Begin finished. "He wants to resolve the status of the West Bank and Gaza, but he doesn't want to invite the PLO or anyone else from the area to participate in the negotiations. He wants to negotiate all of that separately."

"You think that is a problem?" Begin asked.

"I think it will be a problem to implement an agreement covering people who didn't participate in its development. But I think it also reveals something about Sadat and how he sees himself."

Begin nodded affirmatively. "He seems to think he can impose his will on the Palestinians."

"That's precisely what he thinks," Shimon agreed.

Dayan spoke up. "Or, is he simply doing this knowing he can never implement that part of an agreement but negotiating it anyway to see what we will give up?"

Shimon arched an eyebrow. "An exploration. You might just be right."

"A trial run," Begin added.

Afterward, Shimon met Dayan in the hallway. "See, you're better at diplomacy than you think. That part about a trial run was brilliant."

"It was nothing," Dayan scoffed. "If you'd been there at the discussions, you would have caught on to it as soon as Sadat started talking. I just now thought of it."

"You've made good progress with them. This is a very big day for Israel."

"I'm not sure. Sadat still insists on full Egyptian control of the Sinai, which will be a problem for some."

"But you have an opening," Shimon insisted. "Sadat came. He spoke. He and Begin talked. And not just about anything but about substantive issues. That's progress."

Dayan grinned. "And we all lived to talk about it."

SHIMON PERES

"You don't make peace with friends. You make it with very unsavory enemies."

BY 1978, THE FORMAL Middle East peace process still had not produced a solution to the Israel–Egypt problem. In an attempt to prod things along, Bruno Kreisky enlisted the help of Willy Brandt, a former German chancellor, to try a different tactic. Like Kreisky, Brandt had been deeply involved in Socialist International and was a well-known advocate for peace throughout the world. He also was a friend of both Sadat and Shimon and remained deeply troubled by the intransigent nature of Israel's relationship with its neighbors.

Working together, Brandt and Kreisky mounted an effort behind the scenes to bring the two parties—Israel and Egypt—together in an environment conducive to open-ended discussion. A moment when issues could be raised, perspectives aired, and potential solutions proposed without the limitations of formal proceedings or the clutter of aides, policy papers, and the typical trappings of diplomacy.

Kreisky's previous attempt had been by way of a direct approach. He'd contacted Moshe Dayan, then Israeli's foreign minister, and Hassan Tohamy, a well-connected diplomat and official Egyptian intermediary, and arranged for them to meet under the watchful eye of the Moroccan king. All of it aboveboard and straightforward—appointee to appointee, using traditional diplomatic negotiating mechanisms and devices. This time, Kreisky and Brandt decided to try a different approach.

Instead of arranging a formal conference or mediation session with credentialed officials as participants, Kreisky and Brandt turned to Shimon as the Israeli spokesman. Shimon, though a member of the Israeli Knesset and head of the Labor Party, had no official capacity in the Begin government. Nothing he said could be construed as an authorized proposal and he had no authority to strike a binding deal with a head of state. He would be free to simply talk, Kreisky and Brandt reasoned. Sadat from Egypt. Shimon from Israel. Meeting informally and out of the public eye for a nonbinding conversation. It seemed like a great idea to Kreisky and Brandt and they issued their invitation jointly.

Shimon was surprised by the offer and glad to receive it, but it placed him in a somewhat awkward position. It seemed like the perfect opportunity to make genuine progress toward finding new and workable solutions, but for most of his adult life he'd been accused of conducting his own foreign-affairs campaign. To his detractors, this invitation from Kreisky and Brandt would give them demonstrable confirmation of what they'd been saying—that Shimon had been going behind everyone's back to further his own ideas and his own career. Still, he wanted to attend and thought that avoiding it would be a terrible mistake.

In an effort to forestall his detractors, Shimon informed Moshe Dayan of the invitation and promised to do nothing about it until he received official permission to respond. Dayan discussed the matter with Begin, then gave his consent. "But be careful," Dayan warned as he conveyed the news. "Begin and his cronies were already suspicious of you before."

"And now?" Shimon asked with a sigh.

"He was impressed that you submitted a request through proper channels."

Shimon's shoulders sagged. "Do you think they'll ever give up questioning my motives?"

"I doubt it." Then a smile broke over Dayan's face. "But think of it this way—at least they're predictable."

"What good does that do me?" Shimon grumbled.

"It tells you in advance what their position will be."

Shimon smiled. He'd never thought of it that way and the notion that his detractors couldn't help revealing themselves at the slightest opportunity struck him as humorous, just as it had Dayan.

✦ ✦ ✦

As Kreisky and Brandt had planned, Shimon and Sadat met at the Hofburg, a former royal palace in Vienna, Austria. Both arrived in the city on other business and entered the building without notice. They met in a drawing room off the rear hall.

"The Labor Party is committed to peace," Shimon began as they sat down together. "If Begin wants peace, the Labor Party will support him completely. But I want you to know, whatever we talk about today, I will share with them."

"As I would expect," Sadat replied. "And I shall share what we say with my people, too."

"I just want you to know," Shimon reiterated, "I'm here for peace. Not politics."

"Good," Sadat agreed. "Let's talk."

For the next five hours, Shimon and Sadat discussed a broad range of issues. Gaza and the West Bank. Jewish settlements constructed in the West Bank. Settlements in the occupied areas of the Sinai. The Golan Heights. And more. As they talked, however, Shimon sensed from the tenor of Sadat's voice that the biggest issues they faced were control of the Sinai and the status of Jewish villages there.

"We cannot tolerate Jewish settlements in the Sinai," Sadat had repeatedly warned. "They must be removed. All of the Sinai must be returned to Egypt."

"From our viewpoint, settlements might be negotiable," Shimon responded. "But we also have air bases located there. We need those bases."

Sadat's forehead wrinkled in a frown. "Forever?"

"Perhaps not forever," Shimon conceded, "but at least for the next. . . fifty years."

Sadat looked askance. "Why is that so?"

"If we lose those bases, we will be forced to reposition the aircraft stationed there, which means moving them north. If we move them north very far at all, they will become tempting targets for Syria. Perhaps irresistibly so."

"You make a point," Sadat noted. "Moving them north might solve one problem, only to create another. And neither of us wants to see a war erupt with Syria."

"Precisely."

Sadat thought for a moment. "Fifty years would be workable," he replied finally. "I could convince my people to allow the bases to remain for fifty years. But not the settlements," he wagged his finger. "The settlements must be removed."

Although Shimon and Sadat parted without reaching a definitive conclusion, from their long hours of conversation the vague outline of an idea for peace seemed to emerge. One Shimon hoped could be pursued in a thoughtful and deliberate manner.

When he returned to Israel, Shimon reported the details of his conversation with Sadat to Begin and Dayan. To Shimon's surprise, Begin thought Sadat's proposal was the most workable solution he'd heard yet. After an exchange of diplomatic messages, a working summit was convened at Ismalia near the Suez Canal to promote those ideas floated in Vienna toward an actual agreement.

With progress being made, and with Egypt and Israel insistent on solving their problems without including other neighboring states in the discussion, US president Jimmy Carter lay aside his reluctance to enter bilateral negotiations. After the Ismalia summit concluded on a positive note, he invited Sadat and Begin to continue their talks in the United States.

That September, delegations from Egypt and Israel accompanied their respective leaders to Camp David, the presidential retreat in the Catoctin Mountains of northern Maryland, sixty miles outside Washington, D.C. Working in small issue-oriented groups and also in one-on-one sessions between Sadat and Begin, the two sides talked for thirteen days.

The sessions at Camp David proved quite contentious, due in part to the historically hostile context between Israel and Egypt, but also because of Sadat's insistence that they address issues related to Gaza and the West Bank. Almost from the beginning, however, all parties chose to avoid the most divisive issue—the status of Jerusalem—and instead focused their attention on matters that were far more solvable. Issues like troop withdrawals and settlement removal, to name but two.

All day and into the night, the parties argued, shouted, and cajoled their way through a maze of topics, addressing each other with unprecedented frankness and honesty, and when they'd finished they produced a pair of agreements known collectively as the Camp David Accords.

The first agreement, entitled *Framework for Peace in the Middle East*, addressed resolution of the Palestinian–Israeli conflict and the status of Gaza and the West Bank. The other, entitled *Framework for the Conclusion of a Peace Treaty between Egypt and Israel*, focused on resolution of the issues directly affecting both countries.

The first agreement included provisions that impinged upon countries and peoples not included in the negotiations. It was ultimately rejected by the United Nations. The second, however, offered real progress in finally resolving matters between Egypt and Israel. By its terms, Begin agreed to surrender control of the Sinai in its entirety and to remove all Jewish settlements from the region, a move that would require the use of force in some instances. In exchange, Sadat agreed to restrictions on the kinds of military units Egypt would place in the

Sinai, assured Israel's free access and use of related waterways—the Suez Canal, the Straits of Tiran, and others—and agreed to establish normal diplomatic relations between the two nations.

Afterward, the agreements were submitted to the Knesset for approval. As he'd indicated earlier, Shimon led the Labor Party to support the entire peace package—both agreements, as drafted at the conference, including the provision regarding settlement removal.

"Life doesn't give us perfect choices," Shimon offered. "This was a negotiated agreement and in any negotiation one must gather what can realistically be obtained and move on. And," he reminded Labor Party members, "always remember, we are opposed to Menachem Begin and the Likud government, but we are not opposed to peace."

After the Knesset vote, Shimon went to see Golda Meir. Since leaving politics, she had wrestled with health problems and that December had been hospitalized in serious condition. Shimon visited her to discuss the Egyptian peace process and the details of the Camp David Accords. Golda listened as he outlined the basic points of the agreements, then engaged Shimon in an amicable discussion of the matter.

When they'd exhausted their discussion of Egypt and the Sinai, Meir seemed in good spirits, so they moved on to talk about their respective views of government, politics, and foreign affairs in general.

"It's true," Golda admitted. "The party has always been first in my life. I've been a member since before Israel existed. Before any of this," she amplified with a sweeping gesture. "The party rescued me and gave me purpose. It is very dear to me." She took a deep breath and her eyes were full. "The dearest, in fact."

"And Israel has always been foremost with me," Shimon responded. "The future, mostly. Not the past. And not so much the present, either."

"Always looking beyond the next hill."

"Trying to figure out what might lie ahead for us."

"I think we both want the same thing," Meir smiled. "We just differ on how to achieve it."

In a new and deeper way, Shimon realized Golda truly was a labor devotee, but not in the negative way he'd thought before. She was thoroughly committed to the idea that labor was redemptive; to the notion that labor could free one to achieve one's destiny and through that destiny build a country worth having. He, on the other hand, was more attuned to the Western liberal idea that humans have the capacity to move themselves toward an increasingly better way of life. It required effort, he readily agreed, but not in the sense of the labor movement's understanding.

Late that evening, when Shimon left Meir's hospital room, they parted as friends. Whatever had separated them in the past, their relationship was now at peace. It was a bittersweet moment, though. Shimon was glad to have come to a resolution with her, but sad that it took so long to reach that sense of rapport.

A few days after their visit, Golda Meir died.

SHIMON PERES

"We should use our imagination
more than our memory."

WITH THE SIGNING of the Camp David Accords, peace seemed finally at hand in the Middle East. Yet, forces were afoot—ancient forces emerging in new and far more destructive forms—that threatened with a dark and sinister gloom unlike anything the region had ever experienced before.

Near the close of the nineteenth century—about the time modern Zionists began returning to Palestine—scientists discovered a substance in pitchblende, a black mineral-rich compound that emitted radioactive waves. The substance was identified as uranium with small amounts of radium.

The discovery suggested that elements common in nature might provide a source for exponentially larger amounts of energy than anything experienced before. Far more efficient than the combustion of fossil fuels and unbelievably more destructive than the detonation of conventional explosives. This new power became known as nuclear energy. The bombs it produced were labeled "atomic."

Before World War II, many of the scientists exploring the nuclear question lived and studied in Germany. As the Nazis came to power, politicians in the West were convinced that Hitler had initiated a project to create a weapon using this new source of energy, a possibility they viewed as threatening the world with what would bring catastrophic results.

Beginning in 1939, development of nuclear weapons proceeded at a frantic pace in the United States, driven by the perceived need to beat Germany in creating these new master weapons. That effort resulted in the world's first atomic bomb detonation, which took place in the desert of New Mexico during the summer of 1945. A month later, two devices of similar design were dropped on targets in Japan, bringing World War II to a swift but devastating end.

That's where nuclear weapons stood at the time of Israel's independence. Only the United States possessed them. Those circumstances changed the following year, however, when the Soviet Union successfully detonated its version of a nuclear bomb. Even then, there was no cause for alarm in Israel, as both the United States and the Soviet Union had exhibited if not a friendly relationship with Israel, at least a non-hostile one: the United States by recognizing the new state immediately upon its declaration of independence; the Soviet Union by providing weapons through Czechoslovakia in support of Israel's war for independence.

In the 1950s, England, France, and China acquired nuclear arms and in the 1960s, India began its own development program. Although the spread of nuclear weapons seemed inevitable and, indeed, alarming in terms of global security, the presence of weapons in these countries posed no direct threat to Israel. But when news arrived in Tel Aviv that Iraq had begun a nuclear-development program, government officials sat up and took notice.

Most of Iraq's initial atomic exploration involved indigenous research—they received very little outside help—but even work at a remedial level caused concern among Israeli military and intelligence leaders. Mossad kept a close eye on developments there and in 1970 began infiltrating the Iraqi program with agents who monitored key aspects of the program from the inside.

As Iraq's experience with nuclear technology deepened, its program expanded and intensified. It also began searching for a partner to help take that program to a new level. First on the list of potential supporters was France.

When Iraqi officials approached the French government about the acquisition of a reactor capable of producing plutonium, Israel lobbied the French government to refuse. The French acceded to the Israeli request and declined to participate. The Italians did likewise. However, in November 1976, after lengthy discussions, the French reversed their earlier position and agreed to sell Iraq a research reactor, supposedly capable of producing only forty megawatts of power. Actual construction on the project got underway in 1979.

From the time the Iraqi program first began, Israeli administrations discussed potential reactions to it. None of those prior administrations, however, faced the very real possibility that Iraq might actually obtain nuclear weapons. Now, as the reactor project moved toward construction, the threat was no longer theoretical. Iraq was on the verge of possessing both the technology and the fuel needed to make its own version of atomic weapons.

Confronted by an unavoidable threat, Menachem Begin ordered IDF to intensify its preparation for a military response. A model of the Iraqi reactor was constructed at a remote location in the Negev, and IDF pilots began training for potential bombing missions to destroy it. At the same time, Mossad activated its covert teams already inside Iraq. Those teams attempted to sabotage the reactor in an effort to delay its completion but their efforts had only minimal success.

✦ ✦ ✦

Meanwhile, on the streets of Tehran, Iran, the first of many student demonstrations against the shah began. They went largely unnoticed by the West until 1978, when Shah Pahlavi disappeared from public view to take cancer treatments at his retreat on the Caspian

Sea. In his absence, and in the absence of public comment from the Iranian government, rumors about the shah's whereabouts energized the demonstrators. Students clashed with state security forces in increasingly violent confrontations and the size of the protests grew dramatically.

In September, Iranian police fired on demonstrators, killing and wounding many. That action transformed what had been a civil demonstration into an open revolution. A nationwide strike in October paralyzed the country and, with conditions continuing to deteriorate, the shah departed Iran, supposedly to travel abroad for additional medical care.

President Sadat invited the shah to make his permanent residence in Egypt, which eventually he did. For all practical purposes he was gone from power as soon as he left the country.

Whatever kind of leader the shah had been in the previous years, by the end of his reign he was seen by many as a corrupt, non-dynamic ruler. For many in the West, his ouster came as a complete surprise, but to Shimon and those who dealt with him on a regular basis, his fall from the throne was understandable and not unexpected.

With the shah removed from office, Sayyid Ruhollah Khomeini, an obscure Islamic cleric, emerged as the real leader behind Tehran's student revolution. Known to the few aware of his existence as the Ayatollah Khomeini, he quickly became the putative leader of Iran.

Khomeini was born in Khomeyn, Iran, and educated from the age of six in Twelver Shia Islamic tradition. He went on to study at the Islamic seminary in Esfahan, then transferred to the seminary at Qom. As an adult he was a lecturer at Qom and Najaf and wrote more than forty books, most of them dealing with matters of Islamic law and teaching.

In the 1960s, Khomeini began publicly opposing the shah, primarily regarding government programs and initiatives that he saw as Westernizing and corrupting of Iran's Shia tradition and culture. His opposition became increasingly vitriolic and in the mid-1960s he was forced into exile—first in Turkey, then in France.

From Paris, the ayatollah conducted a subversive campaign using messages recorded on cassette tapes and distributed to his followers in Iran. When the shah left Iran for the last time, the ayatollah returned to a triumphant welcome, eventually becoming the nation's Supreme Leader.

The development of Iraq's nuclear program and the Islamic Revolution in Iran occurred at a time when Shimon served in the Knesset and led the Labor Party but was not part of the ruling Israeli government. Yet both events had a profound effect on Israel's foreign policy and would influence Shimon's political life in ways not foreseeable at the time.

✦ ✦ ✦

Following the conclusion of the Camp David Accords, Begin and Sadat reached a peace agreement that resolved issues between Israel and Egypt that had remained unsettled since the Yom Kippur War. That peace agreement was signed in March 1979. Issues regarding Gaza and the West Bank, however, were left unresolved.

At the time it reached an agreement with Egypt, Israel already was obligated by a number of other agreements and international instruments, not the least of which were United Nations Security Council Resolution 242—which obligated Israel to withdraw from territories occupied during the 1967 Six-Day War—and Resolution 338—which imposed the cease-fire that ended fighting in the Yom Kippur War, embraced 242, and required its immediate implementation. In addition, Israel had adopted and approved the Camp David Accords in their entirety, including the *Framework for Peace in the Middle East*. Although that agreement was ultimately rejected by the United Nations as unenforceable against the Palestinians, Israel nevertheless agreed to their terms and was at least tacitly bound by them.

Prime Minister Begin never liked the provisions of the Accords that dealt with the Palestinian issues and only agreed to them as a means of obtaining an agreement with Egypt regarding the Sinai. Like Ben-Gurion, Begin saw Israel as surrounded by enemies on all sides. Security of the nation required that she eliminate as many of those enemies as possible. Doing so from a military perspective was not possible, but by making peace with them Israel could achieve the same goal and more.

Eliminating Israel's enemies through bilateral peace agreements required negotiations. In the exchange necessitated by such a diplomatic undertaking, her enemies would be placed in the position of recognizing Israel diplomatically, thereby legitimizing it in an international sense and acknowledging Israel's right to exist as an independent nation. For Begin, that was the real issue and the larger goal. Agreeing to Sadat's Camp David proposal regarding treatment of the Palestinians was simply the cost of doing business. Besides which, it was an agreement he was certain Israel could finesse to suit its own purposes—which was precisely what he attempted to do.

After the peace treaty with Egypt was signed, Israel faced international pressure to implement Resolution 242. That resolution was written in circumspect language, which Begin reinterpreted to allow for treatment of issues regarding Gaza and the West Bank as an internal Israeli matter. As a means of reinforcing his view that the issues were internal Israeli affairs, Begin excluded Dayan, the Israeli foreign minister, from ensuing discussions with the Palestinians.

Moshe Dayan favored withdrawal of IDF troops from both occupied areas and the opening of the border into those regions to permit free trade between Israel proper and the occupied zones. He understood Begin's decision to exclude him from the Gaza and West Bank meetings as a decision based on their differing views of Israeli policy.

To make matters worse from Dayan's perspective, Begin approved the use of private Arab land to expand Jewish settlements in the West Bank. Dayan, a member of the Knesset as an independent representative, voted against the measure and, like Shimon, felt that further settlements in the occupied territories violated Israel's obligations to any number of agreements and UN resolutions. Consequently, in October 1979, when Begin approved settlement expansion in the West Bank, Dayan resigned from the government.

With Dayan gone, Yitzhak Shamir became foreign minister. Shamir, eight years older than Shimon, was born in Poland and came to Palestine in 1935. He was tough, secretive, and outwardly suspicious. An old-style Irgun hardliner, he held to Revisionist Zionist ideals and was devoted to the idea of Greater Israel—that Jews should control the entire region, all of the area held by the Davidic Kingdom at the height of its glory.

✦ ✦ ✦

In September 1980, Iraq invaded Iran in a conflict that became known as the Iran–Iraq War. As fighting raged along the border between the two countries, Iranian jets bombed the Iraqi reactor site. Damage to the site was minimal but French technicians left the country, and France considered withdrawing from the project altogether. Even with those difficulties, Mossad estimated that the reactor would be repaired, fueled, and operational by June 1981, some nine months away. Begin informed the cabinet of that assessment and in October 1980 the cabinet voted to bomb the reactor to prevent that from happening.

After an intense diplomatic effort, French nuclear technicians returned to Iraq. Repairs were made to the damage inflicted by the Iranian attack and, as predicted by Mossad, the reactor project soon was back on schedule.

Now that Dayan was no longer in the government, Shimon lost his primary channel for information from inside the Begin government. Even so, not long after the cabinet vote, he began hearing rumors about the planning for a strike on the Iraqi reactor. One of those rumors suggested the attack would be a joint operation with the Iranians. That sounded preposterous to Shimon, both from an Iranian and an Israeli perspective. "Shamir doesn't have the imagination for it," he opined. Still the rumors persisted and he decided to find out whether there was any truth to what he'd heard.

Although Menashe Beinart came with Shimon to work for the Labor Party, Yohai Cohen remained at the Defense Ministry. If anyone knew the truth about Israel's preparations for a strike against Iraq, Yohai would. One day that fall, Shimon invited him to lunch. They met in a café on the beach in Tel Aviv.

"I keep hearing rumors," Shimon began.

"About Iraq," Yohai added.

"Yes. Are they true?"

"The cabinet voted to attack. It should have been included in your regular briefing. You've heard about that, haven't you?"

"Yes. But I've heard other things, too."

"Like what?"

Shimon leaned forward and lowered his voice. "Like the attack will be a joint attack with the Iranians." Yohai gave no response and when he remained silent Shimon's eyes opened wide. "It's actually true?"

Yohai wiped the corners of his mouth on his napkin and nodded toward the door. "Let's go for a walk."

Once outside the café, Shimon and Yohai started up the street. In the next block Yohai said, "I can't tell you details."

"Okay. But what's going on here?"

"The enemy of my enemy is my friend." Yohai smiled. "That's what's going on."

"That never works."

"Well," Yohai sighed. "I think we're about to learn that lesson all over again."

"Friends like that always go back to hating you after the crisis passes."

"They understand that," Yohai agreed. "At least on some level. But they also know they don't want our planes to get shot down over Iraq or Iran."

"So, what are they doing?"

"You remember the Iranians hit the reactor last year?"

"Yes."

"They already know the way to get in there," Yohai explained. "Which places to strike. Which ones to avoid. *And*," he added with emphasis, "they can get recent photographs of the site."

"Ah." Shimon had a look of realization. "And they're willing to share."

"I can't say any more."

"Begin understands this is happening? He's aware of what's going on?"

"Yes."

"And he's on board with it?"

"He doesn't object."

"He can be one ruthless guy," Shimon chuckled.

"Yes, he can."

Shimon thought about asking more but didn't want to put Yohai in any more of a compromising position than he might already have created just by meeting with him for lunch. So he kept the rest of his questions to himself. Instead, at the next corner they came to a coffee shop and Shimon suggested they stop in for a drink.

Over the next several weeks, IDF pilots stepped up their training for an attack on the Iraqi site. Those efforts quickened further as the reported delivery of a second uranium shipment, set for the summer of 1981, drew near.

As events unfolded, that uranium delivery was scheduled for a date shortly after French elections. Shimon, ever alert to issues of foreign affairs, was troubled by the juxtaposition of those events and by the timing of a potential Israeli response, especially in light of the rumors about discussions taking place within the Begin government.

In the spring of 1981, Francois Mitterrand was elected president of France. After the election but before his inauguration, Shimon met with Mitterrand at an International Socialist conference in Madrid. They talked about the Iraqi reactor, the pending delivery of uranium, and Israel's concern about what that might mean. Mitterrand promised Shimon he would not allow the second uranium delivery to take place in any manner that violated the agreement with Iraq regarding limitations on the amount of fuel they could possess at any one time.

When Shimon returned from Madrid he went to see Begin at the prime minister's office and reported on his conversation with Mitterrand.

"I understand Mitterrand means well," Begin offered. "And I appreciate you telling me these things, but you are not a minister and any promise he might have made is really no promise at all. Don't you think that is why he told you these things, rather than talking to Shamir?"

"He told me because I was at the conference. Shamir was not."

"Still, if he wants to talk to me about it, or to Shamir, he should give us a call. I am right here at the office most of the time. I'm sure he has the phone number. Or one of his assistants can get it for him. We aren't difficult to find."

"I don't know all the details about what you are planning to do against Iraq—"

"And there is no reason for you to know them," Begin snapped. "You are not a minister."

"I understand that. But I hear rumors, and those rumors say you intend to launch an attack on the reactor in May. The French presidential inauguration is set for May. The reactor in Iraq is a French reactor. Built by French construction companies. Work on it is overseen by French technicians. If we bomb in May, while the French are inaugurating a new president, we will risk offending one of our major international friends."

"Friends?" Begin's voice had an imperious tone. "You think of the French as *our* friends? I think it is more accurate that they are *your* friends."

"They have been a major arms supplier to us and—"

Begin interrupted, "Now we have the Americans. They are selling us F-16 aircraft."

"One day."

"No," Begin corrected. "They intended to sell them to Iran first, but with the shah gone and the Muslims in control, the Americans have refused to sell them any more weapons. We will get the planes that would have gone to them. They will be here in. . . days."

"Well," Shimon sighed, "think about this: When we bomb that reactor—whenever we bomb it—French technicians are going to die. I don't think we want those deaths to occur on the day of the French president's inauguration."

"And why not?"

"Because, Menachem," Shimon exclaimed with frustration, "like I've been saying, doing it then would be an insult to the French government and to the French people. Just delay it one week. That's all. Just a week."

Begin looked away. "I will think about it."

Three days later, Begin sent Shimon a message telling him that the bombing had been postponed for one week. Events pushed the date of the attack back an additional week and on June 7, 1981, Israeli F-16 jets dropped sixteen bombs on the reactor site, at least eight of which hit the containment building. At the time, Israeli analysts calculated the attack set back Iraq's nuclear program by ten years. Later assessment on the ground indicated the bombing had destroyed Iraq's nuclear program completely.

✦ ✦ ✦

Even with military action pending against Iraq, a general election had been scheduled in Israel for June 1981. In preparation for that election, Yitzhak Rabin attempted a political comeback and challenged Shimon for Labor Party leadership. Their old rivalry emerged once more and the two campaigned hard against each other. With help from Menashe Beinart, Shimon defeated Rabin and retained control, which made him the Labor Party candidate for prime minister in the coming election.

Although Menashe Beinart was in charge of the party's message, Shimon asked Amiram Nir to head the overall campaign. Nir, a journalist, took a leave of absence from his job to work full time for Shimon's election. The campaign went well and many thought Labor would win a resounding victory. The result was better for Labor than before but fell short of giving the party enough seats in the Knesset to take control of the government.

When the votes were counted, Likud, with Menachem Begin in control, held forty-eight seats—an increase of only three. Labor held forty-seven, up from thirty-three in 1977, but not enough to have the first attempt at forming a governing coalition. That prize went to Likud, which easily formed a coalition with several right-wing parties. For yet another election cycle, Shimon remained out of the top spot, though still a member of the Knesset.

✦ ✦ ✦

Later that fall, Anwar Sadat attended an annual parade held in Cairo to commemorate the Egyptian army's crossing of the Suez Canal at the beginning of the Yom Kippur War. As he sat in the reviewing stand, a soldier approached. Thinking it was part of the show, Sadat stood to salute him. Rather than saluting the president, the soldier tossed three hand grenades, then opened fire with an automatic weapon. Three other gunmen on a nearby military truck opened fire as well. Sadat was wounded and immediately fell to the ground. Dozens more were struck as well.

Security personnel reacted immediately, killing the first soldier, then wounding the others. The three remaining attackers were arrested and the wounded were transported to local hospitals. Two hours later, Sadat died of his injuries. Ten others were dead from the attack also. Egypt's vice president, Hosni Mubarak, was injured in the attack but recovered and assumed office immediately. A former career air force officer and later deputy minister of defense, he'd been appointed to the vice presidency by Sadat and assumed the role of president seamlessly.

Shimon was shocked by the news of Sadat's death, but he had little time to grieve or process what had happened. Just ten days later, Moshe Dayan died in Jerusalem from a sudden heart attack. The loss of Sadat saddened Shimon. He and Sadat had been much more than mere acquaintances. The loss of Dayan, however, was devastating. They had been more than friends. Much like brothers, they argued over many things but never about their commitment to each other or the ties that bound them together as friends. Dayan had been his comrade, his chief supporter, and a friend when he needed one the most. Shimon had valued his loyalty, but even more his honesty.

SHIMON PERES

*"The Palestinians are our
closest neighbors.
I believe they may become
our closest friends."*

BY 1982, THE LEBANESE Civil War had been going
on for seven years. In June of that year, operatives from Abu Nidal, a
Fatah organization, attempted to kill an Israeli ambassador in London.
Begin responded with an air strike against facilities in Beirut that
housed Fatah headquarters and its sister organization, the Palestine
Liberation Organization. The PLO responded with rocket attacks
against northern Israel. Those attacks were launched from PLO bases
in southern Lebanon.

Begin and most members of Likud favored a military response,
though most of them wanted a limited incursion designed to deal with
the bases from which the rockets had been launched. Ariel Sharon,
who had replaced Ezer Weizman as defense minister, wanted a large-
scale military operation. The two plans were each favored by different
groups within the Begin government, but rather than choosing one or
the other Begin allowed both to develop at the same time.

Begin ordered IDF units into southern Lebanon in an operation Sharon described to the press and everyone else as a limited cross-border action. In reality, IDF had launched a large-scale invasion—the plan Sharon favored but which included no real goal and no end game. Moreover, once the approval order was given and the operation commenced, Begin stepped out of the picture, leaving full control to Sharon.

In rapid succession, the IDF swept across the border and rolled up the PLO camps that had been harassing northern Galilee, but it didn't stop there. Syrian army units that held positions just north of the red line were driven back, then forced into a pell-mell retreat. Lead Israeli units reached the outskirts of Beirut in a matter of days and put the city under siege.

Faced with an Israeli onslaught, Yasser Arafat and the PLO fled from Lebanon and set up a new headquarters in Tunisia. Likewise, the Syrian army withdrew from Lebanon altogether. Shortly after that, an international peace-keeping force, including a contingent of US Marines, arrived in Beirut and attempted to position itself between the warring Lebanese civil factions and the IDF.

With the country descending into chaos, the Lebanese parliament met to select a new president and chose Bashir Gemayel for the position. An Israeli ally, Gemayel seemed to give Begin and Sharon a path out of the conflict—keep IDF troops there long enough for Gemayel to form a stable government, help put reforms in place to quell the fighting, then withdraw from an otherwise successful military operation. That all changed in September, though, when Gemayel was killed in a bombing. The following day, IDF troops entered West Beirut.

From its beginning, the Lebanese Civil War had created an enormous refugee crisis. Camps were set up in numerous locations around the country to deal with the hundreds of thousands who fled the fighting. Two of the largest camps were at Sabra and Shatila. After Gemayel's death, members of the Phalange, a Lebanese Christian political party, approached Sharon and asked for permission to enter those two camps, supposedly to search for terrorists who were responsible for the attack on Gemayel. Sharon gave his permission.

In actuality, the supposed search for terrorists had been merely a ploy for Phalange members who only wanted to avenge Gemayel's death on any Palestinians they might find. That night, they entered the refugee camps and by the next morning more than a thousand Palestinian refugees lay dead.

When news of the refugee killings reached Tel Aviv, protestors took to the streets in mass demonstrations. The international community was outraged, too. So much so that near the end of September, Begin was forced to appoint a commission of inquiry to investigate the matter. The group was chaired by Yitzhak Kahan, the Israeli Supreme Court president, and became known as the Kahan Commission.

Sadly, in the midst of the refugee controversy, Begin's wife, Aliza, died. Those closest to Begin could see the emotional energy drain away from him. Unlike many politicians, Begin was close to his wife and family. "They are why I do what I do," he said more than once. And he meant it. He soldiered on, continuing in office even as Israeli support for the war faded, resistance mounted in Lebanon, and IDF casualties rose, but his heart was no longer in it.

✦ ✦ ✦

Meanwhile, along with its nuclear research, which continued at Dimona, Israel also invested heavily in satellite and rocket technology. The program began in the 1970s and continued into the '80s, though few knew of its existence—fewer even than knew of the nuclear program.

Progress with satellite and missile development progressed ahead of schedule and early in 1983 IDF intelligence agencies were on the verge of launching their own version of a military spy satellite. It was one they intended to place in a geosynchronous orbit above the Middle East. From there IDF analysts would be able to continuously monitor all of its neighbors and increase the window of advance warning from a matter of hours, as it had been at the time of the Yom Kippur War, to weeks—and in some cases, months.

When officials in the United States learned of Israel's program and its intentions, they became concerned that it would provoke others in the region to do likewise. "This isn't merely a new weapons system," one official argued. "This changes the status quo. Nothing you could do short of deploying your own nuclear weapons would have as much effect as this. If you launch even one satellite, Saudi Arabia, Iran, Pakistan, and Egypt will do the same. And they all have the means of developing or acquiring the technology." Still, Israeli officials would not back down and the program continued toward a scheduled launch date.

In order to prevent a Middle East space race, the United States offered Begin and the Defense Ministry an alternative. They could end the satellite program in exchange for real-time intelligence from the region provided by US agencies from all US sources operating in the Middle East—satellite and otherwise.

Faced with the insistence of Israel's primary ally, Begin had little choice but to acquiesce. In a matter of weeks, the intelligence-sharing arrangement was formalized in a Memo of Understanding, which was signed and exchanged between the two countries.

In order to implement the US end of the deal, US intelligence agencies were required to instruct analysts on details of the arrangement and create a mechanism for sharing the intelligence with their Israeli counterparts. One of the US agencies affected by the terms of the deal was the Navy Intelligence Command. Analysts there were briefed at a week-long conference at which they were shown copies of the Memo of Understanding, drilled on the kinds of information that would be shared, and instructed on how to access and use the mechanism for transferring it. They were also told about procedures for reviewing the information before its release and the criteria for redacting content not relevant to the program.

Attending that meeting was Jonathan Pollard, a Jewish American who was sympathetic to Israel. Pollard was a senior analyst and an expert in Middle Eastern affairs. He also was brash, cocky, and not afraid to speak his mind. Unlike the others, Pollard asked questions about the Memo and the scope of its application. "The memo says we are to share real-time information," he noted.

"Yes," an instructor replied. "You have a problem with that?"

"I'm just thinking, if the information is real time, that means it's live. Arriving here and going there in a live feed. So if we're sharing this live feed with Mossad or IDF, how will we have time to conduct the review you mentioned? And why are we reviewing it in the first place?"

"Well... obviously... " the instructor stammered uncomfortably. "We're talking about building in some slack in the timeline."

And that's when Pollard realized United States officials had no intention of sharing anything in real time. Whatever was shared with Israel would not be a live feed, as the Memo required. Just another sanitized version of the truth like those handed out to every other country Americans wanted to control. The American version. Not the raw information necessary to make an informed decision, which was the goal for which Israel had designed its satellite and which the United States wanted to deprive it.

Pollard was angry over the way his supervisors applied the Israeli arrangement, but at first he did as he was told and made sure the information he forwarded for transmission met their requirements. On his own, though, he maintained a log of information he was ordered to remove or which his agency avoided sharing with Israel. Information Pollard thought fell within the meaning of the Memo and was crucial to Israel's defense.

After weeks of complying, however, Pollard could stand it no more. "Look at this," he said to his wife one evening as they sat at the kitchen table. He reached inside his briefcase and took out four photographs and half a dozen documents. "This is the kind of stuff they're withholding," he declared, thrusting the papers toward her.

She took them from him and scanned over them. "Are you supposed to have these?" she asked with a look of concern.

"I have clearance."

She glanced back at the documents. "Clearance to bring this home?"

He attempted to avoid her question. "Don't they seem important to you?"

Two of the documents were transcripts of intercepted communications between Syrian units operating near the Golan Heights. The photographs were of a missile installation. "The intercepted conversation seems to be important," she agreed. "But I don't know about the photographs. What are they?"

"Iranian missiles. They were about to run a test on them. Two days ago." He pointed to his briefcase. "We intercepted the telemetry from the flights. I have that, too."

"And they aren't sharing that, either?"

"No."

"So, why did you bring these home?" She looked up at him. "Why are you telling me about this?"

He leaned toward her. "I have to get this information to them."

His wife frowned. "To the Israelis?"

"Yes."

She glanced over the documents once more. "Won't that get you into trouble at work?"

Pollard had a sly grin. "Not if they don't find out. My supervisors are. . . they'll never know. They'll never figure it out."

His wife laid the documents on the table. "So, why did they set up an arrangement with Israel and promise them information if they weren't going to provide it?"

Pollard leaned away from her. "They do this kind of thing all the time. This is their standard way of operating. Say one thing, do another. It's the American way. Information is control, so they think. And they like controlling everything."

"But, Jonathan, we're Americans, too."

"I am Jewish," he responded in a prideful tone. "First and foremost, I am Jewish."

It was a crucial moment for Pollard. And for his wife. A moment when they turned from being merely upset to becoming active participants in a scheme that would affect both the United States and Israel in deeply troubling ways. And would reach Shimon as well.

✦ ✦ ✦

That same year, the Kahan Commission issued its report on the massacre that occurred at the refugee camps in Lebanon. The commission found that direct responsibility for the tragedy lay with Phalange and its members who entered the camps and conducted the murderous rampage. It further found that no Israelis were directly involved in the events of that fateful night. However, the report went on to conclude that Israeli defense minister Ariel Sharon was personally responsible for ignoring the danger implicit in his authorization for Phalange members to enter the camps, and for failing to take action in advance to prevent the killings. The commission quickly recommended that Sharon be dismissed from office.

In response to the committee report, Begin refused to dismiss Sharon, and Sharon refused to resign. As they had with controversies in the past, Israeli citizens took to the streets of Tel Aviv to register their objections to the underlying conduct at the camp and to the administration's response to the report. At one protest rally, someone tossed a hand grenade into the crowd, killing one demonstrator and wounding dozens.

With the country once again in an uproar over the government's conduct, Sharon resigned from the Defense Ministry. However, Begin, loyal to the bitter end, allowed him to remain as a minister without portfolio.

By then, Israel's military was bogged down in Lebanon with no plan for staying and no plan for leaving. Begin tried repeatedly to reach an agreement with Lebanon officials, and with the warring factions, that would allow Israel a graceful withdrawal from its engagement but those efforts failed.

At the same time, Israel's economy spiraled downward, trapped between rampant inflation and rising prices. Pressure for Begin to resign, which had risen steadily from Shimon and the Labor Party, now came from within Likud as well.

Ever the fighter, the notion of quitting ran counter to everything Begin believed and he longed to remain in office, to serve to the end of his statutory term, if for nothing else than to deny Labor the satisfaction of seeing him go. But he was weary. He'd been working for the Revisionist dream of Greater Israel his entire adult life and had devoted every ounce of himself to that cause. Now, with his wife gone and Israel's future bleak, he had reached the end of his career. "I have no more energy for it," he said at last.

In August, Begin resigned from the premiership. Yitzhak Shamir, the foreign minister, was appointed by Likud to complete the term, which was not scheduled to end until November 1985.

SHIMON PERES

"Our problem is not to submit to the
differences but to overcome them."

AFTER MENACHEM BEGIN resigned, Shimon began maneuvering in the Knesset for early elections. Shamir was reluctant to give up even a single month from the remainder of the term, but the country was in trouble and in the end he was convinced he could find a way to blame the difficulty on the Labor Party. After several rounds of negotiations, the election date was rescheduled for July 1984.

In the spring, before elections in July, Shimon again turned his attention to the issue of peace. The Palestinian problem cried out for a solution and he wanted to find one. He also wanted to address Israel's long-term security. Left unresolved, the Palestinian issue threatened the stability of both Israel and Jordan, where many Palestinian Arabs still resided. "There has to be a way for us to solve this together," he insisted. "Peace with Jordan. Peace with the Palestinians. It would be a win for all of us."

Still not a part of the governing coalition, Shimon was powerless to reach a binding agreement with anyone on any of the issues that concerned him, but he was convinced that the political situation was going to change with the coming election. Israelis were tired of the war in Lebanon and scared of the rampant, uncontrolled inflation that robbed them of their economic power. He was certain they would not return Likud to office, no matter whom the candidates were, and he wanted to be ready when the country's leadership was handed to Labor.

As an initial step in that direction, Shimon asked Menashe Beinart to take over the Jordan peace project and see if a way could be found to move forward with King Hussein. Beinart contacted Abdel Mousa, an acquaintance who worked in the Jordanian prime minister's office. They met for dinner in Jerusalem. "Tell me," Mousa began when they were seated in the restaurant, "What is an honest journalist like you doing with the Israeli Labor Party?"

Beinart laughed. "That is a good question."

"I mean it," Mousa insisted. "You should be reporting on them for a newspaper or television station. Not assisting them."

"I support most of what they stand for."

"Most."

"And I believe wholeheartedly in one of their key initiatives."

"And what is that?"

"Peace."

"Ahh." Mousa nodded approvingly. "And on that we are in wholehearted agreement."

For the next thirty minutes they talked about a wide range of issues, most of which they agreed upon. But when it came to the question of trying again to memorialize those points of agreement in a peace treaty Mousa shook his head. "King Hussein is as interested in these matters as you and I. But he will not undertake to reach an agreement with Israel on his own."

"We've tried multilateral talks before," Beinart replied. "They didn't work."

"Yes." Mousa nodded. "I know."

"The problem is always the same."

"Syria," Mousa said with a scornful expression. "It has always been that way with them. For us. For our ancestors. For *their* ancestors. All the way back."

"They will participate in meetings and they will talk a thing to death, but they won't agree to anything and that's as far as it ever goes."

Mousa smiled. "But we are not suggesting that discussions should involve all of the parties."

Beinart's eyes widened. "So, we wouldn't have to include Syria?"

Mousa shook his head. "Syria is not the key."

"Okay. . . " Beinart thought for a moment. "You mean Egypt?"

Mousa's face lit up with interest. "Convince the Egyptians to support your ideas—and get them to do so publicly—and King Hussein will be more than willing to talk to anyone you send our way."

The next morning, Beinart told Shimon about his conversation with Mousa. Shimon was pleased to know that Hussein remained amenable to the idea of peace but not so confident about getting the Egyptians to support the effort. "Mubarak is not Sadat," he opined. "And I'm not sure how to approach him, either. I don't know him very well. We need more information on him."

Beinart grinned. "And I know just the right person for that."

"You can't do it yourself?"

Beinart shook his head. "Not this time."

"Well, make sure you use someone reliable. I don't want news of this to get out. They'll start all of that 'Shimon making his own foreign policy' talk again."

Later that week, Beinart met with Arik Caspi, a recent graduate of Technion—the Israeli Institute of Technology—Israel's oldest university. Beinart and Caspi's older brother were long-time friends. He'd known Caspi most of his life.

Like many Israelis, Caspi was fluent in multiple languages besides Hebrew, including Arabic, Farsi, and English. Unlike many, though, he also was an expert in the emerging field of computer technology.

In the '80s, before the advent of personal computers and the World Wide Web, the digital world existed as a subculture, one that valued the free exchange of information and cared little about ethnic or cultural distinctions. As a result, Caspi was friends with members of all races and religions in the global technology community. One of those friends was Salah Azer, the youngest son of Hamdi Azer, an Egyptian entrepreneur and friend of Hosni Mubarak. He brought Caspi by the office one day to meet Shimon.

"I'm in favor of using technology," Shimon commented after Caspi was gone. "And I am certain the industrial age is about to be revamped by the application of computers and all they can do. But diplomacy remains a personal thing. It always comes down to a one-on-one relationship with a person. Why do we need a technology expert?"

"You're right," Beinart agreed. "We don't need technology for this. We need Caspi."

Shimon frowned. "You're sure about this?"

"Positive."

At Beinart's request, Caspi passed a message to Salah, who gave it to his father, asking for a meeting. Two weeks later, Caspi responded.

"Next month," he told Beinart, "we will attend a technology conference at MIT."

Beinart gave him a dour look. "We?"

Caspi gesture between them. "You and I."

Beinart looked perplexed. "And why would I attend a technology conference?"

"Salah is expecting you," Caspi explained. "And I want to attend the conference."

Beinart nodded knowingly. "And you expect me to pay for it."

Caspi shrugged. "The cost of doing business."

As arranged, Beinart and Caspi traveled to Boston the following month and attended the conference. While there, Caspi introduced Beinart to Salah. After the conference ended, Salah took them to New York and introduced them to his father, Hamdi.

For three hours, Beinart and Hamdi sat in an apartment overlooking Manhattan's midtown district and discussed a wide range of topics affecting the Middle East—the Palestinian issue, Syrian aggression, how to avoid the spread of nuclear weapons throughout the region, and many other unresolved issues. But when the conversation turned to Egyptian support for a peace agreement between Jordan and Israel, Hamdi shook his head. "Mubarak knows that you want his help. We have discussed it many times. But he will not give it."

Beinart's forehead wrinkled in a frown. "Why not? We have an agreement between our countries. Why not help us reach a similar agreement with Jordan?"

"It is not about Jordan," Hamdi explained. "In fact, Mubarak would very much like for you to have such an agreement with them."

"Then what is the problem?"

"Taba," Hamdi said flatly.

Beinart was confounded. "Taba? The tiny village on the Gulf of Aqaba?"

"That is the one."

"So if we could solve the question about Taba, we—"

"If you resolved the issue with Taba, you would have the full assistance and support of President Mubarak and the Egyptian government for an effort to ease matters with Jordan—or with any of the other countries in the region, for that matter."

A perennial point of contention, the village of Taba—less than one hundred acres in size—located at the top of the Gulf of Aqaba had been the subject of a long-standing dispute over international borders; a dispute that dated to the time of the Ottomans. When Israeli troops invaded the Sinai Peninsula during the Yom Kippur War they took control of Taba. After finally reaching a peace agreement with Egypt, Israel removed the last of her troops from the Peninsula and handed over control to Egypt. The withdrawal had been total, full, and complete—except for a small contingent of IDF soldiers that remained in Taba.

A few days after his meeting with Hamdi Azer, Beinart returned to Israel and reported to Shimon. "That's the holdup?" Shimon asked with a pained look after hearing about Taba.

"Yes," Beinart replied. "That is the issue."

"He would refuse to help bring peace to the entire region over an ancient dispute about one little village?"

"It's not a little village to them."

"Then what is it?"

"Sovereignty," Beinart explained. "And the need of Egyptians to be accepted with dignity by their neighbors. Something we know a little about."

Shimon's countenance softened. "Indeed we do." He gave a heavy sigh. "So, how would they like to resolve it?"

"They would like us to leave Taba. But, short of that, I think they would be satisfied for now if we agreed to submit the matter to arbitration."

"They've said that before," Shimon noted.

"And I think they really mean it."

Shimon ran his fingers through his hair while he continued to think. "I don't know. . . "

"Arbitration would give everyone a chance to tell their story," Beinart continued. "And it would give the losing side a way to bow out gracefully."

Shimon had a thoughtful expression. "No one would have to surrender. They could simply say, 'the arbitrator told us it wasn't ours.'"

"Yes," Beinart said. "And that would be a good thing."

For the remainder of the year, Shimon mulled the idea over in his mind, trying to figure out a way to maneuver the Taba issue toward resolution. Moving this, to get that, to make the third thing happen. He thought he could find a way to make it happen, a way to fit the pieces in place, but it all hinged on the results of the upcoming elections.

✦ ✦ ✦

In the election that July, Shimon and the Labor Party won the most seats, claiming a total of forty-four places. The most—but not enough for an outright majority. Likud, led by Yitzhak Shamir, held forty-one. Without an absolute majority from its own members, Labor was forced to form a coalition. Doing so, however, was complicated because the Orthodox parties—the only source of sizeable swing votes—favored Likud. After a week of bargaining, cajoling, and arm-twisting, Labor controlled sixty seats, but Likud hadn't sat by quietly, waiting to see what would happen. Its members had also been trying to form a coalition and controlled sixty as well. Yet neither side had enough Knesset support to form a government.

With the two sides deadlocked, Shimon approached Shamir—whom he'd just defeated—with a proposition that astounded political pundits and leaders everywhere. "What if we formed a unity government," Shimon suggested.

Shamir was impassive. "Unity?"

"The two parties. Labor and Likud. Coming together to form a governing coalition."

"How can there be unity? Our parties are on opposite sides of the spectrum. Labor favors territorial compromise as a way of finding peace. Likud supports Greater Israel. You want peace. We want victory."

"We won the election," Shimon reminded him. "And yet we are willing to form a coalition with the party we just defeated. Doesn't that speak to a sense of unity that transcends our differences? Isn't Israel bigger than either of us? More important than the political parties we represent?"

"This is ridiculous," Shamir grumbled. "It would never work."

"It would work if we tried. We can divide the premiership's statutory fifty-month term. Each of us serving for twenty-five months."

"I don't know. . . "

"There is no other way. We can't simply allow the government to operate without leadership."

Shamir gave an offhanded shrug. "The cabinet can run it."

"*What* cabinet?" Shimon was thoroughly frustrated by Shamir's lack of interest. "There *is* no cabinet. And without a governing coalition, there won't be one for the foreseeable future, either."

Shamir shook his head. "I don't know. . . "

Shimon left that first meeting angry and astounded at Shamir's response. He'd been offered the most magnanimous gesture anyone in Israeli politics could make, yet Shamir treated it like Shimon was groveling.

When Beinart heard about Shamir's response he suggested that Shimon talk to Ariel Sharon. "He and Shamir are good friends. They go back a long way. Shamir will listen to him."

Shimon was intrigued by the suggestion and went to see Sharon. "That's a great idea," Sharon bellowed after hearing Shimon's plan. "You actually made him that offer?"

"Yes."

"I am amazed."

"But how do we get Shamir to agree? He won't commit. Just grunts and sighs and shakes his head."

Sharon laughed. "You leave Shamir to me."

A few days later, Shamir's assistant called Beinart and the two met for coffee at a secluded restaurant in Jerusalem's Old City. After thirty minutes of discussion about the details, the two sides reached an agreement. Shamir would be named foreign minister. Yitzhak Rabin would serve as defense minister. The remaining Ministry positions would be divided evenly with an executive committee comprised of top ministers to decide the most contentious issues. And Shimon would serve as prime minister first.

✦ ✦ ✦

That September, Shimon took office as prime minister. Menashe Beinart became cabinet secretary, a position that set the agenda for cabinet meetings and coordinated communication with the ministers. He kept the top echelon of the government informed about what each of the departments was doing and communicated the government's legislative bills to the Knesset. In form, the position was administrative. In function, however, Beinart was one of Shimon's closest advisers.

The first issue Shimon addressed was withdrawal from Lebanon. Working with Rabin, he settled on a plan for that to occur in two phases. Over the next several months, the IDF would withdraw in an orderly manner, leaving troops in only a secure zone along the Lebanon–Israel border to prevent the PLO from harassing northern Galilee with rocket attacks—which initially had been the primary goal of the incursion from the start.

At the same time, Shimon began working to put the country's economy on a sound footing. Inflation was rampant. Real income was down. Shimon's economic team, which had been working on the problem since before the election, came to him after he took office with a set of proposals. The measures were serious, precise, and supported by overwhelming data. But they were also drastic and potentially costly from a political perspective. Price controls and devaluation of currency, among other items.

After considering their plan, Shimon decided to try something less risky—incremental budget cuts, a smaller devaluation—in the hope that a bonus could be derived from the reduced military commitment in Lebanon. None of those changes, however, had any effect on the economy.

Reluctantly, he turned once again to his economic team and asked them to review the country's economic situation. A few weeks later, they returned with the same proposal they'd given Shimon at the onset of his term. This time, he decided to implement it.

As a preliminary move, though, Shimon traveled to the United States and met with members of the Reagan administration. After reviewing Shimon's plans for righting Israel's economy, US treasury officials gave their approval and President Reagan pledged a $1.5 billion financial aid package for Israel as a safety net.

When he returned to Israel, Shimon began implementing the economic team's plan, imposing a large currency devaluation, together with price controls, wage controls, and steep government budget cuts. The plan was presented to the cabinet and, after an all-night debate, the measures were passed and put into effect. By autumn, inflation had dropped from twenty percent in June to only two-and-a-half percent.

✦ ✦ ✦

As summer faded into fall of that first year of Shimon's term, Mubarak still refused to talk with Israel about anything other than Taba. Yet Shimon had been unable to bring the Taba issue to a resolution. Undaunted in his desire for peace, he decided to try again to negotiate an agreement with Hussein, even without Mubarak. Perhaps things had changed since the previous discussions. Maybe there was another way.

Beinart had handled Shimon's earlier broach of an agreement months before the election. Now, however, he served as cabinet secretary, which occupied most of his attention. Instead, Shimon asked Yohai Cohen, still working at the Defense Ministry, to take over the effort. Without hesitation, Yohai resigned from his position and came to work in the prime minister's office as a special adviser.

Although Beinart had little time to devote to the cause, he arranged an introduction for Yohai with Abdel Mousa from the Jordanian prime minister's office. Yohai and Mousa warmed to each other immediately and met on several occasions for extended discussions.

A few weeks later, Yohai reported to Shimon, "Hussein will talk to us, with or without Mubarak, but he is only interested in doing so within the framework of an international conference—one that includes the five permanent members of the UN Security Council."

"And Mousa didn't say anything about Egypt?"

"No, but I think he's still in the same position, just talking about it differently."

"What do you mean?"

"He wants someone to cover for him. Another Arab leader to say it's okay for him to agree with us. He's not willing to do this alone."

"He thinks a conference setting will get him a better deal. And he's right."

"How so?"

"The West feels guilty over the Palestinian situation. Arabs know it and are certain that if they can get us into an international conference the West will side with them and we'll be forced to do whatever they say."

Yohai scoffed. "Not much chance of that happening."

Shimon had a dour expression. "People other than our own, dictating terms and conditions for us they would never accept for themselves—I hardly think so."

"The West *is* very sympathetic to the Palestinian cause."

Shimon concurred. "And they will do whatever the Palestinians want. If we're a participant in an international conference, that will force us to comply while giving the Palestinians a pass on doing. . . anything."

Yohai was thoughtful. "Maybe we should look at this a different way."

"What way?"

"An international conference without the part that we object to."

Shimon was perplexed. "I'm not sure I understand what you mean."

"We give Hussein his international conference but one that doesn't permit someone else to force their views on us."

"But how could that work? A conference, but not a conference?"

"We hold the conference, invite all the players. They gather for an opening session, then each of the countries from the region break off into individual groups to meet with us. We have negotiators talking to all of them individually, narrowing the differences. Then you circulate among those groups answering questions only you can answer. Keeping the discussions moving in the right direction."

"But then Hussein or someone else will just object to whatever we propose, the dispute will be referred to the full session for resolution, and they'll jam something down our throats."

"Not if there is no right of referral."

Shimon's forehead wrinkled in a deep frown. "No right of referral?"

"That's the part we leave out. Hussein gets the part he wants—the conference with all of the players participating—but we get the part we want—no right of referral. All issues must be resolved in the one-on-one groups. Whatever is done must be done between the two parties."

Shimon shook his head in frustration. "But why would the international community want to participate in something like that?"

"We bring them in for the enforcement. Their role is to hold the parties to what the parties agree to. But the agreement is between the parties. Israel and Jordan. Israel and Syria. Israel and the Palestinians. The affected parties decide the issues. They agree on the solutions. The others help them enforce the agreements."

Shimon thought for a moment. "It might work," he agreed finally.

"We have nothing to lose. I mean, we have nothing now. The worst that can happen is Hussein rejects the idea and we have nothing then. But we already have nothing, so we'd be no worse off."

"And," Shimon added, thinking ahead, "we'd get Hussein in the room to talk—at least to talk about whether we can agree on a conference. It would be talking about talking, but that's further ahead than we are right now." He smiled over at Yohai. "This is a good idea. Now, see if you can get Hussein to agree to meet with me to discuss holding an international conference."

"We'll need a sponsor."

"I can take care of it. That part won't be a problem at all. A dozen countries will want to host us. Get Hussein in the room with me and let's see if we can get this started."

31

SHIMON PERES

"In many ways, the media today makes dictatorship impossible. But it also makes democracy intolerable."

AFTER SHIMON TOOK OFFICE, Amiram Nir, who had managed Shimon's 1981 campaign, was placed in charge of Israel's terrorism-response policy. In May 1985, Nir attended a UN conference in Paris on the changing nature of terrorism and its increasingly global scope and threat. During a break between conference sessions Nir ran into Sidney Thompson. They had become friends years earlier when Thompson had been a student at American University and spent a term studying in Jerusalem. That night, they met for dinner at a restaurant in Le Meurice, a Paris hotel located across from the Tuileries Garden.

"I never thought I would see you here," Nir commented as they were seated at a table. "Not at *this* conference."

Thompson looked surprised. "Why not?"

"I didn't think of you as someone who'd be interested in the topic."

"But I knew *you* would be here," Thompson answered with a grin.

Nir responded with a raised eyebrow. "That's interesting, because I didn't know I'd be here until a week ago. Someone else was supposed to attend, but she was reassigned at the last moment, and since the expenses were already paid I took her place."

"That's how I knew you'd be here."

Nir realized his attendance at the conference had been manipulated and was curious about how that had been accomplished, but he decided to let it pass for the moment. "What was so important that I needed to be here?"

"You are familiar with Robert McFarlane?"

"President Reagan's national security adviser? I know his name and I've seen his picture in the magazines. But that's about the extent of it."

"McFarlane would like for someone from the Israeli government to meet with Michael Ledeen, a scholar from the American Enterprise Institute."

"The conservative think tank in New York."

"Right," Thompson acknowledged. "When they asked me about it, I naturally thought of you."

"What would this meeting be about?" Nir wondered.

"Ledeen is an historian by training but he's researching counterterrorism options for a group at the White House. They're looking into policy and strategic options and they're interested in his work."

"A group at the White House. Are these people officials in the Reagan administration?"

"Some of them."

Nir had a knowing smile. "You mean McFarlane is interested in it."

"Yes." Thompson glanced away. "So, Ledeen would like to meet with an appropriate person in Israel who might be able to help with his research."

"You mean McFarlane would like for him to meet with someone."

Thompson looked over at Nir. "I wouldn't be here if McFarlane hadn't sent me. So, yes, this was his idea."

"Why didn't you just pick up the phone and call me?"

"I asked the same question," Thompson replied. "They said this way was better."

"Why?"

"I think so you would know how serious they are about this."

Nir paused to wipe the corner of his mouth on a napkin. "I would be glad to meet with Mr. Ledeen. But that's all."

"I understand."

"I'll meet with him and listen to what he has to say, but I'm not agreeing to more than that without authorization from my superiors."

"You mean without authorization from the prime minister."

Nir looked him in the eye. "I think we both know what we mean."

Three weeks later, Ledeen arrived in Tel Aviv and met with Nir. "What sort of research are you interested in conducting?" Nir asked.

"Actually," Ledeen replied, "it's not research."

"I suspected as much. Go on."

"As you are aware, several US citizens are being held in Lebanon. The administration is interested in gaining their release. They were wondering if you or someone you know might be able to help with that."

"They are being held by Hezbollah?"

"Yes."

Nir thought for a moment. "What you're proposing would require the approval and assistance of officials in Iran."

"That is why I am here," Ledeen noted. "We are aware that members of your government have worked with Iranian officials in the past—on the bombing of the Iraqi reactor, for instance."

Ledeen had an odd expression, but the fact that he came by way of a friend, and apparently at the behest of a high-ranking US official, left Nir reluctant to dismiss the request out of hand. "I'll take your request under advisement," Nir said. "We'll see what we can do, but like I've said before, I'm not committing to anything more than that. Not today."

"I understand, but I—"

Nir cut him off. "Should I respond to you, or to someone else?"

"Respond to me for now."

That afternoon, Nir met with Shimon and reported on his meeting with Ledeen. "I would be glad to help," Shimon announced after hearing the details. "But only if George Shultz is involved in the arrangement." Shultz was the US secretary of state. "We need to make sure Ledeen's request is legitimate and that we're actually dealing with the government, not just someone with an idea and personal initiative."

Nir agreed, "My thoughts exactly. What they're talking about would be an Iran–U.S. prisoner swap, no matter how they dress it or what they call it."

"Yes."

"And we would be in the middle of it."

"That's why I want you to check it out." Shimon looked him in the eye. "And check it out thoroughly. Don't cut any corners."

To keep the hostage release effort away from journalists, Nir operated outside ordinary diplomatic and military channels. At Shimon's suggestion, he asked Al Schwimmer to coordinate the details.

Schwimmer had been instrumental in Ben-Gurion's efforts to acquire American bomber aircraft during the War of Independence. After the war, Schwimmer moved to Israel, became an Israeli citizen, and founded the nation's first aircraft-manufacturing company. He was well versed in business transactions and logistics, skills Shimon was certain would come into play if the matter with Ledeen went beyond mere talk.

Nir met with Schwimmer and found him more than eager to participate. "I will do whatever Shimon Peres needs me to do."

"For this to work," Nir explained, "we will need Iranian approval. Hezbollah won't do anything like this without Tehran's involvement. So we need to find someone in Iran who will work with us and who has connections with the government at a decision-making level. We need a player on that end of the deal or this will drag on forever."

Schwimmer nodded. "I don't know anyone personally, but I may know just the guy to help us find someone."

Later that week, Schwimmer contacted Yaakov Nimrodi, a former Israeli military attaché who had served in Iran. With Schwimmer's approval, Nimrodi approached Eshaq Salehi and Hassan Larijani, members of the Iranian government who were politically moderate—committed to the Islamic Revolution that brought them to power but not blindly antagonistic to the West. Salehi and Hassan indicated they could gain release of the American prisoners but needed military hardware as a quid pro quo. "We are at war with Iraq and need weapons with which to fight the Iraqis," Salehi explained. "If you could arrange help for us in that regard, we might be able to arrange help for the Americans."

"You mean if we provide weapons, you can provide release of the prisoners."

"We are willing to buy them," Hassan noted quickly. "We just need access to them."

"What kind of weapons do you need?"

"Missiles," Salehi answered without a moment's hesitation. "We need missiles."

"US missiles," Hassan added.

"HAWK antiaircraft and TOW antitank missiles, to be specific."

Nimrodi nodded. "Very well, I will pass your response to my superiors and to the Americans and let you know their response."

Salehi had a questioning look. "Do you think this is in the realm of possibility?"

"Yes," Nimrodi replied. "I think it is."

"Good," they both beamed. "Very good."

Nimrodi met with Schwimmer and discussed the Iranian response, then together they briefed Amiram Nir, who reported the matter to Shimon. "Okay," Shimon agreed. "We know the parameters of the deal. US missiles to Iran in exchange for the release of US hostages being held by Hezbollah in Lebanon."

"Right."

"But I still want to know that someone besides Ledeen knows about this. Have you contacted Shultz?"

"I've talked to people in McFarlane's office, but not Shultz. I think he's over my head."

"You're probably right," Shimon agreed. "Go ahead and report back to Ledeen. Tell him what you told me about what the Iranians had to say. I'll talk to Shultz and be sure we're straight with him."

A few days later, Nir met with Ledeen in his New York office and briefed him on the Iranian response. Ledeen was favorably impressed and passed that information on to Paul Jackson, who worked in McFarlane's office. Jackson came to New York and met with Nir at a hotel near Times Square.

After hearing the details for himself, Jackson authorized Nir to go forward with the arrangement. "But we will need for you to provide the hardware from your own inventory and arrange for its delivery."

"You mean you want the Israeli government to sell weapons to the Iranian government?"

"I know it's a stretch but it's the way this has to be done. I don't see any other way."

"And the U.S. will replenish our stocks?"

"Yes."

"And you will deliver them to us at your expense."

Jackson grinned. "Once the deal is complete, we will replace the missiles. It's just that if someone finds out about this, we don't want it to look like you were merely the conduit. Israel has to be more than merely a way station in an American transfer. Our people want deniability."

After Shimon was briefed on the matter, he met with Yitzhak Rabin, Israel's defense minister, who approved the deal. Nir arranged for the actual transaction to be handled by Adnan Khashoggi, a Saudi businessman acting on behalf of the Israeli Defense Ministry, and Manucher Ghorbanifar, an Iranian arms dealer acting on behalf of the Iranian government. Schwimmer arranged for the aircraft necessary to transport the weapons and hired pilots to fly them clandestinely. Shortly after the delivery was made, the first hostage, Rev. Benjamin Weir, was released by Hezbollah.

In the wake of that initial transaction, Jackson and others from the United States expressed interest in learning more about Islamic groups operating in Lebanon and Iran. They seemed to know very little about the dramatic changes sweeping through the Islamic world; Nir did his best to bring them up on the latest information, though he was amazed that US officials could be so woefully ignorant of issues Israelis had struggled with for more than a century.

"And," Jackson informed, "we still have American citizens who are being held in Lebanon."

"You want them all released?"

"Yes," Jackson responded. "All of them."

✦ ✦ ✦

Meanwhile, in the United States, Jonathan Pollard had compiled a long list of information collected by US intelligence agencies but withheld from their Israeli counterparts; information Pollard was certain fell within the requirements of the memorandum of understanding reached between the two countries. Yet, in spite of his resolve to make that information available, he still had not located anyone to whom he could pass the necessary documents—and he had assembled quite a trove, copies of which were kept in a suitcase at his home.

When Pollard learned of the arms-for-hostages deal arranged with Iran through Israeli agents, he became even angrier than before. Angry that the United States would withhold information but use Israel for its own purposes.

Not long after learning of that exchange, Pollard attended a meeting at the NSA. Aviem Sella, a retired IDF colonel, was at the meeting. Over lunch that day, Pollard struck up a conversation with Sella, during the course of which he told Sella of his own Jewish background and his interest in Israel. When Sella responded appropriately, Pollard asked if they could meet later to talk about their mutual interests. They arranged to meet at a bar in Virginia the next afternoon.

That night, Pollard told his wife, Anne, about meeting Sella and about their plans for the following evening. "I don't know," she commented. "I think you should check him out."

"I will," Pollard responded with some irritation. "I'm not stupid. But it's just a meeting. I'm not giving him anything. Not yet."

"I know you're not stupid. But this is dangerous. For both of us."

"I'm just meeting him for a beer."

"Just meeting the wrong person—being seen with the wrong person—that's all it takes."

"Okay," he agreed finally. "I'll look into him. But I'm certain this is going to work out well for us. I just know it."

The following morning, Pollard checked the agency's database and learned that Sella really was an IDF colonel. He'd enjoyed a long and distinguished military career, then retired to work at the Israeli embassy in Washington as an IDF specialist. Pollard was excited about the possibility of working with someone from the Israeli government on issues that seemed to really matter. At last, he told himself, he had found someone to whom he could divulge the documents he'd collected. His life, it seemed, was at last turning toward a purpose, a real purpose. Something bigger than himself.

As planned, Pollard and Sella met that evening at the bar in Virginia. They talked awhile, then Pollard steered the conversation around to the memorandum of understanding.

"We really had little option but to agree," Sella offered. "The United States is our most powerful ally. We depend on them for many critical weapons systems. If they cut us off, we'd be in trouble."

"But they haven't lived up to their end of the agreement," Pollard argued.

Sella looked interested. "What do you mean?"

Pollard lowered his voice. "The U.S. has been withholding information from Israel. Information that should have been turned over under the terms of the memorandum of understanding."

Sella's expression became one of concern. "You know this for a fact?"

Pollard was barely able to contain himself. "Even better, I have documents to prove it." He glanced around, checking, then leaned even closer. "Would you like to see them?"

Sella appeared suddenly wary. "Wouldn't documents like that be classified?"

"Do you have a security clearance?"

"I'm not sure that—"

"Even if you don't," Pollard interjected quickly, "you wouldn't violate any laws just by looking."

"Well—"

"Take a look," Pollard urged. "That's all. Just take a look. See for yourself."

Sella shrugged. "I don't know. This is a touchy area. Guys like me get in big trouble over stuff like this. I'll have to think about it."

When he got home that night, Pollard went to the closet in the hall and took out the suitcase where he kept the documents he'd been accumulating. "What are you doing?" Anne asked.

"I met with Sella. I'm going to give him some of these documents. A sample. Just enough to show him I know what I'm talking about."

"Then what?"

"Then after they're on the hook, I make them pay."

"Pay? I thought this was about Israel."

"It is. But if we're bearing the risk, we should get some reward, too."

She backed out of the way as he pulled the suitcase into the hall. "Are you sure this guy is legitimate?"

"Yes," Pollard nodded. "I'm certain he is."

"I don't know." Her voice had a worried tone. "Maybe this isn't a good idea."

"Look, if I get into trouble I'll call you. If it's really bad, you can leave. Go to your sister's house. I'll catch up with you later."

"A phone call won't work. They will hear you," Anne argued. "And anything you tell me will implicate me *and* you."

Pollard looked over at her as he unzipped the lid on the suitcase. "So, what are you saying?"

"If you're going to call, we need a code word," she decided. "A signal, or something. To warn each other if there's trouble."

"Okay," Pollard said as he shuffled through the contents of the suitcase. "I'll say. . . cactus."

She had a puzzled frown. "You'll say what?"

"Cactus."

Anne shook her head. "That's a stupid word."

"I know, but it'll work."

"No, it won't. It's too obvious."

"Then, what?"

"How about. . . dinner."

"Dinner?"

"Yes."

"That's even stupider than cactus."

"Dinner with the Garzas," she continued. "Remind me that we're having dinner with Hank and Jennifer Garza. That's our code."

"Okay. Dinner with the Garzas. Or, dinner with Jennifer and Hank."

"And make sure you sound interested when you say it," she added. "Not your usual 'why do we have to go there' tone."

"Okay," Pollard nodded. Then he caught himself. "But maybe I should just play it straight. I hate going over there. If I say it like I'm interested in going to see them it really will sound fake."

"Okay," she conceded with a shrug. "But that's the code. Mention dinner with the Garzas."

Pollard gestured at the suitcase. "Now help me carry this to the kitchen table."

SHIMON PERES

"I've been controversial for most of my life. Suddenly, I've become popular. I don't know when I was wrong, then or now."

OF ALL THE THINGS that required Shimon's attention as prime minister, attendance at the weekly ministers' meeting was his least favorite. After enduring a lifetime as the victim of backbiting and infighting, he had little patience with the sort of office politics that were seemingly unavoidable. Still, doing his job required that others did theirs, which necessitated some form of regular communication to keep everyone abreast of developments affecting the government in its entirety and to ensure accountability in the performance of their individual functions. The weekly meetings remained the most effective tool for doing that.

Early in Shimon's term, Avraham Shalom, head of Shin Bet—Israel's internal security service—had been away on a trip outside the country. As a result, he missed the ministers' meeting; Reuven Hazak, Shin Bet's deputy director, attended in his place. After the meeting concluded, Hazak asked to speak with Shimon. The prime minister had been warned ahead of time that Hazak might approach him and he dreaded the thought of the conversation that would follow. He knew what Hazak wanted to talk about and he didn't really want to hear it.

In April 1984, near the end of Yitzhak Shamir's government but before Shimon became prime minister, four Palestinians had hijacked a passenger bus traveling from Tel Aviv to Ashkelon. Shin Bet responded and chased the bus into Gaza, where a shootout followed. In the exchange of gunfire, one passenger and two hijackers were killed. The remaining hijackers surrendered, were arrested, and led away. By then, news of the incident had leaked to the press and journalists had responded. The prisoners were photographed being arrested and taken into custody, all of them looking very much alive at the time.

Later, a government spokesman told reporters at a press conference that two hijackers had been killed in the confrontation and two had died on the way to the hospital. Newspapers published pictures of the hijackers as they were being arrested—pictures that showed them plainly alive and walking under their own power. Accompanying articles raised troubling questions about the government's version of events. As reporters continued to dig into the story, a controversy ensued and a committee of inquiry was appointed to investigate. After the committee's report was issued, three agents from Shin Bet were dismissed. Others involved in the incident were exonerated. And that's where the matter rested until the day Hazak asked to speak with Shimon.

Shimon and Hazak met in Shimon's office. "You know about Shin Bet and the bus incident," Hazak began.

Shimon nodded. "Yes, and I must say, I find this conversation highly irregular."

"I find it irregular, too," Hazak said. "But I have no choice but to tell you about it."

For the next twenty minutes, Hazak recounted in detail an intricate and large-scale cover-up regarding what had really happened with Shin Bet, the bus incident, and the two hijackers who died after being taken into custody. According to Hazak, a cover-up of the affair was orchestrated by Avraham Shalom, one that involved witnesses who intentionally misled the committee of inquiry, Shin Bet agents who gave intentionally false testimony, an inside man on the committee of inquiry, contrived physical evidence, and much more.

By the time Hazak had finished, Shimon was visibly agitated by what he'd heard and by Hazak for telling him. "If it was really this bad, why didn't you do anything about it at the time?"

"I did," Hazak insisted. "I confronted Shalom at the time of the incident."

"And what happened?"

"He told me the cover-up had been approved by Shamir."

Shimon's forehead wrinkled in a heavy frown. "Yitzhak?"

"Yes," Hazak answered sharply. "Shalom told me Shamir had approved the cover-up. Shamir was prime minister. Shalom was head of Shin Bet. One approved it. The other made sure it happened."

"And you went along."

"They were my superiors. It went all the way to the top. So, no, I didn't push it any further than to confront Shalom."

"And now?"

"Now I can't stand it any longer. Now I'm doing something more about it. Now I'm coming to you. Shalom acts like what they did with that incident is what we're supposed to be doing. That Shin Bet can do anything and our superiors will cover for it."

"That's not really what they think, is it?"

"Yes," Hazak insisted. "But no agency can operate that far above the law. Two men were murdered. Taken off a bus. Handcuffed. Driven to a field. And shot. That's not security. That's the act of thugs. And it's not what we're supposed to be doing."

"Those are serious accusations."

"I realize that," Hazak nodded. "But that's exactly what happened. You've seen the pictures. They were led away in handcuffs. They had no way to resist. They had no way to fight. Yet less than an hour later they were dead. They weren't killed as a matter of self-defense. They were killed while in our custody. Now you tell me, if we didn't kill them, who did?"

"No one disputes that they were killed," Shimon replied coldly.

"But everyone disputes how they died," Hazak argued. "And I'm telling you, the prime minister and the head of Shin Bet covered up what really happened. And in doing so, they subverted the cause of justice and the very principles on which this country rests. And not only that, they empowered the people who did it. If this isn't addressed, it will happen again."

Shimon didn't like that Hazak was raising the matter now, or the manner in which he raised it. The entire affair seemed like a prime example of office politics—the one element of government service he'd come to detest the most. Yet if what Hazak said was true, it was his duty as prime minister to set things right, even though the incident and alleged cover-up took place before he came to office. "Okay," Shimon decided at last. "I'll look into the matter and get back to you."

"Do you want names?" Hazak asked. "I can give you names of others who will corroborate what I am telling you."

Shimon answered dismissively, "No, I prefer to look into this on my own."

✦ ✦ ✦

Meanwhile, in the United States, Jonathan Pollard tried repeatedly to contact Aviem Sella but with no result. He was about to give up and abandon the project altogether when Sella contacted him.

"I've been out of town," Sella explained. "But I'm back now."

Unbeknownst to Pollard, Sella had been digging into Pollard's life and now was satisfied Pollard really was the person he claimed to be. Sella also had made a trip to Israel, where he discussed Pollard with his Mossad contacts. They were intrigued by what Sella told them and interested in exploring the connection with Pollard further.

The following day, Sella and Pollard met for lunch. Sella asked about the documents Pollard had mentioned earlier that supported his accusation that the United States had withheld information that should have been shared with Israeli authorities under the terms of the memorandum of understanding. "My superiors would be interested in reviewing any documents you can provide that substantiate what you've said."

"Okay," Pollard replied, excited by his apparent progress in establishing a contact with a genuine Israeli operative. "I can give you copies, but not here."

"Where?"

"Tonight, at the Hy-Vee grocery store in Silver Spring."

"Okay."

"You know the location?"

"I can find it."

"What will you be driving?" Pollard asked.

"A Ford sedan. And you?"

"A pickup truck."

After work, Pollard followed his normal routine and returned home to have dinner with Anne. He hadn't noticed anyone watching him but he didn't want to give anyone a reason to by deviating from his usual activities.

While Pollard and his wife ate, he reminded her of the code they'd previously chosen to alert each other in case either of them got into trouble. "Dinner with the Garzas. Don't forget it."

"I know," she replied. "It sounds silly now. Even sillier than when I thought of it before."

"It was a good idea. We need to be able to warn each other if this all falls apart."

"Do you think it will?"

"No." He avoided her gaze. "I think it will all be fine."

"And we'll get some money from it?"

"I think so," he nodded.

"That would be a good thing. We could use it."

Later that evening, Pollard drove to the grocery store parking lot in Silver Spring, Maryland. Sella was parked on the far side beneath a scraggly oak tree. Pollard brought his truck to a stop beside the sedan and each man lowered the driver's window in his vehicle.

"You want to sit in here?" Pollard offered.

"Sure," Sella replied. He left his car, made his way around the truck, and got in on the passenger side. As he closed the door, Pollard took a document from the center console and handed it to him. A stamped warning in the upper margin indicated the document was classified top secret. It contained details about Middle East intelligence that had not been disclosed under the terms of the memo with Israel.

Sella scanned the document quickly, then looked over at Pollard. "You have more like this one?"

Pollard nodded. "Lots more."

"How soon can you get them to me?"

Pollard answered nervously, "Let's talk about that."

✦ ✦ ✦

After conducting an initial inquiry into the things Hazak had told him about the Shin Bet bus incident, Shimon asked Hazak to return to his office. "I've looked into the things you told me," he began.

"You've talked to Avraham Shalom. Did you talk to anyone else?"

"I did my review," Shimon snapped. "And I believe Shalom is telling the truth."

"Which is?"

"That he had nothing to do with the incident or any cover-up. That there was no cover-up. And that you are complaining now because you want his job."

"You are accusing me of—"

"I'm not accusing you of anything," Shimon cut him off. "I know how these situations can get. You work for years beneath someone and you see the mistakes they make. Convince yourself you could do better. Then convince yourself you deserve to be in charge. I understand."

"You don't understand anything," Hazak countered angrily. "You don't understand what happened. And you don't understand me. And you refuse to talk to the people who could open your eyes to the real truth."

"Look," Shimon retorted sternly, "I'm trying to give you a way out."

"I don't want a way out," Hazak retorted. "And I don't want Shalom's job. I want the truth to come out, and for people to know what really happened. We will never have peace in Israel as long as we treat the Palestinians like they don't matter. If we treat them like second-class citizens they will act like second-class citizens. Much of the trouble we experience we bring on ourselves. And it's incidents like this one that put fire in the Palestinian cause."

Shimon winced at the tone of Hazak's voice and the biting nature of his words. He'd been an advocate for peace. He'd said many of those very same things. Now here was someone saying them to him. Anger rose up inside him and he wanted to shout. The very idea of someone. . . a junior-level officer. . . coming to him. . . the prime minister, and talking like this.

Instead of reacting from emotion, however, Shimon took a deep breath and kept his thoughts to himself. "I understand what you are saying," he replied calmly, "but this is my decision. I think you should consider requesting a transfer to a different position. Somewhere else. Under other supervision."

Without a word further, Hazak turned toward the door and disappeared up the hall. The following day, he and the men he'd mentioned to Shimon and with whom Shimon had refused to talk—all of whom witnessed what happened with Shin Bet, the bus incident, and the alleged cover-up—scheduled an appointment with a deputy state's attorney. She listened to their account of the incident and its cover-up, then suggested they talk to Yitzhak Zamir, Israel's attorney general and chief law-enforcement officer. "I can call his office for you," she offered. "If you'd like, I can set up an appointment for you."

They all agreed and the next day Hazak and the others met with Zamir. For several hours, each of them recounted their version of the incident, responding to questions along the way.

"Well," Zamir declared when they'd finished, "I can't promise anything. Except this: I'll investigate the matter a little further, take a look at the transcripts of the statements given to the committee of inquiry, and if I find your stories check out, we'll meet again." He looked over at them. "But if I find out you're lying to me, or that this is all about retribution for some personal matter, you'll be the ones in trouble."

"We're not lying," Hazak assured. "We're telling you the truth."

✦ ✦ ✦

Convincing Aviem Sella to pay for documents that US intelligence agencies should have provided anyway turned out to be easier than Jonathan Pollard imagined. Still, he didn't want to make himself irrelevant by inundating Sella or his contacts with too many documents at once. Instead, Pollard slowly fed documents to him, a few pages at a time. Just enough to keep Sella interested and the price as high as possible. That arrangement seemed to work well for both parties, and their mutual sense of trust grew as they became more familiar with each other.

Then one day Pollard saw an intelligence summary that indicated the PLO was using a private yacht called *Opportunity* to shuttle people, arms, and information out of Lebanon to a PLO cell in Larnaca, Cyprus. The summary had been prepared for inclusion in the president's Daily Brief—a compendium of overnight developments collected by the intelligence community from sources maintained at locations throughout the world and presented to the president each morning. Some of the information included in the summary detailed recent intercepts in which Syrian officials were overheard mentioning a Syrian nerve-gas program—a program with which the PLO seemed to be acquainted and appeared to be urging the Syrians to use against key targets in northern Israel. When Pollard read the document, he checked to see if the information it contained had been disclosed to Mossad or IDF military intelligence. Records indicated it had not, and Pollard went to see Rick Lancaster, his immediate supervisor.

"Well, you know," Lancaster smirked when confronted by the omission. "Jews get nervous when you talk about gas. They don't need to know about that. As to the rest, well, no point in provoking an incident."

"But doesn't this fall within the information covered by the memo?"

"Not if we don't tell them."

"I think we should."

"Pollard," Lancaster said tersely, "the decision has been made. Now, I think you have plenty to do and you had better get to it."

Pollard left Lancaster's office incensed by the remark and infuriated by Lancaster's brazen, arrogant dishonesty. Instead of continuing with his assigned work, he returned to his cubicle, placed a copy of the intelligence summary in a plain brown envelope, then tucked the envelope inside his briefcase.

With the case in hand, Pollard started toward the door and headed up the hall. When he reached the building exit, the guards simply smiled and nodded. "Have a good afternoon, Mr. Pollard."

"And you, too," Pollard replied, a forced smile hiding his smug sense of self-confidence.

Five miles away from the office complex, he stopped at a Fast Copy store and made a photocopy of the document—it bore a unique control number that prevented him from simply handing it over to someone. He could have copied it at the office but office photocopiers required entry of a billing code in order to assign the cost of the copy to an expense account, and besides that Pollard was suspicious that Lancaster secretly monitored documents scanned by the copier.

When he'd finished making a photocopy of the intelligence summary, Pollard walked up to the corner and called Sella from a pay phone. After a brief conversation, they arranged to meet that evening.

An hour later, Pollard returned to the office and placed the intelligence summary in the locked filing cabinet where it belonged—one maintained by analysts to store documents while they worked on various projects and issues.

At the end of the workday, Pollard left the office at his regular time and met Sella at the park-and-ride in Bethesda. He handed Sella the document. "Take a look at this. Nerve gas," Pollard mumbled while Sella read. "PLO shuttling people from Lebanon to Cyprus. Weapons, too. And they say it's not relevant under the memo with Israel."

"When did this information arrive?"

"Today. It was provided to the president this morning as part of his Daily Brief."

"This is a summary?"

"Yes. That's what we do. Most of it, anyway. We summarize things. This summary was handed up to whomever at the CIA actually pre-pares the Daily Brief."

Sella pointed to a place on the second page of the document. "This looks like a reference to something else."

Pollard glanced at the indicated line. "That number identifies a series of photographs." He pointed with his index finger to a place farther down the page. "That number right there identifies the satellite that took them."

"Any idea what they show?"

"The yacht referenced in the document. As I recall, most of them were of people standing on the aft deck."

"Any possibility I could get a look at those photographs?"

"Photographs are kept in a separate building. It's a big deal to get in there. And they aren't easily copied." Pollard gestured to the document. "But that proves they have the information and it proves the information is relevant."

"Yes," Sella noted. "It certainly does."

They talked awhile longer, then Sella took an envelope from his pocket and handed it to Pollard. "I'll forward the document to someone who knows what to do with it. I'm sure they'll have a response."

"Tell them to be careful with it," Pollard cautioned as he took the envelope.

"I'm sure they'll be discreet," Sella replied as he opened the door and stepped outside.

✦ ✦ ✦

When Pollard arrived at the office the next morning, Lancaster was waiting for him and took him aside to a conference room. "I understand you left here yesterday with some documents in your possession."

"No. I didn't," Pollard replied in a belligerent tone. "Who said I did?"

"You know I can't tell you that."

"Yet you're perfectly free to accuse me." Pollard shook his head in an expression of disgust. "You people think you are so smart. I do my job. I'm a good employee. I'm never out on sick leave. I'm always here. More than anyone else in this department. And yet you accost me in the corridor, herd me into an interrogation room, and assail me with baseless statements dreamed up by anyone who wants to make them."

"I have no choice but to follow up on it," Lancaster replied in defense. "We do the same with every suggestion involving matters of this nature."

"Fine," Pollard scoffed. "Follow up on it. Check things out. See for yourself."

"We're searching your cubicle."

"Search it." Pollard gestured in frustration. "Search the files, too."

"We are," Lancaster answered curtly.

A few minutes later, someone appeared at the doorway and caught Lancaster's attention, then gave a shake of his head. "Well, okay," Lancaster said. "I guess that checks out. Must have been a mistake."

"You think?" Pollard stood to leave.

"Be careful," Lancaster warned. "Next time you might not get so lucky."

Pollard didn't like the sound of that—or the implication that Lancaster thought he was up to something—but he pushed the moment aside and opened the door. "You should vet your complainers better before you start accusing people. We have rules about this sort of thing, you know." Then he stepped out to the hall and started toward his cubicle.

✦ ✦ ✦

Within hours of receiving the intelligence summary from Pollard, Sella had boarded a jet owned by the Israeli government and departed from Dulles Airport. He arrived at IDF headquarters in Tel Aviv by midmorning the next day. Before lunch, Pollard's intelligence summary was in the hands of Mossad analysts.

Later that month, using the information provided by Pollard, an IDF patrol boat with Mossad agents aboard halted a yacht bearing the name *Opportunity* as it traveled from Beirut on a course for Cyprus. On board they found Faisal Abu Sharah, a commander in the PLO's Force 17, an elite commando unit. Sharah was arrested, removed from the yacht, and detained.

A few weeks later, the PLO responded by attacking an Israeli yacht off the coast of Cyprus. Three Israelis on board the vessel were held at gunpoint and told they were about to die. Facing imminent death, they asked to write notes to their families. Inexplicably, their PLO captors allowed them to do that, then executed them all. When the boat was found, the messages written by the hostages were found on their bodies. More than merely bidding loved ones a fond goodbye, the notes detailed what had happened in the capture of the boat. When news of the executions became public, Israelis were outraged.

Shimon and Shamir met with Yitzhak Rabin, the defense minister, to discuss a response to the PLO's action. They were joined in that discussion by Moshe Levi, the IDF chief of staff. Several options were mentioned, including an air strike against the PLO headquarters in Tunis, a target Shimon and Rabin preferred and decided to hit.

After the meeting, Rabin and Levi began planning the operational details necessary for the attack. In the course of that planning, IDF intelligence analysts cast about for information about the PLO headquarters, the nature of Tunisian defenses, and other information that might be helpful. Someone contacted Sella, who contacted Pollard and asked for his help.

The next day, Pollard located the latest information on the region and prepared a dossier on Libyan defenses, which he sealed in a plain brown envelope and took from the office. As he'd done before, Pollard called Sella from the pay phone on the corner near the Fast Copy store and arranged for them to meet at the park-and-ride in Bethesda. Sella arrived in the same Ford sedan he'd used before and again parked alongside Pollard's pickup truck. Pollard lowered the driver's window of the truck and handed him the brown envelope.

A hundred yards away, David Payne, an agent with the Naval Investigative Service (NIS), watched Pollard and Sella through the telephoto lens of a camera as he snapped pictures of them and their vehicles. Alerted by Pollard's supervisor, Payne had been following Pollard for three days. He'd seen little that raised any real suspicion but now he was witnessing an obvious exchange between Pollard and someone he'd never seen before.

Payne followed Pollard back to his home, then returned to his office and sent the film from his camera to the agency's lab for development. The next morning, the package of photographs was waiting on his desk.

One of the photos was of the Ford sedan Sella was driving. Payne ran a check of the license plate and learned the car was registered to an Israeli company doing business from a facility in Virginia. A check of sources told him the company was a front for Israeli intelligence. Digging a little deeper, he learned of Sella's identity and his connection to the Israeli embassy. That's when he wrote up his observations and forwarded the report, along with the photographs, to his supervisor.

Not long after that, eight Israeli F-15s took off from Ramon Air Base in Israel. They refueled over the Mediterranean and bombed the PLO headquarters in Tunis, destroying the building and killing sixty PLO members. Arafat was not present at the time and fortuitously escaped a similar fate. The attack was made possible by information obtained from Pollard and forwarded to IDF by Sella.

✦ ✦ ✦

Ten days after the Israeli Air Force bombed PLO headquarters in Tunis, David Payne and an NIS team searched Pollard's office cubicle at night and turned up a trove of documents related to the PLO, along with prints of satellite images showing PLO headquarters in Tunis. "Didn't the Israelis bomb that building the other day?" someone asked.

"Yeah," Payne replied. "They destroyed it."

"You don't think he had something to do with that, do you?"

"Looking more and more like it," Payne replied. "Check the file logs."

By morning, the search of Pollard's cubicle had expanded to include filing cabinets on the floor, files in the adjacent building, and finally, an agency-wide quest as the full extent of Pollard's work slowly became apparent.

When Pollard arrived at the office he noticed different cars in the parking lot and different agents manning the building entrance checkpoints. He was suspicious but knew that running would only make things worse. If they were on to him, they were on to him. And besides, he was sure he could nuance his way out of whatever awaited him. His wife, however, might not be so capable. After moving past the checkpoint, he stopped at a downstairs pay phone and called home. His wife answered the phone. "I just wanted to remind you about tonight," he said. "We're supposed to have dinner with the Garzas. But you'll have to go on ahead of me. I have a full schedule today and won't be able to leave early. Which means I won't get out of here in time to pick you up and get over there, too. So I'll meet you there."

"Are you sure?"

"Yes. You know how Hank and Jennifer are when people are late, so you go on ahead of me and I'll meet you there."

"Okay. But don't skip out on me. I don't want to be there by myself."

"I'll be there," he chuckled.

After the call ended, Pollard continued upstairs to his office, where he was immediately surrounded by FBI agents and placed under arrest.

Meanwhile, at home, Pollard's wife retrieved the suitcase from the hall closet and took it next door to their neighbor. "Can you keep this for me? I have to go out of town right now and I don't want to leave it in the house."

"Okay," he agreed, "but where's Jonathan? Is he going with you?"

"I don't have time to explain." She set the case at his feet and turned away. "If you see him over here, tell him you have it. Otherwise, I'll get it when I get back." By then she was down the steps and crossing the driveway toward her car. A moment later, she backed out to the street and drove away.

Not long after Pollard's wife took the suitcase to the neighbor, FBI and NIS agents arrived. Pollard's wife was gone, which meant agents were forced to break open the door to the house. The commotion alerted the neighbor to their presence. After the agents gained entry to Pollard's home and the initial excitement calmed, the neighbor made his way across the driveway and told them about the suitcase. When they opened it, they found it was stuffed with copies of classified documents.

SHIMON PERES

*"Israel will not have permanent
security without peace."*

AS SHIMON'S TERM in office unfolded, Yohai Cohen continued his attempts to convince King Hussein of Jordan to meet with Shimon to discuss terms of formal negotiations. It was an effort as frustratingly complex as the topic itself, and proved nearly impossible to complete.

Finally, after repeated attempts ended in failure, Yohai went to Shimon with an alternative idea. "What about the UN," he suggested as they reviewed the matter.

"What about it?" Shimon asked.

"Aren't you scheduled to speak there?"

"Next month," Shimon replied.

"What if you used that public platform to announce your interest in negotiating with Jordan and, at the same time, invite Hussein to participate? It's just the sort of thing UN delegates seem to enjoy."

"Yes, that's true." Shimon glanced out the window in thought. "Actually," he said after a moment. "That's a pretty good idea. And it might just work."

Later that fall, Shimon delivered his speech to the UN General Assembly. In it, he proposed his idea for negotiations with Jordan. "Direct negotiations," he outlined, "between Israel and Jordan, but within an international framework to support those talks. Not one that will dictate solutions to the two parties, but a framework that will help them keep the commitments they make between themselves. And today I am inviting King Hussein to meet with me for the purpose of discussing the terms and conditions of such a negotiating framework."

As Yohai had suggested, the speech was well received by the international community. In the Israeli government, it was met with silence but, as Shimon noted, not with rejection by the opposition.

"I'm not sure that means they support the idea," Yohai noted.

"Well, yes," Shimon conceded. "But I'll take anything less than open opposition as a good sign."

Privately, however, Shimon took Likud's silence to mean the party agreed with him and, thinking he at least had Likud's acquiescence—if not its outright support—he prepared to move to the next phase in dealing with Hussein. That would involve face-to-face talks with Hussein about establishing the details for the negotiations he envisioned. He was excited by the apparent progress and felt certain they could reach an agreement, both about the nature of the proposed talks and for peace once those talks began.

In order to assist Shimon's effort to follow through on his UN speech, representatives from the US State Department contacted Richard Murphy, an attorney in Washington, D.C., and asked about his contacts in Israel and Jordan. Murphy's firm represented clients in both places and he knew most of the players. At the State Separtment's insistence, Murphy became an intermediary between Shimon and Hussein.

For the next several months, Murphy shuttled back and forth between Jerusalem, Amman, and Washington, hammering out a draft of a ten-point agreement between Jordan and Israel. When he'd finalized the details with representatives, he showed it to Shimon.

"Seven of these points are acceptable," Shimon commented after reading the document. "But three of them cause me a problem."

"Which three?"

Shimon pointed, "This one here. Hussein wants the Soviet Union to participate."

"You're opposed to that?"

"No. But if we're going to participate with the Soviets, they need to restore diplomatic relations with us and permit Russian Jews to immigrate freely to Israel."

"Okay. What's the second thing?"

"Hussein wants the PLO to participate in talks."

"Hussein and Arafat are close and Hussein doesn't want to move forward with you on his own issues or on Palestinian issues without involving Arafat."

"I'm not talking to Arafat about this. He's been after us for years to engage him in one-on-one negotiations, and our consistent position has been that the Palestinians do not constitute a sovereign nation and that he is not their elected leader. He thinks that by getting us to negotiate with him directly it would lend authenticity to his claim to be the leader of the Palestinian people. We've never negotiated with him in the past. I'm not doing it now."

"At all?"

"If he will renounce terrorism, recognize Israel as a state, and affirm its right to exist, I'll consider talking to him."

"You said there were three things that bothered you. I've heard two. What's the third problem?"

"This includes a referral clause."

"I know you didn't want that. Hussein added it."

"The international conference is to include a plenary session that is largely ceremonial. The real work would be done in committees—Israel–Jordan, Israel–Syria, Israel–Lebanon."

"Hussein wants to include a provision that if the committees can't reach a decision, a member can refer the matter to the plenum for resolution."

"Which gives the conference body the power to impose a decision on Israel without Israel's agreement. We will never agree to that, and avoiding that situation was the whole reason for creating a conference like the one I proposed." Shimon gave a heavy sigh. "We should have met face-to-face. We could resolve these issues if we just talked."

"Hussein thinks that's just a ruse to get him to meet with you and when he does you'll start negotiating substantive issues."

"Even if I did, he could walk away."

Murphy smiled. "Ah, he thinks if he did that, you would tell the world that he walked out on the talks. And he thinks that may very well be what you really want anyway. To belittle him in public."

"He can't possibly think that," Shimon scoffed. "I've never treated him that way. None of us have."

Murphy tried once more to resolve the three remaining issues but was unable to do so. As a result, talks between Israel and Jordan reached a stalemate. Yohai and others on Shimon's staff were at a loss for what to do next, but Shimon refused to give up on the idea. "There must be a way," he repeated over and over again. And he kept meeting, too, regularly convening sessions with staff members to thrash out every detail of the matter, tossing around creative options, unwilling to give up on peace.

✦ ✦ ✦

Shimon wasn't the only one frustrated with attempts to reach an accommodation with Hussein. Hussein was as well, and in an effort to keep the process moving forward, he continued to meet regularly with Richard Murphy. At the same time, Hussein also was engaged in discussions with Yasser Arafat and the PLO, trying to convince them to join him in negotiating with the Israelis. Trying to work out the terms of their mutual approach to peace. Trying to move Arafat toward acceptance of conditions and a framework that Hussein thought Israel might realistically accept.

Rather expectedly, Hussein's efforts to create a path to peace with Israel left many in the PLO suspicious of his motives. They also saw Arafat's attempts to cooperate with Hussein as a sellout of the PLO and its objectives. As a result, the more radical elements of the PLO broke free of Arafat's control, formed their own organization, and resolved to wage war against Israel rather than accept peace or even discuss the topic with Israeli representatives.

Dealing with Arafat, however, proved as difficult for Hussein as it did for everyone else. After months of listening to Arafat always talking but never agreeing to anything, Hussein found himself exasperated to the point of giving up. Finally, in an attempt to back Arafat into a corner, Hussein gave a speech in which he talked past Arafat and PLO leadership to address the Palestinian people, calling on Palestinians to decide for themselves which of the competing voices really and truly spoke for them—Arafat, the PLO, or one of the PLO splinter groups. Most people interpreted his remarks as a challenge to Arafat's leadership.

In reality, Hussein had perhaps finally come to realize how far beyond Arafat he had progressed in his willingness to deal with Israel and the Palestinian situation. Arafat, for his part, saw only that the ground beneath his feet was crumbling away in every direction. Talk of peace—which Arafat knew was the only way forward for the PLO, but which radical PLO members saw as the end of their existence—had created serious fractures within the organization. So serious, in fact, that Arafat's life was at risk.

No doubt, Hussein also realized the PLO posed a threat, but he saw it as a threat not only to Arafat's position but also to his own. In an effort to resolve the matter amicably, Hussein invited Arafat to what would prove to be one last meeting for a final attempt to iron out their differences. The meeting took place in Amman. They discussed the peace process and Hussein's speech, but rather than resolving their differences both men became intensely angry and the meeting ended abruptly with matters between them worse than before. Rather than being a moment that facilitated their reconciliation, it became the moment that marked their final and irrevocable break.

Not long after the last Hussein–Arafat meeting, Richard Murphy, still shuttling between the two capitals, arrived in Amman, where he met with Hussein to review the situation. Hussein told him about the failed meeting with Arafat and that he and Arafat were no longer on speaking terms. "I am ready to proceed with Israel on my own. Alone," Hussein announced. "Shimon Peres and I will conclude our own peace between Jordan and Israel."

Murphy was surprised. "You are no longer asking for PLO participation?"

"No, and not only am I not asking for it, I don't want them there, either. Even if they ask, and even if Shimon wants them present, I do not want them present."

After talking with Hussein, Murphy traveled to Jerusalem and reported the latest development to Shimon. "He's really dropping the demand?" Shimon asked.

"Yes," Murphy acknowledged. "He's really dropping it."

"This is great!" Shimon was excited and it was obvious in the tone of his voice. "We have a real chance to reach an agreement."

"But," Murphy cautioned, "you still have one more issue."

Shimon looked puzzled. "What issue is that?"

"The Soviets."

"Hussein still insists the Soviets must participate?"

"He no longer wants Arafat there, but he still wants the Soviets."

"Okay. I'll see if I can work out that part with them."

"Do you want my assistance with that?"

"No," Shimon replied. "I can deal with this on my own."

A few weeks later, Shimon prepared to return to New York to attend a UN general assembly. It was to be a brief trip, over to New York and straight back, but he was certain he would have time to talk to his Soviet counterparts about the one issue still standing in the way of peace talks with Jordan—restoring diplomatic relations between the Soviet Union and Israel.

As Yohai Cohen briefed him on last-minute details for the trip, Moshe Levi, the IDF chief of staff, appeared at the doorway to Shimon's office. Shimon stood to greet him as he entered and Yohai excused himself, leaving Shimon and Levi to talk in private.

"I'm sorry to bother you," Levi began, "but I wanted to see you before you left for New York."

"What's the matter?" Shimon asked in a concerned tone.

"Jonathan Pollard."

Shimon frowned. "The American?"

"They arrested him."

"I heard. But I'm not sure you and I should talk about this."

"Not about the details, no," Levi agreed. "But about him. . . as a person." Levi seemed to search for words. "It's just that. . . he helped us. We. . . owe him, I think."

"Owe him?"

"He's in prison. And we need to get him out."

"I suppose I could ask about him when I'm in New York. But they have me on a tight schedule. We're not going to Washington and I don't know if I'll see anyone from the United States who has anything to do with Pollard."

"You understand, he helped us with the strike against the PLO in Tunis."

"I understand. But tell me this—did we pay Pollard for his help?"

"He received money."

"Was it money that came from us? We authorized payments from us to him?"

Levi chided, "Now, Mr. Prime Minister, I would have to join you at this point in saying perhaps we shouldn't talk about this part too much. It's probably better if you don't know too many details."

Shimon was no longer interested in pursuing the conversation. "Well, if I have time, I'll see what I can do. But I'm not promising anything."

"It's just that he—"

Shimon cut him off. "I understand. Pollard put himself in a bad spot, he did it for us, and the attack on the PLO headquarters was a success because of it. But I don't—"

"There's a little more to it than that."

"How much more?"

"Well. . . "

"Okay." Shimon dropped onto the chair behind his desk. "Go ahead. You might as well tell me about it. I don't want to stumble into something and have it catch me unaware."

"You remember this all started when Mossad seized those people from that yacht off the Lebanese coast."

"I think you mean it started with the PLO smuggling weapons and people out of Lebanon."

Levi nodded. "To Cyprus."

"And from there to who knows where."

"Right. Well, we were able to intercept that yacht because of information provided by Pollard. He was the one who tipped us off that the PLO was doing that."

Shimon had a curious expression. "That wasn't the first time they did that."

"No, sir."

"And the Americans knew about it and failed to share that information with us."

"Yes, sir. Not just failed but refused."

"So Pollard saw the intelligence information and took it upon himself to get it to us."

"Yes, sir."

"He violated US law when he did that."

"But he did it for us."

Shimon answered softly, "For us."

"So there's a little more to it than simply the air strike against PLO headquarters."

"He was in this from the beginning."

"Yes, sir. From the very beginning."

While in New York, Shimon met with Eduard Shevardnadze, the Soviet foreign minister. They talked for an hour about the possibility of the Soviet Union reestablishing diplomatic relations with Israel and about the immigration of Jews from Russia to Israel. Their discussion was cordial, but they failed to reach any agreement on resolving the issues.

When the meeting ended, Shimon walked out to the corridor and started toward the Israeli offices. As he made his way in that direction, Alice Delaney, a US official with whom he was acquainted, walked toward him. Shimon approached Delaney and asked for a moment to talk. They stepped into an office, just the two of them, and Shimon asked about Jonathan Pollard.

"It's not as simple as it might seem. Did you know he was paid?"

"I'm aware he received money. I'm not sure who gave it to him or why."

"And that is the problem."

"What? That I don't know is a problem?"

"No. The lack of transparency."

"Transparency?" Shimon blurted out. "Whatever information we might or might not have received, and I'm not saying we did, but if we did, whatever we received was information you were supposed to be sharing with us in the first place."

"I'm sorry, Shimon," Alice answered, "but I can't help you on this one. You'll have to talk to Shultz or Casey on this. I can't touch it. And I doubt they can, either."

After meeting with Delaney, Shimon and his team left the UN for the airport and the return flight home. At the airport, an aide received a message from the Soviet consulate asking if Shimon could meet with Shevardnadze that afternoon. Shimon agreed and, instead of boarding the plane, left the airport and drove to the Soviet consulate.

When they arrived, Peres was ushered into a conference room where Shevardnadze was already seated and waiting. "I thought we should make one more attempt regarding diplomatic relations," Shevardnadze explained.

"And the immigration of Russian Jews to Israel," Shimon added. Shevardnadze shook his head. "I cannot help you with that today." "Why not?"

"It is too much for us to accomplish today. But diplomatic relations, that is something we can explore with the expectation of success."

Shimon realized that since their first meeting just a few hours earlier, Shevardnadze had been in touch with officials in Moscow. He settled into a chair beside the foreign minister and for the next two hours they discussed again the issue of restoring diplomatic relations—an issue with roots in Soviet support of Egypt and Syria during the 1967 Six-Day War.

✦ ✦ ✦

A week or two after Shimon returned from New York, Yitzhak Zamir, the Israeli attorney general, asked Shimon for permission to interview members of Shin Bet regarding the death of the Palestinians who attacked the bus and who subsequently died after being taken into custody. Shimon took the request under consideration and a few months later gave his approval.

Based on information gleaned from those interviews, Zamir requested permission to formally investigate Shin Bet. This time Shimon refused, arguing that Shin Bet operated in an area of secrecy—a gray area—but one vital to Israel's security. An investigation by the attorney general might compromise other operations and endanger the lives of Shin Bet members and agents.

With Shimon refusing to permit an investigation, Zamir filed a formal complaint with the chief of police, Rafi Malka. Shimon, angered by Zamir's actions and by the exposure an investigation by the police posed to Shin Bet, replaced Zamir with Yossef Harish under the assumption Harish would side with him and dismiss the complaint. After Harish was sworn in to office, Shimon asked him to do just that.

To his dismay, Harish refused, saying the complaint should go forward to a conclusion, however uncomfortable that might be.

Facing certain court action and exposure of Shin Bet secrets beyond those related to the incident in question, Shalom and his colleagues agreed to resign, but by then the police investigation was already in motion and officials said it had to go forward even after Shalom's resignation.

To end the affair, Shimon approached the Israeli president, Chaim Herzog, and asked him to intervene. "And what would you have me do?" Herzog asked.

"Pardon those involved."

Herzog took a few days to consider the matter, then agreed and issued pardons to all who were implicated in the matter. The pardons put to rest an uncomfortable and complicated incident legally, but only added fuel to the opposition's accusations against Shimon—that he was a liar, that he only served his own interests, that he could not be counted on to stand up for the truth.

✦ ✦ ✦

All the while, the US deal with Iran—arms in exchange for hostages being held in Lebanon by Iran's client Hezbollah—continued to play out. After the first transaction and the release of Benjamin Weir, Amiram Nir gradually took over the operational side of Israel's involvement. The policy side, however, was coordinated at the highest levels of the Israeli government, with all participants fully informed—Shimon, Shamir, and Rabin were involved in every major decision each step of the way. Mossad was kept fully in the loop as well, and played a role in the deliberations. Everything on the Israeli side was completely aboveboard.

A month or two after the Shin Bet pardons were issued, Shimon traveled to Washington, D.C., and met with President Reagan. Based on their conversation, Shimon thought the American process had worked as openly and frankly as the Israelis. That Reagan understood and approved the details of the arms-for-hostages deal with Iran, with Israel as an intermediary.

After meeting with Reagan, Shimon had lunch with George Shultz, the US secretary of state. While they ate, Shimon launched into a review of the Iranian deal. When he glanced across the table, he saw Shultz's eyes were opened wide.

"What are you talking about, Shimon?"

"The deal McFarlane set up through Ledeen. TOW and HAWK missiles to the Iranians in exchange for release of the hostages in Lebanon."

"This has happened?"

"How do you think the hostages were released?"

"I didn't know."

"You didn't know? How could you not know?"

"Look, there is no consensus among administration officials about how to handle the Middle East. Weinberger has different ideas about what we should be doing. The joint chiefs have their ideas. The national security adviser wants to do something else. Why didn't you ask me about this before you got involved?"

"Ledeen came to us through a known source. Said he was acting on instructions from McFarlane. We contacted McFarlane, who confirmed Ledeen's story. I talked to President Reagan just a little while ago. He seemed to understand."

"He knows nothing of this," Shultz replied sharply. "I assure you of that."

"We thought it was all on the up-and-up."

"I'll find out what's going on," Shultz promised. "I'll get to the bottom of it."

34

SHIMON PERES

"The nuclear option is that most of our neighbors, who want to destroy us, believe that Israel has the capability to destroy them. Their suspicion is our strength."

IN NOVEMBER 1986, Arik Caspi attended a technology conference in San Francisco. While there, he was approached by Victor Yudin, a professor on loan from the University of Moscow. They were acquainted with each other professionally, having served on peer-review panels, and struck up a conversation one afternoon as they waited for a conference session to begin. "You are friends with Menashe Beinart?" Yudin asked.

"Yes," Caspi replied. "I know him well."

"I am told you can get a message to him. This is correct?"

Caspi nodded. "I can do that."

"Tell him Nikolai Zamenhof says this." Yudin smiled, then lowered his voice to a whisper and began to recite as if speaking from memory. "In the spring the Soviet Union plans to allow Jews to immigrate to Israel at the rate of five hundred per month. And at that time the Soviet Union will restore full diplomatic relations with Israel."

When Caspi returned to Tel Aviv he went to see Beinart and gave him the message from Yudin.

"Who is Nikolai Zamenhof?" Beinart asked.

Caspi smiled. "A Soviet diplomat. He works at the Kremlin. Is this good news?"

"The best," Beinart replied. "The best."

When Caspi was gone, Beinart went to Shimon's office and told him what Caspi had said.

Shimon grinned from ear to ear. "This means the only thing preventing peace talks with Hussein is the referral clause."

"But that's a pretty big issue."

Shimon shook his head. "Not really. I'm not sure Hussein will insist on it now."

"But what about Mubarak and the Egyptians?"

"We don't really need the Egyptians to get Hussein to talk to us."

"No," Beinart agreed. "But we need Mubarak to make Hussein actually do what he says he will do."

"Good point," Shimon conceded. "We should see where we stand with Mubarak."

"I think we're right where we were before."

"Check anyway. See what you can find out."

To learn where Mubarak stood on the Taba issue, Beinart contacted Hamdi Azer, the Egyptian entrepreneur and friend of Hosni Mubarak whom he'd met through Caspi. They arranged to have dinner in Tel Aviv one evening while Hamdi was in town on business.

"I suppose," Hamdi spoke when they were seated, "that since the Taba issue remains unresolved with Mubarak you are interested in learning where Mubarak stands on that topic."

"You would assume correctly," Beinart replied in a friendly tone.

"President Mubarak is in precisely the same position as before. The area is rightfully part of Egypt and he insists IDF abandon it and return it to Egyptian control."

"The dispute over that area has been going on for a hundred years—maybe longer—and he expects us to simply walk away?"

"President Mubarak would be satisfied if Israel agreed to submit the matter to arbitration."

Beinart leaned back in his chair. "No Israeli leader will ever agree to turn this issue over to the UN for resolution."

"It would not have to be resolved through the United Nations."

"Then where?"

Hamdi shrugged. "The Court of Arbitration, perhaps."

"At The Hague?"

Hamdi nodded. "Yes, The Hague, for instance."

"For instance?"

"I'm just saying it doesn't have to be arbitrated through a United Nations court. It could be done somewhere else. The Hague. Or. . . a commission we created for this specific purpose."

Beinart shook his head. "If Israel chooses half of the arbitration panel and Egypt chooses half, the panel would never reach an agreement."

"I agree. We were thinking more as in you choose one, we choose one, and then the rest would be comprised of people from outside the region."

Beinart was intrigued. "Okay. We could resolve it like businessmen."

"Yes," Hamdi concurred with a satisfied smile. "Just like businessmen."

This, indeed, was good news from Hamdi, and Beinart was sure it was the break they'd been looking for. Israeli politicians—and Israeli individuals, for that matter—had a disdain for outside groups that attempted to impose their will on Israel, but the Permanent Court of Arbitration in The Hague was different. Established in the nineteenth century, it had a long-standing reputation for impartiality. Not only that, arbitration was a familiar device used by many to resolve business disputes. If this turned out to be Mubarak's official position, things could move forward quickly on the Taba issue and resolution of that matter would open up the real possibility of sitting down with King Hussein for substantive talks.

The next day, Beinart met with Shimon and told him of this latest development. Shimon was relieved. "We could do this. We could get this to arbitration."

"The cabinet will agree?"

"I think so. It might be a fight, but I think we could convince the cabinet to authorize that kind of arbitration."

Shimon and Beinart worked to prepare the Taba issue for the cabinet to consider, reviewing the history of the dispute, the nature of arbitration in The Hague, and the likelihood a ruling might go against them. When the matter was finally submitted for cabinet consideration, Shimon found the opposition more entrenched than he'd expected. Cabinet members were evenly divided along party lines, but Shimon would not give up and refused to recess the meeting. All night they debated, argued, cajoled, and finally, as dawn approached, one Likud member switched sides and voted to support arbitration.

A few months later, the issue of which country held proper claim to Taba was submitted to arbitration before an independent commission comprised of one Egyptian, one Israeli, and three from outside the region. Arbiters heard testimony and reviewed evidence, then ruled in Egypt's favor. When the ruling was final, IDF units withdrew and handed control of Taba to Egypt, putting to rest a long-standing dispute over the small area of land at the head of the Gulf of Aqaba.

While the Taba issue was making its way through arbitration, Shimon and Beinart worked to improve life in the West Bank and Gaza. They were hoping to show Hussein the sincerity of their intentions toward the Palestinians. Shimon was convinced that improved economic conditions would go a long way toward resolving the social and political problems in the occupied areas. Not that they could buy Palestinian loyalty, but that they could bring the two sides into a more amicable relationship. With Beinart's help, Shimon implemented new economic and agricultural programs, authorized exports from Gaza directly to Egypt that served to introduce direct international dialing from Gaza to the world.

In spite of those improvements, however, Hussein remained suspicious, thinking that Shimon made the effort only to improve Israel's image—and the image of occupation—to the world, making occupation more palatable to the international community. As a result, he failed to understand the urgency of the moment.

Like Shimon, Hussein viewed Likud's lack of objection to Labor's pro-Palestinian measures as an indication that Likud supported the underlying intent to actually resolve the Palestinian question. "I think we have time to deal with Shamir and Likud when the premiership changes hands," Hussein said in a meeting with his advisers. "They are as supportive of peace as Shimon Peres and perhaps we will even get a better deal from them than from Shimon."

Abdelsalam Al-Majali, president of the University of Jordan and one of Hussein's closest advisers, was not convinced. "Are you certain Shamir and Likud support the effort for peace?"

"Of course," Hussein replied. "Otherwise, they would have spoken out against it when Shimon made the first proposal."

Zaid Rifai, Jordan's prime minister, sided with Al-Majali. "I am not so certain that is a correct assessment."

"Oh?" Hussein had a look of surprise. "And why not?"

"Likud has been against territorial compromise from the beginning," Rifai explained. "I do not think they have suddenly switch positions now. And I am not so sure the premiership will change hands, either."

Hussein had a puzzled expression. "You think Shimon would refuse?"

"I think he *should* refuse."

"As do I," Al-Majali added.

"But that would mean the collapse of the government." Hussein seemed perplexed. "Surely, Likud would abandon the coalition and demand elections."

"And Peres would win on his own," Rifai observed. "With no need of a coalition."

"And he would be in a much stronger position than he is now," Al-Majali added.

"That might not be so bad, either."

"No," Rifai acknowledged. "But if he lost, peace would be lost and not dealing with him now, while he has the power to do something about it, is a gamble."

Al-Majali nodded with a serious expression. "With Shimon Peres, there is peace. Without him, there is none."

As his term neared an end, Shimon repeatedly sent messages to Hussein urging him to agree to talks about scheduling an international conference, trying to explain to Hussein the political landscape that awaited them under Shamir. Beinart met with Rifai and Al-Majali, both of whom understood the situation in its starkest perspective, but still Hussein delayed, and the momentum Shimon had worked so long and hard to obtain slowly slipped away.

✦ ✦ ✦

Faced with Hussein's intransigence, Shimon put aside the issue of peace with Jordan for the moment and prepared for the coming rotation of the premiership. Shamir was set to assume the office of prime minister, with Shimon moving to the post of foreign minister. That transition required a series of meetings, selecting staff and packaging the work they'd done into briefing papers that could be handed to Shamir. Beinart worked diligently to assemble everything in order, but he was not at all satisfied with the way things were coming to an end.

"It will be okay," Shimon assured him—while trying to reassure himself. "We can get Hussein to the bargaining table, even after the rotation."

"I don't think so," Beinart responded. "Shamir might have agreed if we'd reached an agreement during your term, but on his own he will never agree to anything with Jordan, Syria, or the Palestinians." He paused a moment and caught Shimon's eye. "Do you really intend to follow through with the rotation?"

"You sound like Levi Bennett," Shimon quipped. Levi Bennett was a Labor Party official who'd been arguing for months against the rotation.

"Yeah, well," Beinart sighed, "Levi has a point."

"I can't refuse the rotation," Shimon said emphatically. "I would be the liar and the cheat they accuse me of being. I would prove their accusations true."

"Okay," Beinart responded, conceding the argument for the moment. He could see that Shimon was becoming upset. "But they want to talk about it anyway."

"Who?"

"Bennett and the others."

Shimon's eyes blazed. "You've been talking to them?"

"Yes," Beinart replied. "That's my job. I talk to many people. I think you should at least meet with them."

Shimon turned away to look out the window. "Okay," he said finally. "If they want to talk, tell them to come over to the house tomorrow night." He glanced back at Beinart. "Can you be there?"

"Yes. Of course."

"We'll meet then. But I'm telling you right now, I'm not refusing the rotation."

The next evening, Shimon, Beinart, and a group of party officials gathered at Shimon's house. Sonia was present, too. After a few simple opening remarks, Shimon asked for comments.

"You must refuse to hand over the premiership," Levi quickly responded. "You can't let Shamir take the office."

"Likud will resign," someone countered.

"Then let them resign," Levi argued. "The government will collapse. We will hold new elections. And we will win."

Around and around they went, arguing this way, arguing that. Finally, late in the evening, Sonia spoke up in a calm, even voice, "Shimon, you must uphold your end of the bargain. You must be a man of your word, no matter what." Others continued to talk for a while, but everyone in the room knew from the look in his eyes that Shimon's heart had been won and the issue settled by those few words from Sonia.

After the meeting ended and everyone had gone, Shimon and Sonia sat at the kitchen table and talked. "You can't go back on your word," she repeated what she'd said earlier. "All you have in this world is your personal integrity. You can't trade that for a mere political office. It's not worth that price."

As she spoke, Shimon remembered the accusations he'd heard about himself—*Shimon is a dreamer, a liar, a cheat.* "I know," he sighed. "But if I do this, if I go through with the rotation, do you think they will finally realize they were wrong about me? Will they see me for the person I really am?"

Sonia answered softly, "Shimon, they will *never* see you for the man you really are. They will *never* see you for the man I have always known you to be. They see you through their own eyes, and those eyes are prejudiced against you by their narrow-minded view of life and their intellectual limitations."

Tears filled Shimon's eyes. "Well, do you think Shamir will continue with the peace effort?"

"Shamir is Lehi," Sonia stated flatly. "He will let you talk to whomever you want to talk, but no matter what you do, he will never agree to anything with the Palestinians. He only wants to defeat them and control the entire region. In his mind, Jordan should not exist. Gaza should be under our control and settled by our people. The West Bank should be rid of Arabs completely."

Shimon had a troubled expression. "You really think he's that much opposed to the peace process?"

"About those places, yes." A grin spread over Sonia's face. "He's a little ambiguous, though, about how much of Lebanon we should control."

"Ha," Shimon laughed, then he leaned over and kissed her gently on the lips.

✦ ✦ ✦

In October 1986, Shimon's term came to an end and Shamir took over as prime minister. As previously agreed, Shimon assumed the role of foreign minister. Menashe Beinart came with him as the Foreign Ministry director, responsible for the Ministry's day-to-day operations.

As he settled into his new role, Shimon met with Beinart to discuss renewing their efforts to arrange a meeting with Hussein.

"Even if we convince Hussein to talk, will Shamir allow us to negotiate?" Beinart wondered.

"How can he refuse?"

"I'm sure he can find a way."

"Not if we resign from the government," Shimon countered.

Beinart frowned in response. "You would do that?"

Shimon raised an eyebrow. "I might."

Beinart was far less certain about Shamir's willingness to negotiate, much less his willingness to actually reach an agreement. To ease his mind, he turned to his assistant, Rafael Lotz, who was friends with Ilan Ravid, one of Shamir's supporters who worked in the cabinet secretary's office.

As instructed, Lotz met with Ravid. "Shamir is not troubled by having Shimon Peres talk with King Hussein, or anyone else from Jordan," Lotz explained. "He doesn't think anything will come of it. Shamir thinks Hussein and Shimon will never work out an arrangement that gets them both what they want. Aside from that, the substantive problem for Shamir is Hussein's insistence on conducting negotiations in the context of an international conference."

"Even if we give him a conference that can't impose its opinions on us?"

"I don't know about the nuance," Lotz replied. "This is the first I've heard of a conference like that. But I know this: Everyone in Likud thinks everything Hussein has said so far has been merely a ruse to lure us into the trap of a conference where they can get people from outside the region to impose their views on us. Shamir thinks—we all think—Hussein has been playing Shimon and doing a very good job of it."

"You don't think Shimon knows when someone is serious and when they aren't?"

"Shimon's obsession with peace and his 'dreams' for Israel have blinded him to the absolute necessity of national security and to the fact that Hussein, the Arabs, the Palestinians have one goal—the elimination of Israel and the removal of all Jews from the region."

"I want to make certain I understand you. This is Shamir's opinion, not just your own?"

"Yes. Shamir will let Shimon Peres talk to Hussein as long as he likes, because Shamir is confident that in the end it will all come to nothing."

Lotz reported to Beinart, who relayed the information to Shimon, who continued to insist on moving forward anyway. "Shamir can't oppose this," he kept saying. "If we can address all of his worries, neither he nor Likud as a party will be able to oppose it."

"But how?" Beinart asked. "How do we do that? In practical terms, what do we do to address their concerns *and* get Hussein to talk?"

"All we have to do is give him a chance."

"Shamir?"

"No." Shimon looked frustrated. "Hussein. He's the one we have to convince. Once we get him to agree, we can manage the rest."

"What do you mean?"

"I mean by now Hussein must realize he made a mistake in not dealing with us earlier. All we need to do is give him an opportunity."

"Okay, but back to my earlier question. How do we do that? How do we get him to talk?"

"I think we need a new approach," Shimon explained. "Who do we know who knows Hussein well enough to set up a meeting?"

"A meeting?"

"A discreet meeting. A gathering. Just you, me, Hussein, maybe someone he brings. Just the four of us. Who do we know who can arrange that for us?"

"Here? In Israel? Or in Jordan?"

"No. Not here and not there. Somewhere else. Where no one will notice us. Who do we know who could set that up?"

They thought for a moment, then Beinart mentioned a couple of people who lived in France. Shimon shook his head. "I'm not sure France is a good location. Too many connections that might taint the effort. What about Victor?"

"Victor Mishcon?"

"Yes. I know him and I think he knows Hussein, doesn't he?"

"Yes," Beinart acknowledged, "Mishcon's daughter, June, attended Oxford with Hussein's sister, Basma. The two families met there. They've remained friends ever since."

"Good." Shimon was energized. "Contact Mishcon. Ask him to arrange a dinner at his home. Hussein, me, you, and a couple of others but not more than five or six of us. I want to talk to Hussein one-on-one. We should have thought of this long before now." Shimon rubbed his palms together. "This will be great. I think this will work."

✦ ✦ ✦

Victor Mishcon was a London attorney and a mutual friend of Shimon and Hussein. Beinart contacted him and explained the situation. Mishcon was eager to help and arranged an informal meeting between the two over lunch at his home. The gathering was set for April 1987.

When the details were in place and Hussein confirmed his commitment to attend, Shimon met with Shamir and briefed him on the planned meeting. Shamir was acquainted with Mishcon but they were not friends.

"Do you object to the meeting?" Shimon asked.

Shamir shook his head. "I do not object. I am sure you and Victor Mishcon will be very. . . discreet."

"If I can convince him to actually sit down with us to negotiate a peace agreement, will you agree to negotiate?"

"Not at an international conference."

"What if that conference was designed so that we settled all of our disputes with Jordan in bilateral talks?" Shamir offered. "Just us and the Jordan representatives. With the conference having no authority to impose anything on us that we and the Jordanians did not agree to first. Would you consider such a conference?"

"An international conference where the international community only attends but does not act?"

"Yes, something like that."

"I would like to see such a thing," Shamir laughed. "No one would agree to that."

"If I can convince Hussein, will you consider it?"

Shamir chuckled. "I will consider it. But I think it will never happen."

When Shimon had gone, Shamir's assistant looked over at him. "He is conducting his own foreign policy behind their backs."

"I don't think anything will come of the meeting." Shamir had a dismissive tone. "Just more of Shimon's dreams. Hussein knows he is a liar and a cheat. And besides, they can talk all they want. Unless the prime minister agrees, nothing can be concluded. And I am the prime minister."

In April, Shimon and Beinart flew to London for the planned lunch at Victor Mishcon's home. Hussein was accompanied by Zaid Rifai, Jordan's prime minister. In order to preserve the secrecy of the meeting, the Mishcons gave their staff the day off. Mishcon's wife, Joan, cooked and served lunch. Afterward, Hussein suggested that he and Shimon help clean up the dishes. They met in the kitchen and talked. The discussion covered a broad range of topics, but the issue of an international conference remained an impediment to moving forward.

Determined not to let the moment pass, Shimon kept talking, slowly separating the larger idea of an international conference into its constituent pieces, resolving each question one by one, slowly resolving issues he knew Israel could not agree to. One of those issues concerned the delegates who might be invited to attend.

"We need all of the members of the UN Security Council," Hussein suggested flatly.

"That would not be a problem in and of itself," Shimon replied.

"And," Hussein continued, "we need representatives from the Palestinians."

Shimon stepped back. "We need to address that."

"How so?"

"Who would attend for the Palestinians?"

"Whomever they chose," Hussein answered.

"You mean Yasser Arafat and members of the PLO."

"He is their leader." Hussein seemed tense. "Or, at least, he is *one* of their leaders."

"The Palestinian representative can be part of your delegation."

Hussein looked surprised. "Our delegation?"

"If they accept UN resolutions 242 and 338," Shimon added quickly.

That sparked a vigorous discussion that went on for almost an hour, and finally Hussein agreed. He also accepted Shimon's position on the referral option—an international conference as a framework, but solutions would come from the mutual agreements of the parties, not as an imposition from other attendees.

When they'd ironed out their differences, Hussein and Shimon reduced their agreement to writing. Shimon suggested they present the document to the United States and ask their leaders to offer it as an American proposal. Hussein liked that idea and immediately following the meeting, Shimon arranged for a courier to deliver the document to George Shultz at his Washington, D.C., office. Once the courier was on his way to make that delivery, Shimon flew back to brief Shamir.

Shamir listened to Shimon's explanation of the meeting and reviewed the document, but was noncommittal. "I will have to study the proposal further before I can answer," he commented as he started toward the door with the document in hand.

"Where are you going?" Shimon asked, cutting him off.

"To make a copy of this," Shamir replied, gesturing with the pages in his hand.

"I don't think you should do that," Shimon said.

Shamir turned to face him. "What do you mean?"

"For this to work, there must be absolute secrecy."

A look of anger flashed through Shamir's eyes. "You don't trust me, the prime minister, with a document?"

"We may be in government together, but we are members of opposite parties," Shimon explained. "I worry that someone on your staff may leak it for political purposes."

Shamir was incensed. "You reach an agreement and reduce it to writing. That much I understand. But then you give the American secretary of state a copy before you show it to me. Surely *you* have copies in your own office. And yet you tell me that I, the prime minister of Israel—the prime minister of our own country—cannot have a copy for myself?"

"I'm just saying, I—"

"I think you've said quite enough." Shamir returned to his desk, still with the document in his hand. "You may go now," he ordered coldly. "I've talked to you enough."

When Shimon had gone, Shamir called Moshe Arens to the office and asked him to find out what Shultz thought of the agreement. The next day, Arens reported to Shamir that Shultz was excited but not sure he could raise the matter as an American idea.

"But they would be supportive?" Shamir asked.

"Quite enthusiastically so."

Shamir was still angry but kept quiet. He mulled over the matter for a day or two, then sent Arens to meet with Shultz and deliver a message: "If the United States offers the proposal, or takes actions to move forward with it, such conduct would be viewed by the Israeli government as a gross meddling in Israeli internal affairs."

Based on his discussion with Arens, Shultz notified Shimon that he was refusing to offer the agreement as a US idea and that the United States would not participate in its implementation. He sent the same message to King Hussein.

With Shultz's response, the arrangement reached in London collapsed. Shimon was angry. Hussein was furious and felt he'd been betrayed.

"This is the work of Likud," Rifai explained. "They are the ones who scuttled the effort. Shimon Peres is from the Labor Party. Labor would give us this arrangement. Shamir will give us nothing."

"I should have listened to you before," Hussein responded. "I should have worked with Shimon when he was prime minister. You tried to warn me of this."

"It is too late to worry about that now. We must find a way forward with the Israelis."

"I don't think that is possible."

"Then there will be trouble," Rifai replied in a remorseful tone.

Rifai's insight proved correct and in December 1987, the first Palestinian Intifada began. Palestinians throughout the region rose up in acts of civil disobedience and oftentimes in acts of violence. Shamir responded by ordering the IDF to impose greater restrictions on the Palestinians. Raids of Palestinian strongholds followed and hundreds of Palestinians died.

35

SHIMON PERES

*"We know that the new opportunities
reside in the campuses of the scientists,
rather than in the camps of the army."*

IN 1988, statutory limitations brought an end to Yitzhak Shamir's term as prime minister under the shared agreement with Shimon. Elections followed with Shimon standing as the Labor Party candidate against Shamir for Likud. Both sides campaigned vigorously for office and when the results were tallied, Shamir and his party were victorious.

The Likud Party, however, failed to obtain an absolute majority in the Knesset, which forced Shamir to form a coalition government. This time, however, Shamir turned to several of the conservative religious parties for support rather than Shimon and the Labor Party as he had done the term before. Doing so allowed him to serve as prime minister in his own right. That notwithstanding, the Labor Party held the second largest bloc of Knesset seats and Shimon was named vice prime minister and minister of finance.

One of the key issues Shamir faced early in his new term was that of Jewish immigration from the Soviet Union. In the late 1980s, Soviet premier Mikhail Gorbachev loosened restrictions imposed by previous regimes and allowed all Russian citizens unrestricted immigration to wherever they wanted to go in the world. Thousands of Jews who previously had been unable to leave the country took advantage of the change and departed. The United States, trying to be of help, granted Russian Jews refugee status on a more-or-less unrestricted basis, resulting in a major influx of Russian Jews to America.

Although not unsympathetic to the plight of Russian Jews, the idea of a Jewish homeland in Palestine was always a much bigger issue for Shamir and Likud members than merely a political perspective. It was a fundamental concept underlying the whole Zionist statehood process, a key element of which was the right of all Jews to return to Israel—or "make Aliyah."

Now, as prime minister, Shamir was faced with a perplexing predicament: Russian leaders had allowed Jews to leave without hindrance, but Israel's largest and most significant ally was, unwittingly, syphoning off that flow of emigres. "They should be coming here," Shamir often stated. "They are Jews. This is their homeland. Not the United States."

Just months into his term, Shamir found himself arguing with his US counterparts that Jews leaving the Soviet Union weren't refugees at all—at least not in the traditional stateless sense—as they already had a homeland in Israel. "They are only going to the U.S. for economic reasons," he countered. "A practice which current US policy encourages."

Eventually, Shamir convinced the United States to stop issuing refugee visas to Soviet Jews. As a result, large numbers of Jews immigrated to Israel from the Soviet Union. Though not readily apparent at the time, their arrival would have an incredible transforming effect on Israeli society, culture, and politics.

✦ ✦ ✦

In 1989, after serving two terms as vice president under Ronald Reagan, George H. W. Bush became US president. Bush appointed

James Baker as his secretary of state. Baker, an attorney from Texas with years of experience in government service—including terms as Reagan's chief of staff and as treasury secretary—was well acquainted with the Middle East. Early in 1990, he and President Bush decided the time was right to try again to restart Middle East peace talks.

Baker proposed that Israel begin the renewed peace process by negotiating with the Palestinians. Shimon, as vice prime minister and minister of finance, supported the effort and demanded that Shamir accept the proposal. Shamir angrily refused to meet with the Palestinians. "I will never negotiate with terrorists," he vowed.

Incensed by Shamir's response, Shimon began searching for a new way forward, a path more conducive to peace than merely serving out his term as a minister in Shamir's cabinet. He didn't have to wait long for an opportunity to emerge.

When Shamir refused Baker's proposal, Rabbi Ovadia Yosef appeared on Israeli television in support of negotiations with the Palestinians. In his remarks, Yosef talked about a change he'd experienced in his political perspective toward exchanging land for peace with the Palestinians and with Israel's neighbors.

That shift in perspective was quite dramatic, as the notion of such an exchange—land for peace—had been opposed by Shas. Shas was a conservative rabbinical party that Yosef co-led with Aryeh Deri, a longtime political operative who served as Shamir's minister of internal affairs. Shas was part of Likud but far more tolerant than most of the other factions within the party.

Through his devotion to the value of human life, Yosef had come to see that an Israeli future dominated by war and conflict was no future at all. Certainly not for those who favored life over death. As a result, peace became more important to him than the cause of Greater Israel and he was deeply troubled by Shamir's staunch refusal to negotiate with the Palestinians.

Excited by the political possibilities Yosef's statement seemed to portend, Shimon met with him and Deri to discuss how they might react to Shamir. Over the next few days they reached an agreement for Shas and Agudat Yisrael, another of the conservative parties in Shamir's coalition, to break with Shamir and support a no-confidence vote in the Knesset—Agudat by voting in favor of the measure and Shas by abstaining. The vote, assuming it went as planned, would bring an end to Shamir's government and give Shimon an opportunity to form one with Labor in control, something that seemed easily obtainable given the obvious support of the two men.

When Beinart heard news of the plan, he rushed to Shimon's office where he found Shimon seated at his desk. "You aren't really serious about bringing a no-confidence motion to a vote, are you?"

"Yes, I'm serious," Shimon nodded. He pushed back from the desk and looked up at Beinart confidently. "It's all set. All I have to do is introduce the motion."

"This will never work," Beinart warned.

"It's a done deal. Shas and Agudat are on board. Why wouldn't it work?"

Beinart took a moment to catch his breath. "Okay. You might prevail on the motion, but that's as far as it will go. Shas and the other conservative parties will never support you as prime minister."

Shimon had an amused expression. "Why not?"

"Because you favor giving up land in exchange for a peace agreement."

"But Yosef already came out in support of that very plan. On national television, no less. You heard him. You know what he said."

"That was his own—"

Suddenly the door flew open and Arik Caspi burst into the office. "I just heard. You can't do this."

"Do what?" Shimon asked, still seated at his desk.

"The deal with Shas and Agudat. You can't do it. It will never work. Shas and the other religious parties might support an end to Shamir's government, as a form of protest, but they will never support you as prime minister."

"That's what I was just telling him," Beinart agreed.

"But they've already gone public with their support of the peace process," Shimon argued. The look on his face mirrored the frustration in his voice. "They've already said it. From their own mouths. Exactly the thing you say they won't do. They've already said they support it."

"But they didn't say they supported you for prime minister," Beinart noted. "They said they supported land for peace."

"And that's what they said on television, too," Caspi added. "Land for peace. Not you for prime minister. They don't see this the way you do. You see them as one and the same. They don't see their support for peace as support for you. They will never vote to put you in office as prime minister."

"Why not?" Shimon continued to argue. "I keep asking you this and neither of you has given me a good answer. If they support land for peace, why wouldn't they also support me for prime minister? I'm the one person in Israeli politics who has staked his future on this very idea."

"The rabbis in America will oppose you," Beinart said flatly. "That's why they won't support you."

Shimon threw up his hands in a gesture of frustration. "And what do the rabbis in America have to do with this?"

"Everything," Caspi answered. "They have everything to do with it."

In spite of all that Beinart and Caspi had to say, Shimon offered a no-confidence motion in the Knesset the next day. As planned, Agudat voted in favor of the motion and Shas abstained. Their actions allowed the motion to pass and Shamir's government came to an end.

With Shamir's term ended, Israeli president Chaim Herzog asked Shimon to form a government. Shimon went to work assembling a new coalition but soon ran into trouble when news began to spread that Yosef and Deri were uncertain whether they could support a Labor candidate for prime minister. Caspi was dispatched to find out why.

"The problem is with the rabbis," Caspi explained. "They're opposed to any cooperation with Labor."

"Which ones? I'll talk to them."

"That won't be easy."

"I know how to talk to rabbis," Shimon insisted. "Give me their names."

"Elazar Shach, for one."

"I know him. Who else?"

Caspi took a deep breath. "Menachem Mendel Schneerson."

"A Lubavitcher," Shimon muttered. The Lubavitch were the oldest and largest Hassidic group. Devoutly religious, they represented a major force in Judaism on any issue they chose to address. Schneerson, the group's chief rabbi, held sway over them in an absolute manner and though he lived in New York, his word on any topic could turn the entire group's opinion.

"Schneerson sees the exchange of land for peace as a desecration of Israeli soil," Caspi explained. "He's let them know he's opposed to cooperating with anyone who supports any version of a land-for-peace policy. All of the Orthodox rabbis have lined up behind him."

Shimon leaned forward and rested his head in his hands. "There must be a way around this. There must be."

That afternoon, Beinart canvassed the Knesset, but no other members were willing to join the Labor Party in creating a new governing majority. A final head count indicated Shimon was one vote short of a coalition.

With Labor unable to form a government, Herzog turned to Shamir and the Likud Party. Agudat Yisrael, the party that just days earlier had voted to end Shamir's government, threw its support to Shamir and joined Likud in forming a new coalition. Shamir was returned to office as prime minister and head of his third government, only this time without Shimon and Labor as participants. Shimon remained a member of the Knesset and leader of the Labor Party, but he no longer held a ministerial position.

✦ ✦ ✦

In August 1990, the army of Iraq, at the behest of Iraqi president Saddam Hussein, launched a military invasion of Kuwait, a tiny nation located between Iraq and the Persian Gulf. Very quickly, Iraqi troops swept through Kuwait and took control of the entire country. The United States responded to that action by assembling an international military coalition to oppose the invasion and restore the tiny country to Kuwaiti control.

After an intensive military buildup, the international force led by units from the United States army, launched an offensive into Kuwait and defeated the Iraqi army, destroying most of it in the process. The liberating operation, known as Desert Storm, lasted about a month and by the end of February 1991, Kuwait was once again a sovereign nation.

Following the defeat of Iraqi forces and the liberation of Kuwait, the United States experienced a period of goodwill among Arab states in the Middle East. President Bush, along with Secretary of State Baker, sought to capitalize on that goodwill as a means of again restarting the Middle East peace process. Near the end of October, they announced plans for an international conference to be held in Madrid, Spain, and invited all nations from the region to participate.

Shamir, still leery that non-Israelis would impose their solutions on Israel without Israel's consent, opposed the talks. In response, the Bush administration declined to approve a series of pending loans to Israel that had been devised to help offset increased expenses incurred by the Israeli government due to the rise in the number of Jews emigrating from Russia. Pressure, both domestic and international, mounted against Shamir to change his mind. He held out for several weeks but eventually relented and agreed, albeit reluctantly, to participate in the conference.

The conference lasted three days and produced little of substance except for a two-track framework for future peace talks. That framework consisted of bilateral talks to be held between Israel and each of the Arab states with multilateral talks to be held between countries from outside the region—much like the model Shimon had proposed to King Hussein of Jordan when they met in London.

Although the conference only moved the peace process forward by a minimal degree, even that small progress proved too great of a move away from Likud's basic support of the Greater Israel concept. Shas and other conservative religious parties that had formed Shamir's coalition remained in opposition to any discussions with the Palestinians that smacked of cooperation, and were not at all interested in pursuing talks that led toward exchanging land for peace with any of Israel's neighbors. When the results of the Madrid Conference were announced, the conservative parties withdrew their support from Shamir, the Likud coalition collapsed, and Shamir's third government came to an abrupt end.

SHIMON PERES

"The Arabs are not our enemies. The terrorists are enemies of both of us."

WHILE OUT OF POWER during Shamir's third administration, the Labor Party reorganized with Shimon serving as its interim leader. As general elections approached near the end of Shamir's government, Labor conducted party elections to choose its candidates. Yitzhak Rabin, who had recently emerged as a party activist, ran in that election and defeated Shimon, making Rabin the party's leader and candidate for prime minister. Many of Shimon's friends and colleagues switched their support to Rabin to make that happen, a fact that was bitterly disappointing to Shimon. Still, the two were party stalwarts and the fact that Shimon lost the election did not change that. For Labor to be successful in the upcoming election and in leading the country, Shimon and Rabin would certainly have to find a way to work together. Once again, Giora Eini emerged as a mediator between them.

By then, the composition of Israel's population had changed again, this time due to the anticipated immigration of large numbers of Jews from the Soviet Union. Most political analysts expected those new arrivals to join the other immigrant groups and gravitate toward Likud, but the Russian Jews were of a different sort than previous groups. For one thing, many of the Jews from Russia were highly educated intellectuals. Moreover, their cultural orientation was quite different from that of immigrants who came from Africa. The Russians assimilated more rapidly, too, and as they adjusted to life in Israel they found a ready home in the Labor Party. With their help, Labor won the 1992 election and Rabin again became prime minister. Shimon, who finished the election high on the Knesset list, was appointed foreign minister. He brought Menashe Beinart, Arik Caspi, Yohai Cohen, and Uri Savir with him as members of his staff. Savir was named director general of the Foreign Ministry and took charge of the day-to-day operations.

As foreign minister, Shimon dedicated himself completely to the goal of obtaining peace between Israel and its neighbors. At the time, the peace process still was on the two-track structure, which had been achieved at the Madrid Conference. Rabin remained suspicious of Shimon and took responsibility for the bilateral talks—the direct talks between Israel and representatives from each of the regional states, talks that addressed past conflicts and grievances. Shimon was placed in charge of the multilateral side—negotiations that included non-regional international powers and dealt with issues related to the future, looking forward to the way Israel's relationship with the world might develop in the years ahead.

The international context had changed dramatically since Israel achieved statehood and even since the Madrid Conference that established the current negotiation framework. Near the end of 1991, the Soviet Union finally collapsed. Though most in the West understood this in terms of the Cold War, the demise of the Soviet Union altered the status quo of the Middle East. Previously, most Arab states viewed the Soviet Union as the model to which they aspired, a blend of collective control and individual freedom—the use of government to marshal national resources to achieve political and economic goals. Now that model was gone. In its place, a new order emerged in

Russia and a new order also emerged in the Middle East. At the same time, changes in Russia left it less free to meddle in Middle Eastern affairs.

Change had occurred in China, too, with the emergence of a market economy and a more capitalist approach to managing it. India's worldview had been altered by the realization that Arabs of the Middle East supported Pakistan, India's nemesis.

Among Arabs, Saddam Hussein's aggression against Kuwait, a fellow Arab state, and the Islamic Revolution in Iran that brought Khomeini to power, put the lie to the idea of a transnational Muslim fellowship. Being Arab came to mean very little among fellow Arabs. No one was safe. Despots threatened them all.

In spite of his assigned area, Shimon still wanted a Jordanian option as a means to move Israel and its neighbors toward regional peace. In the years since he and King Hussein met in London, he'd had time to think and develop new ideas about how to accomplish that goal. His latest proposal was to place the West Bank and Gaza under a trust administered by joint Israeli–Jordanian control. He'd also devoted more time to his idea of creating a region-wide economic zone—not unlike the way European nations addressed their trade priorities or the way the United States had created a free-trade zone in North America—one that permitted a free flow of goods, services, and people back and forth across the region, at least as far as Jordan and Israel were concerned. A plan under which both countries would remain separate political entities, and the West Bank and Gaza would exist as somewhat autonomous, but all would share a mutual economy. The best hope of achieving that had been lost when Shamir quashed the agreement with Hussein, but Shimon hoped to get it back now that Labor was in office.

Rather than approaching King Hussein directly, however, Shimon decided to focus on creating a Palestinian option first. One he could use as a means of leveraging Israel's neighbors—not just Jordan, but Syria and Lebanon, too—into a peace agreement that settled all of their grievances and provided a way toward his broader regional goals.

Analysts in the West, and indeed most of the international community, saw the Palestinian problem as a single, unified issue. That perception, however, proved to be erroneous. Not only were the two regions dominated by different political groups, they also posed unequal obstacles to the peace process.

The situation in Gaza, for instance, was tragic. Everyone, Arab and Jew alike, agreed that Gazans were trapped in horrible economic and social circumstances. Both factions also agreed that the situation needed to be remedied. Consequently, addressing those circumstances posed the fewest obstacles for Israelis in general and for the government in particular.

The most difficult questions, however, involved the West Bank. That was because resolving the status of the West Bank ran headlong into the heart of the problem with the Palestinians and the Arab states—the status of Jerusalem. The West Bank situation was also complicated by the presence of Jewish settlers that had moved into the occupied zone and established Jewish settlements as a means of further eroding Arab territorial control.

So, instead of seeking a complete solution, Shimon decided to begin with an interim agreement. One that began with Gaza First.

Following the Madrid Conference, there had been an exchange of letters, followed by a series of meetings, between representatives of Israel and the PLO. At the same time, direct bilateral negotiations began in Washington, D.C., between Israel and a joint Jordanian-Palestinian delegation. None of the members of that delegation were current PLO members but several had been in the past. The delegation, however, took its orders from Yasser Arafat and other PLO higher-ups who worked from their headquarters in Tunisia. At the time those talks began, Shamir was prime minister. He had not been interested in pressing the matter, and as a result the discussions moved slowly. By the time Rabin was elected, the talks had made very little progress.

Shimon, now as Israel's foreign minister, suggested his government begin an effort with Gaza by adopting a new approach. "We should invite Arafat to move himself and the PLO headquarters to

Gaza," he opined. "Make him an insider. Force him to stand for election, lead the Gazans, and represent them in negotiations."

Yohai Cohen thought the idea was brilliant. "How do we do that? We can't just make the bald offer."

"We need to get the idea on the table."

Yohai suggested, "Leak it, like the Americans."

"But we can't get away with that. This isn't America."

"Okay," Yohai nodded. "Then how?"

"We need someone else to get the discussion started," Shimon suggested.

"We could write an opinion piece for the newspaper."

Shimon consider that. "Yes, but we also need to know if others are interested in the idea. Leaders. Government leaders."

"The Egyptians. I'm having lunch with Osama El-Baz this week. He's one of Mubarak's advisers. We could give him a message to pass to Mubarak."

"We don't want a paper trail," Shimon retorted. "Not yet. What if you just talk to El-Baz. Float the idea. Just lay it out there and let him respond. If he likes the idea, he will take it to Mubarak without us asking."

Later that week, Yohai met with El-Baz and casually broached the notion of Arafat moving to Gaza. El-Baz liked the idea and discussed it with Amr Moussa, an Egyptian diplomat, before taking it to Mubarak himself. Before long, the suggestion reached PLO headquarters in Tunis, along with Shimon's greater idea of addressing Gaza First. They were favorably impressed and eager to pursue both, but formal negotiations in Washington remained, and Shimon's new ideas were on the verge of fading before they got started.

In the summer of 1992, Forskningsstiftelsen Fafo, often understandably referred to simply as FAFO, a research foundation created by the Norwegian Confederation of Trade Union, sent a team to conduct social and labor research in Israel's administered territories. While doing that work, FAFO's director, Terje Rød-Larsen became acquainted with Menashe Beinart, who by then was deputy foreign minister under Shimon. Rød-Larsen heard about Shimon's interest in regional peace and wanted to help.

At the same time, FAFO's work caught the attention of the Norwegian government and in September of 1992, Jorgen Garborg, Norway's minister of labor, visited Israel to review the project. While there, he talked to Beinart about Shimon's ideas for regional peace and economic cooperation. "Norway would be interested in helping establish a back channel between Israel and the PLO," Garborg offered. "If that would assist the process."

Beinart reported Garborg's comments to Shimon. "You and Yohai have been looking for a way to get things started again. This might be a way to do that."

"Yes," Shimon replied. "But we need to proceed with caution. I'm not sure Rabin will like it and I'm not sure what would happen to the Washington talks if we opened another channel."

"You don't think the PLO could keep this quiet?"

Shimon chuckled, "I don't think they can keep *anything* quiet. Subtlety and nuance are not their strengths. This would have to be a truly back-channel matter."

"I need to give Garborg some kind of response. What if we used people unconnected to the government?"

"That might work even better," Shimon agreed. "Find a couple of academics somewhere who can take up the matter with him."

Later that week Beinart talked to Garborg, who handed the project to Rød-Larsen, who'd already been working in the country. Beinart put him in touch with Yair Hirschfeld and Ron Pundak, faculty members at the University of Haifa.

At first it seemed nothing would come of the matter, but in December Hirschfeld received a word forwarded to him by a relative in London. The message was from Abu Ala'a—a banker, member of the Fatah Central Committee, and one of Arafat's confidants—and suggested that Hirschfeld attend a human resources conference being conducted by FAFO at Sarpsborg, near Oslo, Norway. The conference was set to convene the following month.

In January 1993, Hirschfeld, accompanied by Pundak, arrived in Oslo to find, as they suspected, that the conference was nothing more than a ruse for a meeting with Abu Ala'a and others. Hirschfeld and Pundak represented Israel. Abu Ala'a, Maher el-Kurd, and Hassan Asfour represented the PLO.

The Palestinians brought with them a three-point proposal: Gaza First, with Israel out in two or three years; a trusteeship for Gaza under Egyptian supervision or that of some other suitable country; and talks regarding West Bank autonomy. A mini Marshall Plan for the West Bank and Gaza that was to be funded by the international community would expand and invigorate the economies of both. And intensive economic cooperation between Israel and the Palestinians—the free-trade zone Shimon had been talking about for years.

When Hirschfeld and Pundak returned to Israel they briefed Shimon on the discussions. Nothing in their comments indicated major difficulties that could not be addressed. Confident that they could continue with the talks, Shimon briefed Rabin. He was interested enough to allow the process to continue, and the five negotiators met again in Oslo the next month to work out more of the details.

After lengthy talks, the issues needing resolution were boiled down to four areas: jurisdiction—defining the geographic areas involved; Jerusalem—the PLO wanted East Jerusalem Palestinians to be able to vote and stand in elections; arbitration—a means of resolving future disagreements; and security—delineation of IDF activity and control in the interim.

When the February meeting went well it was followed by a third in March. As the fourth meeting approached, Shimon sensed a need to give the Palestinians something more than simply Gaza First and economic assistance. That's when he raised the question of adding IDF withdrawal from Jericho to the package. Rabin was agreeable and when Hirschfeld and Pundak returned to the Oslo talks, they added that suggestion to the discussion.

Following conclusion of the fourth Oslo meeting, Rabin met Egyptian president Mubarak in Ismailia to discuss the regional implications of the talks. Mubarak brought with him a map of the area and began discussing Gaza First plus Jericho. The map, however, included Allenby Bridge with a note indicating it would be exclusively under Palestinian control. Rabin was taken aback. The topic of bridges had not been discussed at the Oslo meetings and he hadn't expected Mubarak to address the matter. Rabin handled the issue in a diplomatic manner, but later in Tel Aviv he took Shimon aside.

"Why was Mubarak talking to me about bridges?" Rabin demanded. "This was not something you told me about."

Control of the bridges was a minor issue. The real problem was the way Mubarak handled it, and the fact that he seemed to presume something not specifically offered at the meeting. Shimon knew from past experience that this was the point at which previous discussions often had fallen apart. Offenses over minor things had often been a big problem. If the Oslo talks were to proceed, he needed to guide Rabin away from that trap.

"I didn't tell you about it," Shimon responded, "because it hasn't been discussed yet. We haven't suggested it to them. They haven't brought it up with us. I'm not sure why Mubarak mentioned it or why it was on the map."

"I don't like this," Rabin proclaimed flatly, still upset. "We give them one thing; they act like we're giving them something else. Are you sure this discussion is under control?"

"Yes," Shimon replied. "It's very much under control. Look, no one has committed themselves to anything yet. And we don't have to agree to anything we don't want to agree to. I'll have our team take it up at the next meeting, but I think we should push that issue to the side for now. It should not be a problem if we solve the other things first."

"I understand, but I want to make it perfectly clear. I am interested in talking but I have not made a final decision yet on any of this."

Shimon was trying his best to keep an even tone. "This kind of thing happens when people who aren't in the room express an opinion about things they don't fully understand. Mubarak isn't in the room. Don't let him derail you. We've made a lot of progress. We don't want it to come apart because Mubarak makes assumptions about something he's not involved with."

"But you must keep this under control," Rabin insisted, emphasizing his earlier comment. "I'm not giving away the whole package just to get some signatures on a piece of paper that doesn't mean anything to the other side."

After talking to Rabin, Shimon returned to his office and convened a meeting with Hirschfeld, Pundak, Beinart, and Yohai Cohen to discuss the situation. When he'd explained the incident between Mubarak and Rabin, Hirschfeld spoke up. "Does Rabin realize how far we've come with them?"

Shimon ventured, "I think so. But we have to keep on top of this. We need to minimize any disinformation or misunderstanding."

"It's not so much misunderstanding," Hirschfeld added, "but lack of trust."

"Trust is a big issue," Pundak agreed. "I suspect Arafat has been talking to Mubarak, trying to figure out if we mean what we say. And I imagine Mubarak's map represents some of that discussion—a mix of what we said in Oslo and what they said in processing what went on at the talks."

Beinart spoke up. "Caspi has learned from sources in Egypt that Arafat is having an internal sales problem with his fellow PLO members."

Pundak nodded. "I would think so, but it wouldn't surprise me if many in the PLO think this is all a ruse."

Shimon nodded. "I was thinking about this earlier and how it would be a problem for Arafat to convince others in Fatah to go along with him, if we ever get to a final agreement."

"And if it's a problem for Arafat," Beinart noted, "it's a problem for us. Whatever agreement he reaches with us, he has to sell it to his people in order for the process to work at all."

"I think also," Hirschfeld continued, "they're still a little unsure if Pundak and I are close enough to the government for the talks to mean anything."

"And from talking to them," Pundak added, "I think they're worried that Gaza First may turn out to be Gaza First and Last. That this is all they're going to get."

"That's the reason I suggested we add withdrawal from Jericho to the discussion," Shimon explained. "Make it Gaza First, plus."

"Maybe we still need to give them something else," Beinart offered. "Something small but sends a big signal."

Yohai spoke up. "Let's send Uri Savir to the next meeting. Let him go back with Hirschfeld and Pundak when they return to Oslo. He's connected to the government."

"That's a good idea," Beinart said.

Shimon hesitated. "I don't know. We've offered them Jericho. If we send Savir it might be giving them too much too soon."

Beinart pressed the point. "Uri is director general of the Foreign Ministry. Ala'a will know who he is and what his presence means. I think he would get the message."

"And," Yohai noted, "we offered them Jericho last month. Sending Uri this month wouldn't seem like we were giving them several things at once."

They discussed the matter awhile longer and Shimon slowly came around to agreeing with Yohai and Beinart—for the fifth meeting in Oslo, Savir would accompany Hirschfeld and Pundak and the team would raise the issue about control of the bridges. "But do it carefully," Shimon cautioned. "We need to address it, we need to be able to tell Rabin we brought it up, but we don't want to destroy the talks over this. Not now."

As Beinart predicted, Uri Savir's presence at the Oslo talks made a favorable impression on Ala'a. When the Israeli team raised the issue of the bridges, Ala'a offered a less-strident position—total Israeli control with joint Israeli–PLO patrols. From the manner in which it was offered, the proposal seemed to be one the PLO staff had already given much thought to, a fact that Savir noticed as a positive development.

In spite of the issues that had been discussed and the progress that had been made, Shimon and the negotiating team came to realize that getting to an agreement with the PLO would require still more movement on their part. "We will need to withdraw from some other place," Shimon stated finally. "A place that lets them know we really are serious and that this is not just a game."

"Yes," Beinart agreed. "But where?"

"I'm thinking Hebron might be a good place."

Beinart frowned. "Can we do that? For the rabbis, and for many Israelis, it's second only to Jerusalem in importance. The place where David was crowned king of Israel. Likud will resist."

"Let them resist," Shimon snapped. "They've been resisting since. . . the beginning. We have to do this. Can you think of a better move?"

Beinart sighed. "No, I can't."

At the June round of talks in Oslo, PLO representatives suggested that the proposed agreement include the Gaza First idea they'd been discussing—without addressing control of the bridges, which proved to be more intractable than it seemed at first—along with the Jericho arrangement, but expanding it to make Jericho the Palestinian administrative center for the West Bank. Savir, now permanently part of the negotiations, liked that idea. He also proposed a further withdrawal of IDF troops, "From an unspecified area, but somewhere of significance."

Ala'a and the PLO team liked the idea. "Any suggestions as to where that might be?"

"We've been discussing Hebron."

Ala'a eyes lit up. "That would be a big step for you."

For a moment, panic struck Savir. Ala'a clearly realized the significance of the offer. *Did we overstate our position? Do they think we'll give them anything they want just to get an agreement?* Then he remembered what Shimon had said more than once—they didn't have to agree to anything. They could always walk away.

"It's a suggestion," Savir added. "We're open to discussion."

The meeting continued and another followed after that, but Ala'a raised nothing more contentious than the question of patrolling the bridges that linked the West Bank to Israel. In the days ahead, negotiations moved toward a Declaration of Principles, reducing the points they'd agreed upon to writing.

By mid-June the discussions turned to more detailed legal requirements. Lawyers and diplomats were drawn into the talks to address historic precedents, specific terminology, and the technicalities of diplomatic language. The PLO wanted a self-government that resembled an actual government with a two-house parliament, cabinet, and an executive branch. Israel wanted something less formal and proposed a type of trusteeship for the occupied territories, but that came with the implication, derived from historic usage, that the arrangement was a step toward anticipated full and complete independence. All of that had to be hashed out, and doing so took time.

Finally, a Declaration of Principles was prepared and signed in Oslo on the morning of August 19, 1993. Uri Savir and Yoel Singer signed for Israel, with Yair Hirschfeld and Ron Pundak standing with them as witnesses. Abu Ala'a and Hassan Asfour signed for the Palestinians. Shimon was present for the signing ceremony, then returned immediately to Israel to brief Rabin.

Afterward, Shimon and Rabin traveled together to the United States. By then, Bill Clinton was president and Warren Christopher was secretary of state. Neither of them knew the full extent of the negotiations in Oslo, nor of the parties' success in reaching a statement of principles that would guide them to a formal agreement. After reviewing the statement, Christopher indicated the United States would support and participate in the effort to reach a final peace agreement.

An official public signing ceremony took place in Washington in September, followed by detailed discussions and further negotiation at Taba, but the basic work had been done. It was a moment of historic proportion for Israel and the Palestinians. For Shimon, personally, it was a big step toward his lifelong goal of peace and regional cooperation. They had the principles of a deal. Now if they could just follow through and build on it.

✦ ✦ ✦

Early in 1994, Shimon and Rabin made yet another overture to King Hussein, suggesting they should talk to settle their differences lest, after concluding final arrangements with the PLO, Jordan might be left out. The two sides began tentative discussions, with Hussein consulting Mubarak of Egypt and Assad of Syria each step of the way.

"Mubarak is encouraging Hussein to find an agreement with us," Yohai reported.

"And Assad?" Shimon asked.

"Assad is telling him he should talk but not sign."

"Typical," Shimon replied. "I'll get someone to help him understand what's at stake."

Shimon relayed the information about Hussein to Warren Christopher, who in turn discussed it with President Clinton. Not long after that, Clinton placed a series of telephone calls to Hussein reminding him of the loans outstanding between the United States and Jordan and promising to forgive that debt if he entered the talks and reached an agreement.

In July, Yasser Arafat took up residence in Gaza and transferred the PLO's headquarters there. In the days that followed, he established a police force and appointed members to the Palestinian Council, a precursor to a Palestinian legislature contemplated in the Declaration of Principles.

That same month, Rabin and King Hussein met in Washington under the sponsorship of President Clinton. After several rounds of negotiations, the two sides signed an agreement to negotiate terms of a treaty—an agreement to agree, known as the Washington Declaration.

Extensive negotiations followed immediately and in October Israel and Jordan signed a peace treaty. Rabin signed for Israel. Abdelsalam Al-Majali, Jordan's prime minister, signed for Jordan. Israeli president Ezer Weizman, US president Bill Clinton, and Warren Christopher observed.

The previous two years had witnessed unprecedented progress in the cause of peace for the Middle East. For their effort in that regard, Shimon, Rabin, and Arafat shared the 1994 Nobel Prize for Peace. They had come a long way from the confrontations during Israel's first fifty years, but still there was much to do and the effort continued unabated.

In September 1995, Shimon and an Israeli delegation met with Palestinian representatives at Taba to negotiate an interim agreement, which had been contemplated by the Oslo Accords. Work on that agreement went quickly and was completed before the end of the month. The agreement was signed in Washington on September 28. That agreement, known as Oslo II, was designed to broaden Palestinian self-government and open the way for mutual economic cooperation between Israel and the occupied areas.

Things had gone well to that point, but age-old disputes still loomed and there was trouble in the offing. Some of that trouble stemmed from the peace agreements themselves. Not the least of which was Oslo II.

Language in some sections of the Oslo II Accord, particularly sections describing the physical jurisdiction of affected areas, was vague. Perhaps intentionally so. Those vague sections left the Accord open to interpretation by both sides. Arafat and the PLO interpreted the language broadly. Shimon and the Israelis interpreted it narrowly. Almost immediately following the official signing, the differences in those two interpretations became obvious and both sides grew tense.

For their part, PLO hardliners felt Arafat had negotiated away pieces of Palestinian territory. Orthodox Jews and members of Likud, on the other hand, thought the agreement gave Palestinians a permanent claim to portions of Greater Israel, a claim they viewed as a desecration of land given to Jews. Various acts of terrorism erupted from both sides, particularly from among radical Palestinians and Israeli religious conservatives in the settler movements.

On November 4, Rabin and Shimon appeared at a rally in Tel Aviv meant to be a celebration of peace. The square where the meeting was held was packed with supporters. With Shimon flanking him, Rabin delivered a beautiful speech that was received with jubilation by the crowd. When the speech ended, Shimon and Rabin stepped away from the podium. They'd arrived in separate cars and headed in opposite directions toward them.

As Rabin neared his car, an Israeli nationalist named Yigal Amir, disgruntled about the future of Jewish settlements in the occupied territories, rushed forward. When he was just a few feet away, Amir drew a pistol and fired repeatedly at Rabin. Bullets from the pistol struck Rabin multiple times and he collapsed to the pavement.

Security personnel responded quickly and Rabin was rushed to the hospital. The bullets, however, had caused extensive internal damage. Doctors operated in an attempt to save him but were unable to do so. A few hours after the shooting, Rabin died.

✦ ✦ ✦

With Rabin gone, Shimon again became acting prime minister. Implementation of Oslo II went forward and Palestinians living in the West Bank and Gaza conducted elections. Representatives were elected to the Palestinian Council, a body that replaced the one appointed earlier by Arafat, and Arafat was elected to the Palestinian presidency.

Both sides attempted to implement provisions of the Oslo agreements, but details on the ground caused problems. Israeli checkpoints, closed areas, and exclusive roads accessible only to Jewish settlers limited Palestinian mobility in the West Bank. Very quickly, many came to see the agreements as only serving to solidify Israeli control over the territories rather than freeing them.

Tensions were high and in the spring of 1996, Hamas—by then active in Gaza—launched a rash of suicide bombings against Israeli targets. The agreements, so carefully crafted by negotiators from both sides, teetered on the edge of collapse.

SHIMON PERES

*"You're as young as your dreams,
not as old as your calendar."*

AMIDST GROWING PRESSURE from the conservative parties, elections were held in early 1996. Shimon, yet again head of the Labor Party, stood as the Labor candidate for prime minister. He was opposed by Benjamin Netanyahu, the Likud candidate. Campaigning went well for Shimon but Netanyahu had garnered strong support from religious conservatives and members of the settler movement. Even Election Day exit polls predicted Shimon would win, as had polls earlier in the election season, but the final total gave Netanyahu a narrow victory—by less than one percent of the vote. Nevertheless, Netanyahu had won the direct vote for prime minister, Israel's first direct election, and was entitled to form a government.

Because Likud lacked an absolute majority in the Knesset, Netanyahu was forced to work with a coalition. He created that coalition through the support of the religious and conservative parties. As a result, Shimon was excluded from the cabinet.

Netanyahu and Likud were opposed to the policy of exchanging land for peace and remained deeply committed to the cause of Greater Israel, as were the members of his governing coalition. Israel, however, was committed as a nation to the Oslo Accords. Netanyahu was forced to place those provisions into effect but doing so put him in the untenable position of promoting policies both he and his government opposed. By then, however, Arafat had become dissatisfied with the circumstances on the ground—the way the Oslo Accords had been interpreted by Israeli leaders and the restrictions their interpretation seemed to foster. Following the election, both sides tacitly delayed implementation.

In response, President Clinton and Warren Christopher pressured Netanyahu and Arafat to move forward with the agreements, trying to prevent the peace process from collapsing. Both Clinton and Christopher stressed the issue of legal precedent with Netanyahu—the notion that the agreements reached by his predecessor were legally binding—and emphasized the likelihood that, should he walk away from the Oslo Accords, no one would reach an agreement on any matter with Israel in the future.

The implications for Netanyahu and Arafat were obvious. Neither could thrive in the international community without support from the United States. Bowing to pressure from Washington, both sides negotiated an agreement regarding withdrawal of IDF troops from the city of Hebron, a matter that Uri Savir and the negotiating team had suggested earlier in the Oslo process. The agreement was signed in January 1997.

The Oslo Accords envisioned an IDF withdrawal from the West Bank, too, but as of the first year of Netanyahu's term, none had occurred. To address that requirement, Netanyahu proposed a withdrawal from nine percent of the area. Arafat and other PLO leaders considered that amount far too small and tensions in the region began to rise once more. Rather than waiting for things to get worse, President Clinton invited the parties to return to the United States for more talks.

✦ ✦ ✦

By then, Shimon was almost seventy-five years old. Though he remained a member of the Knesset, he no longer held a seat in the prime minister's cabinet. To many of his friends, it seemed that he was entering the twilight of his political career. Several of them were concerned about how Shimon would adjust to what they saw as a permanent change in his life. They approached Yohai Cohen with those concerns. They also had ideas about what Shimon could do to remain active in the areas that continued to interest him. After listening carefully, Yohai decided to take their ideas to Shimon over lunch a few days later.

"What do you see yourself doing now?" Yohai asked.

Shimon had an amused grin. "Are you worried about me?"

"Not me so much. Some of the others are a little concerned."

"Why are they concerned?"

"You've lived an active life," Yohai explained. "Most of it at the center of the country's political affairs. You were with Ben-Gurion from the beginning. Before the beginning, actually."

"And now?"

"And now you're still a member of the Knesset but—"

"Now I'm getting old," Shimon interrupted, finishing the sentence. "Is that what you were going to say?"

"Neither of us is young, Shimon. Younger men are ready to step up. Take their place."

"To take *our* place?"

"To take *their* turn."

"Netanyahu isn't as young as he seems," Shimon observed.

"Comparatively speaking, though," Yohai countered, "he's noticeably younger than we are. And even if his current coalition collapses, which seems a real possibility, he isn't going away anytime soon. He's going to be around for a while."

"He's in Likud. We're in Labor. I'm not really worried about it."

Yohai persisted. "It's the same with the Labor Party. Younger faces are taking their places. Party members are talking about fielding younger candidates."

"The *party regulars*, you mean," Shimon corrected with a hint of disdain. "They were still in school when I ran in my first election."

"And that's what we're up against." Yohai gestured with his index finger to emphasize his point. "You sound like the old guard we faced when we were their age."

They ate in silence a moment, then Shimon spoke, "So, these people who are concerned about me, did they have something in mind they want me to do?"

"They were wondering if you would be interested in establishing a permanent organization to fulfill some of your dreams."

"You think I won't get back into office?"

"As a minister?"

"Yes."

"I think the possibility of that happening diminishes every day. You need to consider the future from a different perspective. Maybe something other than serving in government."

"I'm not so sure I like the sound of that," Shimon replied.

Yohai nodded. "I know. And I told them that. But they made one point that is unavoidable."

"What was that?"

"The day will come when Shimon Peres will no longer be here. And when that day arrives, who will carry on the work you have started; and who will advocate for the things you've spent a lifetime trying to establish?"

The words struck home with Shimon and he looked over at Yohai. "They said that?"

"Yes. They did."

Shimon was intrigued enough to continue the conversation and agreed to sit down with a small group of friends to discuss the possibilities they'd raised. The following week he and Yohai met with Beinart and Caspi to discuss the idea of forming an independent organization.

"What would we do about funding?" Shimon asked.

"Funding would not be a problem," Beinart answered. "All you have to do is ask. Leaders of the world, public and private, respect you. They will be glad to support an organization established to continue work on your vision for the Middle East."

"It would need to be something beyond politics," Shimon offered. "I'm not interested in creating an Israeli equivalent of an American political action committee."

"Certainly. No one wants that. We were thinking you might want to create a vehicle for pursuing your ideas beyond the political level."

"An organization that could work on those ideas of cooperation you like," Beinart added.

Shimon's countenance brightened. "Economic cooperation?"

"Yes."

"We haven't gotten to that yet," Shimon observed. He had a distant look in his eye, as if gazing at a prize that lay just beyond his grasp. "Helping Gazans obtain access to markets in Israel and throughout the world. And helping them obtain medical care."

"It could begin with something as simple as children playing soccer together," Beinart noted, a reference to some of Shimon's earlier ideas and efforts in creating ball fields.

Shimon smiled. "Children have a way of getting along without regard to their parents' limitations."

"And it would bring their parents together, too," Caspi added. "They'll come to watch because their children are involved."

That conversation was only the beginning, but it led to many more discussions as they slowly worked through the details. Meetings with lawyers followed and other individuals were recruited to join the effort. Finally, after months of work and preparation, Shimon and a group of close friends founded the Peres Center for Peace, a nonprofit organization designed to continue his vision of peace and advancement in the Middle East.

✦ ✦ ✦

In response to President Clinton's invitation, Netanyahu and Arafat traveled to the United States and met to negotiate details regarding the implementation of the Oslo Accords. Madeleine Albright, who replaced Warren Christopher as US secretary of state, served as mediator. The agreement they reached became known as the Wye River Memorandum, after the site where the meetings took place.

The Wye River Memorandum and Hebron Agreement, along with the IDF withdrawal from the West Bank facilitated by them, put a strain on Netanyahu's governing coalition. Conservative members of the government responded by introducing a no-confidence motion in the Knesset. When the measure came up for a vote, Netanyahu's government collapsed. An election to choose his replacement was set for May.

After losing to Netanyahu earlier, Shimon had chosen not to stand for election as leader of the Labor Party. Members chose Ehud Barak for the post. When Netanyahu's government dissolved, Barak became the Labor Party candidate for prime minister. Netanyahu remained Likud's candidate, but dissatisfaction with his initial term put him at a disadvantage. Barak defeated him handily. Shimon, still a force within the party, was appointed minister of regional cooperation.

During the campaign, Barak had pledged to withdraw all remaining IDF forces from Lebanon. A limited number of troops had remained there after the end of the Lebanese civil war to maintain a security zone that protected northern Galilee from PLO terrorists. Within weeks of taking office, Barak made good on that promise and brought the troops home.

As President Clinton neared the end of his final term of office, he approached Barak and Arafat about trying again to obtain an agreement on the final status of the occupied territories. Barak, facing growing dissatisfaction at home and rising clamor for early elections, was interested in pursuing the matter. Arafat, however, was hesitant, claiming he needed more time to prepare.

Nevertheless, in July, Clinton invited Barak and Arafat to Camp David to discuss final status talks—yet another talk about agreeing to talk. Very quickly the participants realized the two sides were far apart. Arafat and the Palestinians wanted a state that occupied the area generally denoted by the UN partition of 1947–48. Doing that would have required Israel to surrender territory it obtained as a result of each of the major conflicts that had marked its fifty-year history. Arafat and the Palestinians also wanted East Jerusalem as their capital. Both of those demands were conditions even a Labor Party prime minister would never accept.

In response, Barak offered the Palestinians control of eighty percent of the West Bank with Abu Dis, a town outside East Jerusalem as their capital. He suggested further that Abu Dis could be renamed Al-Quds, the Arabic term for Jerusalem. Arafat declined and the meetings ended without an agreement.

In 2000, Israeli president Ezer Weizman resigned and elections for his replacement were announced for July. Largely a ceremonial office, the position of Israel's president had often gone to an elder statesmen. Someone who'd played an instrumental role in the life of the country and who was given the position as a seat of honor. A way to keep their hand in the game without requiring participation in the prime minister's agenda.

At the urging of his friends, Shimon stood for the office as the Labor Party's candidate. Moshe Katsav was the candidate from Likud. In the short campaign that followed, Shimon pledged to support Ehud Barak in the peace process and to continue the effort to reach a conclusive peace agreement with the Palestinians.

When the election was held, Shimon lost to Katsav by six votes. Most thought his support for Barak and the peace process cost him the election. Shimon viewed his position as merely being true to himself and to the issues he'd devoted his life to resolve.

Katsav was the first Likud Party member to hold the office of president. The statutory term was seven years. At the moment, it seemed the sun really was setting on Shimon's political career.

SHIMON PERES

*"Optimists and pessimists die the same
way. They just live differently."*

IN JANUARY 2001, George W. Bush became president of
the United States. At the beginning of his term, his administration
distanced itself from the Middle East and the Israeli–Palestinian
problem. As a result, peace talks between Israel and the PLO continued
to languish.

Without the talks to provide a sense of hope, Palestinian terrorists
increased their attacks on Israeli targets. Tension rose among Israeli
citizens as Ehud Barak seemed unable to do anything to stop them.

Finally, in February, Barak's government reached a crisis and he
called for a special election. He ran for reelection as prime minister
and was opposed by Ariel Sharon, the Likud candidate. Although
Barak had much to offer the country, he lost that election and Sharon
became prime minister.

In the aftermath of the election, Labor turned once again to
Shimon and chose him as its leader. With Barak no longer a factor,
Shimon and Labor joined with Likud to form a governing coalition,
creating another National Unity government. Shimon was appointed

foreign minister, a position from which he hoped to continue the push toward peace with the Palestinians. Sharon and his government, however, turned away from further negotiations and focused their attention on other areas.

Shimon did his best to keep the hope of peace alive but with negotiations nonexistent, and with no interest from Sharon in restarting talks with the PLO, he and the Labor Party withdrew from the coalition. Sharon's government collapsed and elections were scheduled for later that year.

As expected, Sharon stood as Likud's candidate for prime minister. Shimon ran as the candidate from Labor. Sharon won handily, giving Labor a bitter defeat. However, Shimon remained leader of the Labor Party and, in 2004, when Sharon embraced a policy of military disengagement from Gaza, he led Labor back to the governing coalition.

In 2005, ahead of regular elections scheduled for the following year, the Labor Party held an internal party election to choose its leadership and to prepare its slate of candidates. Shimon stood for election as party chairman but lost at the hands of a revolt led by younger members, a rising group of politicians in the process of eclipsing the older, established power brokers. Their primary activist, Amir Peretz, became party leader.

Labor's change in leadership portended a shift in policy, one that Shimon felt turned away from the party's historic focus on the peace process. Consequently, he resigned from the party, the organization that had been his political home for some sixty years.

At the same time, Ariel Sharon resigned from Likud and formed a new party known as Kadima. Shimon aligned himself with Sharon and brought with him several former Labor Party cabinet members and more than seventy mayors. "In light of changes within Labor," Shimon explained, "Kadima offers the best hope of leading the way toward peace with the Palestinians."

Although he had switched parties, Sharon remained in office as prime minister, pending elections the following year. In January, however, he suffered a stroke and lapsed into a coma. With Sharon no longer able to continue in office, Kadima regulars, most of whom were from Likud, chose Ehud Olmert as party leader. In elections later that year, Olmert was elected prime minister. Shimon served as vice premier and minister for the development of the Negev, Galilee, and the regional economy—next to peace two of his greatest interests.

By 2007, Shimon was eighty-four years old. He'd held every major position in the Israeli government except one—the presidency. In the summer of that year, Moshe Katsav, who held the post, came under suspicion of criminal activity and resigned from office to challenge those allegations. Elections were scheduled to choose his replacement and Shimon entered the race.

In the first round of voting, Shimon received fifty-eight votes out of the total one hundred twenty seats in the Knesset, more votes than any of the other candidates but not quite a majority. In the second round, two of those candidates dropped out and endorsed Shimon and after a second round of voting, he was elected president of Israel, winning by a margin of eighty-six to twenty-three.

With his election to the presidency, Shimon resigned from the Knesset, a position he had held since 1959. At the time of his resignation he was the longest-serving member of the Kensett in Israel's history. He was sworn in to office as president on July 15.

Once in office, Shimon devoted his time and energy to uniting the nation, extending its sense of goodwill to the international community, and in furthering the development of the Negev and northern Galilee. A founder of Israel's technology sector, he continued to promote the development of research and business centers. At the same time, he did his best to keep the hope of peace alive and encouraged the Israeli government to reach an agreement with the Palestinians.

A year after Shimon became president, Ehud Olmert faced corruption charges and was replaced as leader of Kadima by Tzipi Livni. Olmert stepped aside as prime minister and Livni became acting prime minister. Elections were set for the spring of 2009. Benjamin Netanyahu ran as the Likud candidate against Livni and, for the second time, was elected Israel's prime minister. He took office in March of that year.

Shimon kept an eye on Israeli politics but as president there was little he could do to shape the electoral outcome. By then he'd come to realize that, for him, politics and international bargaining had run its course. It had achieved all it could and no longer offered a path to the goals he wished to achieve. Peace, it seemed, now was in the hands of the people. The bakers, mechanics, nurses, and store owners who defined the region by the lives they led. Peace was up to them, and Shimon was more interested in helping them than engaging in political debate.

In December 2009, the Peres Center for Peace moved to a permanent home at the Peres Peace House, a building located on the shores of the Mediterranean Sea in the Ajami neighborhood of Jaffa. With a permanent location, the Center focused on four areas—healthcare, education, business, and innovation. And while he never neglected his presidential duties or confused the two, Shimon devoted as much time as possible to the Center's chief aims.

✦ ✦ ✦

One morning in January 2011, a security guard at Shimon and Sonia's apartment in Tel Aviv noticed that Sonia had not come downstairs for her newspaper. Later that morning, her grandson came by for a visit and discovered her lying lifeless in bed. She had passed away sometime in the night.

A doctor was summoned and after a check of her vital signs turned to the grandson. "We must notify the medical examiner, since she died at home."

"Was she in pain?"

"I don't think so. From all appearances, she died in her sleep."

"At least she went peacefully."

The doctor agreed. "Yes, she went peacefully. Where is the president?"

"At his office, I suppose."

"You should call him," the doctor suggested, "and let him know what has happened."

The grandson suddenly felt awkward at the thought of telling his grandfather she'd died. "I suppose I should," he muttered.

The doctor walked out to the living room and while he waited for the young man to place the phone call he wandered across the room to a desk that sat near the window. A document lay on the desktop and he glanced down to see that it was a certificate thanking Sonia for volunteering at a nearby hospital.

After a moment, the grandson joined him and the doctor commented, "I never knew she was a volunteer at this hospital."

"She went there three times a week, just to visit patients," the grandson explained. "Usually she visited the terminally ill, though she tried to get into the psych ward a few times. They wouldn't let her, of course, but she was rather persistent about it. She said those patients were some of the neediest."

"She was right. They are very needy indeed."

"She couldn't convince them to let her go in, but she spent a lot of time with the terminally ill. And at the physical therapy wing with patients who were disabled."

There were other papers on the desktop and the grandson pushed them aside to take out another certificate. "She received this one last month for tutoring," he gestured to the document.

The doctor glanced at the notice. "That organization works mostly with Arab children," he noted.

The grandson nodded. "She loved everyone."

The doctor shook his head in disbelief. "I never knew this side of her."

The grandson smiled. "And that is the way she wanted it." He choked back a tear and the doctor glanced over at him. "Did you reach your grandfather?"

"Oh. Right. I saw you over here and got distracted." The grandson took a cell phone from his pocket and placed a call to

Shimon's office. An assistant answered. "May I speak to my grandfather?"

"I'm sorry," the assistant replied. "He's in a meeting."

"Interrupt him, please," the grandson instructed. "This is important."

✦ ✦ ✦

Shimon served as president until the end of his term in July 2014, at which time he announced he would not seek reelection. After leaving office, he devoted all of his time to working at the Peres Center for Peace and to supporting its programs through writing, study, and fundraising efforts. As Beinart had suggested when they formed the Center, leaders from around the world were eager to help.

One bright, sunny day in the summer of 2015, Shimon sat on a bench at a sports field with Oded Lurie, one of the young staffers from the Peres Center. On the field in front of them was a group of young people, about twelve or thirteen years old, playing soccer.

"I was their age when I first arrived in Israel," Shimon observed. "Mandatory Palestine, actually."

"That was a long time ago."

Shimon chuckled. "Don't remind me."

"You played sports back then?"

"Everyone played basketball then. It was all the rage when I arrived here. In the neighborhood. At school. I'd never played sports much back in Belarus. Never had many friends back then, either. Then suddenly, there I was, in a neighborhood filled with boys. At a school packed with kids. And they were doing all the things I'd never done as a child and doing them well. So I tried to play but it didn't really work out so well."

"They wouldn't let you play?"

Shimon smiled at the memory, "Oh, they let me play. Then spent most of the time laughing at me."

"Laughing?"

"They used to call me Two Left Feet."

"Ah," Lurie nodded. "You were awkward."

"I kept tripping over my own feet. Stumbling into people. It was awful. Same thing happened when I tried to dance."

"Yeah," Lurie grinned. "Everyone's bad at that at first."

"After the first time," Shimon continued, "Sonia made me practice so I wouldn't cause a scene in public. She didn't like having her toes stepped on or having me bump into people on the dance floor."

"I guess that was a little disconcerting."

A wide grin lit up Shimon's countenance. "She laughed the whole time. So it was okay."

"Sounds like she was an interesting lady."

"She was more than an interesting lady." Shimon's eyes were full. "The greatest person I've ever known." He looked away and sighed. "I miss her every day."

THE AUTHOR'S
AFTERWORD

ALTHOUGH THE STORY you've just read is fictional, it is based on historic events. Some of those events have been altered for the sake of the story line. Events and people have been compressed or combined with others to create a fictional narrative. One thing that is very much true, however, is the account of events surrounding Shimon's grandfather, Zvi Meltzer. He really was cantor rabbi at the wooden synagogue in Vishnyeva, Belarus. He served there with my great-grandfather, Michael Katznelson, who was the chief rabbi. They served together and died together when the Nazis locked them and many of their followers in the synagogue, then set the building ablaze.

Through my involvement with the people of Israel, I have come to know many Israeli politicians and civic leaders. In the course of that work, Shimon and I became good friends. Selfless and tireless in his quest for peace, he was one of the greatest men I've ever known.

In 2010, I began the initial work on a museum and research institute, which I planned to locate in Jerusalem, near the Old City. That idea grew and matured to become the Friends of Zion Museum. It opened to the public in 2015.

As we developed the organization to support the museum, we held lengthy deliberations about the composition of the board of directors and the appointment of key executive staff. One thing that didn't require lengthy deliberation was the person we wanted as our international chairman. Only one person could fill that position—Shimon Peres.

After we'd made that decision, I had to recruit Shimon to the position. So I invited him to dinner at a restaurant in Jerusalem and we talked about the institute I wanted to create. He asked what I wanted that institute to accomplish and I explained, "We want to tell the story of non-Jewish people who have helped support the people of Israel. Those who came to the aid of the nation when it was formed and who stood by it in the struggle for independence, and in the struggle to maintain the freedom that followed."

"And you are right," Shimon agreed. "It has been a struggle. One we could not have won without the help of our friends. How can I help you with that?"

"I would like for you to serve as our international chairman," I said. "I know you're busy and have many constraints on your time, but will you do us that honor?"

He smiled at me. "It takes a lot less energy to make friends than it does to make enemies. I will do it."

In an effort to promote the museum and to further its work we established the Friends of Zion Award, given periodically to those who have shown the same kind of support for Israel as the historic figures we honor in our museum displays and programs. The first award was scheduled to be presented to former US president George W. Bush at the Presidential Library in Dallas, Texas. I wanted to ask Shimon if he would present the award but he'd already agreed to serve as international chairman, so I decided to wait and ask him about it later.

As we continued to talk that night in Jerusalem he asked, "What are your dreams? Tell me two of them."

"The first was that you would become our international chairman," I replied.

"And the second?"

It seemed like an opportunity so I took a deep breath and said, "My second dream is that you would come to America and present our first award to George W. Bush."

He laughed, "You need to dream some more."

Later that year, Shimon traveled to the United States and presented the Friends of Zion Award to George Bush. Two years after that, he accompanied me to Monaco and presented the award to Prince Albert II of Monaco.

Not long after that, Shimon and I visited with Pope Francis at the Vatican. When we arrived, Shimon and the pope met privately. In the course of their conversation he told the pope about me, mentioning that I was named for my great-grandfather, Michael Katznelson, who was a rabbi from Vishnyeva, Belarus, the same town as Shimon and his family.

After their private visit, Shimon and the pope came out to the room where I was waiting. We had a painting of Abraham that we presented to him and as I handed it to him I said, "This is a picture of the first Holy Father."

The pope studied the picture a moment, then turned to those who accompanied him. "For two thousand years we have said that Peter was the first Holy Father. Now the Jews have come to set the record straight." We all laughed good-naturedly, then the pope turned to me. "You are a Jewish man."

"Yes," I replied. "I am a Jew and a Christian."

"President Peres has told me the story of your great-grandfather. Can you tell me how you as a Jew came to faith in Jesus Christ?"

As succinctly as possible, I recounted the story of my early life—how my father abused us, the night I thought I was going to die, then Jesus appeared to me in my bedroom. As I shared that account I began to cry. Pope Francis began to cry, too, and so did Shimon.

Later that evening over dinner Shimon said, "You and I have become very close these past couple of years. Like family."

"Yes. It has felt that way for me, too."

"Today I realized why I felt that way about you. I went to Israel because of my grandfather, Rabbi Meltzer. Everything in my life has occurred because of him. He was my hero. But your great-grandfather was the chief rabbi of that synagogue. They died together. Burned to death by the Nazis in the same synagogue—your great-grandfather and my grandfather." Then he looked at me and said, "You are truly family."

Shimon Peres lived a long and very productive life, holding every major office in the Israeli government and bringing Israel closer than anyone else to actual, lasting peace with the Palestinians. He remained active in that effort after leaving political office and worked every day to see his ideas transformed into reality.

At the age of ninety-three, Shimon suffered a stroke and was hospitalized at Sheba Medical Center. I was in Israel at the time and went to see him on the afternoon that he was admitted. He obviously was not well but was stable and able to discuss a book we planned to write together. One we'd tentatively entitled *The Wooden Synagogue*, about what happened to our family members during World War II. It was his last meeting that day and, as events turned out, the final meeting of his life.

ACKNOWLEDGMENTS

My deepest gratitude and sincere thanks to my writing partner, Joe Hilley, and to my executive assistant, Lanelle Shaw-Young, both of whom work diligently to turn my story ideas into great books. And to Arlen Young, Peter Glöege, and Janna Nysewander for making the finished product look and read its best. And always, to my wife, Carolyn, whose presence makes everything better.

BOOKS BY: MIKE EVANS

Israel: America's Key to Survival

Save Jerusalem

The Return

Jerusalem D.C.

Purity and Peace of Mind

Who Cries for the Hurting?

Living Fear Free

I Shall Not Want

Let My People Go

Jerusalem Betrayed

Seven Years of Shaking: A Vision

The Nuclear Bomb of Islam

Jerusalem Prophecies

Pray For Peace of Jerusalem

America's War:
    The Beginning of the End

The Jerusalem Scroll

The Prayer of David

The Unanswered Prayers of Jesus

God Wrestling

The American Prophecies

Beyond Iraq: The Next Move

The Final Move beyond Iraq

Showdown with Nuclear Iran

Jimmy Carter: The Liberal Left
    and World Chaos

Atomic Iran

Cursed

Betrayed

The Light

Corrie's Reflections & Meditations

The Revolution

The Final Generation

Seven Days

The Locket

Persia: The Final Jihad

GAMECHANGER SERIES:

GameChanger

Samson Option

The Four Horsemen

THE PROTOCOLS SERIES:

The Protocols

The Candidate

Jerusalem

The History of Christian Zionism

Countdown

Ten Boom: Betsie, Promise of God

Commanded Blessing

Born Again: 1948

Born Again: 1967

Presidents in Prophecy

Stand with Israel

Prayer, Power and Purpose

TO PURCHASE, CONTACT: orders@timeworthybooks.com
P. O. BOX 30000, PHOENIX, AZ 85046

MICHAEL DAVID EVANS, the #1 *New York Times* bestselling author, is an award-winning journalist/Middle East analyst. Dr. Evans has appeared on hundreds of network television and radio shows including *Good Morning America, Crossfire* and *Nightline,* and *The Rush Limbaugh Show,* and on Fox Network, *CNN World News,* NBC, ABC, and CBS. His articles have been published in the *Wall Street Journal, USA Today, Washington Times, Jerusalem Post* and newspapers worldwide. More than twenty-five million copies of his books are in print, and he is the award-winning producer of nine documentaries based on his books.

Dr. Evans is considered one of the world's leading experts on Israel and the Middle East, and is one of the most sought-after speakers on that subject. He is the chairman of the board of the ten Boom Holocaust Museum in Haarlem, Holland, and is the founder of Israel's first Christian museum located in the Friends of Zion Heritage Center in Jerusalem.

Dr. Evans has authored a number of books including: *History of Christian Zionism, Showdown with Nuclear Iran, Atomic Iran, The Next Move Beyond Iraq, The Final Move Beyond Iraq,* and *Countdown.* His body of work also includes the novels *Seven Days, GameChanger, The Samson Option, The Four Horsemen, The Locket, Born Again: 1967,* and *The Columbus Code.*

✦ ✦ ✦

Michael David Evans is available to speak or for interviews.
Contact: EVENTS@drmichaeldevans.com.